ALSO BY LOIS-ANN YAMANAKA

Saturday Night at the Pahala Theatre

Wild Meat and the Bully Burgers

Blu's Hanging

Heads by Harry

Father of the Four Passages

The Heart's Language

Name Me Nobody

Behold the Many

FARRAR, STRAUS AND GIROUX

NEW YORK

Behold the Many

Lois-Ann Yamanaka

Farrar, Straus and Giroux
19 Union Square West, New York 10003

Distributed in Canada by Douglas & McIntyre Ltd.
Printed in the United States of America
First edition, 2006

Library of Congress Cataloging-in-Publication Data
Yamanaka, Lois-Ann, date.
Behold the many / Lois-Ann Yamanaka.— 1st ed.
p. cm.
ISBN-13: 978-0-374-11015-4 (alk. paper)
ISBN-10: 0-374-11015-8 (alk. paper)
1. Women—Hawaii—Fiction. 2. Tuberculosis—Patients—Fiction.
3. Abandoned children—Fiction. 4. Sisters—Death—Fiction.
5. Orphanages—Fiction. 6. Hawaii—Fiction. 7. Guilt—Fiction.
I. Title.

PS3575.A434B44 2006
813'.54—dc22

2005019875

Designed by Cassandra J. Pappas

www.fsgbooks.com

10 9 8 7 6 5 4 3 2

For Asha, Aki, Annie, and beloved brother Charles Medeiros

For Claire E. Shimizu and Melvin E. Spencer III

For ye were sometimes darkness,
but now are ye light in the Lord:
walk as children of light.

—Ephesians 5:8

Behold the Many

Kalihi Valley

1939

The valley is a woman lying on her back, legs spread wide, her geography wet by a constant rain. Waterfalls wash the days and nights of winter storms into the river that empties into the froth of the sea.

In the valley, the rain is a gossamer cloth, a tempest of water and leaves. The rain is southerly with strange foreboding. The rain is northerly with cool rime.

The rain glistens on maiden fern, the wind rustling the laua'e, the palapalai touching her there where it is always wet and seamy.

The valley is a woman with the features of a face, a woman whose eyes watch the procession of the celestial sphere; a woman with woodland arms outstretched and vulnerable, a woman with shadowy breasts of 'a'ali'i and hāpu'u, lobelias and lichens; a woman, a womb, impregnated earth.

O body.

When they find her, she is shiny, she is naked, she is bound, but for her legs, spread open and wet with blood and semen. Tears in her eyes, or is it rain? Breath in her mouth, or is it wind? Her thicket of hair drips into her mouth, sliced open from from ear to ear. She is pale green, *the silvery underside of kukui leaves*; her eyes and lips are gray, *the ashen hinahina*; her fingers and feet are white, *the winter rain in this valley.*

O body.

O beloved Hosana.

ANAH KNOWS her daughter is dead at the very moment of her passing. She is sitting early dawn in the honey house, surrounded by the hum of the wild swarms outside. Then the dead of a strange silence. Light enters the room in a strand that illuminates the particles of dust, the luminescence of bees' wings. Hosana enters the room in a flowing orange dress. She stops where the sunlight stills.

"Hosana?" Her daughter has been gone for weeks. Gone at fourteen with a man who called her beautiful. Gone to the other side of the island of O'ahu.

"Remember always, Mother," Hosana says without moving her lips, "love is sweet."

Honeybees move in the thick smell of the honey house.

She follows her daughter's slow gaze around the room as if placing the honey bins, the amber-filled bottles, the broken smoker, the dust of kiawe pollen, wooden frames, the scent of nectar, and finally her mother's face in her memory.

When the light fades, so does she. And then comes the wailing rain from a cloudless sky. Days of rain.

1916

The valley is a woman crying, a child's lonely wailing. Nothing but the river moaning down the mountain.

The valley is a woman's breath, a child's whisper. Nothing but the language of wind in trees.

In this valley, Anah's little sister died. On the night of her death, Anah walked down the steep staircases of the orphanage, Aki behind her holding on to the back of her nightdress. It was dark beyond midnight; the nuns were asleep in their small cells on the second floor. Anah stole a bottle of honey and a cube of honeycomb from the kitchen.

No one knew that Leah had died but Anah and Aki who sat beside her bed as she choked on sputum and blood. Her labored breaths grazed her throat, then crackled with hollow relief in her tiny chest.

"Okaasan coming tomorrow," Anah told her. *Don't die.* "And Charles, Charles too. He coming. *Don't die, don't die.* You have to be well so they can take us home for Easter dinner."

"Liar," Aki whispered. She looked away from Leah. "They never coming back for us."

Leah turned her face to the porcelain bowl with blue flowers on the bed stand beside her. She heaved thick strands of blood from the side of her mouth, missing the bowl. "He coming," she said.

"Yes, I promise," Anah told her, gently taking her hand.

"Who?" Aki asked. "Who coming?"

"No, Dai, no!" Leah rasped, her eyes fixed on the ceiling. "Dai, no!"

She died that night, that moment with her eyes open, horrified and stunned.

When little Leah died, Anah stole a bottle of honey from the kitchen, poured it on her face, a glaze over her sleeping eyes. *You're sleeping, that's all.* She poured it over her hair, brushed it to a glossy shine. *Never mind Sister Bernadine cut off your beautiful hair.* She rubbed the cube of honeycomb over her bloody lips, then placed it in her warm mouth. *In remembrance of me.*

Anah took her tiny right hand, Aki her left, and they bit off her fingernails. Anah cut off a thick strand of her hair with a kitchen knife. She placed these relics in the empty honey bottle filled with Leah's baby teeth and hid it in one of the dark closets on the third floor.

Then hand in hand, they waited for morning.

1939

Ezroh finds his beloved Anah sitting in the honey house. He is holding their daughter's hand.

"Get out, quick, the bees swarming!"

Their child in a young woman's body, sings a child's song:

Sweet dreams for thee, sweet dreams for thee.

Anah sits in the midst of this odd, mad swarm, the certain pitch and hum at their untimely displacement.

"Why you naked?" he yells, waving his arms at the furious swarm.

There's not a comb of honeybee,

so full of sweets as babe to me.

He tries to pull her shirt over her head, then urges her to run. Their woman-child laughs at bees crawling on her hands, her father brushing them away from her face. He pulls her away from the honey house.

And it is o! sweet, sweet!

Anah sits in the blur of the old hive, stares at the green stinger barbs writhing in her hands, face, breasts, belly, thighs, and feet. And when she is fully pierced, she walks out of the honey house, the swarm emitting a high pitch behind her.

O BODY.

SHE PLACES the corpse of her firstborn, her beloved Hosana, on a long table covered with her best lace tablecloth in the parlor. *Watch,*

O Lord. She lights beeswax candles blessed by Father Maurice. *Those who weep tonight.* She folds her daughter's hands on her breast with the knotted sennit rosary. *Bless your dead ones.*

A snail slides across the threshold.

The woman-child sings:

Worm, nor snail, do no offense.

A rice sparrow hits the window.

The woman-child sings:

What nestlings do in the nightly dew?

An owl cries from the ironwood trees.

The woman-child sings:

Night is come. Owls are out.

She covers her daughter with foliage from the Koʻolau Mountains: woodland arms of kukui; breasts of ʻaʻaliʻi and hāpuʻu; hair of hinahina and lichens; body of palapalai and lauaʻe. She rains holy water on Hosana's body. And then she anoints her daughter with royal jelly, brushing honey into her beautiful long hair. She kneels before her daughter, then prays for her soul all night.

O beloved Hosana.

When Father Maurice and Sister Mary Deborah arrive in the morning, she is holding her daughter's cold hand. She kisses her face in this house one last time.

Glory be to the Father. The horse-drawn buggy pulls away.

To the Son. The church bells echo.

And to the Holy Spirit. She follows the body deeper into the valley.

As was in the beginning. The valley is a woman lying on her back.

Is now and ever shall be. The rain is a gossamer cloth.

World without end. Her many dead ones surround her.

Amen. A vincible God resides in this valley.

Someone is praying. The prayers do not end:

"Hail, holy Queen, Mother of mercy, my life and my hope, to you

I do cry, poor banished child of Eve; to you do I send up my sighs, mourning, and weeping in this valley of tears.

"Hail, holy Queen, Mother of mercy, my life and my hope, to you I do cry to ask the Father on my behalf:

"Tell me how, O Lord," Anah cries, "how have I so offended thee?"

1

1913

Little Leah was the first to be taken to the orphanage deep in Kalihi Valley.

For months, Anah watched as Okaasan quietly burned the strips of old rice bag into which Leah had coughed up her contagious blood. Okaasan did not want Dai to discover their littlest one's illness. And she did not want Leah to infect the rest of the family.

Anah and Charles did as Okaasan had asked, collecting the soft tips of the a'ali'i and white ginger blossoms as the crippled kahuna lapa'au la'au who lived among the Chinese in Pake Camp Two had instructed. His Hawaiian herbal remedies had helped many of the plantation's immigrant workers. So at the kahuna's behest, Okaasan instructed Anah to cut stalks of young sugarcane from the field behind their house in Portuguese Camp Four.

She held her sister Aki's hand as they watched their mother extract all of the sweet liquid from these plants in her hidden nook furnished with wooden crates and planks behind the makeshift furo house Dai had built far away from Japanese Camp Three.

The eldest, Thomas, skulked around the banana trees. "Go do your schoolwork right now, Thomas and Charles," Okaasan said in her native Japanese to her first and second sons. "I do not want the mean-spirited teacher to chastise you again." Okaasan twisted and squeezed the cheesecloth she had taken from the noisy tōfu-ya lady from Fukuoka-ken to strain the juices of the flowers and plants. "And you," Okaasan said to Aki, placing a kind hand on the little one's face, "go watch for your father. I heard the pau hana whistle. Give me a warning as soon as you see him coming." Aki's small body disappeared beyond the furo house.

"Okaasan, what about Anah?" Thomas yelled in anger. "She has schoolwork too. How come you never scold Anah?"

"Never mind about Anah. She is not your concern. She is helping me," Okaasan said to him. "Go, go, hurry. Get out of here," she said to Anah, pushing her back, "or Thomas might—"

"Okaasan!" Aki called in warning from the front of the house.

"She is over there again in back of the house," Thomas reported to Dai in his native Portuguese, "making her useless plant medicine. She never listens to you, Father. She has not ironed your shirts. She has not made your dinner. And she is always talking in secret to the crippled kanaka man from Camp Two."

Anah moved to the opening of the nook to shield her mother from Dai's sight. Okaasan began pouring the juices together, haphazardly swiping the remnants of stem and leaf onto the ground.

Dai appeared as a huge, grotesque shadow in the shade of the nook. He pushed Anah out of his way, knocking over crates and planks. "Sumi," he called to his wife, "whassamatta you?" Homemade mead on his breath, he grabbed the tin can from her, sniffed it, then threw it over his shoulder.

"No, no! Baby sick-u, baby sick-u, Tomasu," Okaasan cried. She coughed into her hands to demonstrate the child's illness.

"How come you no cook my kaukau? Pau work, past pau hana time," Dai said, pulling Okaasan toward him by the sleeve of her cotton kimono. Okaasan would not respond. Dai was drunk. He spoke in Portuguese even though Okaasan did not understand. "My house is always filthy. And there is no food on my dinner table. My mother cooks better, anyway. Thomas and Charles," he called to his sons, "I am eating dinner with your grandmother. You can come with me or go hungry with your damned useless sisters."

Thomas followed Dai. They would eat a hearty Portuguese ham hock stew with sweet bread that Okaasan was forced to bake twice a week for Vovó Medeiros and various other Portuguese in-laws in the large community forno that the haole owner of the O'ahu Sugar Company had built for his immigrant workers at the center of Portuguese Camp Four.

Anah helped her mother off the ground. She dusted herself off, then rushed to the kitchen to boil corn tea for their dinner of rice and pickled cabbage.

Anah motioned for Charles to follow her into the mountains above Kīpapa Stream to gather more sugarcane, a'ali'i, and white ginger. In the dark of evening, in the nook behind the furo house, Anah extracted the juices of these plants.

Okaasan smiled at Anah when she presented her with the pulp-filled can. She sniffed it, dipped a finger, tasted it, and nodded. She quickly poured some of the liquid into little Leah's tea, then forced Anah, Aki, and Charles to drink the rest of the bitter tonic.

IT RAINED the day they took Leah to the orphanage in Kalihi Valley cradled deep in the Ko'olau Mountains, one of two volcanoes that formed the island of O'ahu. Freshwater streams and waterfalls ran from the wet upper peaks of Kalihi Uka to lower Kalihi Kai to Ke'ehi Lagoon, just west of Honolulu Harbor but many miles away from the O'ahu Sugar Plantation.

"Tuberculosis is highly contagious," the haole camp doctor had whispered to Dai in the quiet of the front room. "Many people world-wide, Tomas, living in unsanitary conditions I might add, have become infected by this epidemic. A terrible, terrible contagion." He tsked-tsked.

Dai nodded, utterly afraid for years of the leprosy that took a second cousin, then an older sister, then an aunt to the dreaded peninsula of no return, Kalaupapa, where a leper colony was established on Molokai's rugged north shore in 1886 by royal order of King Kamehameha V. Afraid of the bubonic plague that swept through an overcrowded and filthy Chinatown in 1900, the Board of Health forgoing quarantine and disinfection in favor of a purging by fire, leaving thirty-eight acres of slum in rubble and ash. Afraid of the epidemic of cholera, the worst outbreak since the maʻi ʻōkuʻu that swept the Sandwich Islands in 1804, this time taking a paternal grandmother who shared living quarters with the Medeiros family soon after her arrival from the Azores in early 1889. Afraid of the influenza, typhus, whooping cough, the polio that crippled his younger brother, the smallpox that killed the newborn and the elderly. And now very ashamed of the stigma of the consumption that threatened his entire extended family living in Portuguese Camp Four. And all because of *his* infected youngest daughter.

"I realize that on your luna's pay, you cannot afford the sanatorium at Leahi Hospital, Tomas," the doctor said, snapping his bag shut with authority. "So it is my urgent recommendation that you make arrangements for your daughter to be taken immediately to St. Joseph's. Mr. Campbell has instructed me to make absolutely certain that the child infected with the consumption is gone by—"

"Haibiyo?" Okaasan stammered.

"Yes, Mama-san, tu-ber-cu-lo-sis," the camp doctor enunciated loudly as though she were deaf and stupid. "Con-sump-shun. Very ki-ta-nai. Very pi-lau. Very su-jo." He looked pleased to speak the word *dirty* in many plantation languages.

"Akachan no come home?" Okaasan asked the doctor.

"Your daughter is *not* a baby, Mama-san."

"*Akachan* no come home?" Okaasan repeated.

The doctor shook his head. "She will receive adequate care from the Sisters of the Sacred Heart," he said. "Many plantation workers in your si-tua-tion—no more mo-ney. Send sick child St. Joseph get better. When sickness all gone, maybe your child come home, Mama-san."

"No, me, I go," Okaasan insisted, patting her chest. "Me go with akachan. Me Mama. You talk to Nihon-jin doku-toru?"

The doctor, agitated and insulted now, knew of the Japanese doctors she referred to. "I am a better physician," he told her. The Japanese doctors were brought to eight sugar plantations in 1886 by edict of the Bureau of Immigration.

In his anger, he began making large, impatient gestures as he tried to explain to her. "Over there in mountain, Mama-san, there are German brothers and priests—very nice, very good men of God. They build very big foundling home." He paused, not wanting to frighten her with an explanation of *orphanage*. "Hos-pi-tal, three-story, Mama-san. Plenty nuns. Way inside the mountain. Clean air," he said, exaggerating a deep, robust breath. "Proper diet—tabe-mono. Consumption all gone. Girl must go now, Mama-san. You listen to me or else—"

"No, no," Okaasan told the doctor. "Way *in* mountain?" she asked. She did not wait for his answer. "No. Tomasu—" She turned to Dai. "You talk to the Japanese doctors the plantation brought to help us," she said to him in her native language, panicked and unable to find the words in pidgin.

"No, Mama-san, the girl must go now," the doctor insisted. "Very bad, very bad. You have four other keiki and family relations living close by. The girl is ki-ta-nai, Mama-san, *dirty*," he said with great impatience and import.

"Me take her back to Nihon," Okaasan said. "Maybe they can provide proper treatment in Japan," she consoled herself in Japanese.

"We have no money. The poor send their children to orphanages.

It must be done or Mr. Campbell will take away my job," Dai said in an angry Portuguese. "It cannot be helped. It is God's will."

She did not understand his words.

"We no mo' money, Sumi-san. Listen doctor," Dai said, taking her face in his hands. "No mo' money for sanatoria. All kine family in plantation same-same. Children sick, go St. Joseph." He would have hit her had the doctor not been there. "Meu família," he said at last with great concern, looking out the window toward Vovó Medeiros's house. "I no like them sick from this *Japanee* illness—" He stopped, catching himself.

"*Your* family. You only think about your own kind. Your own kind is filthier than the pigs," Okaasan said in Japanese. "The Portuguese do not even bathe every night. Even the women are covered with hair. Your kind stinks worse than the Chinese. Our daughter was infected by the Portuguese."

"Speakee English," he said, glowering at her. "You listen me. And you listen doctor. All pau. No mo' talk." Dai looked at Leah lying on the futon by the window. "She go today," he said to the doctor. "You tell Mr. James Campbell, Medeiros like stay luna. Me listen Mr. James Campbell. Me not troublemaker." And then he muttered in Portuguese, "I will take her there myself if I have to."

Anah helped her mother, who collapsed into a chair. Dai left the house with the doctor, slamming the door behind him.

ANAH RODE with Charles and Leah in the back of the Andrade Dairy buggy full of empty milk cans and bottles. The smell of spoiled milk soaked deep into the wooden bed. Okaasan rode up front with Manuel Andrade. It would be a long day's trip from the O'ahu Sugar Plantation over the dry 'Ewa plains and into the city of Honolulu. The heat at sea level made the smell of sour milk unbearable.

They rode past groves of tall coconut trees, Chinese rice plantations, and taro farms near the huge ancient Hawaiian fishponds, twenty-seven in total, built by a chain of native men and boys from mountain to sea who moved rocks shoulder to shoulder to build the walls of the ponds. Hundreds of acres once the royal property of area kings and queens lined the coastal lands of the Pearl Harbor lochs.

They passed through the endless fields of rolling cane as they traveled along the train tracks of the Oʻahu Railway built by a young, entrepreneurial Benjamin Franklin Dillingham. The train tracks, for years many called "Dillingham's Folly," would soon find the support of King David Kalākaua in 1889, the train tracks that brought king sugar to port, the train tracks that would lead Anah, her mother, brother, and little sister on this day to the city of Honolulu.

From the train station near the piers, Manuel Andrade clopped-clopped the horses along King Street, bustling with women under plumed hats and parasols, Chinamen mea ʻono puaʻa vendors, stray cats, a Japanese funeral parlor, haole businessmen in formal suits, the candy man, fish peddlers, soldiers and whores, babies tied to the backs of mama-sans, noisy street merchants, and oxcarts filled with bags of rice or Japanese and Korean picture brides straight from the docks at Honolulu Harbor.

Anah listened to the slow squeak of the bed and the solemn creak of the wheels on the unpaved road. She had never seen the big, modern city of Honolulu, but fearing for the welfare of the little one, she turned her attention toward comforting her.

The buggy headed up into the mountains, past haole mission homes with vast lawns, Japanese flower growers, Okinawan piggeries, wet Chinese taro patches, and Portuguese and Hawaiian dairies, finally dropping them off on the deserted, narrow road leading to Kalihi Valley.

Charles hurried out of the back, Anah passing little Leah to him, as Okaasan bowed and bowed to Manuel Andrade, offering him bentō, fresh produce from her garden, and a loaf of sweet bread that she had packed for the long journey. He smiled briefly with a tip of his straw hat. They did not exchange words. He accepted her obligatory gifts, then spit tobacco juice on the ground with a quick jingle of the harness. He pulled the buggy away.

It began to drizzle. They walked to the orphanage in the rain on a dirt road that followed Kalihi Stream, the muddy smell of the taro patches and duck ponds at the foot of the Kapālama Hills, the debris of fallen mangoes, pungent, the fuzzy gray seeds slippery underfoot.

Anah tended to little Leah, who began falling behind when the road became a meandering mountainous trail, the mud deepening with the whipping rain. She was so tiny, this winter of her fifth year. She stopped to fill the scoop of her dress with soft mangoes.

"They get 'ono kaukau ova there," Anah told her, taking the rotten mangoes and wiping the orange slime off her sister's dress. "You eat plenty good food, make you all pau sick."

"And they got real toilet paper so you don't scratch your little ass when you wipe your shit," Charles added. He spoke in the crude Japanese he had learned from the disgraced gannenmono samurai who lived in a lean-to beyond the whorehouse on the banks of Waikele Stream. "Steal some for me when I come to visit you. I can wrap some around my penis to keep it warm at night." He ruffled her wet hair when she laughed, punching at his stomach, then pushing him away from her. Large drops of rain fell from the trees. They took shelter from a heavy downpour.

Leah looked at Anah. "Where we going?" she asked tentatively.

Anah did not answer.

"You staying with me?"

No answer.

"When you all pau sick, I come back fast," Anah said at last, taking Leah's small hand in her own. "No worry, okay? Only chotto you stay ova there," she said with a small space between forefinger and thumb.

Anah hoped that Leah believed her.

Charles took out a long swath of rice bag that Okaasan had used to carry them when they were infants. He tied Leah onto his back like the strong big brother he was to his sisters even though Thomas was a full year older and Anah exactly nine months younger than him.

"My akachan," he said to Leah as she rested her cold face on his back. She always loved to pretend she was *his* baby.

"My paipa," she whispered into his ear, "my chichi." He always loved to pretend he was *her* father.

"Mine," Anah said, "my paipa!" She reached for Leah as Charles ran ahead. "My daddy, my chichi!"

Leah laughed at their game of keep-away.

Okaasan trudged on ahead of them, crying, wiping her face with both hands. She had no one, no family to turn to, disowned from Nihon to Hawai'i to Amerika to Kanada to Buraziru. She had disgraced the aggressive village matchmaker from Yanai City and her own desperate father by running away from her marriage contract, running from the docks of Honolulu Harbor with the filthy, hairy Porutogaru-go.

Anah stopped on the trail when she saw the foreboding three-story orphanage run by the Sisters of the Sacred Heart, built plank by plank at the turn of the century by two holy brothers, master carpenters from Germany, who were called on to serve the blessed church by Bishop Lanfranc Deusdedit, the third apostolic vicar of the Hawaiian Islands.

With a work crew of brothers and natives, the bishop himself had supervised the arrival, inventory, then hauling of each truss, joist, and main beam from Honolulu Harbor up the ominous valley by buggy. The holy brothers loaded their supplies onto mule wagons, then hand-carried them to the expansive site when the road narrowed from a horse trail to a mountainous path.

The cross on its rooftop made from chene wood imported from the bishop's native Fain-les-Moutiers stood white against a black sky.

Okaasan walked slowly over the spacious, soggy front lawn. Anah and Charles carried Leah and followed behind her. Then under a grove of mountain apple trees, near a patch of beautiful white ginger, on a bridge over a raging Kalihi Stream, they left her.

She clung to Okaasan as Anah untied her from the sling. And then she held on to Charles, who screamed her name as the nuns pulled her away from him. Leah wriggled loose and ran back to Anah's open arms, the huge white nun restraining her tiny arms and legs.

Anah felt Leah torn from her body, torn from that space in her belly left churning and empty.

Okaasan held Leah's coughing and gagging face in her hands as the nuns tried to separate them, Leah's arms outstretched, the wind pulsating with her cries, "Okaasan! Okaasan! No leave me!"

Her wailing, frantic voice echoed, and echoed, and echoed. A dog's long howling, an owl's plaintive cry, the high whinny of a whipped horse. Anah ran down the rocky dirt road for miles, the road that led them out of Kalihi Valley.

Little Leah's Lament

Rain rain go away come again another day.

No cry Okaasan. Only rain in my mouth. The blood all pau. I like come home.

See Dai. No more blood. I promise. The cough all pau now, Dai. I like come home.

No more pilau.

No more blood.

Only the blood of a lamb. Jesus stay with me now. He the boy with white hair. The one was waiting for me on the bridge.

'Be not afraid,' he say to me.

I not afraid. I Leah.

'Sister of Rachel,' he say.

No, sister of Anah.

'Sister of Zilpah,' he say.

No, sister of Aki.

'Sister of Bilhah,' he say.

No, sister of Charles.

'Daughter of Laban,' he say.

No, daughter of Sumi.

Jesus get all the white ginger.

Make tonic, I tell him. Just like my mama.

'For your long hair. Wear it in your long hair,' he say to me.

But they take me away from him. He stay on the bridge with the white ginger in his hand.

I in the outside room all by myself on a chair I waiting.

"Full of nits and lice," the small one say.

"They are all horribly infested with the vermin," the big one say.

The big one smell like vinegar. Daisy bonnet around her pink face. All white dress, all white, only face and hands I see. Black boots with broken lace. And plenty beads swinging.

The small one smell like honey.

They scrub me with pig soap.

"Filthy filthy full of the krankheit," the big one say. She scrub and scrub my ching-ching, my 'ōkole hole.

Owee owee.

"Hush now. Hush. You are full of the pestilence," she say.

Then she do the head stomach shoulder shoulder.

Owee owee.

Jesus come. Jesus watch.

The big one put the pig soap on my head. Ten fingers scrub, scrub. "The razor, Sister," she say. "The child is full of eggs full of eggs, dreckig, sweet Lord Jesus."

My hair all around my feet. No more hair on my head.

Jesus cry. His white ginger fall in the water.

"Put this on," the big one say.

The big white dress feel rough. The big white panty feel rough. Too big too big.

"Sister, they're much too ill fitting for the child," the small one say. "She is such a slight little lamb the poor little lamb."

Head stomach shoulder shoulder.

"We have nothing this small," the big one says. "Hush your crying now hush."

Jesus walk in front of me. Up the first long stairs then up the next long stairs.

'Be not afraid for I am with thee.'

I not afraid. I Leah.

"Here is your bed, child," the small one says. She smell like honey, little daisy face.

"The children are having their supper," the big one says. "You are to join us—ummittelbar—" She smell like vinegar.

Rain rain has gone away. Another day. No one come see me. I like go home. No one come get me. I like go home. No one but Jesus. Jesus with me now. Jesus is a boy with white hair. Jesus is a sad boy. Jesus is a lonely boy. Jesus is just like me.

I wear the white ginger in my short hair.

(Sister not looking.) I put the white ginger in my soup.

"No," the big one scold. "No more pagan remedies."

(Not looking.) In my milk.

"Nein, I said no more." She hit my hands.

Looking. In my bread.

"Nein! Nein! Nein! Godless heathen!"

Head stomach shoulder shoulder.

The stick on my hand again and again.

See Dai, no more cough. See Okaasan, no more blood. Only blood on my hands.

I in the dark closet. All by myself on the cold floor. I waiting. I afraid.

'My name is—' he says to me.

Who? What? Jesus? I no can see you.

No one come get me. Sun under the door. Moon under the door. Okaasan, I hungry. This food not like home. Anah, I like mango. Why you wen' take the mango. You said they had good food here. Not good. I hungry. This food not like home.

I smell vinegar under the door.

The door open.

She yank me up the stairs then up another stairs to my bed. Push me to the ground.

Licken. Licken.

"Nein heathen practices. Nein pagan rituals. You will confess your sin."

Head stomach shoulder shoulder.

The stick on my head. The stick on my back. The stick on my legs.

Somebody had put white ginger all over my bed.

1914

Aki was taken after Leah to the orphanage deep in the valley.

Aki coughed up blood at the dinner table. The red blood bubbled over the tender catfish Dai had poached from the artesian waters of the rice fields farmed by the Chinese Ma Lee Chong along the western border of the Oʻahu Sugar Plantation.

Dai slammed the dishes off the table. The cat licked the fish head until he kicked her away, spine and tail in mouth. Then he jabbed his finger on Aki's forehead. "You go St. Joseph tomorrow," he said. "We no mo' money for the sanatoria. Let the holy sisters take care you."

But Anah knew. Aki would not go without a fight.

Aki would run away and hide forever.

Aki would wield a knife to keep him from taking her.

"Leah need you," Anah told her as she backed into the corner of the kitchen.

"I go there, I no come back," Aki said, her hand groping for the butcher knife on the sink, "just like Leah."

"She all by herself."

Aki's shoulders slackened for a moment.

It was all the time Dai needed to grab her, first by her hair and then by her throat. "Thomas, go get the rope."

Thomas skipped out the door.

"Tomasu, no!" Okaasan screamed, her hands reaching for Dai. "Leave her alone," she began pleading in Japanese. "No one has to know. Even Mr. Campbell will not know, I promise. I will hide her from the Board of Health inspector. I will hide her from the constable. I will take her with me to Japan. Do not let them take another daughter from me."

Aki flailed wildly in Dai's grasp like a squealing piglet. "Okaasan! Anah!" she rasped.

Anah looked at Charles, who rose from the dining bench.

"Sit your ass down, boy," Dai growled in Portuguese, as he covered Aki's mouth with his huge hand.

Okaasan stood there, holding her breath, her eyes mirroring Aki's panic.

"Clean up the blood," he said to Okaasan.

She did not move, her hands forming fists.

He shoved her against the sink. "Clean the pilau." Anah scrambled for a dishrag. "Clean the filth, Sumi," he said, snatching the rag from Anah's hand.

Okaasan hesitated, frozen in place. She looked first at Charles and then at Anah, who understood in that moment:

Her mother could not save any of them, so she contemplated saving only herself.

Okaasan ran out the back door, bumping into Thomas, who eagerly handed Dai the rope.

The blood dripped into the floorboards as Anah watched him tie Aki's arms behind her. She struggled against the rope while he bound her legs. He dragged her to the outhouse and blocked the door from the outside. He didn't gag her mouth. He wanted Okaasan to hear her wailing throughout the night.

Wherever Okaasan was hiding.

ANAH KNEW the outhouse smelled of Dai's piss embedded in the termite-rotting walls. The urine stank of the mead he swilled with Manuel Andrade who reeked of sour milk sweat, Pedro Torres his uncle who habitually touched his testicles, and Floyd Pacheco his second cousin who had a white eye. The Portuguese were famous for their homemade mead, the Japanese their homemade sake, the Hawaiians their ʻōkolehao. Dai indulged every night in them all for a pau hana oblivion. He drank and drank like many of the plantation men to forget the hardship of their days.

Aki screamed until her throat dried and hissed.

Anah listened to Dai grunting in the next room, Okaasan's quick breath, placating his anger with her numb body. The shucked grass mattress shifted and moved under their bodies. Anah closed her eyes and pulled herself close to Charles when Aki's wailing resumed. He covered her with the small rice bag blanket they shared and put his hands over her ears.

But then, Anah *saw* her:

In the corner near the metal washtub with the broken washboard, Aki pulls her hands, bound behind her, pulls her arms under her buttocks. She moves her buttocks, her thighs, her feet over her arms, her back arched, shoulders nearly dislocating, then falls over to the side, hitting her head on the edge of the washtub, the pop of bone and joint.

Anah listened closely to the sounds of this night, the *flap-flap-flap* of a rooster's midnight stretch, the skitter of cane rats, Aki's pain-filled cry.

Because, Anah *saw* her.

'No, Aki,' Anah spoke with her mind, 'do not bite the ropes.'

The rats smell her blood, big, black cane rats with thick, pink tails. Tools fall. Glass breaks.

"Anah! Charles!" she screamed.

The thudding of her body against the walls of the outhouse, the rats jumping at her, yellow eyes, black claws, her face caught in a spider's web and blood on her hands and feet.

Anah threw the blanket off her, listened to Dai's final moan, Okaasan's padding to the washstand in the corner of their room. Charles held her arm. "Chotto," he whispered, "wait 'til he go sleep. Only little while more."

Thomas stirred on his lauhala mat.

Anah pulled herself away from Charles. Because she saw and heard them all:

The dog scratches at the outhouse door. Cats in heat mewl. Goats cry like screaming babies. Pigs frantically root and growl. The frenzied screech of rats. Aki shrieks.

Anah stepped into the kitchen. The floorboards shifted. The kerosene lantern hissed, the pump creaked, and then the globe ignited with hollow authority. Anah snapped the back door open.

She *saw* her.

Huddled, whimpering, hitting her head against the closed door.

Anah held the lantern up to the night and moved toward the outhouse, a circle of light on the stepping-stones ahead of her, when out of the darkness and into her path, she saw Dai.

"Get inside the house right now. You mind me, Anah," he snarled at her in Portuguese. "You want to get sick too? I already lost two children. You must understand. I do not want to lose another child."

Anah tried to run past him.

He yanked the lantern from her hand, then backhanded her face, knocking her to her knees, kicking her, beating her until she lost all breath, sound and sight funneling far, far away.

Aki *saw* Anah from behind the closed door, huddled, fetal on the grass.

"Anah?"

It was strangely beautiful, hearing her sister whisper her name, breathy and soft, the moment before she lost all consciousness.

"WE WILL VISIT Aki and Leah the first Sunday of every month," Okaasan said in her Japanese monotone at the kitchen table early the next morning. "After all, we are still a family."

Anah cringed as Okaasan wrapped her bruised body with strips of cloth soaked in a mixture of crushed koa bark, noni leaves, and rock salt.

"And they will be home with us very soon, you will see. Your father has promised me. And your sisters will be well again. The holy nuns provide good treatment and care for the poor and sick children."

Anah said nothing.

Okaasan placed more bark, leaves, and a handful of rock salt in her mortar, the slow grind of the pestle against stone.

"Tomas!" Manuel Andrade called, pulling his buggy to a stop in front of their house. "Apressar, Tomas, merda!" He could not afford to lose another day's wages.

Okaasan startled.

The horses whinnied with impatience.

Charles put his face in his hands.

Anah listened to Aki's gutteral moans as Dai pulled her sister like a wounded animal through the vegetable garden. She listened to the thud of her body as he threw her into the back of the buggy, the heavy thunking of the milk cans and empty bottles around her.

"Charles, hele mai," Dai yelled, "appressar, boy."

"We go, Okaasan," Charles begged. "We go Nihon. You, me, and Anah. We take Aki with us."

Okaasan dipped the hem of her apron into the mortar and swabbed at the open welts on Anah's face that burned her eyes to tears. But Anah would not cry.

"And your father has promised that we will bring them home for Christmas," she whispered, her fingers moving slowly inside the cuts, the grit of Anah's angry teeth. "The nuns said we could bring them home for the day. Your father wants to make a feast for them with a suckling pig and his favorite rabbit stew. He will do all of this if I am a good wife to him. I have promised to bear him many more sons."

"Tomas!" Manuel Andrade yelled.

"Charles!" Dai called again, impatient now. "You better get your ass out here right now. You mind my words." Charles feared Dai's earthy Portuguese that accompanied a black eye or bruised ribs, but he lingered a moment longer to beg his mother to leave.

Thomas grinned with a strange glee as he slipped out the back door with his book bag. Their father would never risk sending his first-born son with the infected child.

The horses cried.

"Please, Okaasan," Charles pleaded.

Dai barged through the back door. "You listen to me," he said, grabbing Charles by his neck.

"No, no, Tomasu, I make money. I wash-wash clothes and make bentō for all the bayau man with no wife," Okaasan said, her hands grasping onto Dai's shirt. "I go hō hana in the field. I delivery for the tōfu-ya mama-san. Aki go Nihon. Aki go Leahi."

"The home for the incurables," Dai said in Portuguese with a shake of his head. "They will both be dead before you earn enough money." He shoved Charles toward the door.

"Me go, me go with Aki," Okaasan said, quickly following. "Me help Leah and Aki 'til sick-u all gone."

"No, you stay home with me, Sumi."

"Hah? No, Tomasu, me go with akachan," she insisted.

"You not going, Sumi. I no like you get sick."

"No, me go. Me no like Chazu get sick-u. Me go," she said.

Then Dai struck her across the face with his large hand. "Every night we can make more children. I can have many, many children, but I have only one wife. You are staying with me."

She moaned, helpless and yet strangely resigned.

Dai threw Charles into the buggy. Anah scrambled after him. She would accompany him on the long journey.

"Where you think you going?" Dai yelled, grabbing her from behind.

"Bumbye Charles get lost," Anah said, thinking fast. "Charles dunno para casa. Aki run. I help catch."

Dai looked at Manuel Andrade, who shook his head. "Your second youngest with the Japanee name is a bad girl, ask anyone in Camp Four," he said to Dai in Portuguese. "Ask the priest, ask the schoolteacher, ask any of your relations. She will run from your son and bring the consumption right back to your family—right back to all of us. Your eldest daughter is right. She will help your son bring your bad daughter to the nuns, then assist him in making his way home on foot. It is a long and arduous journey, Tomas. And they are only children."

Dai paused. "Ride up front with Manuel," he said at last to Anah. "Get up front, boy," he said to Charles, pulling him out of the back. "Do not untie your sister until you get to St. Joseph's," he instructed them. "And do not touch her unless she runs. If she comes back home, I will beat the both of you to your deaths."

"Yes, Dai," Anah whispered, burying her face in Charles's shoulder.

The buggy pulled away from the house. Anah turned to see her father drawing water from the drinking barrel. He sipped it hard and fast like a shot of cheap B & W scotch whiskey. There was a stern sadness on his face.

Her mother stood beside him in a defiant nonchalance. She washed her hands, then emptied the water from the dipper onto her tiny feet in wooden geta. She stood there until the buggy pulled out of sight.

Beyond the luna's palatial home, its broad lānai shaded by jacaranda trees in bloom, haole ladies sipped iced tea with mint leaves and fanned themselves on lawn chairs by the haole children on the swings. The luna's prized Irish setters ran across the expansive lawn among the haole men in the middle of their croquet game.

Beyond were the last rows of Japanese laborers' shacks built with old planks and bamboo, their rooftops thatched with dried sugarcane leaves and covered with kabocha vines, open sewage ditches running alongside the children playing with sticks on the dirt road. Manuel Andrade brought the horses to a stop.

"Get in the back and help your pitiful sister," he said to them in Portuguese. "We are all still blood." Thereafter, he said not a word.

Anah hurried over the milky damp floor to get to Aki. Her wrists and ankles were cut open with deep rope burns, the flesh on her arms and face animal bitten, her clothes caked with phlegm and dried blood. Anah spit into the hem of her dress and tried to wipe the blood from the corners of Aki's eyes. Charles put his teeth to the tight knots and tugged hard to undo the ropes. Aki's eyes rolled white, then focused briefly on Anah.

"I saw you," her lips mouthed.

"I know," Anah said, their bodies melting together. "I saw you too. I heard you calling me."

"I know."

Anah cradled her body and rocked her as the buggy followed the train tracks to the city.

Aki's Resolve

I am Aki.

"Breathe the clean mountain air," they tell me.

I hate this place.

"Eat the oatmeal with honey and cream."

No taste good this haole food.

"Bed rest, lots of bed rest."

I hate this place.

"Wear this scratchy white dress."

Where my clothes? This not mine. Hah? Na-ni-wa? I pretend to only speak Japanese.

"Do the morning calisthenics."

I hate this place.

"Feed the hens."

Let them die.

"Bleach your bedding."

I hate this place.

"Harvest the bush beans."

Trample the vines.

"Pray."

God is dead. I will sin.

And I tell them in the language of my mother:

I will take your croquet mallet, crush the cats' skulls, thou shalt, thou shalt kill.

I will steal your holy oil, pour it on my feet, thou shalt, thou shalt defile.

I will shove the jacks into the pigs' eyes, watch them bleed, the devil's in the piggies.

I will throw my pantaloons into the river, run naked over the lawn.

I will steal sausages from the salt crocks, eat it raw in a cave.

I will eat the honeycombs, thou shalt steal it, thou shalt steal it.

Take care Leah? Who talking to me? Anah?

'Leah need you.'

Anah, I need you, Anah. You can see me? You can hear me? Charles? Okaasan?

'Take care our Leah, akachan Leah, baby Leah.'

Shut up, all of you shut up. She's not a baby. I dunno where she stay. Where you stay, Leah? They all so worried about you. Worried about their akachan. But what about me? Who going take care me?

I want to scratch you, run, little Leah.

I want to pinch you, run, little Leah.

I want to slap you. Run.

And I tell them:

I here because of her. She poison me. She infect me. Made me sick. Sick like her. Where my sister?

Nobody tell me.

I ask them all.

Nobody tell me.

Someone whisper, 'In the closet, in the closet, third floor, the dark closet.'

So I find her. She scared. She small in the corner. No be scared, I tell her. It's me, Aki. I not going kill you if you run with me. We go run.

Stay here? We not going get well. The sick ones, they all dying. Coughing up the blood and choking at night. The sick ones like you and me. Stupid akachan. No believe their lies.

"Jesus is here," she tell me in Japanese. "He will save me," she tell me. "See him standing right behind you?"

I turn around. Nobody there. So I hit her and hit her, stupid akachan. Get up off the floor, you all dirty. Who cut your hair? White ginger? What about the white ginger? Where? Get up. Right now.

"Jesus help me. I cannot see."

Jesus no like save you. Jesus not here.

"Okaasan! The light, the light, too bright, too bright."

Okaasan no can save you. Okaasan not here.

Your father ma-ke-die-dead.

"No."

I wen' kill him with the butcher knife.

"Anah!"

No more Anah. Your father ate her.

"Charles!"

No more Charles. Your big brother shove him in the forno where your vovó bakes her bread.

Dead. They all dead. Dead to you and me.

1915

The blood pooled in her hands. She fed it to the pigs. The blood pooled in her hands. She rinsed in the drinking barrel.

The blood pooled in her hands. She spilled it over the vegetables in the garden, mixed it into the bread, the rice, the goat's milk, rinsed it over the pots and dishes, and into her father's cup.

She could have hidden it from him, but she wanted the blood to pour from her lips like thick, red honey all over her father's table, his food, his drink, to infect him who refused them their mother's tonic, who reduced their beautiful mother to a wisp of her former self, who refused them visitation on the first Sunday of every month. They *never* visited Leah and Aki. They were to be in the house of the Resurrection of the Lord Our God.

Anah translated his terrible words to her mother when he said over their meals, "What the hell is wrong with you, Sumi? I raise them to be good Catholics. Pray the holy Rosary for your daughters like my mother and aunts do three times a day for *your* children. Go to Mass, you heathen Japanee. Only God can help them now."

They ate it, drank it, the body and blood of Dai's everlasting covenant:

The Agony.

So he ate and drank it. Of that Anah made sure.

MONTHS BEFORE the blood, Dai said that Charles and Anah would no longer be schooled by the plantation teacher. Thomas was smart. A born leader. "He takes after the Portuguese side of the family, even in appearance, stature, and natural tendencies, thanks be to the Holy Virgin," Vovó always said to Dai. "The second boy and the girl after him are stupid, good-for-nothings. Typical kowtowing Japanee. Just like the mother's side of the family. And they look like Oriental half-breeds. And so dark skinned." Vovó never cared who in Portuguese Camp Four heard her speak of her own grandchildren in this way.

Thomas would continue his schooling. Thomas would eat the best part of the fish, the fattest sausages, the freshest bread. Thomas would drink the richest cream. Thomas had the best blanket. Thomas would wear new shirts and trousers. Thomas would eat at Vovó's table every night.

Charles and Anah would be laborers.

THERE DID NOT seem enough hours in the day, even though they rose before the roosters. Charles began by cleaning the inside of the forno, rinsing the blackened rags again and again in a rusty cracker can. His face and clothes were covered with a fine soot, the black of his labor under his fingernails, an ashy film over the white of his eyes and teeth.

Anah milked the goat, keeping the best cream for her father's coffee and Vovó's icebox, the rest for the bread she baked for Vovó and her assorted relations and in-laws who lived in Portuguese Camp Four.

"You mind me, Anah. Scald the milk, you hear me? I don't want a heavy bread," she scolded in Portuguese, as Anah prepared the dough in the darkness of Vovó's kitchen twice a week.

Anah prayed to God to coax their temperamental hens into laying enough eggs for the bright yellow dough and egg-wash glossy loaves that Vovó demanded.

"Heaven save you, Anah, you better be using only egg yolks," she chided even on days when there weren't enough eggs. "And make sure you put a raw egg in the middle of the dough for *my* family's loaves," she commanded as though every day were Easter.

Anah needed more eggs and more eggs. Charles began feeding the hens a concoction of dandelion and marigold petals with a dash of ground arnotto in their mash as the bayau cockfighters from Ilocos Norte did. He did not want his sister so terribly beaten by Vovó Medeiros for pale, tasteless loaves that were not suited for her pigs.

The hens began to lay eggs with deep yellow yolks. Anah thanked Charles and God for the golden loaves she baked with fewer eggs. Their vovó began selling the bread. And Charles began breeding the bayau's best cocks with Vovó's thick, healthy hens.

All morning, Okaasan wandered the vegetable garden in the haze of her loss.

"Mãe demente?" the Portuguese midwife asked Anah as she removed her family's loaves from the camp's forno.

Anah shook her head, *No, my mother is not crazy.*

Bell peppers popped under Okaasan's bare feet, chives and green onions flattened. Anah quickly escorted her inside.

"Your okaasan, she went crazy, nei," the tōfu-ya mama-san commiserated as Anah finished their deliveries in Japanese Camp.

Anah shook her head, *No, my mother is not crazy.*

Squash vines pulled and ripped between Okaasan's dirty fingers. Charles placed the orange flowers and vine tips in the scoop of her apron as though she were harvesting them for dinner with salted pork.

"Your mother lost her mind when they took her children," the chu-umon tori lady said in Japanese while taking Anah's order for store goods.

"No, not crazy," Anah replied. "Mama hāpai. She having one mo' baby." She feigned the morning illness of a woman with child.

Dai, leather whip in hand, was always hard at work supervising the laborers in row after row of backbreaking field work, hard at work atop his white horse from dawn to dusk:

Chinese weeder women;

Puerto Rican cane seedling cutters;

Japanese hō hana women those who dug furrows for cane seed-lings;

Korean pulapula boys those who planted the stalks of cane;

Filipino harvesters those who went through the fields with cane knives;

Spanish liliko hāpai cane collectors those who bundled up the ma-ture stalks;

Japanese hāpai kō men those who carried the cut cane to mule wagons;

work lines divided along nationality lines, workers kept apart in the fields and in habitations to breed mistrust, jealousy, and innuendo among the immigrants, all penniless indentured slaves.

Dai, working dawn to dusk, would know nothing of Okaasan's con-dition. Charles and Anah did all of her chores. And they did their best to hide her from the sight of her gossiping Portuguese in-laws.

Charles slopped the pigs for her, boiling the rancid leftovers, rot-ten fruit, taro leaves and stems, and assorted maggot hatchlings in a five-gallon can. Anah poured the orange, bubbly, stinking sludge into the troughs.

Anah and Charles swept the floors and scrubbed the front room and the kitchen with coconut husks and broken pieces of lye soap. Dai demanded a clean, Portuguese house of Okaasan, so he would have it, of that they made sure.

Okaasan picked white ginger for Dai's table and played the koto she had brought over the ocean with her, the beautiful zither given to her by the blind priestess at the temple. She combed her long, black hair with scented oils, her fragile spirit terribly broken.

With Dai's house in order and his wife earnest in her carnal penance, he indulged her madness. Her melancholia would come to pass soon enough, he said to himself. But past the midnight hour while Dai drank and gambled at the stables, Okaasan, ghostlike, drifted from room to room, humming, staring, sighing, weeping without sound or tears.

Charles began sleeping beside Anah every night on the mats she once shared with Aki and Leah. She had become her drunken father's dawn whore, until the morning Charles held her and would not let their father take her. He almost died for her, Dai choking him to insensibility.

Okaasan sat in her rocking chair, the full moon spreading light on the fields of cane. Over and over, she repeated the Hail Mary, numbing herself with its holy repetition. Or was it the nembutsu, numbing herself with the Buddhist mantra? Anah could no longer tell.

She let her blood spill all over the spicy boiled pig meat on the table, the Portuguese bread, rabbit stew, rice, pickled radish, and wild cherry tomatoes. Charles cried softly but continued eating from the bloody mess, the strands of red saliva and phlegm hanging shiny from his spoon.

"YOU WILL BE home soon, my Anah. And Aki and Leah, I will see you all, my beautiful daughters," Okaasan called in a shrill Japanese to Anah's back as she walked away from the house. The morning sun was white and hot. "I will be there on the first Sunday of every month. I promise you."

Dai had forbidden her to touch Anah's clothing and bedding. He even forbade her from holding Anah one last time. He would not lose his wife. She could bear him more sons. Many more sons. Okaasan watched as Anah burned everything she owned, as Dai had instructed, in a huge pyre behind the house. She watched as Anah scoured the floors, the table, the crockery, the utensils, and the sink until her hands cracked open from the harsh bleach.

"I promise you, my beautiful daughter," she cried hysterically, reaching out her hands to Anah, "I will see you next Sunday."

Anah did not turn around. Her father would not ask Manuel Andrade to lose another day's wage to take her to the orphanage.

"You know the way. Follow the train track," Dai said that morning. "Manuel has family too. I will not be the cause of consumption infecting his wife and children," he explained to Anah. "House all pau clean, Sumi?" he called to Okaasan.

She nodded, *yes*.

"Fire all pau? Thomas and Charles inside?"

Okaasan composed herself. She did not want to be beaten. She nodded slowly.

"Then go, Anah," he said, a kind of fear in his eyes. "Go on. Go away from here. Do not make me call the constable. Go with God."

It began to rain from a hot white sky.

Anah saw him again when she passed the stables where Pedro Torres and Floyd Pacheco squatted near the small, muddy corral. They drank their mead from large flasks, the other men laughing, the rank smell of horse manure and mud rising in some wet heat.

"Suja puta, get away from here," Uncle Pedro yelled drunk. She did not look back at her own uncle who called her a filthy whore.

"Hey you, hey boy. Come back here," Dai called. "You go home. Go Mass. Pray for your sisters. Come back here."

Anah turned around. Charles was following her on the dusty road.

"Come back, my son. Only my sons left," he said. It sounded like he was crying. "You make them sick, I kill you. Go home, go home." Dai began throwing sticks and rocks at Anah while Pedro and Floyd howled and jeered.

Charles shielded Anah with his body before she pushed him aside and hurled rocks at her drunk father, hitting the horses instead, which began running in frantic circles in the corral. Floyd and Pedro stumbled after her with that look in their eyes, the wild look of her father in the bedroom at dawn.

"Run, Anah," Charles yelled, pulling her arm.

"You wait 'til I catch you, boy," Dai slurred at Charles. "I will beat some sense into your stupid head."

Anah stopped in the middle of the road, Dai and his drunken relations quickly moving toward her.

"Hurry, Anah," Charles said, holding her face in his hands. "We run away together. C'mon—"

"Get out of here, you filthy cunt," Dai spat at her, waving his arms in the air. "Bad luck, just like your mother. I should have left her at the docks. Bad luck like your sisters. As good as dead. All of you, no-good girls."

"Oh, please, Anah, run," Charles cried. "You and me."

But Anah would not move. She looked at her brother and remembered Okaasan who ran out the door to save herself.

"We no can run away. Aki and Leah," she whispered to Charles. "I gotta go St. Joseph take care them."

"Then run, Anah!"

But Anah stood there slinging rock after rock at her father's fast-approaching face, turning to run only when she saw him drop to his knees, blood trickling into his eyes and over his lips.

THEY HOPPED a train car full of stacks of stripped and burned cane. The German brakeman heard nothing over the *chug-chug-chug* of the Leahi's locomotive. Anah's arms and legs tired as she held on over the expansive flat plains, the coastal heat rising up in invisible waves; held on past fields just burned, past the new steam plow with a Japanese crew making dusty furrows, past the green spread of new plantings and the waves of mature cane ready for the harvest.

Charles caught her tired body in his arms when they disembarked at the main station outside of Honolulu. They walked over the River Street bridge and into Chinatown. Charles stole handfuls of sticky lychee and sweet-ripe longan, boiled peanuts, roasted almonds, and warm butbut wrapped in ti leaves from the fruit stands and street vendors. He followed mama-sans with babies tied to their backs with obi in pretend familial relations.

"I going buy this pretty dress for you, okay?" he told Anah as they peered into the window of the Leong Chew Company, a huge dry goods store, three times bigger than the general store at the O'ahu Sugar Plantation.

"And I buy you that bow tie and derby," Anah told Charles, pointing to the back of the store.

Charles hid Anah from the constable who approached on horseback, even though there were no outward signs of the consumption. He shielded her from the sailors who staggered by, sneering at Anah in drunken want.

He gave her the last of the fleshy white longan. "One day, we eat all that we want from there." Charles pointed to the Nanking Chop Sui House above the Benson Smith Drug Store. The sunlight stung Anah's eyes as she strained to look up into the restaurant's windows.

"One day," she said.

Charles took Anah's sticky hand tucked inside his arm like she was a fine lady in a broad hat with white plumage. He held her hand throughout this day, holding on even tighter as they headed past Palama Settlement toward Kalihi Valley.

It was late evening when Anah and Charles arrived at St. Joseph's. He shivered and stuttered, begging the huge Sister Bernadine to let him stay with his sisters.

"My father say he kill me when I go home," he told her. "No, I lie, forgive me, Sister. We no mo' mother or father. I take care of sisters. I hard worker. Tell her, Anah. I know how cook. I know how clean. I make soap. I feed pigs. I clean stables. I know how read," Charles gasped, as he crumbled into Anah's arms.

She stroked his wet hair.

"I stay now. Nighttime, Sister, I scared. I no make it home. I so tired, Sister. I come from far. Too dark. No can see. I beg you. I hungry. I like stay."

Sister Bernadine put her heavy arm around him and silently led him away from Anah.

But when he looked up toward the highest window of the orphanage building, he saw Aki and Leah, their bodies, their faces, their hands pressed to the light-filled glass. Their open palms hit the window, their mouths screaming, "Charles! Anah!"

Anah turned to the rustling of the sister's starched woolen habit and her brother's cursing and flailing as the sister pulled him away toward the bridge over the stream.

"Anah! Anah!" he called.

It would be the last time she heard his voice for five years.

Beloved Charles

'Are you alone, Anah?'

The trees in the valley are full of tiny faces.

'Are you scared, Anah?'

It is night when you leave me. The windows in the orphanage clatter in the wind.

'Does the wind speak, Anah?'

The rain speaks against the glass.

'Do you listen, Anah?'

I listen to the river, boulders rumbling, and crackling trees.

'Are there many, Anah?'

There are nearly twenty of us, *inmates*. Two floors bigger than the community hall near the church. Rows of beds.

'Do you listen, Anah?'

I listen to children crying. The rain on the windows. The wind howling.

'Where are our sisters, Anah?'

I slip out of my bed after Sister Mary Deborah makes her final round.

'Where are our sisters, Anah?'

I crawl across the floor, look at each sleeping face, look for Aki and Leah.

'Find them, Anah.'

I find Aki on the other side of my wing.

'Aki.'

She sleeps fitfully, her head tossing from side to side.

'And Leah?'

Three beds down, I find her under isinglass that covers the top half of her body.

'Is she cold, Anah?'

I move myself under the tent. I place my hand over her mouth. I slide my body under her covers. Her feet and hands are cold. *Shhh*. I remove my hand, then touch her face.

'Does she say your name, Anah?'

Yes.

'Does she cry, Anah?'

She puts her face on my body and cries as I hold her.

'Do you sleep, Anah?'

Beloved Charles, I do not sleep this first night.

'And in the morning, Anah?'

The sun rises behind my head, the chickens crowing. Sister Bernadine pulls me from Leah's bed. The blanket falls to the cold floor.

4

1915

Kalihi Stream swelled for days after Anah's arrival, the thick brown torrent thrashing the low-hanging wiliwili and hau trees. Then orange sunlight broke through the upper ridges of the Koʻolau Mountains, dispersing the lingering clouds. By the next morning, the waters calmed and cleared to a constant flow.

Sister Bernadine paused in the middle of a prayer to bless their collection of pennies for the Holy Childhood Association whose international mission was to rescue pagan babies in foreign lands, pagan babies like the orphans of St. Joseph's.

Anah opened one eye when the sister paused.

The sister continued her prayer. "For it is our Lord's joy to see child helping child as is the mission of our Father's Holy Childhood Association, to help the hungry in the streets, the krank ridden with disease, the hopeless without God—" But again, she paused to survey the sunlight.

"For it was the blessed Bishop de Forbin Janson who collected pfennig upon pfennig, one pence at a time for the poor Chinesin children abandoned to become beggars—mere heathen Orientals, God bless his soul—thus we pray, O Lord—" Sister Bernadine sighed deeply.

Anah opened both eyes and stared at the sister's eyes that widened and followed a strip of sunlight that entered the musty schoolroom. "The dreadful rains might come again, heaven forbid. We must hasten to our neglected chores, Sister," she said in her upper-class German accent to Sister Mary Deborah, who sighed heavily with the sign of the cross. "Young la-dies, we had better bounden our household duties."

Leah stood up at her desk, then took two small steps, moving her cold body into the thin beam of light, warming her feet and hands.

"Young la-dy, you will sitzen immediately," Sister Bernadine scolded. "We will complete our religious instruction with a sincere and heartfelt choral recitation of Our Father. Beeil dich, children." She clapped her hands with impatience. "Hurry, hurry, children."

"I thought we was all pau with religion time?" Aki whispered to Anah.

"Hush your disobedient mouths. We are done when I say we are done and no sooner and no later," Sister Bernadine scolded as she continued. "Thy king-dom come . . . and a Hail Mary for young Aki for so rudely speaking out of turn."

After Aki's solo Hail Mary, the sisters stood all of the girls in a line. Anah stepped out into the warm sunlight, steam dewing the windows and rising in the doorway, all of the girls marching single file to the laundry room near the outhouse. So many days of wet gray, the mud on the lawn oozing between Anah's toes, she breathed deeply the smell of muggy sunshine.

"Good heavens, the rain has caused us to so neglect our laundry," Sister Mary Deborah gasped in her Brighton seaport lilt, which at times confounded Anah, who concentrated on the music of her brogue rather than the meaning of her words. The sister surveyed the piles and piles of soiled clothing and infected bedding gone unwashed since the coming of the winter storm. She rolled up her heavy sleeves and hiked up the layers of her woolen habit, shoving the dirty whites into huge metal tubs, passing washboards, scrub brushes, and bottles of bleach to each girl in line.

"Don't—just—stand—there, dumm mädchen," Sister Bernadine yelled in Leah's face as two Hawaiian girls backed away. The sister was already perspiring, the bonnet around her face rimmed with sweat, her woolen habit rank and musty with the efforts of her labor. "Did our heavenly Father not bless you with any common sense? Must we instruct you in everything? Can't you see Sister Mary Deborah needs your assistance? Beeil dich, sloth," she continued ranting at Leah. "Why won't you hurry along?" Anah moved toward Leah, but the little one turned away from the nun with a strange, wry smile.

Sister Bernadine would not tolerate such impertinence. "Leah, lieb?"

Leah stood still and unresponsive.

"You go down into the cellar right now and fetch the PandG laundry bar for me, lieb."

Leah did not move.

The sister smiled, pleased with her mordant victory, the cellar probably wet and flooded, mossy and without light or breath.

"I going with her," Anah said. She was certain that Leah's separation from her family had harmed her; she would not go into the dark cellar alone; she would stand at the top of the stairway, frightened, white-faced; *dark closet, third floor*; this place so full of many black nooks and spaces.

"Nein, you will not," the sister snapped.

"Please, Sister," Anah blurted.

"Is your name Leah?"

Anah shook her head.

"I thought not," Sister Bernadine said, pushing the older girls out of the laundry room with tubs and bundles of whites. "You with the arrogance of the idle hands," she said, pulling Leah toward the door, "fetch me the laundry bar."

Anah lingered behind, slowly gathering a pile of dark clothes in her arms. She would go to the cellar with Leah if she had to run. Anah knew she had come to this place so that Leah would no longer be the little sister all alone, the little sister afraid.

"Come with me, Jesus," Leah whispered, then held out her hand.

"What you said?" Anah asked, as Leah took a step away from her. "Wait, I like go with you," Anah told her quickly.

Leah did not turn. Instead, she continued walking down the cellar stairs.

Anah looked at Aki, who shrugged her shoulders and rolled her eyes. "Let her go herself," Aki said. "She not scared anymore."

"You, Susanah," Sister Bernadine yelled, "assist Aki in carrying that washtub to the river." She watched as Anah reluctantly lifted the handle of the tub. "Right now, Susanah. I will not permit your disobedience," she said, striking the back of Anah's head, then twisting her earlobe away from the door.

Aki carefully followed the thick mud trail across the lawn, the girls in front slipping with their heavy loads. Anah looked ahead for the path through the trees leading down to the riverbank. "Who Leah was talking to?" Anah whispered to Aki after Sister Bernadine turned around to whip the girl whose bag of clothespins spilled over the lawn.

"She talking to the dead boy," Aki reported, "making like he still alive."

"The dead boy?"

"Seth," Aki answered, "but she call him Jesus. Pa-ke Doh Nee told me he fell from that big tree over there. But this was before Leah came here."

"And Leah talk to him?" Anah asked. "But she never know him."

"I know," Aki said, shaking her head with a grimace. "But she talk to him all the time."

"And how he wen' die?" Anah asked.

"He went *ko-tonk*, right on those rocks." She pointed, her side of the tub falling onto the grass. "Blood and brains and bones all over. Pa-ke Doh Nee told me." Aki laughed, mean, because, "Seth was haole."

"What else you know?" Anah asked Aki.

"She said every time she scared, she tell his name and he come," Aki said, mildly irritated.

"You think she can see him?"

"She said he hold her hand," Aki said. "And tell her all the time, 'I here for you.' "

"I here for you?"

Leah ran up behind them, laughing as though being chased, dodging some invisible hand trying to tag her while she held the chunk of laundry bar above her head.

"Who chasing you?" Anah asked.

"Nobody," she replied, coming to a giddy halt.

"Who, Leah? Tell me who," Anah commanded, grabbing her by both shoulders.

"I said nobody," she said, lowering her head and clutching the bar of soap to her chest.

"Tell Anah," Aki yelled at her. Leah snubbed her. "Tell your stupid secret, incapaz," Aki said. "Everybody know. And everybody think you crazy. Just wait 'til Sister Bernadine find out and put you in the closet for talking to the devil, you little piggie, just like the one in the Bible story, the one who went over the cliff."

"Shut up," Leah whined. "I not the devil. And he not the devil. You the devil." She hurled the heavy bar of soap at Aki's face, then rushed at her. The bar broke into pieces, chunks of hardened soap rolling on the mud, little flakes and ripped paper rising in the wind. Anah tried to pull Leah away from Aki, who managed to get around her. She shoved and punched Leah's face, the two of them fistfighting, rolling on the lawn, their white day dresses, their arms and legs, their faces, their hair, muddied messes.

Sister Bernadine turned in a sanctified, malevolent rage. She hoisted her habit and stampeded across the lawn like a great white phantom beast. In the heat of the sun and the cold of the mountains, steam issued from her nostrils and mouth. She extended her arm, and with a mighty shove, sent Anah tumbling out of her way. She lifted Aki with her left hand, Leah with her right, dragged both of them across the lawn, kicked open the door of the washhouse with one leg, and hurled both of them inside.

Anah did not see Leah for two days.

Anah did not see Aki for three days.

That first night, Anah called with her mind: 'Aki, let me see you.' But she would not be seen.

Anah called with her mind: 'Aki, are you hungry?' But she would not answer.

Anah called with her mind: 'Aki, take care of little Leah.'

And then, the next evening during fancy work, Anah heard her sisters humming.

And the following morning while sweeping the kitchen floor, Anah heard her sisters humming.

And then one night, Sister Mary Deborah's Victrola playing "A Little Night Music," the slow scratch of the dull cactus needle, the winding of the violins slow at first, the serenade of strings, the sister's beloved composer Wolfgang Amadeus Mozart filling the empty dining room, Anah heard her sisters humming.

She followed the humming up one flight of stairs. *Second floor, the dark nook under the staircase*. The music of their voices sounded sweet and sad, the darkness of that night like a cold rice bag blanket, her sisters humming:

Jesus loves me, this I know.

"Leah? Aki?" she whispered under the door. "You o-kay? You in there?"

They did not respond. Instead they hummed:

Little ones to him belong, they are weak, but he is strong.

"Yes," Anah answered.

Jesus loves me.

A Christmas Letter Home

December 18, 1915

Dearest Mother, Father, Thomas, and Charles,

Seasons greetings to you. We hope you are well. We are fine. It is nice here. The holy sisters are nice. The brothers are nice. The food is nice. The beds are nice. Everyone here is nice.

We go to school. We learn our ABC. We learn geography. We learn mathematics. We learn manners and morals. We learn elocution. We learn history. We love God. God is good even to us sinners. We do our chores. We do fancy work. We sing songs. We sleep early and get much rest.

Here is a poem from Aki for Christmas. She has nice penmanship.

Tub tub tub
The old woman stands
At the tub tub tub
The dirty clothes to rub rub rub
But when they are clean

And fit to be seen
She'll dress like a lady
And dance on the green

It is clean here. It can rain or it can be sunny. I stitched a pillow with flowers. It is for Mother. It is her Christmas gift from me. It is my hope that she will like it. When we see you on Christmas, Aki and Leah will sing a song for you about Jesus. They learned it just for you. They sing it all the time.

Here is Leah's favorite prayer. She also has nice penmanship.

Angel of God
My guardian dear
To whom God's love commits me here
Ever this day be at my side
To light to guard
To rule and guide
Amen

Soon it will be Christmas. We hope to see you soon. We can come home for one day. We miss you. Leah is a good girl. Aki is a good girl. I am a good girl. Please do not delay.

Send our best regard to Grandmother and our aunts, uncles, and cousins. Tell them we are well. We wish to see them soon.

Love,
Susanah Medeiros
Aki M. Leah

A Christmas Letter Thrown to the Winds of Kalihi Valley

December 25, 1915

Dearest Mother and Beloved Charles,

Why have you not come? Why do you delay? We are dying here.

We want to come home. It is cold here at St. Joseph's. Where are you?

So many others have come and gone for the day. Even the poor brought gifts of food for the holy sisters. We are dying here.

No one is here but the poor Medeiros sisters. But they are not true orphans. Still, no one has come for them. Some show us pity. Some laugh at us.

We are dying here. And so very sad. It is Christmas Day and we are alone. We miss you with all our hearts.

Please send word of your health. Please come to see us as you promised on the day I left home. Do not delay. We are dying here.

Have you forgotten us?

Have you forsaken us?

Why do you delay?

Mother and brother, we love you so, even with hearts broken into many pieces.

Yours always in love,
Susanah, Aki, and Leah Medeiros

5

1916

Anah counted twelve months. Anah counted twelve Sundays. The first Sunday of every month that passed.

It was Visitation Sunday, the first Sunday in April. Anah attended Mass with Aki and Leah. They wore their clean white cathedral dresses, their bare feet dirty from predawn prayers at fourteen stations of the cross that wound along a mountain trail deep into Kalihi Valley. Mosquitoes swarmed around them. The church bells rang.

Back inside the chapel, Aki sat wedged between the sisters. Her silence in Mass was a protest against everything Catholic. She was refusing the Eucharist, again.

"Lord, I am not worthy to receive you, but only say the word, and I shall be healed," Leah whispered between rasping breaths.

Aki would not kneel but for the force of Sister Bernadine's weight on her shoulders.

"Take this, all of you, and eat it. This is my body, which will be given up for you."

Aki pressed her lips together. The Communion wafer crumbled as the sister tried to pry it into her mouth.

"Take this, all of you, and drink from it."

"This is the cup of my blood," Leah whispered with the priest, "the blood of the new and everlasting covenant. It will be shed for you and for all so that sins may be forgiven. Do this in remembrance of me."

The bitter wine spilled down Aki's chin and onto her white church dress.

"Mass is ended!" Aki screamed before the priest. She bolted from her pew and out of the church, the sisters running after her. Anah found Aki hiding in the arbor near the great monkeypod tree. She was waiting, again, for Okaasan and Charles, as they all did against hope.

Yet every Visitation Sunday, they believed, would be the last time they would wait. They would see their loved ones at last.

Anah took one hand and Leah the other as they hurried Aki to the washhouse. Anah wiped the wine and wafer from her face and then tried to remove the purple stains from her dress. She brushed and oiled her sister's hair. She washed her bare feet.

When the holy sisters were occupied with welcoming visitors, Anah walked with Aki and Leah to the picnic tables where families gathered the first Sunday of every month. A Filipino maid, a Chinese laundress, and a Japanese seamstress, immigrant mothers with wide-open arms, took their sad and sick children into their bosoms, an Okinawan farmer, a Hawaiian fisherman, a Puerto Rican field worker, and a Portuguese cowboy, fathers lifted their children high into the blue sky with a happy spin.

The mothers and fathers of the other children had always managed to make the difficult journey to St. Joseph's at *least* once a year.

Many, many tears, an afternoon spent under the trees, the chatter of brothers and sisters, mothers and fathers, sometimes even grandmothers and grandfathers who spread blankets on the lawn, a Sunday picnic in a park, children running, playing ball while Anah waited and waited with her sisters in the cruel disappointment of their expectations.

Leah was getting sicker, cold hands, dark rings under her eyes, gray lips on a pale face. "They coming," Anah told her. "I know they coming because Visitation Sunday is right before Easter. I know Okaasan like bring sweet bread, your favorite, with the yolk in the middle."

Aki folded her hands on her lap and squeezed them until her fingers turned white.

Leah stared, unresponsive.

"Because Charles love you," Anah told her, "and he said he coming with blood sausage and sweet bread and white ginger for your hair."

She slowly turned to face Anah, her gaze vacant and tired.

Sister Mary Deborah walked over to the three of them.

"We can go inside now?" Aki asked her.

She surveyed their faces.

Anah fought back her tears and her feelings of utter aloneness.

"Fresh mountain air and sunshine is vital to your recovery," the sister said. "Father Maurice wants all of you to breathe the good oxygen into your lungs until Visitation Sunday is through."

"But nobody—" Aki began as her eyes scanned the vast lawn. The faces were unfamiliar.

"Thank the blessed Lord that you have each other," Sister Mary Deborah said. "The others are here alone on every other day of the month when the three of you have each other."

It was all Leah could take. She laid her head on Aki's lap. For once, Aki comforted Leah with the slow stroke of her hand over her sister's hair. "Still early," Aki whispered to Leah. And then she spoke in Japanese. "I think our mother is making some of her special tonic for you so you can get better. You are her akachan, remember? It takes a long time to make that tonic, right, Anah?"

"It is rude of you to speak a foreign tongue in front of me, Aki," the sister began.

"Right, Anah, our mother loves our little sister best," Aki continued in Japanese. "Right?"

"Aki, your rude disobedience will certainly—"

"Right, Anah?" Aki interjected.

Anah nodded slowly. *Liar.* She missed her mother. *Okaasan.* She missed Charles. *Beloved brother.* She loved her sisters, but caring for them overwhelmed her.

"Anah—"

She stood up and ran to the apiary.

"THE INCREDIBLE POWER of the swarm," Sister Mary Deborah said as she approached Anah inside the honey house. Anah sat in the dark corner of the room next to some broken frames still holding jagged fragments of comb. She held out her hand to Anah. "For where two or three are gathered in my name, there am I in the midst of them."

"Go away," Anah told her. "Nobody here. Nobody came. I no like hear scriptures. They never coming to see us."

Leah, out of breath from running, peered out from behind Aki, who stood in the doorway.

Sister Mary Deborah moved her bee hat onto a high shelf, the heavy veil a cool whiff of smoke. She placed her gloves near the extractor. "Some hives are determined to swarm," she said, pointing toward the wild bees circling a rotting knot in an old mountain apple tree. "There's nothing you can do about it." She looked at Anah, then with a gentle wave of her fingers, called Aki and Leah into the honey house.

Aki slumped onto the floor and buried her head in her folded arms.

Anah welcomed the change of subject. "What happen to the queen?" she asked the holy sister, Leah inching around the table, then leaning against her.

"She leaves, quite frankly," Sister Mary Deborah said, "and starts a whole new life of her own with the new swarm."

"Do they ever go back—" Anah began, Leah pressing her body closer.

"No, but the honey from the new hive is always as sweet. The Lord our God makes sure of it," the sister said, her eyes meeting Anah's. "They just need to be coaxed into feeling acquainted with their new home. And soon, they are all settled in with their new family and their new lives."

Leah looked up and stared at the sister. Aki plucked a bee from her sleeve and crushed it between her fingers, watching the green stinger ooze from its abdomen.

"My mother made honey lemon in bottles. She put it on the roof of our house," Leah said, the moment of her memory sweet, the moment of her memory sour.

"To help allay your cough?" the sister asked her.

"Never help," Aki answered, her voice dark and low. "Dai took the lemons out of the bottle and put toads from the river inside so when he drank the juice he could *see* things. One time he saw Okaasan's face melting and big colors between his fingers."

"And fish and red ants and kites flying out of Floyd's mouth." Leah giggled.

"We'll be sure to make some honey lemons," Sister Mary Deborah promised, "without the toads." She made the sign of the cross. She took Anah's hand in hers. Anah stiffened for a moment, then felt the collapse of her muscles and reserve. "When the lemon tree produces fruit this summer, we'll make up a whole batch of your mother's curative." She moved a dusty box from the worktable. "And we'll drink the juice in our tea. Yes, we'll have high tea with sweet cakes on the lawn just like the queen mum herself."

"Not going help," Aki muttered.

"Pleasant words are a honeycomb, Aki," Sister Mary Deborah said, dusting her hands on her heavy woolen habit, "sweet to the soul and healing to the bones."

"Look at her," Aki screamed, grabbing Leah's hair and pulling her close to the sister. "She dead. Look at her. We no can wait for your lemon tree."

Leah screamed a high-pitched wail. Aki shoved her into the great white space of the sister's habit, then bit and scratched at Anah when she tried to stop her from running out of the honey house.

She ran to the mountain apple tree, lifted her arms into the pitch of the swarm, and turned around and around in a dance on the green. The bees followed her out onto the lawn, a black cluster of furious resonance. Aki spun around in the middle of the displaced hive, a laughing, hacking queen, the bees stinging her body until she collapsed on the lawn, putting a premature end to this Visitation Sunday.

Anah's Dirge

The lemon blossoms are in the trees. Too late, too late, the fruit of the summer comes too late.

Leah is dead.

Blessed are the poor in spirit: for theirs is the kingdom of heaven.

No lemon and honey in bottles on the roof of the orphanage.

No thick syrup in a cup of hot tea.

No soft rinds.

No golden pulp.

Only bees gathering pollen from lemon blossoms.

Blessed are they that mourn: for they shall be comforted.

I wash Leah's hands, each line, each finger, each nail.

I wash Leah's body.

I wash Leah's feet, whisper her name, sing her a baby's song.

Lullaby and good night.

She shines, her face and hair shiny with death's honey.

Blessed are the meek: for they shall inherit the earth.

She wears the yellow dress. It is the dress that belonged to me and then to Aki. It is the faded yellow dress Aki hid from the sisters upon her arrival at St. Joseph's. The dress Okaasan sewed from the lining of her old kimono.

Blessed are they which do hunger and thirst after righteousness: for they shall be filled.

Aki runs away in the morning. She is hiding somewhere in the valley. She is crying somewhere in the valley. I can hear her howling. Soon, Father Maurice will send the constable with the bloodhounds to find her, again.

Escaped inmate.

She comes back filthy and naked. Shackled. She is tired and hungry, but they put her in the closet. I do not see her for days, but I hear her screaming in the chapel. She will not kneel down. She will not close her eyes and recall the sin of her days. She will not enter the confessional box. She will not whisper her sins to the priest. She will not express her sorrow to God for what she has done. She is screaming in Japanese:

"Bless me, father, for I love my sister."

Over and over until they drag her out of the chapel and to each station of the cross deep inside the valley.

Blessed are the merciful: for they shall obtain mercy.

I turn Leah's body. I draw her arms into her chest and her knees into her body. Sister Mary Deborah places white ginger in Leah's closed fists. Then she places petals over her body.

Blessed are the poor in heart: for they shall see God.

Sister Bernadine beats Aki's open palms with the guava switch if our eyes meet in religious instruction, singing and elocution, manners and morals, meals or chores. Whenever our paths cross, I lower my eyes. I do not want the sister to beat Aki.

But Aki will not be beaten down by the nuns or God.

"Anah!" she calls from the garden. "Anah!" she calls from the stable. "Anah!" she calls from the river. "Susanah Medeiros!"

And I look for her.

Every day, we bear the stripes of these glances. These moments of want for each other. I put my body between her and the sister's switch. But Aki gets up and runs. I run after her. She is all I have left.

Blessed are the peacemakers: for they shall be called the children of God.

I kiss Leah's face. The honey is sweet on my lips. The sister kisses her face. The priest kisses her face. The bells begin their slow clang. They carry her body on a plank of wood. The children stare. The priest prays. The sister weeps. The children weep. The reins jingle. The bells clang. The buggy pulls away.

Blessed are they which are persecuted for righteousness' sake: for theirs is the kingdom of heaven.

The sky in the valley is blue. I follow the procession. When we cross the bridge over Kalihi Stream, I stop and look back. A hive swarms around Aki, who stands on the bridge. Her hair, her face, her body is covered in the silt of the river but for the white of her eyes. I take a step toward her, but she runs away.

"Come, Seth," she says, taking the hand of the unseen.

For I will be with you until the end.

6

1916

That Easter, Anah waited alone for Leah's resurrection. She hid in the cave in the hills after morning chores, behind the apiary after Mass, near the pigsty during manual work, down on the riverbank after folding laundry, beyond the small stable before fancy work, in the closets, in the basement, in the lava catacombs that wound beneath the orphanage grounds.

Anah watched for her at night from the window behind her bed on the third floor of the orphanage. She would wait to see her rise in the moonlight or in the morning like the Christ of the sisters' stories and ascend with the heavenly host to be with God the Father.

She waited and waited, minutes into hours into days into weeks until she was certain:

Leah was earthbound. She would not leave without Anah partaking of her departure.

After Sister Mary Deborah moved the wild swarm from the mountain apple tree to a wooden hive, Anah began collecting the abandoned honeycombs, chiseling and breaking off shards of wax piece by piece. When she cleaned out the knot in the tree, she melted the chunks of mountain apple–scented wax in a small pot over the fire behind the apiary.

She would make pure beeswax candles, Easter candles like the one on the altar in the chapel, keep the flames lit for Leah to find her way, until Anah knew she rose up from the shallow grave they dug for her deep in the muddy cemetery in the valley, her grave marked by a small river rock that looked like a toad.

Anah spoke to no one for weeks. She placed the vow of silence, the vow of St. Ignatius, on her solemn lips. She would not speak a word to anyone, she would not sleep or eat, but go deeper and deeper into her grief, spiraling to the place where Sister Mary Deborah promised her the spirit of God resided within her broken heart.

Anah wasn't looking for God. She was looking for Leah, the girl in the yellow dress who, in her harried visions, walked ahead of her on a road lined with mango trees and shell ginger.

Anah followed the white petals left for her like a trail of fairy tale bread crumbs that led to a light at the end of the valley with no end.

But no matter how long and hard she walked, Anah could never reach the light pulling farther and farther into the valley with each step she took toward it.

And every time her tired, wandering spirit stopped on the road to look for the girl in the yellow dress, she would appear behind her giggling in some shadowy darkness, the shade of a grove of avocado trees wet and dank around her.

And Anah would begin walking the long road again.

Her silence, her fasting, her sleeplessness continued.

Sister Mary Deborah urged Father Maurice's prayers on Anah's behalf to St. Joseph and the Blessed Virgin for God's intercession:

"Hear the cry and the prayer that your servant is praying in your presence this day."

She petitioned the Reverend Mother Magdalena:

"Do not ignore my plea; hear me and answer me; I cry out to you and to our God most high; listen to my prayer."

The Virgin Mary:

"Holy Mary, mother of God, pray for us sinners now and at the hour of our death."

And finally, St. Joseph:

"O St. Joseph, do assist me in the name of your most blessed son for God's intercession. Hear my prayers and obtain my petitions. O St. Joseph, pray for your daughter Susanah Medeiros."

She sat beside Anah's bed on a moonlit night, placed her hand over Anah's open eyes and pressed them shut. "It is vain for you to sit up late, to eat the bread of sorrows," she said, quoting the Psalms, "for so He giveth his beloved sleep."

Anah began to cry under her warm hand.

"The reverend mother in her gracious wisdom has asked that you assist me in the rebuilding of the grass shack on the north side of the lawn."

Anah shook her head, *no*, under the sister's hand, determined to help her find calm and rest this night.

"It will serve as the centerpiece for the orphanage's nativity scene," she said, stroking Anah's hair and wiping the tears from her face with a fragrant handkerchief. "We haven't done this for many years, so the structure is in great disrepair."

Anah shook her head again, *no*. She would rather continue waiting for Leah's resurrection if she had to die and rise with her to show her the way.

"Aki will help us."

She who had shut Anah out of her head for weeks began to scream:

'Let me out of here! Let me out of here! Please, I begging you. Let me out of here. Please.'

"Aki and you will work with me. Surely the work of your hands will reward you as your labor will be pleasing unto the Lord our God."

"Aki?" Anah's lips moved without sound.

"Yes, Aki," the sister reassured.

Anah placed her hands over Sister Mary Deborah's hand. The warmth and darkness made her breathing deep and secure. Anah nodded, *yes*. And then she fell asleep.

AKI AND ANAH WOULD no longer wait for their mother and brother on Visitation Sunday with the other children. In the final days of her silence, Anah hauled old planks to the broken shack surrounded by a tumbledown stone wall made with river rocks. They carried load after load of lumber, the splinters embedded in their hands.

At night while Sister Mary Deborah listened to "Clair de Lune" by Claude Debussy, a lonely solo piano recording, on her Victrola, she lifted out the splinters from their fingers with a thin sewing needle, humming to ease each initial tear of skin. And she would tell them the news of the day, on this day, her prayers for the thousands of young men from the islands who volunteered for service in World War I. She spoke with eloquence of the soldiers' bravery and families.

Mornings after religious instruction, Sister Mary Deborah taught Anah and Aki to make rope from the sinewy fibers inside the banana trunks. She taught them to strip clean the long strands with their fingernails, then wipe each translucent fiber with old rags before twisting the ropes.

She would tell them as they worked on the lānai of her brother, Lars, an infantryman in the Army of the British Commonwealth, who fought courageously in the Battle of the Somme. They wound the rope into balls, the strong banana ropes used to fasten the planks to the main beams, as they listened to the sister's stories of her childhood on the pebbled shores of Brighton. Stories of afternoons with her beloved brother in the arcades of the new Palace Pier.

Once the structure was completed, after their chores of cleaning the stables, feeding and watering the animals, the sister marched Anah and Aki deep into the thick forests of Kalihi Valley to cut the banana fronds needed to thatch their shack. The sister taught them to bake banana bread sweetened with honey, the heavy bunches of apple banana they began to harvest filling large buckets in the kitchen. As they baked, she informed them of the cancellation of the Olympics in Berlin because of the war and of her great surprise and pleasure at seeing the handsome Olympic swimmer Duke Kahanamoku on one of her supply trips into town.

In the evenings while the other girls did their needlework or mending, Anah and Aki sat on the lānai with Aunty Chong Sum, the cook, who taught them to weave lauhala mats with the hala leaves her eldest son Pa-ke Melvin brought on his donkey each Visitation Sunday when her family came to see her niece Pa-ke Doh Nee. Aunty Chong Sum told stories of the heroic revolutionary deeds of the idealistic and selfless Sun Yat-sen educated right here in Honolulu as she wove the lauhala into even and sturdy mats. With the large mats, they lined the inner walls of their shack, then lay the rest over the deep layer of sweet honohono grass on the floor.

They saved the best pieces of wood for the construction of the manger. When turned upside down, it would be an altar for Anah's secret beeswax candles, the single candle that she would keep lit in the shack day and night like the Easter candle on the altar of the chapel. It would light Leah's way; it would light their way.

On warm summer nights, Sister Mary Deborah let Anah and Aki sleep in their shack surrounded by a fine stone wall they repaired, each new moss rock cradled in their arms from Kalihi Stream, chipped and fit into the places where the wall had crumbled. On these nights, Anah told Aki fondly remembered stories of their brother Charles and stories told to her by their okaasan of Japan's brave young Prince Komatsu, who had visited Hawai'i aboard a mighty warship. She told Aki stories of Okaasan's mother and her mother before her and her mother before her, stories of a lineage of influential women shamans with magical powers who ruled alongside kings.

On Visitation Sundays, the sister baked honey and coconut cake from a recipe sent to her by her maiden aunt Gertie, who lived with ten gray tabby cats in a quaint white Georgian house facing the sea in Kemp Town. They shared this treat in the nativity shack while families gathered in happy reunion on the lawn.

She let Aki and Anah devour the entire cake, then served them an afternoon tea with lemons soaked in honey as she read them stories of Saul and David and Solomon, leaving them on the proverbial cliffs of the story. "Saul lay sleeping a deep slumber given him by the almighty God within the high mountainous cave when there came a great rumbling and all of a sudden—" The sister would shut her Bible.

Aki begged her, "Go on. No stop. Read some more, please, if you will, Sister."

To which the sister would smile and say, "To be continued, my dear Aki."

During the Feast of the Assumption, Anah baked a perfect loaf of Portuguese sweet bread with whole yolks, golden yellow from the marigolds and arnotte seeds she had been feeding to the hens.

She snuck the warm loaf under her day dress to the nativity shack. She placed stolen linen napkins over the manger, then wild ginger and wild orchids in old Crystal Soda Works bottles that Aki had found on the riverbank. The manger was now their altar. From the brilliant light of their beeswax candle, Aki lit the candle Anah had made especially for her.

"Repeat after me," Anah told her. Aki stared back, defiant at first and more interested in the forbidden flickering of the candle's flame. "Repeat. 'I want to hear and I want to be heard.' Say it."

Aki slowly repeated Anah's words.

"The Acts of John," Sister Mary Deborah said, standing in the doorway. "What are we celebrating?" she asked, her eyes scanning the altar.

"The Feast of the Assumption," Anah told her. She lit her candle from Aki's flame. "Sweetness dances," Anah said. "I want to pipe; all of you dance."

Sister Mary Deborah took the candle Anah had made for her. She lit it from Anah's flame. "I want to make you beautiful," she said, looking at both sisters with great tenderness, "and I want to be beautiful."

The space of the nativity shack filled with the smell of mountain apple, wax, honey, and bread. "If you look at me, I will be a lamp," Anah said. "Leah, if you see me, I will be a mirror. If you are a traveler, I will be a road." Anah looked around the room.

Aki lowered her head.

"Repeat after me, Aki."

She would not look at Anah.

"Repeat after me," she insisted. " 'I want to run away. I want to stay.' "

Slowly and almost inaudibly, the words moved out from Aki's lips.

Anah broke a piece of bread from the loaf and placed it between her sister's lips. "In remembrance of Leah." Anah poured honey lemon juice into a tin cup. "Drink from it, the new and everlasting covenant."

"In remembrance of Leah," Sister Mary Deborah said, lifting the cup to her lips, then passing it to Aki. She broke a piece of the bread and placed it in her mouth.

"I want to run away. I want to stay," Aki said, again.

"I have no house and I have houses," Anah said, looking at Aki, who had begun to cry.

"I have no ground and I have ground," Anah continued. "I have no temple and I have temples. This is my dance."

Anah held her cup in the air and looked all around her, the sweet of the lauhala and banana fronds rustling in the trade winds. She drank from it, all of it.

"Answer me with dancing," Sister Mary Deborah whispered.

Anah looked outside the door, a dirty yellow dress fluttering in the trees, many dresses in the trees, a labyrinthine movement of cloth around and over and through the leaves, a confusing, unholy dance, macabre, childish laughter, the dead children caught in the branches of the ironwoods.

Leah Says

o not be afraid, Anah.

Not be afraid.

Be afraid.

Afraid.

Why do you look for the living among the dead?

The dead.

Among the living.

Anah, do you see me through the glass door? I have no legs. See me through the glass door. I have no arms. See me through the glass door. I have no head.

Now I am in the trees. Now I am on the roof. Now I am on the stairs. Now I am in the honey house. Now I am dancing on the bridge. Now I am in front of you.

Anah, the whisper you hear is me. The scent of ripe mango is me. The ball of rope that rolls in front of you is me. The tricycle that pedals beside you is me. The yellow dress that moves in the corner of your eye is me.

Come to me.

I will lead you home.

Do you see our mother? She kills a rabbit. Skin the rabbit. Find his heart, pull it out. Blood on her hands. Rabbit stew. Onions, araimo, carrots, cabbage, kabocha, string beans, boiled crumbled heart, and five special kolī beans in Dai's stew.

Okaasan says, "The Thomas kolī bean."

Thomas sells the blood sausage. Sausage boy no more school you're stupid too you sell the sausage to the whores in Camp Six.

Okaasan says, "The Charles kolī bean."

Charles shines the shoes downtown. Oxblood GI shoes. Panini boy. Hey, red ink. Hey, Charlie boy. Got change for a dime, boy?

Okaasan says, "My Anah kolī bean. You must have grown into the blood. You must need me to tell you what to do. Welcome you, a woman too."

Okaasan says, "Aki kolī bean. Little warrior bean, little descendant of the priestesses of Miwa, keep running, magical small one. Never let them steal your heart, before they do you rip it out."

And Okaasan cries for me. "Little Leah kolī bean. Akachan bean, dead bean, the last one I put in his stew, the last bean round and prickly, the oily bean is for you. He would not let me see my baby one last time. So I put it in his stew. I grind it into powder. I sprinkle it on his bread. I sprinkle it in his tea. I do this my akachan for you."

See him, Anah. See our dai coming home when the rooster crows. No more money in his pockets. All in the Jap gambler's pocket, the bayau cockfighter's pocket, the whore's pocket.

Sake mouth, ʻōkolehao mouth, mead mouth, mean mouth.

"Ana-ta, rabbit stew. Eat, my beloved."

"Leave me, cadela," he slurs. "Bitch."

"Ana-ta, eat yo' kaukau. You feel mo' betta. Eat stew and bread."

"Cadela!"

"Yo' mãe make this stew for you. Yo' mãe hāpai this heavy pot to yo' house," she insists. "Just fo' you, her meu filho."

Beloved son.

Dai eats the rabbit stew. "Meu filho." Dai eats the kolī bread. "Meu filho." Dai drinks the kolī tea.

Soon, Dai is lying on the bed. Bloody mouth, open sores, he cannot breathe, cold, cold, thick throat, hot, hot.

"Mãe, Mãe." Like a baby he says, "Mother, Mother."

But Okaasan does not call his mãe. Okaasan calls no one.

Dai is crying on the bed. All day, all night, all day, he vomits the blood. His biri-biri all green with blood. His shi-shi all yellow with blood.

Dai is dying on the bed.

The doctor comes. "Water, Mama-san, water. Give him water. Mizu, mizu, Mama-san. Arrowroot with poi. Drink this, Tomas, hurry. Eat this, hurry. Whassamatta you, Mama-san? Why you no call me sooner? Someone inform Mr. Campbell. Tell him Medeiros has been very sick. Call his loved ones. Call the priest, Mama-san."

Then:

Dai is dead. Thick yellow seafoam from his mouth one last time. The doggies howl and howl.

Okaasan sits on the rocking chair. *Hail Mary full of grace* or the nembutsu *Namu Amida Buddha*? I do not know.

Dai sits up in the bed. He looks at Okaasan. He rises. He puts his hands around her neck. He squeezes hard as he can. But she keeps rocking and rocking.

Anah, see him through the glass door:

Now he is in the kitchen, but he cannot throw the dishes. Now he is in her room, but he cannot tear her clothes. Now he is gnashing at her face, but he cannot bite her. Now he is in the garden ripping up the vegetables, but they stay on the vine. Now he is chasing Charles in the cane fields because he is laughing, but he cannot catch him. Now he is looking for you, but he will never find you.

So he will stay here and stay here and stay here.

He sees me in the corner of the room with my hand on Okaasan's hand. She rests her head on my shoulder. I am smoothing her hair.

Now he is afraid.

'You are dead, Dai,' I tell him.

He looks at his hands. He looks at his body. He looks around the room. He does not believe me.

'The Lord our God has risen, but you will not,' I tell him.

"Mãe, no," he says. He has no legs.

'Be afraid,' I tell him.

He covers his ears. He cannot stop the laughter. The children have followed me. The children in the trees. They are laughing at him.

Charles is in the room. He is standing over the bed. He is laughing too. The aunties and uncles try to take him away, but he sits with Okaasan and me, the three of us giggling in the corner of that room.

1916

When Anah woke the next morning, she was alone in the nativity shack. She called for Aki, who for the first time in many nights had slept peacefully. Anah stepped into the cool light of the early sun, a single strand of a spider's iridescent web moving before her with each breath.

"Aki?" she called. Because of her disappearances, Anah found great comfort in knowing her exact whereabouts, even when she visited the outhouse. "Aki!" she yelled.

Aki answered her from the high branches of the mango tree, her voice far away. "Go, go, try, c'mon, go," she said, laughing.

"Who go?" Anah asked as Aki reached for a cluster of red hayden mangoes. "How you got up there?"

"And then he wen' climb the tree like Monkey Boy," Aki said, dropping the firm fruit into Anah's hands. "Leah told me he would do anything I tell him. And he went first, so I wen' follow him. 'Cause I climb tree better than all of you." She paused, beating her chest. "Then he fell off the tree, off the tree, off the tree, he fell off the tree."

Her giggling began to frighten Anah. "Get down right now, Aki. If Sister Bernadine see you up there—who fell off the tree?"

"Look, Anah, he standing right by you," Aki said, her voice urgent. "Macaco Boy, thass him, but he keep falling down. He said to tell you that he *like* you," she said, squatting on a thick branch. "No, he said he *love* you." Aki bit into the fruit, the orange juices dripping from her chin and hands.

"Father—" Anah said.

"Who art in heaven," Aki finished.

"No, not that father," Anah said. "Our father—"

"Uncle Haru be thy name," she said, laughing.

"No, Aki, listen to me," Anah begged. The trees went still, the distant roosters silent, the bees, the breeze, the waters solemn. "Dai is dead."

"How you know?" she asked, wiping the orange juices with the back of her hand, thick mango skins falling.

"Leah told me."

Aki laughed mean. "Good, thass good, Anah. Now the dead girl can teach the dead paipa how to play hopscotch in hell, right, Seth?" She hurled a fuzzy mango pit, hitting Anah on the face. " 'Cause thass where they stay!"

"Seth?"

"I said Seth? I meant death." Aki laughed again, screeching. "Death love Anah. Seth love Anah," she chanted in a mad singsong.

Anah wiped the slime from her cheek as Aki scurried higher into a thicket of leaves. "They *have* to let us go to the funeral," Anah said urgently in Japanese. "We can go home. Just like Shizu Kutaka when her grandpa died, remember? They came to get her and then the sisters let her go home for little while, remember?"

Aki's rustling stopped and then Anah saw her face peering down at her. "We going home?" she whispered. "We going see Okaasan?"

"Yes, and Charles," Anah told her.

"Dai ma-ke you sure?" she asked, stunned and yet relieved. "We going home?" she repeated.

Anah nodded. Aki scrambled down the tree, her naked body scratched, her nightdress a white fluttering left high in the branches of that tree.

Anah didn't care about the dress. It was summer. They were going home. They ran laughing and dancing, holding hands, spinning and skipping across the great lawn to the rectory. The reverend mother would be waiting there to tell them that they could go home.

Sister Bernadine saw them from the kitchen window and ran after them from the open door. They tried to outrun the great nun the size of a stampeding albino buffalo. She reached her fleshy arm toward Aki and grabbed her by the hair.

"Cover your shameful nakedness," she said, beating Aki across the head and slapping her buttocks with her thick, pink man-hands. She lifted Aki under one arm, then came after Anah.

Anah backpedaled, then turned to run, but the nun caught her by the back of her loose nightdress, wrapping it around and around her hand until Anah could no longer breathe.

"You, Susanah," she hissed, lifting Anah's feet off the ground, "have abused your privileges." The sister pressed her mouth to Anah's ear. "I told them you were not worthy of our Christian kindness, wilde tiere. You willfully cause your brother to fall. Why is your sister not wearing her nightdress? Oh, I know, yah, I do. You are not your schwester's keeper. Slave of sin," she said as she tightened her grip, simultaneously strangling the breath out of both of them. The other girls had gathered in the kitchen doorway.

"Our father, our father," Anah said, choking, "he, he—"

Aki writhed and kicked to free her body, but the sister locked her head in the crook of her arm, Aki punching at the deep, dusty folds of the sister's habit.

"Young la-dy, not even fifty Our Fathers will help you," Sister Bernadine huffed.

Sister Mary Deborah pushed her way through the gawking crowd of girls, Aunty Chong Sum and Supang the groundskeeper running out behind her. The cook wrapped Aki in a dirty sheet, petting her head, trying to calm her. Sister Mary Deborah put her arms around Anah, urging Sister Bernadine with her eyes to loosen her grip on her dress. Anah smelled the vinegar of her wrathful discipline as she released her. She fell gasping to the ground.

"We received word yesterday," Sister Mary Deborah whispered to Sister Bernadine. "Father Maurice asked that you inform the girls after Mass that—" Her words grew softer and sibilant with increased nodding and the sign of the cross over and over. "And the reverend mother requests that for the girls' sake, that you, we should—" Sister Bernadine's face softened for a moment, but she did not look at Anah or Aki.

"Out, out, move out of the way," Aunty Chong Sum told the other girls, shooing them back into the kitchen then to the dining room. "Go finish breakfast, hele mai, before Supang feed to the pigs. Move along, hele mai."

She sat Anah and Aki at the tiny wooden table near the pile of guava stumps for her old Cabinet Glenwood stove. "Drink," she said, placing tin cups full of hot cocoa in front of them. "Here, kaukau," she said, sliding a plate of warm bread covered in goat's butter and honey.

"Is my father dead?" Anah asked Aunty Chong Sum.

Aki looked up, her eyes begging the truth from the cook. Aki's face and arms were bruised and bleeding, her body shivering uncontrollably, her teeth chattering.

"Is my father dead?" Anah asked Aunty Chong Sum.

Her mouth opened to tell them what she knew.

Sister Bernadine stomped into the kitchen in her scuffed black lace-ups. With her sharp, narrowing ice-blue eyes, she dared the cook to tell them.

"I dunno," Aunty Chong Sum said, lowering her head. "I dunno nothing."

THERE WAS too much pleasure in Sister Bernadine's voice later that evening. She had let Anah and Aki wait through a day full of religious instruction, school lessons, lunch, manual work, dinner, then elocution before calling them into her presence.

She slowly removed her reading glasses, tiny glass circles without frames, and placed her huge wooden quilting ring on the table in front of her. A small fire crackled and spit in the hearth. She excused the other girls, who left their embroidery and needlepoint on their chairs. Each quietly slipped out of the room. The sister folded her hands on her lap, then nodded toward the chairs where she wanted them to sit.

Condescending eyes, insincere sympathy, she lifted a letter from the folds of her habit, then perched her reading glasses on her broad nose. There was too much pleasure, too much, as she read the letter sent to the orphanage by Dai's family:

To Whom It May Concern:

We ask that Susanah and Aki Medeiros be detained at your facility to prevent infection of susceptible family members and loved ones especially the newborn and elderly as the family of the late Tomas Medeiros mourns his passing. We thank you for your prayers and understanding.

The Medeiros Family

Anah recognized the haole plantation doctor's fancy penmanship. She rose from her chair, the tears welling heavily in her eyes. She gritted her teeth and tightened her jaw, hot air moving in and out of her nostrils. She looked up at the ceiling, blinking her eyes, then closing them to keep the tears from rolling down her face. She took Aki's hand and watched as the sister resumed her quilting, a priggish smile on her pasty face, her wrist flicking them out of that room.

AKI RELINQUISHED all hope that night, falling sicker and sicker with each hour, her body surrendering to the disease she fought by sheer will. After midnight, Sister Mary Deborah moved her under the isinglass on the second-floor infirmary where the sick ones remained both day and night, the floors, beds, linens, and washbasins disinfected daily. They would not let Anah see her.

But late at night, Anah stood whimpering behind the locked doors, the glass painted a shabby opaque mustard.

'Aki, hear me. You are my only remaining family.'

With her fingernails, jagged from scrubbing pots and dishes as punishment for not attending to her lessons and her refusal to speak the holy Rosary for her dead father, Anah began to etch a peephole in the paint. Small enough to see her sister, small enough to be undetected, Anah watched Aki through that hole. There was no one beside her bed to comfort her.

Aki emerged from that bed six days later, her body thin and frail, her pallor gray, eyes black rimmed and sunken, her hair brittle to the touch. She breathed heavily through her slack, open mouth, her back bent, and her spirit finally broken. But the spirit that left Aki's body fused with Anah's.

You will never break me. Anah spit into Sister Bernadine's oatmeal before serving her.

You will never break me. Anah endured the whip of her guava switch across her face.

You will never break me. Darkness entered; her heart was a cold stone.

Aki emerged from that bed. She spoke in gibberish. Father Maurice believed her aggrieved and anguished, Sister Bernadine that she was in covenant with the devil as Aki flung crazy, misquoted scriptures at the sister, who became more and more outraged with each biblical exchange with Aki, outraged at her wicked acquaintance with God's word.

Aki spoke openly to Seth in Portuguese, Japanese, pidgin, and Old English she learned from reading the scriptures. "You cold, Macaco? Me too. If your atama so-wa, so-wa, so-wa your head—you put hōtai o suru, plenty bandage with the kanaka's bitter noni juice, aloe, aloe, juicy, thass right, my little Macaco Boy. You better listen for if you believeth in noni, you also believeth in me, because I careth for you, I do."

"Seth?" Aunty Chong Sum gasped as Anah finished wiping the last of the dinner dishes. "Seth Soares?"

"She calling him Monkey Boy," Anah told her. "And Leah use to call him Jesus. He live around here? Maybe he come play with them from someplace around here?" Anah did not want to believe the stories that Leah and Aki had told her about the boy. He had *not* fallen from the tree. He was a *real* boy who came onto the grounds to play with them.

"They *seen* him?" Aunty Chong Sum asked, wiping her hands on her dirty apron. "They *play* with him?"

"Yes."

"*You* seen him?"

"No. Why?" Anah asked her, soaking the baking sheets in the sink.

"No, you no play," she scolded, taking Anah's hands in hers. "No play. He longtime dead." She sat Anah down at her small table and paused as if to consider telling the rest of the story. "No, you listen Aunty Chong Sum—never you play with the dead."

"Please, Aunty, tell me about Seth," Anah said. "He come here. Every day, I promise. I no lie."

The cook placed her face in both hands. She breathed deeply, and when she looked at Anah, she was already crying. "He use to play here when his papa deliver milk to trade for honey with Sister Mary Deborah," she began. "All time climb the mango trees in the back. Quiet boy, nice face, come visit all the time, follow me all over, so I make him work, but he never grumble. He sweet boy. So handsome, the face. All time pick flowers for me, the white ginger flower."

"How he wen' ma-ke?"

"He fall down the big tree. Crack his head wide open. Big mess, blood and bone and brain all over. The reverend mother make me clean it all up with Supang. I so sad for his family, longtime Portagees live in the valley. He good boy, very good boy, but dead, very dead boy."

"He not dead," Aki said, startling Anah and Aunty Chong Sum. "He right here," she pointed at the empty space next to her.

"Where?" Anah asked.

"There," she pointed to the stove. "There," she pointed to the window. "There," she pointed at the ceiling. "There," she pointed at the door.

"You hush your mouth. He ma-ke-die-dead," Aunty Chong Sum said, taking a small step toward Aki. "Sister said you no talk like that. You kaukau some bread with honey. You go upstairs to yo' bed. Go hi-amoe. Go, go moe moe. Go sleep." She moved toward Aki, then stopped abruptly.

The door opened, a cold wind rushing in and sucking out.

"What?" Anah asked her.

Aunty Chong Sum dropped the wooden spoons she held in her hand.

"And Leah came with him." Aki smiled. "But he still like Anah the best, right, little Leah? You see her, right, Anah?"

"Leah," Anah whispered. "Where, Aki?"

She pointed at the open door. And then Aki's mouth fell open, her eyes widening. She gasped, "Dai. No, Dai! Run, everybody, run!" she screamed as she bolted for the door that slammed shut in her face.

She twisted and turned the knob, yanking and pulling at the locked door, finally slapping her palms against it. "Open the door, Aunty," she screamed. Aki scrambled onto the sink, flinging away knives and forks. She looked out of the window. "Seth! Run, Seth! I coming, Seth!"

Anah pulled her down from the sink. The door creaked open. She turned, her breath locked inside her chest. Leah's smoky white face peered in. She smiled at Anah, a cluster of rotten mangoes in the scoop of her dirty yellow dress.

Seth stood beside her, kind eyes, lonely eyes. The moment, a second, a glance, then gone.

Anah felt the blood drain from her face, the skin of her forehead and cheeks pulling back into her skull. Her body weightless, stunned, a wave of nausea rising up to her gasping mouth.

Aki stepped toward their dissipating shapes. "Take me with you," she spoke to the darkness of the kitchen doorway. "To see Okaasan and Charles. We go home. He dead now. Maybe we can all go home." Aki collapsed on the floor.

Sister Mary Deborah ran into the kitchen toward Aki. Aunty Chong Sum helped the sister carry her limp body up two flights of stairs. Anah held the oil lamp to light their way. Aki mumbled, incoherent, "Believeth all things. Let nothing dismay thee. Behold them in spirit."

Sister Mary Deborah moved quickly to tuck Aki into bed. An urgent look in her eyes, she placed a finger over her lips, *be silent, O all flesh*, and with that finger directed the cook downstairs. She petted Aki's face and stilled her murmuring lips. With her tired eyes, she directed Anah to an empty bed beside Aki's.

The quiet of the lamplight, the quiet of the night, Aki bolted upright in her bed, her eyes scanning the room. She did not panic as her face filled with a kind of joyful knowing.

"Time is now," she said.

"Yes, child, it is time for sleep," Sister Mary Deborah whispered.

"Time?" Anah asked Aki. "Time for what? I go toilet with you. You like make shi-shi?"

She smiled and leaned toward Anah. "Time is now, Anah." She gazed in each corner of the second floor, her mouth slack open in fatigue and wonder. "Time to go home."

They Speak in the Tongue of Their Ancestors

Sumi. Sumi-chan. Where are you, my beloved whore? I am still here among you looking for your children, the dead ones you made with your useless body. Again and again you made those girl babies. For what? For me to feed and clothe.

' "Another baby, Tomas?" They all laughed at the cockfighting ring, at the stable, in the fields. Even my own uncles and cousins laughed. And girls, so many girls. I wanted to sell those useless half-breeds to the bayau Ilocos bachelors to take care of my gambling debts, but you made them sick, didn't you, Sumi-chan. All three whores, didn't you.'

"I made *you* sick."

'Sumi? Is that you, my sweet little Sumi-chan? Come closer and spread your legs so I can smell you.'

"Go away, Tomasu. How come you do not know? You are dead now. I cannot make my promise to the priestesses in the heavens with you in the way. Get out of the way. I want to bring my baby home so I can bury her with her baachan and jiichan. And then I will be buried there too."

'Catch her if you can. Come out, come out wherever you are. She wants to play with me, Sumi-chan. She wants me to touch her. And I will. The way I touch you at night, put my hand over your mouth, put my weight on your struggling body, then put my long flesh deep inside you until you bleed. Japonêsa cunt. Did you know that the matchmaker sold you to me for cheap? For a one-way ticket home? He is still around somewhere drinking sake all day all night. I see him all the time. He is a happy drunk. He likes to watch you bleed.'

"Liar."

'Liar.'

'Hey, little one. Hey, little Leah. Come to Dai. Come sit on my lap. Paipa drives a nice buggy. See the big horsey? Let's go for a ride, just you and your paipa.'

'I see the moon and Okaasan smiling when they put you in the ground. Vovó cry like Floyd's fat girl baby. We hate to eat you, said the worms, but we must we must. Jesus love me, Okaasan, and Aki and Anah.'

"I was coming to get you, my little akachan. Charles made money. And me too. To bring you home. But your father, he found the money."

'The moon see me. Fear not! For I am! Thee unto the end! He went to bed and bumped his head and couldn't get up the next morning.'

"Run, run away from him. He took me even with the blood. He will take you too. What have I done? I watched him die. How can this be? Why is he there with you? Look for your jiichan. He has a long white beard and a dwarf bamboo cane. Look for your baachan. She wears a yellow kimono just like your yellow dress. She died with Haru-chan in child bed. Find your baachan."

'God see the moon. The moon see baachan. Uncle Haru be thy name.'

'The good are all gone, Sumi. No good ones here. Just the gamblers and drunks and whores and liars and thieves and rapists and the poor, poor, lonely hearts. And the trees, Sumi, are full of stupid children waiting to go home. But no one comes for the lost, the lame, the bewildered, the beaten, the dirty children who want to go home like your Leah wandering around in that yellow dress. You remember that yellow dress, don't you, Sumi? I will rip it off her before I spread her legs. As soon as I catch her.'

"No, Tomasu, leave her alone. Leave our daughter alone."

'Two will be with me soon. Our two. See the dying, every day they are dying. Then three will be with me soon. Our three. See the whores, every day, they are gone a-whoring. I will sell them all to the matchmaker.'

"Take me, Tomasu. Take me. I am coming to you right now. I am coming to you with child. With another son."

'Promises, promises.'

'God bless me. God bless Okaasan. Stay with Charles. Stay with Anah. Aki says we can fight him. Good soldiers of Jesus Christ thass Aki and me.'

"Do not say such things. My Aki is alive. She will be home soon."

'Lay thee down now and rest. May thy slumber be blessed.'

'You are right, sweet Sumi-chan. She will be *home* soon.'

8

1917

So many dying.

They die at night.

She stole a bottle of honey and a cube of honeycomb from the kitchen. She stole a beeswax candle from the honey house. To anoint the dead.

"Beeswax is the brightest of all candle flames, is it not, Susanah?" Sister Bernadine asked Anah one morning. "Where are all the candles, you who will suffer as a thief the wrath of the Lord our God?"

The sister beat Anah's sinful hands until they bled from open welts, her palms lined with the sister's holy outrage. "Young dieb, thou shalt not, thou shalt not, thou shalt not steal," the whip of her guava switch punctuating her words.

But they were dying every day.

Dying in darkness.

So she kept stealing.

Exasperated with Anah's disobedience, the Reverend Mother Magdalena thought it best that the Lord's wrath be stung into her daily by forcing her to help Sister Mary Deborah in the apiary.

Every day after Anah's hands were repeatedly punished, Sister Mary Deborah boiled honey in a dented little pot over a fire behind the honey house, then applied it as a smooth honey-paraffin salve to seal the open wounds on her palms.

"One cannot conduct the Lord's work without one's hands," she said matter-of-factly as she wrapped Anah's hands with clean rags. "Now back to your labor, Susanah."

But on the night Anah knew Aki would die, she stole again. She ran in the dreadful darkness of the spacious lawn past the pigpens and the stable to the honey house near the apiary. She boiled the entire contents of the last bottle of honey from the kitchen, the sweet, heavy smell of the nectar and bits of melting wax languishing around her. Then from that fire, Anah lit the beeswax candle.

When she returned to Aki, Sister Mary Deborah sat beside her after the last bed check. Anah put her finger to her lips and begged with her eyes for the sister to keep her silence. *Thou shalt not, thou shalt not.* The sister made the sign of the cross, bowed her head for a moment, and left.

Aki was feverish, her body shaking with chills, her neck red and swollen. And every breath she managed to pull into her body entered as if she were pulling air on a thick sennit rope, pulling it down her small throat. She coughed up ribbons of heavy blood. There were tears in her eyes, her mouth open and gasping.

Anah took her hands and smoothed the warm honey into the beaten palms. She ripped the hem of her white nightdress and wrapped Aki's hands as Sister Mary Deborah had done for her.

Aki gasped again, deep and guttural, her whole chest heaving. Anah anointed her face and her hair with warm honey.

"Don't die."

Aki sat up as Anah brushed her short hair, smoothing it away from her face with raw palms.

"Never mind Sister Bernadine cut off your beautiful hair."

Aki closed her eyes tightly and breathed in high and shallow.

"Open your throat, Aki. Don't die."

"Anah." She coughed, flecks of blood spotting her face. "He *is* coming."

"Yes, Charles coming," Anah told her.

"Liar," she said, wincing with her next breath. Then she opened her eyes and stared at the ceiling just as Leah had done and took in a labored breath.

"Aki," Anah whispered, taking her sister's face in her hands. "No leave me."

"Dai, no!" she cried.

Anah placed the cube of honeycomb between Aki's lips. She closed her mouth to its sweet melt, her body melting in Anah's arms. "Stay here, Aki. In remembrance of me," Anah frantically whispered.

Aki's body stiffened. "Go, go 'way, Dai," she said, her words extinguishing the candle on the bed stand. She took in a final breath, held it, then exhaled one last time. A single tear fell from her eye. Anah took her limp hand to her lips and kissed her sister's fingers. She bit off pieces of each of her fingernails to put the relics in the honey bottle filled with her baby teeth.

Anah listened for the holy sister's footsteps, then quickly raised a small paring knife to cut a strand of Aki's hair. But Aki returned to struggle one last time against the threat of knife and the coming of death. She scratched at the air and then at Anah's face.

"Mentirosa," she hissed at Anah in their father's Portuguese.

And then she left, calling Anah with her last word:

Liar.

Her mouth was open, her eyes horrified and stunned.

Hand clenched in hand, Anah waited for morning.

THEY LIFTED Aki's thumb in rigor mortis, lifted her finger, another finger, finger, finger, her hand stiff and splayed, her other hand a fist clenched.

"We are one family always," Sister Mary Deborah whispered to Anah. "Pilgrims on our earthly journey, the deceased in heaven, and the dead who await entrance into heaven."

Pilgrims.

She helped Anah to stand from the chair next to Aki's bed while Supang the groundskeeper and Fukunaga the janitor lifted Aki's dead body from the bed.

"Her eyes, Sister, onegai shimasu," Fukunaga said. "Please, close the eyes, please, Sister."

"Oh, the smell."

"Ai-ya, dirty, dirty, dirty. All the pilau shi-shi and biri-biri on the floor."

"Tend to all of that later," the sister said. Her heavy habit shifted as she disappeared across the room. "I'll prepare the body in the wash-house after Mass," Anah heard her tell them, the sound of their foot-steps diminishing down the steep staircases.

Anah kneeled beside Aki's empty bed. *Love is sweet.* Bodily fluids dripped off the bed's steel frame, puddling around her.

Thou shalt not hunger or thirst.

She smelled the pillow, still with the scent of Aki.

Anah had no prayers. No thoughts. She heard nothing, even that which was spoken to her.

Bless me father, for I love my sister.

Nothing but grief and breath. She closed her eyes and wept at her uselessness. At Aki's last word to her:

Mentirosa.

"Take care of Aki and little Leah," Okaasan had said to her. "We will come to see you soon, I promise."

But they never came.

Anah told her sisters again and again that she was sure they would indeed come on the *next* Visitation Sunday. She wanted to keep their hopes up, to keep them well.

She was not a *liar*. She believed that her mother and brother would come to get all of them.

The smell of white ginger rose from under the cold sheets. Then Anah climbed into that bed. And she wept.

She felt someone's cold hand on her head, comforting her, *O death*, comforting her, *O Seth*?

Anah slowly lifted her eyes, her heart pulling upward against skin, quick palpitations inside her chest, beating and pressing inside her nightdress. Her teeth began to chatter, her skin moving as death crawled over her.

"Seth?" So afraid, the utterance of his name, the acknowledgment of his presence at last seemed her last breath. Anah's body shivered in cold sweat, and then she saw him as if through glass.

He knelt beside her, his hands folded in prayer.

'Glory be to the Father, to the Son, and to the Holy Spirit.'

He cried.

'As was in the beginning is now and ever shall be.'

Anah cried with him for Aki.

'World without end.'

"Susanah Medeiros! Why are you lying in the wet bedding? Get up! As the door turns on its hinges, so the slothful turns on his bed. Beeil dich, go wash your face. Right this instant. I said hurry. Go brush your teeth. Go comb your hair. Clean yourself, Susanah."

But she could not.

And then she awoke in her own bed. She did not know how she had gotten there.

"Anah? Eat. Neck soup make you feel better. Aunty Chong Sum save the chicken neck special for you, Anah."

Time passed. She heard the sister's voice at her bedside.

"Young la-dy, repeat your scripture lesson: 'My life is an instant, a fleeting hour.' Repeat, bitte. 'My life is a moment, which swiftly escapes me.' Repeat, bitte. 'O my God, you know that on earth I have only today to love you.' Repeat, *please*."

She listened to the voices that spoke to her at night.

'Anah? Come out, come out wherever you are. One whore. Two whore. Maybe three whore. You, like your sisters, will die there. No visitors, please. Only the dead leave there. We can be one, big, happy family. Dai and his three whores. Hurry now, Dai is tired of waiting.'

She would not take food or drink.

"Eat, you must kaukau, Anah. Kabocha soup with rice juk good for you. Make you strong. I make special for you, Anah."

She listened at night.

"I will bring you home soon, Anah. I will make more money, Anah. I will send Charles and Thomas for you, Anah. I promise you, Anah."

She heard Father Maurice.

"Do you believe in God the Father, Susanah? Do you believe in Jesus Christ? Do you believe in the Holy Spirit? Do you believe in the holy Catholic church? Susanah? Do you reject Satan? Susanah? Thanks be to God. Amen."

She heard the bells echoing in the valley, the bells calling the pilgrims to Mass, the bells resounding for the dead.

'Anah, you must listen.'

"Aki!"

Anah heard the children cry, the children laugh, hideous laughter. They pulled at her hair, pinched her, slapped her, scratched her face, her hands, her arms until she bled.

'Anah, quick, take the journey down, the journey down, follow me, follow me through the catacombs. Our Queen Lili'u is dead. Our Queen Lili'u is dead.'

Anah followed Seth's shadow. He moved like breath from her lips on cold mornings in the valley. She stopped. She looked for him on the steep staircase. She stopped. Listened. The bells clanged, slow.

'Follow me.'

Anah followed Seth's shadow. The children scratched at her, biting her flesh. Blood dripped from her eyes and fingertips. Seth's urgent hand beckoned Anah to the washhouse.

"Mass is ended!"

The chapel doors pulled open.

The washhouse door pulled open.

O body.

'Wash her, Anah.'

Children cried, children laughed. They hid in the trees. They hid in the washhouse. Seth stood alone, a shivering white light in the dark corner.

O Aki.

Anah removed Aki's nightdress, filled the washbasin with cold water and a piece of bath soap. She scrubbed the slimy film from her sister's stiff, dead body, rinsed out the chunks of rock salt they shoved inside her every orifice. She washed her sister's dress.

'Love is sweet, Anah.'

She anointed her sister with royal jelly.

'Tend to the dead, Anah.'

She covered her naked sister with foliage: silver kukui leaves, palapalai, white and yellow gingers, tiny heliconia, red and green ti. She took Seth's hand and rested her head on his shoulder; he comforted her, comforted her.

She anointed herself with royal jelly, washed her dirty feet, removed her bloody dress. She put on Aki's nightdress, wet with the scent of flowers.

"Susanah Medeiros! What in heaven's holy name? Are you desecrating your sister's mortal body? God is so angered by the wicked, the heathen and pagan rituals that you continue to practice even in this holy place. I warned them that you were not worthy of our patience. We should have buried her days ago. Susanah, come back here!"

She ran after Seth across the lawn. Seth in the trees, Seth among the flowers, Seth on the wind. He released the goats from their pen, the pigs from the sty. She opened the rabbit cages, the chicken coops, the duck pen. They laughed, pixilated laughter that echoed in the valley.

The children reveled in the trees at the cacophony of animal frenzy, the freedom of their colors, the flurry of nuns in woolen habits and orphan girls in starched white church dresses, the dogs barking, the cats skittering away, the cook, the groundskeeper, the janitor scurrying about the delirious flutter of feather and fur. Children laughed in the trees.

And the valley rang with Aki's voice:

'O pilgrims, follow me.'

Aunty Chong Sum's Comfession

Bless me, Father, for I have sin. It has been maybe three four day since my last comfession.

I think I sin a bad one. The girl, our Anah, make me see the ghost again. I try change since I accept the Lord Jesus Christ in my life as Lord and Savior, but I see all the ma-ke keiki again.

"I cold, Aunty Chong Sum," the keiki tell me. "I hungry, Aunty Chong Sum," they tell me. Always laughing by my knee. And scratching my face when I no listen them. Reverent Mother ask me how come my face and arm all cut up. I tell her I clumsy with knifes.

I so sorry I sin. I tell lie to the Reverent Mother, which is big number one commanment thou shall not give false testimary. What I going tell her? The ghost been bust me up 'cause I no listen them?

So I listen the ghost. I make big fire in the stove when they cold. I put plate hot bread and sweet cocoa outside when they hungry. I listen them and they no scratch.

But I comfess to you, Father, that I know it is sin in the holy word when I listen to ghost.

The girl, Father, you seen Anah? Her too all scratch up from the ghost. I seen the blood come from her eye like tear. No can stop the blood from the eye, you know. The towel, the bed, the clothes all blood. And the blood come off her finger all frip, frip, frip all over the place, I tell you.

She try no listen too. But she no can help. Just like me. I no can help. They like us listen.

I hear the Aki giggle, giggle, giggle. She the bad one throw stone at the kitchen window. She let go all the animal nighttime, Father, that one is a bad girl, no listen nobody. All the time naked even when they put her in the grave.

Anah no let the holy sisters put the dress on her. "No," she scream. "No, no, no," like one cat she scream. "My sister no like wear your clothes. Only the flower and plant on her body," she scream. "Look, my sister running over there. You no can see her? Whassamatta you?" she scream. "You kill my sister," she tell Sister Bernadine. "You cast your pearls before swine," she yell at the sister. "You never catch my Aki no more," she tell, and she climb the tree over the small grave.

And when they lower the dead one on the plank all cover with plants, she yelling, "Seth! Seth!" And she climb higher in the tree 'til no can see her.

You was there, hah, Father? You seen all this, hah? You seen the boy, Father?

That one is another sin of mine. The boy been coming see me again. You remember how Seth love his Aunty Chong Sum? Always bring me the special cream from his favorite cow. Or the cow tongue for me cook Pa-ke style for my niece Pa-ke Doh Nee come better from the cough with the special Chinee food.

You remember, Father, he come all the time with his papa deliver the milk. Then he fall off the big tree and ma-ke, and I make vow to the Holy Mary 'til this day, I never been seen the boy no more.

But the dead boy, now he all over the place with the girl. Everyplace I see the girl, I see the Seth with her. Holding hands too, you know, Father, just like best friend, just like lover, she talk to him all the time, feed him, give blanket, sing all kine song, say all kine scripture reading. She no so sad when the boy with her. But when the boy no come, she all alonesome, only think about dead, dead, dead.

Poor thing. No more family. She bury two sister all by herself like a good, big sister. And the father ma-ke too and they no come get her for go home say aloha-no to the daddy. What kine family is that? No wonder she make family with the dead boy. Forgive me, Father, for I know it is sin.

The girl lucky Sister Mary Deborah petition intercess for her to the Holy Mary and the Saint Joseph and all them other saints in the chapel.

Oi Virgin of virgin, my Mother, to thee I come, before thee I stand sinful and sorrow!

Oi Saint Joseph, patron of departing souls, do assist me by your powerful intercess!

Oi merciful Jesus!

I repeat all that from the holy sister. I make my own intercessor for me and Anah. And I make intercessor for the kanaka Queen. Our poor Queen Lili'uokalani, no mo' kingdom, no mo' palace, her too ma-ke. So sad, so sad.

I better go back inside kitchen before the big sister accuse me of sloth again. Every day at least one two time I sloth. Sometime I have mouth of folly. Sometime I dumm. Sometime I sluggar. Sometime I shiftless fool. Most times I do works of the devil. Thass what the big sister say all the time 'pecially if she hot and hungry.

Ai-ya, my God, I am so sorry I offend thee, and I detest all my sins because thy just punish me but most of all because I offend thee, my God, who is all good and deserve my love. I firm resolve with the help of you, I no sin no mo' and pass the near sin.

Father? You there? Father Maurice? You listening me, your humble servant Aunty Chong Sum? You hot in there? You hungry?

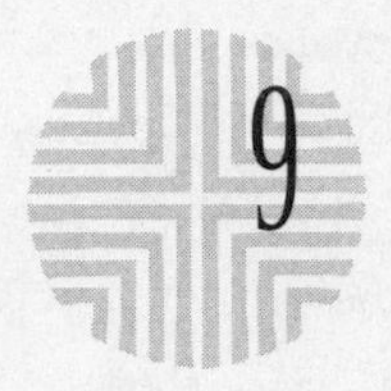

9

1918

And on nights with no moon, Aki released all of the animals.

And in the rain-wet mornings that followed, Anah was to capture all of the animals at Sister Bernadine's behest. She convinced the reverend mother that Anah snuck out like a banshee wraith on these nights to do the ritualistic working of Satan.

Anah never even tried to tell them that it was Aki.

Anah smelled her at the moment her mind wandered in sleep. Aki spiraled her earthy hands about her sister's face, then breathed her phlegmy, bloody wheeze. Anah smelled her hair, the sweet sweat of her neck, the spaces between her dirty fingers and toes.

Awake in bed, Anah heard Aki running down the hall, the padding of her bare feet over the wood floors. She heard Aki bounding up and down the staircases, slamming doors in and out of the closets, sliding down the banisters, giggling her sinister trill.

Sister Bernadine convinced the Reverend Mother Magdalena that it was Anah. Anah was incorrigible. A miscreant. An abomination. A wicked, wicked changeling. She had seen Anah disappearing into the night's darkness with her own eyes, a girl and then a white mist.

The sister dragged Anah to the reverend mother's small office near the rectory and sat her on a wooden chair.

Anah smelled Aki. She giggled in Anah's ear.

The reverend mother stared at her from above her chipped reading spectacles. She pursed her thin lips sphincterlike. "Sister Bernadine," she began, "on the matter of Susanah Medeiros, please inform me plainly, posthaste sister, there's the Lord's work to be done, much work, viel, viel arbeit—" She sighed heavily.

"Reverend Mother, forgive the forthright nature of my words, but at your behest I speak expeditiously." She paused, pleased at the complexity of her English, for she was the pious but horse-faced sixth daughter of Count and Countess Otto Bettleheim von Solms educated at the Convent of St. Walburga in Münster, Germany, who lorded her nobility over the Reverend Mother Magdalena, the daughter of a widower shoemaker from the industrial north's Rhine Province, her working-class dialect thick and distinguishable.

"I have spent many hours in prayer and meditation," Sister Bernadine continued, "on the matters concerning this young la-dy, Susanah Medeiros, and I firmly believe, Reverend Mother, that the girl—" She made the sign of the cross slowly and paused to look at Anah.

"Yes, Sister?"

"That the girl is incapable—" She made the sign of the cross again and held her rosary to her lips.

"Yes, go on."

"The girl is incapable of being educated as a proper Catholic," she blurted out in German, then made the sign of the cross a third time, "completely unable of becoming a good citizen of the Territory of Hawai'i with religious values, manners, respect, and discipline." She pressed her hands together in prayer and brought them to her face, shielding her lying eyes from the reverend mother, further emphasizing her harrowing revelations about Anah with each shudderful sob.

"What?" the reverend mother gasped. "What are you saying, Sister?"

"There are far too many other girls, aboriginals at that, who *deserve*, please dear Mother, forgive my frankness. What I mean is, there are many other girls who *exhibit* a proclivity for tutorship and edification—" she said with her mighty arrogance, ice-blue eyes piercing Anah.

"Sister Bernadine," the reverend mother interrupted, rising now from behind her cluttered desk.

"Reverend Mother, pardon my candor, bitte," the sister said, wiping a tear from her eye, then clasping her hands together with great drama, "but we do not have enough tables and chairs for all of them," she sobbed, "not enough paper and pencils and textbooks, the room is so warmen, I beseech you to request assistance—the girls, Reverend Mother, so many of them are witless and illiterate even in their native tongues." Anah smelled the vinegar of her pessimism and failure. "We do them a disservice when we do not heed the holy word of the Lord's servant Job, 'Gold and crystal cannot be equal—' "

The reverend mother sent Anah out of her office with a stern finger. She shut the door softly, then listened to them whispering in a viscious English-German consonance about her and a few of the other girls.

Anah could barely read, add or subtract, Sister Bernadine told the reverend mother, and no amount of schooling would remedy her innate immigrant's stupidity. Under the close supervision of Sister Mary Deborah, she implored, Anah would instead benefit tremendously from vocational training from Aunty Chong Sum, Supang, and Fukunaga. The girl was their *kind*. Half-witted, uneducable, uncultivated, Oriental Oceania ancestor and idol-worshipping heathens, field laborers, rice paddy stock.

"But they are *all* their *kind*," the reverend mother sighed, "or even, shall I say God help them, *worse* off than their kind. However, we are not engaged in a proverbial losing battle, Sister, for we are soldiers for the Lord our God. We will continue to be vigilant in prayer so that we do what must be done in the name of our beloved Lord Jesus Christ, Sister—" And then she acquiesced. "We will do what is in the best interest of our young charges."

And so she decided. Anah would not be schooled any further; however, she would be indoctrinated with Catholicism in every other way. Anah and a mildly retarded girl, Shizu, would be removed from the sister's classroom but be vocationally trained, upstanding Catholic young women.

Anah along with Shizu, free of Sister Bernadine's oppressive and repetitive school lessons, gladly followed Supang around the grounds as he tended to the animals. Anah hoisted heavy five-gallon kerosene cans from the river to fill the murky animal troughs and buckets. Shizu filled the barrels of drinking water and cooking water for Aunty Chong Sum, carefully replacing the mosquito netting and screen to keep the bugs and rodents out of the clean water.

They slopped, watered, and cleaned the sty for the wild mountain pigs that Father Maurice domesticated and bred with a fat, pink, imported European boar generously donated to the orphanage by the Portuguese dairyman Rex Soares.

The mottled piglets pranced about Anah's feet and nibbled at her toes, picking up scraps of wet bread and biscuits. They grew fat and happy on boiled taro leaves and stems, rotten avocado, mango, tangerine, guava, and assorted worms in a simmering stew of leftovers.

Much to Supang's delight, Shizu worked like a man, shoveling out load after load of chicken manure from under the coops. The smell, the work, and the sweat never bothered her as she fertilized the vegetable garden where Anah grew large sugar beets, bush beans, sweet corn, and hearty herbs that Father Maurice liked to flavor his chicken roast or drink as afternoon tea with his treasured weekly edition of *The Pacific Commercial Advertiser*.

Shizu shoveled rabbit manure from under the many hutches and fertilized a special garden that Fukunaga and Anah started for Aunty Chong Sum, who would cook special foods that reminded them of their homes. The spicy gobo, the tangy daikon, purple shiso, and slimy araimo grew healthy and tall, and kabocha vines bearing large green pumpkins crawled over the bamboo poles and string trellises they built. Aunty Chong Sum made tsukemono from the cabbage they grew. And on cold days, she made chicken feet soup filled with vegetables from Anah's garden.

Supang showed Anah how to coax the temperamental egg layers with a dash of paprika in their feed, just like her brother Charles once showed her. Anah added dandelion and marigold petals. Supang marveled at her concoction that did indeed produce eggs with bright yellow yolks. Anah let the tame hens roam the grounds by day, then carried them back one by one to their coops in the evening.

Shizu gathered the red pullet feathers for Anah in an old jar she found buried near the banana trees. She told Anah that she would help her to fly away from this place one day. Anah promised to take Shizu with her as they filled the jar with feathers.

On sunny mornings, after the difficult chores, Sister Mary Deborah allowed Anah and Shizu to go to the water lily patch, a swimming hole up the road from the orphanage. "Take the buckets and nets with you, dear ones, so you can bring some prawns and river shrimps home for the cats," she said with a wink, "and I'll have the cook sauté the large ones in butter for you, you like?"

"You going kaukau some pa-wawns wif us too, Sister Mary Bee?" Shizu asked. She spoke loudly with a sloshy mouth that made her words seem like one long slur.

"I'll eat them only if you peel the shells and take the dreadful heads off for me," she said, heading back toward the apiary. "And don't forget your bee work today, young ladies. The hives are very full, and I will surely need your assistance in the harvest."

These were good days, such good days, days without fear or shame, days without Aki's constant presence.

Sister Mary Deborah fashioned a makeshift bee suit for Anah from some old crinoline she found in a church donation box and then a bee hat with a heavy veil. Shizu would have to wait for her suit, but she was in charge of preparing the tools for the harvest and filling the smoker with old coconut twine. She lit the rope and vigorously pumped the bellows, filling the honey house with thick, cool smoke.

"Now, now, dear." Sister Mary Deborah coughed and hacked. "Let's save the smoke for the hives."

Anah took the smoker from Shizu. "Me, me," Shizu said, not letting go. "Mine, this smoker."

"I no like the bee sting you," Anah told her softly.

"Wait right here for us, dear," Sister Mary Deborah said to her. "We'll be just a wee little while. I promise, you'll be in charge of the extractor upon our return with the frames."

"I like bee clothes too, Sister Mary Bee-borah," Shizu sloshed. "Because I no like stingers. I like bee hat too."

"Yours will be next, of that I am certain," the sister reassured, as Shizu reluctantly waved good-bye.

Anah followed the sister past the first few wooden boxes, then puffed the smoker at the one she pointed out as she opened the hive. She lifted the full, glistening frames, gently brushing off the groggy bees.

Anah was mindful of the sister's safety and welfare. She swept the disgruntled bees from the sister's veil, repositioned the bulky lids, pried the honeycombs from the walls of the hives, then hoisted the heavy wooden frames for her. Then Anah took the smoker from her and tucked it under her arm.

The sister smiled at Anah, a small, quiet smile, then placed her hand on Anah's face. "Thy merciful kindness be for my comfort," she said.

Anah looked at her beautiful face in the last hours of this day. "How sweet are your words to my taste," Anah began, "sweeter than honey to my mouth. I gain understanding from your precepts; therefore, I hate every wrong path."

"The psalmist spoke to the Lord our God," she said, mildly irritated at Anah's misuse of scripture.

"But when I think of those words, I think about you."

"Those words were intended for the glorification of our God," she said, definitive and indignant. "You must *never* use the scripture for vainglorious—" She stopped and looked at Anah struggling with the load she did not want the sister to bear.

Anah lowered her eyes.

The sister put her hand on Anah's shoulder. "But aren't the psalmist's words beautiful, Susanah? And how impressive your recitation." She began humming as she guided Anah back to the honey house, her hand on the small of the girl's back. "Very impressive indeed."

On the night of no moon, near the first whelping time for the gray mother rabbit, Anah slept in the nativity shack as the animal midwife. She had already assisted many of the animals in birth, for she loved them all. She prayed for their souls as she welcomed them to the world, baptised them in the name of the Father, the Son, and the Holy Ghost, and offered last rites when it came time for them to die. She knew each of them by name, even the newborn.

But on that night, alone in the nativity shack, she heard *them* calling her name.

'Anah.'

These were different voices.

'Anah.'

She would not answer.

'Look, Anah.'

She would not look.

'In the trees, all around you.'

She shut her eyes and ears.

'We are many.'

"Seth!"

He came immediately to her and stood at the doorway to the shack. He beckoned her with his hand to *Come, come*, but she would not.

'Anah.'

"No, Seth. I scared."

'Anah.'

"Little Leah?"

'Anah!'

"Aki? Thass you, Aki?"

'Anah, look.'

But Anah would not look. "Aki, you cannot see or what?" And then she spoke to her sister in Japanese. "These are good days for me. I am happy now. You must leave. I do not want to see you." She covered her eyes with her hands.

'Anah, listen.'

She would not listen. "Go away from me, Aki. Leave me alone. They blame me for the things you do at night." She covered her ears.

'Anah.'

She should have looked. Aki's voice was fading. "Leave me alone, Aki. Go away."

'Anah.'

She should have listened. She could barely hear her.

'Behold, Anah.'

But even then she did not.

'Behold the many, Anah.'

But she did not.

'Mentirosa.'

And for refusing to heed her command, Aki began scratching at

Anah's arms, catlike, with thin, razored claws, translucent pink, a trinity of talons that pierced her flesh again and again, moving underneath her skin like a reckless trio of maggots.

Anah scuttled to the corner of the nativity shack, swabbed her arms with her bedding, and covered her huddled body.

Aki bit Anah's cheek as she wrangled with air. Aki had no form, she who laughed as she bit her sister's neck, back, belly, and then buttocks, leaving the mark of her purple teeth all over Anah's body.

Anah was certain she screamed. Anah was certain she fought. But no one heard her, no one came.

So Aki pinched her over and over, and at last, without any fight left in her, Anah let her, the pain becoming painless with the numbing of her body; it felt languidly comforting, Aki twisting and pulling at the softest flesh until it bruised, every inch of Anah's skin a purple-black blotch.

'Anah.'

"What you like, Aki?"

She answered in Japanese. 'Home. I want to go home. I want my mama.'

"Don't you understand? She is never coming to get us. We are never going home. There is no Mama. She is dead to me, just like you."

'I have a mama.'

"No. No mo'."

'I have a brother.'

"No. Him too. No mo'."

'I have a home.'

"No."

The winds screamed and tore at the nativity shack as a shudder of cold passed over Anah's torn body. She had not realized that she was naked. The thatched roof lifted off, turning in a small cyclone as if in a puppeteer's hand. And then it went still but for a brush of leaf, the chirp of chick, the cry of rabbit. Anah smelled her sister's earthy hands above her, her phlegmy, bloody wheeze. She crawled for the door.

'We are many.'

'Mama!'

Mama!

They all began calling for their mothers. A sad longing, the pitiful wailing of the lost and forgotten children. But there was nothing Anah could do. Not even for her beloved Aki.

"I will be your mama," Anah said to them.

'You are not! Mama!'

Anah wrapped her bedding around her, kneeling in the doorway, readying herself to run. She stepped onto the lawn, but they knocked her down, pinning her to the floor of the shack.

And in her vicious, consciousless child's anger, Aki slashed the thin membrane over the orb of Anah's eyes, red and blue veins spider-webbing inside, filling her eyes with bloody tears. She sliced open the delicate skin of eyelids with the precision of light, each cut intended for Anah to see no more what she did not want to see until the weight of skin and tears, blood and pus, sealed her eyes shut, blood issuing from every hole on her face.

'Behold, mentirosa,' she commanded.

But Anah could not.

Voices Amid Delirium

"Has the girl been violated, Sister Bernadine?"

"I do not know, Reverend Mother."

"Is this the work of our groundskeeper or our janitor, Sister Mary Deborah? Did you not say they treated the girl like their own?"

"Yes, Reverend Mother, I mean, no, Reverend Mother. Mr. Supang and Mr. Fukunaga were sent home for the weekend. Susanah, Shizu, and I were managing their chores until Monday."

"And was the retarded one with the girl? Was she also harmed?"

"No, Reverend Mother. She spent the night under the isinglass on the second floor."

"Was not the girl under your supervision, Sister Mary Deborah?"

"She was, Reverend Mother. I took some cinnamon toast and milk and a fresh lantern for her after my last bed check. The gray mother rabbit had only begun labor, so we walked to the hutch to check on her progress. She had already begun preparing a nest of grass and fur, in fact, she had begun pulling fur from her—"

"Sister, what time was it?"

"About eleven-thirty, after the last bed check."

"And you heard nothing, nothing at all? I find that completely implausible, Sister. The girl has been horribly, horribly brutalized."

"It must have been later at about three in the morning. I heard the animals, Reverend Mother, the goat bleating, the dogs barking, the rabbits crying, the cats, the pigs, the chickens thrashing their bodies against the sides of the coops, the donkey braying until the ropes cut into his neck."

"Were all of the animals secured, Sister? Did the girl release all of them again?"

"Reverend Mother, all of the animals were in their pens. But I heard them screaming, each and every one of them, the wind was howling madly in the trees. I ran outside to check on the animals when I found Susanah benumbed in a state of shock in what remains of the nativity shack."

"The girl did that which was evil in the eyes of the Lord our God and she has wrought evil onto this place."

"Hush, Sister Bernadine."

"Forgive me, Reverend Mother, but the prudent forseeth the evil; however, our Sister Mary Deborah hath not."

"I caution you, Sister Bernadine. Let your mouth transgresseth not into judgment."

"You, Sister Mary Deborah, it is you who called good evil and evil good; it is you who shutteth our eyes from seeing."

"Judge me not, Sister, lest the Lord our God—"

"Sisters, please! Your angry words do nothing but fill this room with your rancorous animosity. When the girl awakens, we must encourage her to conduct a thorough examination of conscience by confession and penance. And we will discipline her by the rod. The girl must seek good and not evil, so that she too may be delivered unto the light."

"Will you be calling the authorities, Reverend Mother?"

"No, Sister Mary Deborah."

"And what of Father Maurice? Have you spoken to him, Reverend Mother?"

"No. He has been preoccupied in his preparations for Bishop Deusdedit's inspection, rather, *visit* to St. Joseph's."

"Will you be calling the constable?"

"No, Sister."

"A doctor?"

"No, Sister. We will take care of all matters concerning Susanah Medeiros ourselves."

10

1919

"Hup hup, get me aloe. I make you sweet bread and coffee," Aunty Chong Sum ordered Supang. "I already pick the pōpolo leaf and mash with rock salt fo' make paste put on the girl sore."

Supang hesitated in the dark of the doorway. "They no like us make no good plantation medicine on Anah. I no make humbug for me and Fukunaga. Me like job. Maybe you no need mo-ni. Me need mo-ni," he said, pounding his chest with his hand. "I get plenny keiki. One mo' baby come pretty soon. You go get aloe." He picked up his lantern from the small table.

"What kine man you? Anah follow you like dog and do your work like dog and you no can kōkua her," she scolded. "Why you no like help her?" She looked at Supang's guilty face, yet recognized his genuine concern for his many children. "Never you mind," she said, dismissing him with a flick of her wrist. "I ask Pa-ke Melvin bring the 'ulu for the scratch all over the body. Get plenty breadfruit fo' make 'ulu medicine in his yard. And the noni juice for the deep cut. Noni berry numba one good kine medicine. I mix with rock salt too—"

"You tell your nephew, Chong Sum, he going get big pilikia with the big mama. You watch out, you no mo' job, you nīele them." And then he spoke to her in Cantonese. "You must mind your own business, Chong Sum, or you will be in big trouble. Too bad for Anah. I feel badly about her condition, but I do not wish to stick out my neck and become a penniless, headless chicken for her sake. And you should also think about yourself and your family."

"You *seen* Anah, or what? I think you seen her you know why I like make medicine. Eye no can open. Poor thing, our Anah. She scream when the sister wash-wash her with vinegar. And no good the other haole medicine—"

AND IN THE SAME MORNING'S DARKNESS of the second-floor infirmary, Anah listened to all of their voices from the expansive blackness that enveloped her.

"Even if she writhes in pain, hydrogen peroxide sizzles when it is battling her infection," Sister Bernadine whispered. "So we *must* apply it three times a day to the fresh wounds. And we must continue bathing her with a vinegar wash."

Sister Mary Deborah, urgent in her worry, kneeled at Anah's bedside. Anah breathed in the sweet fragrance of her hands. "Her wounds are not healing, Sister. We must be extremely careful and extremely vigilant in preventing any further infection, as her consumption may worsen."

"Ich wissen, Sister. I know. Do you not think I am gravely concerned about Susanah's condition?" She swabbed the cuts on Anah's cheek with a heavy, angry hand. "I do not appreciate your implication that I—"

"Careful, please, Sister, I implore you, especially the cuts around her eyes. We have not been able to adequately treat the wounds with conventional medicine. May I have your permission to seek the assistance of the cook who has suggested a salve made from plants and herbs found here in the valley?"

"Sister Mary Deborah, we will not resort to pagan remedies," she began, placing the bowl of vinegar on the nightstand. "How many times must we impress upon you the importance of modern medicine and conventional treatments?" Anah stirred, her forehead furrowed in great pain, a tear falling from the corner of her eye.

Sister Mary Deborah began to weep. "But never in my life have I ever seen or treated," she sobbed. "I am utterly—please, forgive me, Sister." She turned her eyes away from Anah's body that continued to sizzle with the effects of the peroxide. "Susanah's condition is extremely troubling," she said, composing herself. "I recommend we consider the native remedies, as there is some merit in their curative properties. Especially for the stitches on the girl's face. The peroxide is causing her such great discomfort. I fear I must inform Father Maurice, as my heart is with great heaviness—"

"Sisters?" the reverend mother interrupted.

"Yes, Reverend Mother."

"Seek the counsel of our cook, posthaste," she said to Sister Mary Deborah, who stood quickly and hurried out of the infirmary. "The child's infections worsen by the hour."

"But—"

"No, Sister Bernadine. You will obey my orders. The girl's fieber rises higher and higher," she said, placing the back of her hand on Anah's neck, then forehead, sending a shiver through Anah's body. "You will attempt the use of the aboriginal remedies. Do you understand, Sister? And Father Maurice is not to be troubled by this matter. The bishop arrives any day now. Do you understand, Sister?"

"Ja, Reverend Mother."

THE SUN CAME UP from behind the Ko'olau Mountains. Sister Mary Deborah thrummed her fingers on the small table as she sat waiting with Aunty Chong Sum in the kitchen. They watched Sister Bernadine lead the girls like a line of ducklings to the river with the week's laundry.

"No worry, Sister," Aunty Chong Sum said, placing a cup of māmaki and lāpine tea before her. "The boy coming pretty soon. Mr. Rex have no time for such things as this when no rain and the cows have no food. Him and the paniolos take the cows go up mauka this morning. But the boy know what the Mr. Rex know. He come pretty soon make medicine for Anah."

From his grandmother born in São Miguel in the eastern Azores and her grandmother and her grandmother before, Rex Soares had passed the tradition of Portuguese folk medicine to his eldest son as many of the immigrant peoples had. They adapted the herbal remedies of their homelands with the traditions of the kahuna lapaʻau laʻau in the treatment of common ailments.

The sister deeply inhaled the smell of the herbal citrus brew in the teacup before her. "Will you need some fresh honey, Chong Sum?" the sister asked after her first sip.

"Yes, Sister. The boy said we need the honey. I wen' get um from the honey house—" She stopped to listen to the approaching rider on horseback, flinging back the curtains from the kitchen window. "Fukunaga! Bring Ezroh inside. Get watercress?" she yelled. "Good, good, we make into juice with the flaxseed and green mustard leaf with honey," she muttered as she busied about the sink area.

Sister Mary Deborah stepped onto the small porch, Chong Sum behind her. "Very fresh. Nice watercress. You bring mortar and pesto? Good, good, poi pounder with rock okay too."

Ezroh led his horse to a waiting Supang. He handed his bags full of herbs and plants to Chong Sum. "My father coming after he bring the herd back down the valley. He said fo' me stay o' here help you with the medicine 'til he come back."

"Yes, please stay," Sister Mary Deborah said, stepping aside to let Ezroh into the kitchen. "We will prepare a bed for you."

Ezroh began sorting the different leaves, seeds, vegetables, roots, and branches on the huge table in the middle of the kitchen.

Chong Sum smelled each one, taking tiny bites of the plants unfamiliar to her. "Ezroh, you tell me what Mr. Rex say about this medicine," she said of the bounty before her.

"My father said drink most of this as tonic." He pointed to the left side of the table. "This you mix with honey and put um on as salve. This one you put on pus. This one for face only with plenny honey."

"It makes complete sense," Sister Mary Deborah said, hiking up the heavy sleeves of her habit. "The honey for nourishment and for her wounds; when boiled and applied, honey joins the separated parts of the body."

"And he said fo' Aunty make poultice with ti leaf and pulu bandage for the eyes bumbye no can see. Soak everything, ti leaf and pulu in water. Better holy water. Boil with onion skin and koa bark. Then drink um with tea."

Sister Mary Deborah smiled. "She ingests what we apply externally to accelerate healing. Will you assist us in the infirmary, Ezroh?" she asked.

"Yes, Sister."

IN THREE DAYS, Anah woke briefly for the first time.

Anah's Wakening

Seth? My eyes. I think I can open. Seth? Muito obrigado, my Seth, thank you, thank you for bringing me special medicine, just like my mama made for Leah, Aki, and me. Your medicine just like home."

"Seth? Muito obrigado? Portuguêsa?"

"No, Anah, you no talk like that. I told you how many days not, this not Seth. This one Ezroh. The brother came kōkua you. Seth make. She not well. You drink this tea. Be quiet your mouth."

"Seth? How you know my brother Seth?"

"No, she dunno. Anah, this one not Seth, I said. You better listen your Aunty Chong Sum before I—"

"Seth, help me up."

"No, lie down, you Anah. You still little bit lōlō. You dunno what you talking. Go back hiamoe. Sleep now. She have the gallop, you know, the cough. Just little bit crazy still yet. Hush up yo' mouth."

"Is everything all right over there, Chong Sum? What is all the commotion?"

"Yes. I mean, no. I mean, yes, Sister Bernadine. Everything numba-one okay over here on this side. No troubles. No pilikia o' here."

"Seth, my eyes feel better. I like see you now, Seth."

"Aunty, please tell me. How she know my brother?"

"Shhh! Lie down, I said. She dunno him. He long time ago ma-ke, long time before Anah come live St. Joseph. No, she lōlō. You, Anah, you no talk like that. Here, Ezroh, you put aloe o' here. Be careful no drop on floor."

"Your hands, Seth—"

"Seth? Aunty, she think I Seth."

"Sister Bernadine!"

"Chong Sum, there is no need for yelling in the infirmary. What is the matter with you today? What do you want? And please, do not shout."

"I going let Ezroh take Anah outside on lānai for sunshine on her cut. I just put aloe and noni juice. Sun good before I put bandage on her arm. Thank you, thank you, Sister. Go, go now, you Ezroh. Wiki-wiki, go now, hurry before Sister come."

"Where we going, Seth?"

"Outside."

"Your voice—no be sad for me."

"Here, sit in this rocking chair. Here, nice blanket keep you warm."

"Thank you. I knew you would come. Was you made me better? I knew that was you by me every day. No leave me. Stay with me. I no mo' family. Only you. Take this off my eye. I like see you."

"No, Anah. The sunlight. Too bright. Leave um on. No take off the bandage—"

"Seth?"

"My name is Ezroh."

1919

Anah awoke one morning as if from a long dream. What day it was, she did not know. She heard the birds in the pine trees outside her window. She was on the second floor in the infirmary on the bed closest to Sister Mary Deborah's cell. She was alone, the beds on the entire floor empty and made military-precise.

It was morning. Anah was sure of it. She had awakened this morning as if from a long dream. She was sure of it.

What day? What month?

She listened to the birds. She looked at her arms covered by ti leaf poultices wrapped neatly with sisal twine like gifts of broken, infectious flesh.

She moved her eyes to the left. Sunlight through the open French doors, a light wind pushing the white curtains. She was awake.

She moved her eyes to the right. A small crucifix hanging against the white wall, immaculate white. She was awake.

She opened her hands, a rosary of knotted sennit with a hand-carved wooden cross cured with sweet kukui oil. *Was it Sunday?*

She was alone.

It was morning.

Anah closed her eyes, straining to hear familiar sounds. Fukunaga's mop bucket wheeling slowly on the floor above, Aunty Chong Sum stirring oatmeal and frying blood sausages in her heavy cast-iron pots, girls in the chapel reciting the Lord's Prayer, Hail Marys, Our Fathers, Glory Bes.

Nothing.

Nothing but the birds in the pine trees.

She lifted her head to the morning. The room began to spin. Below her window on the green lawn, a gathering of girls and nuns, happy dogs, a cook, the always hungry cats, a janitor, busybody chickens, a groundskeeper, and a priest, all moving in a dizzying, kinetic arch around *Shizu*.

Anah's best friend, her only friend, Shizu Kutaka. She wore her white, starched Mass dress. *Sunday? Yes, Sunday.* She held her Bible and a huge bouquet of yellow and white ginger. *Of course, it is Sunday.* On her head, her thick, black Okinawan hair pomaded shiny, she wore a crown of gardenia and rose pikake.

A woman in a simple cotton kimono embraced Shizu. A man in a stiff Western suit and a straw hat lifted Shizu's small wicker suitcase onto the back of the buggy, then held out his hand to help her in.

When did this happen? How many days had passed? How many weeks, months? Shizu cured? By the doctor? No, he let them all die. By the sisters? No, they slept as the children slipped away into death. By the reverend mother? No, Shizu didn't even deserve schooling, how could she deserve a healing? By Father Maurice? No, he read the last rites like empty words over and over. By God?

Then it must have been God. By the grace that Shizu repeated over and over in a child's singsong, "God's gwace, God's gwace, God's gwace."

How many days as they did their chores together, Anah listened as Shizu prayed for a miracle with her sloshy way of speaking. She prayed to each saint she knew for God's intercession, to the blessed Virgin, and to Christ Jesus himself. Anah laughed at her senseless faith in a God who had cursed her with the consumption that she now so fervently believed he would take from her.

"I rh-ove you Ghee-sus, above all. Wit' your shtripes I am all pau con-shump-shun," she yelled as she scraped impacted manure from the donkey's hooves.

"Be it accodian to yo' will. Fo' he heal every shickness and di-shease," she prayed, closing her eyes and lifting a bunch of harvested radishes to the sky.

"O Ghee-sus, heal the shick, which is me and all the gurlz on the shecond flo', even on the shab-bash which is a holy day unto dee," she said as she scrubbed rose apples and peaches in the wash barrel.

"O Rhord," she prayed one day, stopping as they hoed a deep row for gobo and daikon, "in your gweat generoshity, heal my shickness, pwease. And Anah's too, pwease. I beg you be mer-shee-fool. Wash 'way our de-filth-ment." As they walked to the pigpens, she shouted, "Behold the handmaids of the Rhord, me and Anah! O that yo' loyal shervants, me and Anah, shall be all pau with our shick!"

While she stepped barefooted in pig manure and mud, God must have heard Shizu. She would leave for her father's small taro farm on the North Shore while Anah remained at St. Joseph's. She would live while Aki and Leah died. While Anah lay dying.

Anah could not bear it. Shizu had not even come to say good-bye. But she watched as Shizu frantically waved her hand as the buggy squeaked and shifted toward the grove of mountain apple and avocado trees. Anah listened to the dissipating sounds of whinny and wheels, a jingling harness as the buggy approached the bridge over Kalihi Stream.

She watched Shizu's huge hand waving at her, as she lifted her eyes to Anah's trapped in the window on the second floor. Anah hit her hands against the glass so hard that they began to bleed again. Shizu's hand waved her back, back into that place.

How would Anah bear the days to come without her? They never made her a bee hat with crinoline veil. They never harvested the sweet corn or picked the huge kabocha with her name etched in its skin from the healthy vine they planted behind the chicken coops. Anah never showed her how to bake a loaf of Vovó's sweet bread. Shizu never showed Anah how to make andagi doughnuts in hot coconut oil.

"Come back! No leave me here! Take me with you! Come back!"

Shizu's hand waved her back into that place, the place of Anah's hollow heart.

SHE AWOKE one morning as if from a long dream. Aunty Chong Sum and Sister Mary Deborah changed the dressing on the wounds that covered Anah's body, the horrid slashes of her sister's wrath, wet skin and thick yellow pus lifting like strands of saliva from each gash.

It seemed to Anah that she had been asleep for a long time, listening to disembodied voices around her like the buzzing of the bees, intermittent intrusions that intensified then subsided as she drifted in and out of what felt like a death.

She never recognized the voices or the faces.

Until the morning she awoke.

"Yes, Chong Sum. We are to provide temporary lodging for the boy in Supang's quarters. Please supply him with fresh linens and towels twice weekly. You will treat him as a welcomed guest." Sister Mary Deborah gently fluffed the pillow under Anah's head.

"The mama leave him o' here? When she wen' leave? How come?" Aunty Chong Sum asked as she straightened out Anah's sheets with sharp tugs. "The boy is good boy. I always say that lady is a no good wahine always making keiki, keiki, too much keiki. Some of her babies no even look like Mr. Rex. You ask me, I think the kanaka cowboy, the one with nice Sepania face, he the one make the baby with the wahine."

"Now, now, Chong Sum. The holy book says, 'He who spreads slander is a fool, but he who holds his tongue is wise.' " The sister placed her hand on Anah's forehead and brushed away the loose hair from her closed eyes.

"I not one fool," Aunty Chong Sum huffed. "Thass what Fukunaga told me. Maybe he the fool, tell me all kine story, that damn Japanee fool. I neva even ask him nothin'. He tell me from *his* side. I no ask nothin'. He the one like talk story with me alla time talk-talk." She ran her hands briskly over the bedspread. "He the one say the wahine take all the small keiki go follow the Portagee sailor on the boat back to the Azores. No good, that wahine. Not even the sailor keiki, thass the kanaka keiki," she muttered on. "But she leave Ezroh, poor thing. I dunno why. Maybe he help the papa on the dairy. Maybe he the only one from Mr. Rex, what you think, Sister?"

"Now, now, reckless words pierce like a sword. Please tend to Susanah," the sister instructed firmly. "The tongue of the wise brings healing, Chong Sum." She poured fresh water into the washbasin on the bed stand. "Mr. Soares has asked us to supervise Ezroh until he returns with the herd."

"Mr. Rex, he so sad. Thass what Fukunaga told me." Aunty Chong Sum rinsed a washcloth in the clear water. "Mr. Rex no take care himself. No shave, no bathe, drink the 'ōkolehao all night with the paniolos at the stable. He no feed the boy." She tsk-tsk-tsked. "And give um dirty lickens for nothin'. But he so sad thass why. I think he take the herd up mauka pastures 'cause he no can tell the boy how come the mama run away. What you think, Sister?"

"He took the herd up into the mountains because of the mild drought, Chong Sum. Enough of your unfounded gossip. The prudent keep their knowledge to themselves, but the hearts of fools blurt out folly."

"How many times I tell you I not fool. And I not folly."

"When you are done with your morning chores, please ask Mr. Fukunaga to accompany you to the Soares dairy to gather the boy and his belongings. God bless Mr. Soares," the sister said, making the sign of the cross. "He has been so generous in his provisions for the orphaned and the infirmed. And he has harvested so many plants and herbs to help the children's consumption and Susanah's wounds."

"Only Mr. Rex plants help our Anah."

"Only our blessed Lord sustains Susanah."

ANAH AWOKE one morning as if from a long dream. She saw Seth's beautiful face above hers haloed in a white seraphic light.

"Seth? I dead?" Words stumbled from her lips. "Where is God? Take me to him. Tell him make Aki stop hurting me." Seth reached out to touch her face. "Where Aki? Leah all right? Take me with you. To God, Seth."

"Shh, no talk. Be quiet. Be still."

She closed her eyes slowly, once, twice, and when she opened them, she saw Ezroh cleaning her fresh wounds with tender hands. "Ezroh?" He smiled at her, his touch warm and gentle. Seth pulled back his hand and stood against the wall.

"How long have I been—" she asked him in Portuguese. "What day, how long? Where is Shizu? Please tell me." Tears began welling in her eyes, burning the slashes at the outer edges.

He was startled at her fluency in the tongue of his father as he put pieces of koa bark and rock salt in his mortar. "You have Portuguese blood?" His pestle moved in circular precision.

"Yes," she answered. "Now tell me. How long?"

"It has been months, Anah," he answered in the familiar music of Portuguese. It soothed him to hear the language of his father and extended family at the dairy. But he did not look at her as he spoke. "It is the twenty-fifth of May, a Friday." He poured water into his mortar from a small glass vial. "Holy water. Do not tell Father Maurice." He winked. "You can use all the help you can get."

"May?" she gasped.

"My father tended to Shizu's consumption with his plant tonics when they realized their curative value because of your wounds," he said, removing coarse strands of bark from his mortar. "And all of the sunshine and chores with the animals helped her to get better. That is what my father said. He helped her until his wife . . . until he could no longer . . . and then she took my brothers and sisters . . . so he took the herd into the mountains. And he sent me here to—help."

"Oh, Shizu—" Anah moaned. Was she happy for Shizu's recovery or jealous over her leaving? It was a little of both. "Why have I been asleep for so long?"

"Look," Ezroh said, pulling loose the sisal that bound the ti leaves around her arms. "Every time your wounds began to heal, new gashes appeared. They thought you were hurting yourself."

He dripped the koa juice onto the infections on her right arm and held her hand as it burned deeper and deeper. Anah felt herself falling back into the darkness behind her closed eyes, her head spiraling down, down into the softness of her pillow.

"Anah!" he kept calling her. "Anah, come back!"

She listened to his urgent voice and willed herself back, held on tight to Ezroh's hand and pulled herself back. She had to know what had happened to her, where all those months had gone.

Her eyes opened slowly. She surveyed the scratched and torn flesh on her arms. "I did all of this to myself?"

"No," he said, resting her arm on a sheet rolled into a small bolster warmed by a strand of sunlight. "Sister Bernadine herself sat with you all day and all night for three days to find out if it was you—"

"What happened?"

"Nothing."

"Nothing? Then why am I still—"

"When they woke on the fourth day, it was as though someone had taken a small knife to slice open each of your bindings. And with that small knife, cut you again and again. You were covered with blood.

Then Sister Mary Deborah sat with you. And it happened again. Then the reverend mother herself. And it happened again, but each time worse than the time before."

Ezroh moved to the other side of the bed. He began removing the poultice. "You shield your face with this arm whenever you are being assailed. There are many more wounds on this side." He rinsed the mortar and pestle in the washbasin. "But thank the Lord our God for your sleep. I do not think you would have been able to tolerate the pain otherwise."

Anah watched as he began grinding taro leaves and rock salt. "Who is doing this to me?" She looked past Ezroh to the corners of the room. Leah looked at her from one, her face concerned.

Little Leah?

"Father Maurice said it is you. He suggested they tie your arms to the bed frame. When the ties were found cut for the third time, he finally called Bishop Deusdedit. He will be here again. Any day now. Aunty Chong Sum said—" He took Anah's hand in his to prepare her for the pulpy green tonic.

But as she gripped his hand, she saw Aki. She stood in another corner, her hand over her mouth stifling back her laughter.

Aki!

"I do not want you to leave us again," Ezroh said as he poured extracted juice of taro leaf onto her wounds. "Hold on, Anah." Her mouth and eyes open, the juice seeped in liquid flames down to her bones.

She saw Seth crying in another corner, his finger pointing at his chest:

'Me. It was me.'

Aki clutched at her belly, her body bent over, laughing. 'No, me!' she squealed.

"Seth?" Anah winced in a painful delirium. "You? No, it was Aki."

"Seth? Aki? Stop it, Anah. My brother is dead. And your sister is dead."

"I know, but—" She started, noticing Ezroh's face confused. "Ezroh, what did Aunty say about this?" she managed to ask.

"To ask *you* what is happening. That you *know* who is doing this to you." His grip on her hand loosened, and he began binding her arm with fresh taro leaves. "Tell them, Anah."

"They would not believe me." She searched for Aki. But she was gone, her trill giggling on a gusty breeze. "You would not believe me." Seth followed her, a mournful wailing wind.

"Ezroh," Aunty Chong Sum called from the door. She held a tray with a bowl full of steaming broth. "I made plenny. Had plenny meat and soup bone. You like me bring some up for the Yamada girl? Your father keep sending meat and plants. He neva come home from up mauka yet, huh? The old paniolo, what his name, the old cowboy? Tora-san, he bring the meat and bone."

Ezroh lifted a spoonful of the delicate soup to Anah's lips. It smelled of the ocean's brine, a light broth with tender slivers of beef. It warmed her entire body.

"What I put on you, I put inside you," he said. "Make you come better mo' fast. This what my father did fo' Shizu." He took out a small silver snuffbox from his pocket. "Hinu honu oil. I wen' trade with the fisherman Kepo'o down Ke'ehi Lagoon. His fresh turtle for our milk, oxtails, and tongue."

"When your papa come back, he going be proud you, Ezroh," Aunty said, placing her hand on Ezroh's head. "I tell him how you make all kine good medicine fo' us when he no stay."

Ezroh pulled himself away from her. "No tell him nothing," he said.

"I tell what I like," she muttered, startled by Ezroh's angry reaction. "You no tell me what to tell when I tell what I like tell. You one good boy is all I saying," she continued, leaving to get another bowl of soup.

Ezroh shook his head and opened the snuffbox. He dabbed his finger in the precious turtle oil. "The hinu honu oil makes the scars go away," he whispered to Anah in Portuguese, gently massaging the oil on the cuts that covered her face. "One of the cowboys at the dairy told my father about the healing properties told to him by his great-grandfather from Punaluʻu on the southern shore of the island of Hawaiʻi."

"How will it make *all* of these scars go away?"

His fingers moved across her forehead, then down to her cheek, and slowly over her lips and chin. "You do not let them cut your face anymore," he said, his eyes searching hers for acknowlegment and promise.

Them.

She nodded, a tear slipping down her face, Ezroh blending it into her scars with another dab of turtle oil.

"Finish your soup," he said, standing to begin his morning chores with Supang. "You need to get out of that bed soon." He looked at her, something rising and spinning between them. "The animals miss your care." He turned to leave, but at the doorway, he stopped and reached into his pocket. "Shizu asked me to give this to you when you woke up."

Anah felt her throat tighten.

"She needed help rebuilding the nativity shack for you. We spent many days working together, and she wanted me to tell you—"

"What?" Anah asked. "Tell me what? Tell me."

"But I told her to give me the words. I wrote them down the best I could." Ezroh walked back to Anah's bedside. "Here," he said, holding it out to her. "Take the letter."

Shizu's Letter

February 28, 1919

Dearest friend Anna,

By the time you read this I will be gone. I going home to my brothers and sisters, mother and father, aunties and uncles, you name it, we all live on the taro farm plus lots and lots of pigs and dogs and cats and chickens and goose and ducks and my usume's canaries. Oh how my grampa love those little canaries. I came say good-bye to you every day but you was asleep all the time. I try wake you up but sister Bernadine catch me and whip my hands with the stick for disobey and one time I had the closet when she said enough of my insolen.

I said many prayers to Our Blessed Virgin who is Jesus beloved mother and St. Joseph who is our patron saint and Jesus beloved daddy. They will ask their son in my name and kiss his head for me so his Father hear my prayers for you to wake up and not die.

Please do not die, Anna. I was thinking that the Holy Virgin and St. Joseph are like a mommy and daddy to me since mine had bring me here to get cure when I got the consumption. They can ask Jesus to ask his daddy cure you like He cure me. Remember how I use to pray real loud when we feed the pigs and water the donkey and goat and you tell me hush up Shizu but in a nice way? Mostly I think you scared the mama sow attack us again for making a lot of noise around her babies. We sure got stink when she knock us over in the trough.

Your my best friend, Anna. I know that nobody like me because I talk in a funny way and talk stupid things but no matter what you was always kind to me. I ask God all the time how come Anna the only girl over here that is kind to me. Please do not let her be the one to die. Even the sisters not nice to me in fact they the meanest especially Sister Bernadine. Maybe sometimes Supang nice to me when he in good mood not too many times but sometimes. And lucky I had the animals because they always kind to me. And now Ezroh. He is nice. I told him if he would marry me but he said no thanks in a nice way because he already has a girl who is in his heart. I ask him who is that girl but he does not want to tell since it is a secret.

But you Anna I wish you could come with me to the taro farm with my family. I could tell my brother Kiyoshi marry you if you like. He is shy but the kindest brother with brown hair and strong teeth. He can draw very nice pictures. But he so quiet everybody say he will not find a good wife. You would be a good wife to Kiyoshi because you know how to wash pigpen and make good slop. If you marry him you would be my sister and you would live with us.

You never tell me anything about your mother or father or brother. I only know that you had two sisters name Aki and Leah who die here and you cry at night in your bed for them. And on Visitors Sunday nobody came see you and I watch how you look so sad. I wanted to tell you come be in my family but maybe that make you mad at me.

You know how sometimes you get mad at me like the time I told Fukunaga that you like marry him. That time you got mad. You said you rather marry the pig or maybe the donkey. But later on I went back and told Fukunaga that I mean that I like marry him when I get big not you. But he said no thanks. How come everybody say no thanks when I ask them to marry me? Lucky I no get mad back or watch out I could knock them out with one punch in the nose.

Your my very dearest friend, Anna. That's why I fix the nativity shack for you, me and Ezroh and Supang help too even Sister Mary Deborah came help put up the roof again. Maybe come Christmas time you light a special candle for me and I will go to mass and light one for you. But here is the big secret. When you wake up and read this letter I want you to go inside the shack and dig in the corner by the place

I plant the squash vine. It is my special bottle of red feathers. I want you to have it. Ezroh said he will help you to find some more feathers to fill it to the top. You can make wings and fly away from St. Joseph's in case your mommy and daddy don't come back at least you can fly over the valley and go home.

I will say a lot of prayers for you every day even if you would tell me to hush up in a nice way. I said prayers for you all the time inside my own head and you did not even know.

Your friend forever,
Shizu Kutaka

P.S. Sister Mary Deborah used to always tell us this when we got the honey with her. Remember always my children love is sweet. Please listen to Sister Mary Deborah and remember always Anna.

12

DECEMBER 1919

It was the morning of December 24. In this season of glad tidings, Prince Jonah Kūhiō Kalanianaole and Governor Charles J. McCarthy had been unsuccessful in their bid for Congress to consider Hawai'i for statehood. In this season of glad tidings, Prohibition was law. But it was Christmas at St. Joseph's.

The girls began leaving the remote orphanage one by one. They would be allowed to spend two days at home with their families. Fathers and mothers arrived from far points on the island of O'ahu, bearing the bounty of a poor man's gratitude to the holy sisters of St. Joseph's:

loaves of bread

bags of rice

cans of fruit cocktail

bottles of pickled daikon, onion, cucumber, cabbage, eggplant, fish, achiote oil, kochu jang, bagoong, and patis

small baskets of dried fish, octopus, gandule, chickpeas, sweet potato, and star fruit bundles of squash flowers, ong choi, bok choi, fern shoots, burdock root, and kale

packages of candied vegetables and fruits, dried seaweed, jasmine and chrysanthemum teas

plates of yokan and kanten, haupia and kūlolo, gau and jin dui, suman and puto, sweet rice fritters, chestnut and date balls, and fried taro cakes

Anah leaned on her rake and watched them all leaving from behind the māmaki trees by the gazebo. The little Filipina Edwina Estrella left with an elderly manong uncle for the 'Ewa Plantation. The Japanese sisters Miki and Anne Torige left with a married brother for the Waialua Sugar Plantation. The robust Pa-ke Mai Lee Chong went home with her mother and brothers to her family's fruit stand in Chinatown.

The clannish Korean Kang girls went home with their seamstress picture bride mother, the Puerto Rican Mercado girl with her field worker father, the Hawaiian Makua girl with her poor fisherman uncle, the Portuguese Teixeira with her older sister, the Okinawan Heima with her pig farmer grandparents, the Spaniard Baldomero with her blacksmith father's apprentice—all who came for their ailing loved ones.

Anah had convinced herself that she didn't need a family. Her family had only caused her pain.

A little one whose death made her heart despair for three years now.

Aki who tormented her on nights when she neglected to wear the sennit-knotted rosary around her neck, sprinkle Hawaiian rock salt, and splash ti leaves dipped in holy water around her bed like Aunty Chong Sum had instructed her.

A father who aggravated her sleep with his mead-scented breath during Lent then Easter as if mocking the resurrection with his drunken stupor.

She had no mother.

She had no brothers.

She had not heard from or seen any of them for four years now.

She raked the leaves of the māmaki trees into neat piles and watched Ezroh hold the hands of the pretty girls as they climbed onto buggies or on horseback. She watched the girls giggle and steal kisses from him when the sisters weren't looking.

He already had a *girl in his heart*. That was what Shizu's letter had told Anah in Ezroh's own hand. How she had hoped while she recovered from her injuries that the *girl* was her. But Ezroh's presence in school, in chapel, and at mealtimes had been nothing less than a divine visitation for each and every girl at St. Joseph's—for Ezroh was the object of every girl's affection and desire.

The girl in his heart was probably Yong Jim Kang, who was an exemplary reader and articulate in eloqution. He told Anah as they picked sugar peas that Yong Jim held his hand as she read him in perfect English the most incredible stories about great biblical heroes.

Or Clydina Ramsey, the only haole girl at St. Joseph's. She played the piano for him after dinner the way her German mother had taught her on the family's prized Bluthner upright piano in Kahuku. He told Anah as they swept the stables how Clydina's soft white leg touched his all the while she taught him how to play "Chopsticks."

Or Glenda Nakaya, who was secretly left-handed but very good at arithmetic and baseball. Glenda always smelled like sweet talcum powder. Glenda even embroidered a handkerchief *with her right hand, can you imagine that*, for Ezroh during fancy work that he kept in his back pocket.

Anah pressed herself against the rough tree bark as Glenda put her hand on Ezroh's face. She blew a kiss to him as she turned to leave with her mother and father for their flower farm near Sand Island. He pulled the handkerchief from his pocket and wiped his brow. It was sickening. Glenda was the girl in his heart. Anah was sure of this.

Ezroh caught her staring and called her over to the front lawn.

"Come, Anah, I want to show you something," he yelled in Portuguese.

She would not listen to him. Who wanted to see a stupid handkerchief embroidered with another girl's right hand?

"Did you hear me, Anah? I said to please come here. I have something for you."

She ran away from him and ducked behind the chicken coops. She knew that he wanted to brag about Glenda's affection for him. Or the many special Christmas gifts from all of the other girls.

"I see you over there, Anah. Do not run from me. Please wait."

Anah peeked out at him, his handsome face turning to catch her glance. "Why are you mad at me?" he asked, exasperated. "Anah, please—oh, never mind." He sighed.

He walked over to the vegetable garden with some gardening tools. They kept each other in sight. He bent over to pull weeds from between the basil and chives when Anah snatched the handkerchief from his back pocket. He chased her around the dry and pokey string bean poles that caught onto her coveralls.

"Give it back, Anah," he yelled, grabbing her wrist and twisting her arm.

His eyes darkened as she clutched it tighter in her fist. "There," she said, wrenching her hand free and throwing it at him. "You want her, you can have her."

Ezroh laughed then pushed her shoulder. "C'mon, Anah. Don't say such things. Glenda is just a—"

"Just a what?" Anah pushed him back, hard, nearly knocking him over.

"Just a—she is just a very sweet girl." He pushed her back, harder. "Not at all like you."

"Sweet?" She shoved him into the tall stalks of corn. "Here, I show you sweet."

They began throwing blows, rolling over the rows of corn and into the row of herbs.

"Stop! Stop! No make like that!" Supang yelled as he trampled over the fallen stalks. He pulled them apart. "Why you fight-fight? How come you make like this? You no make humbug fo' me, gunfunnit you. Look the corn. All broke. All pohō. For nothing we plant this corn. How I tell sister no mo' God's bounty?"

Anah got up, spitting corn tassels from her mouth, dusting leaves from her hair. Ezroh picked up his handkerchief, filthy with mud.

"You, get a-going," Supang said, slapping the back of Ezroh's head. "Tora-san came take you home for Christmas. Good thing the Prohibit come law of land bumbye the old man all pilut with the sa-ke. Go, go, he in front talking with Chong Sum."

"I no like go home," Ezroh said, lowering his eyes. "Nobody stay. I like stay here."

"Nobody here too," Supang said. "Everybody go home. You go too. Get to the front before you no mo' ride."

Fukunaga hurried toward them, picking up the garden tools strewn along the way. "Anah, you go wash-wash before the Sister Bernadine see you all dirty. Why you fight with Ezroh?" he asked, trying to straighten the bent stalks of corn. "He your numba-one tomodachi now you no mo' Shizu-chan as yo' best friend."

"He not my best friend," Anah said, glaring at Ezroh. "Nobody my best friend."

"Ai-ya, nuff already. Okay then, no need best friend, you. No pa'i pa'i. All pau hit-hit, fight-fight," Supang said, pushing Ezroh's back to hurry him along. "This the eve of our Lord birthday, gunfunnit you."

IT WOULD BE Anah's first Christmas alone. A couple of the very sick girls, a Korean five-year-old and a lonely Chinese near certain demise, lay under the isinglass. And two true orphans, Mie and Emi Omori, sat without speaking in the dark, empty dining hall. On Christmas Eve, Anah and the Omori sisters sang Christmas carols with Sister Mary Deborah after Mass for the two sick girls on the second floor.

The holy sisters had begun constant adoration in the chapel, spending hours in Lauds and meditation, Terce, Sext, None and litany, Vespers, Compline, and Matins. This left very little time and energy for the girls.

Anah stood at the doorway to Aunty Chong Sum's small room as she prepared to leave after dinner. "Merry Christmas, Aunty," Anah told her, placing three small packages wrapped in twine on her bed.

"What this?" she asked.

"For you, Supang, and Fukunaga from me," Anah told her. "Give to them before you go."

"I take to them," she said, lifting one of the packages to her nose. "Mmm." She smiled. "My favorite. When you grow this?"

"Shizu and Ezroh wen' plant the bitter melon when came little bit cold. After she went, I make sure cover each one so the bugs no sting—" Anah paused, thinking of the crinoline for the bee hat she never made for Shizu. She had used it to cover the young bitter melons.

"I remember now," Chong Sum said. "Shi-chan said maybe *you* like eat bitter melon when you pau sick. 'Bee-taa-me-yon make Anah shtrong,' thass what Shi-chan said. You know how she talk funny kine, huh? Yeah, yeah, now I remember."

"And I remember how you said Pa-ke Melvin and Doh Nee like when you cook bitter melon fo' them with salty black bean. With little bit pork belly."

"You such a good girl, Anah," Chong Sum said.

Anah's eyes began to fill with tears, but she would not let them fall. Not in this place. Not now. "And I put some shiso leaf for your pickle vegetable and some mitsuba for tempura or maybe miso soup. My haha used to put it on hot rice for me—"

Anah did not want to remain in this moment, this moment that hurt her someplace deep inside. She remembered now how her brother Charles so loved their okaasan's vegetable tempura. She knew Aunty Chong Sum would be gone for just a few days. This good-bye should have been easy. But Anah would remain at the orphanage for Christmas. Alone. She began to back away from the cook.

"I give to Fukunaga and Supang family," Chong Sum said, quickly packing Anah's gifts into her bag.

Anah backed out of the door into the hallway. "That huge kabocha with my name and Shizu on the skin"—she pointed—"will taste ono if you cook with ebi."

Aunty Chong Sum took her hand. "I would take you with me, I promise you, Anah. Doh Nee always asking how you. I ask the reverend mother please I like take Anah with me, but she say that . . ." She turned, lifted her bag, and hurried down the stairway.

"What she said?" Anah called to her. But the cook would not answer.

Anah followed her out the kitchen door. "What? Tell me!"

Down the narrow lane. "Say it!"

Across the bridge. "No! Susanah Medeiros stay here, alone, forever! Thass what she said?"

Anah watched her disappear down the valley, her words and screaming echoing behind her, Sister Mary Deborah running out to stop her.

LATE THAT NIGHT, Anah sat with Sister Mary Deborah near the fireplace. They listened to the sister's most recent acquisition from her grandmother back in Brighton of a beeswax recording of Bach's "Air." The strings lulled tinny, breathtaking phrases on the Victrola. A small fire prickled shards of flame up into the flume.

The sister whispered the Joyful Mysteries:

"Mary, my Mother, I see you telling the angel: you are ready to be the Mother of God."

Anah would not be able to finish the embroidered handkerchief she wanted to give Ezroh for Christmas. The night was still, the sister whispered:

"Thank you Jesus for becoming her child for love of me."

The handkerchief she would give to him to say sorry for being so unkind and envious of his affection for Glenda, the sister whispered:

"Teach me to be kind and to help in every way I can."

To say Merry Christmas to him, she whispered:

"He was born for love, to save our souls."

To say thank you for saving her life with his herbs, the sister whispered:

"Offer Jesus to the Heavenly Father for me that he may forgive my sins."

To say she loved his company just like she loved Shizu's company:

"Mary, my Mother, I love you."

She put the small embroidery hoop on the table. When the music paused, she listened to the amplified crackle of a cactus needle space break in wax. She heard a tap on the window.

Sister Mary Deborah lifted her eyes and her sibilant prayers ceased for a moment.

And then another tap.

She looked up at Anah ever so slightly. And then at the window. And then back at Anah.

"I will be tending to our afflicted ones, then retiring to my cell to rest awhile before midnight Mass," she said to Anah. The sister looked to the window and smiled, small but sure. "I will see you later in the chapel for Mass, Susanah."

Anah held the lamp to the window. Ezroh's face warmed that light. He smiled and waved her out with his hand. Anah ran to the kitchen door, tripping over a small basket of mountain yams. She pulled the heavy door open and saw him, Ezroh, standing in the cold.

He put down his bag and led a huge milking cow into the small light of the lamp. She stopped to munch on the tiny heather flowers near the doorstep.

"Miss Donna Choo," he said to the cow, "this my best friend, Miss Susanah Medeiros."

"Hello, Miss Donna Choo," Anah said, bowing her head. "Merry Christmas to you and yours." The cow mooed.

"She said, 'Same to you.' " Ezroh laughed, holding out his hand to Anah. She stepped outside barefooted onto the cool grass. "Tora-san said my father wanted to give our best milker to the sisters," he said in Portuguese. "We better let her sleep so that she will provide for them sweet cream on Christmas morning."

"You could have come in the morning," Anah told him as they led the cow to the stable.

"I know," he said, holding her hand even tighter. "Your hand is so warm." He lifted her hand and pressed it to his lips.

"There was nobody at home," he began, "and after we had some miso soup, Tora-san passed out drunk on his sake. So I put a blanket over him and sat by myself in the dark for a long time."

Anah said nothing as she watched Ezroh settle the cow on a bed of dried honohono grass. He did not let go of her hand, drawing it to his heart.

"I have nobody too," she said at last. "No mother, no father, no sisters, no brothers."

"We are alike, you and I," he said, holding Anah's face, her gaze, her breath in the palms of his hands. "Come," he said. "I have presents for you."

They walked to the nativity shack. Anah hung the lamp on a nail. "I do not deserve anything. I have treated you so unkindly. And I have nothing to give to you in return," she said as he settled down next to his bag. He opened it slowly. Anah thought about her horrid gift on the table near the fireplace, the embroidered stitches hurried and clumsy. An afterthought. An unsightly imitation.

Ezroh put a small gold package with a beautiful red ribbon in her hands.

"I cannot accept this. I have nothing for you."

"Please, Anah," he said. "It is Christmas."

Anah opened the package slowly, straightening out the folds in the gold paper over her leg. She put the paper and the ribbon in her pocket.

A piece of milk chocolate. "I never tasted chocolate before," she stammered. She stared at it in great wonder, then lifted the piece to her nose and inhaled deeply of its sweet, dark fragrance.

Ezroh took it from her hands and broke it in half, placing the bigger piece in Anah's mouth, the smaller piece in his. She closed her eyes to the warm melting of sugar and cocoa and cream that lingered over her tongue, then slid in a sweet river down her throat.

"Wait, I have another present for you." He reached into his bag and took out a shiny red apple.

"Where did you get that?" she asked. She had never seen an apple so big and red except for the apple her father brought home one Christmas and ate by himself as the rest of them watched, asking questions about its taste and texture, the ambrosial perfume in the space between his greed and their want.

"Tora-san gave me a dime for Christmas, so I went to Chinatown," Ezroh said, slicing the apple in half, then carving out the seeds with his small pocketknife. "There were so many people and so many shops," he said with much excitement. "I will take you to Chinatown one day with me, Anah. We can buy more apples and chocolates."

He cut a fan of slender apple wedges and placed it on Anah's hand. She lifted a shiny piece, looked at it in the round, then placed the crescent in Ezroh's mouth that moved slowly over the sweet apple.

He took a wedge from her hand and placed it in her mouth. The sweet juices moved inside of her with each slow crunch. This did not taste like the waxy mountain apples they harvested in the summer or the tart rose apples they shoved whole into their mouths, spitting out the pits at each other. Anah closed her eyes and breathed deeply.

She could have never imagined this taste. Watching her father eat his apple slice by slice, she did not even come near to conjuring up this flavor in her mind. Ezroh licked the blade of his knife, and when the apple was gone, they licked the palm of Anah's hand.

"Merry Christmas, Anah," he said.

She lifted the lauhala mat from the place she had hidden the beeswax candles she had made for her own Christmas Mass in the nativity shack. With each flicker of flame, she would remember:

Leah dancing on the lawn in Anah's yellow dress.

Aki swimming naked in the diving pond after laundry.

Shizu announcing the Hail Mary to the chickens.

Seth standing over her bed when she was sick.

And Ezroh.

She lifted the sennit rosary from around her neck, put the wooden cross to her nose to take in the sweet kukui nut oil, then placed it upon her lips. She put it around Ezroh's neck.

"Now you have somebody," she whispered.

He began to weep. She placed her two hands on his beautiful face, kissed his forehead, then each of his tear-stained cheeks.

"Merry Christmas, Ezroh."

The Gift of the Magi

What I can do fo' Anah? And then Doh Nee tell me go give present like the magi story to Anah numba-one brother.

I so happy. "That is good present fo' Anah," I tell Doh Nee. She smart girl, Doh Nee, just like you. So we go on trolley car, go little while on train, walk, walk, ride the back of taro buggy, go far to 'Ewa see your brother. Yes, Anah, your brother, Charles.

He tell me to tell you everything he say. Make promise, make promise, Aunty, you tell my sister Anah all what I tell you because I no know how write. Older brother he say, "Too much schoolwork. No can write letter fo' you to sister. Too busy, must study, leave me alone." Charles say, "Lucky fo' him Vovó say he go back school."

He like me tell you he see you nighttime in his dream. He say you look mo' beautiful and strong than the day you go. He like you get well.

Every day since you go, he pray fo' get the cough so he can come here take care you. I tell him this place no place to be. No mo' boys o' here. Only Ezroh. No make the sick come on him.

He say you every minute on his thoughts, every day, especially now

Christmastime. He remember how you make the sugar cookie and star fruit candy for him.

But he think he no-good boy. Big coward him. He know how fo' get here. But he scared come see you. You no love him no mo'. He no come fo' so long. And he so sorry, Anah. He say if you no can forgive him, he unnastand.

Your mama tell him no can go. No, no, no. She hit him with the stick on his face when he tell he going get you, go say aloha-no to Aki and Leah. Crack his teeth, black his eye with the iron, no can walk his leg all pa'i from the whip. Bumbye you bring the cough back. He still no listen her.

He like come see you. Then the Portagee uncle come give him pilau lickens. Choke the neck, he no can breathe, punch and kick, all broke the rib. Now no can walk. Then he listen.

Your mama, Anah, she yell at me, "Obaasan, go away. I no mo' wahine keiki. Me have no children."

Yo' vovó say mama can stay even after husband ma-ke. She can stay with the Portagee so long she promise numba-one son go university. He need good education because life is so hard fo' him since he hapa. He yo' dead papa's namesake even if he half-breed.

Your mama spend all her day work, work, work make mo-ni fo' vovó. She wash and iron fo' the Pilipino, make bentō fo' the Japanee no mo' wife, clean the haole luna house, go delivery fo' tōfu-ya lady.

Charles make mo-ni fo' brother go school. He shine shoe Hotel Street stable fo' sailor boy. He pick kiawe bean sell ten cents bag to dairyman. Make mo-ni but all fo' brother. Charles no go school how many years now. All his friends akamai. Him stupid. Pretty soon he work the fields.

He say he no like you come home. They make you slave too. All fo' numba-one boy. Only have nuff fo' numba-one.

I tell him yo' life no better over here. How sad your life. How you watch sisters ma-ke one by one. Poor thing you get lickens no can wake up long time almost ma-ke too. Charles cry, cry, cry.

Anah, maybe you beg Sister go intercess fo' you go learn A-B-C, 1-2-3. You go learn with Ezroh and be akamai girl. Or you like be stupid girl and scrub pot, hō hana field worker all day? You go back inside and learn. Maybe one day you teach Aunty Chong Sum how read the good book, huh?

You go now. We talk story too much.

Yes, Anah. I already tell you. He say he see you all time nighttime when he close his eye go hiamoe. He say make sure Anah no ma-ke. Make my Anah stay well.

Tell my sister Merry Christmas.

He see you again. Very soon come nighttime. He see you then.

13

1920

Seth appeared sadder and sadder, his body diminishing with each passing day. His eyes darkened into hollow orbs as he watched Anah spend her days with Ezroh, who became the center of her world and she the center of his.

Seth, the fair-headed little boy who had befriended Leah in her aloneness, the boy she mistook for the blessed Christ child, took her hand and led her through a five-year-old's darkness. He no longer smiled at Anah from the corner of rooms.

Seth, the silent companion of Aki after Leah's death, who followed her into days and nights in the dark closet on the third floor, hummed songs to her, stroked her hair, scared away the rats. Seth no longer stood above Anah as she opened her eyes in the morning, his beautiful face awakening each of her days.

Anah spent all of her days with Ezroh even after Rex Soares returned to the ranch with the herd. He asked the reverend mother to provide Ezroh with a sound Catholic education in exchange for his own hard labor and his donation of milk products from the dairy owned by his father before him, João Soares, one of the founding members of the Dairymen's Association who had advocated for the first pasteurizer in the Sandwich Islands.

"Mr. Soares, you have been more than generous in your charitable assistance to us," the reverend mother told him, her hands pressed together under her chin. "We will gladly take your son into our tutelage."

The sisters needed Rex Soares's patronage to build beds and desks, repair broken windows, wobbly pews, bookshelves, crumbling stone walls, leaky roofs, and the sagging stable; they needed him to provide tonics and herbs for the growing number of orphans at St. Joseph's.

He sent Tora-san and a couple of his cowboys to paint the chapel and then repair the termite-eaten eaves and floorboards of the rectory. They built a huge smoker for wild turkey and pig, elaborate fish-drying drawers, and many more wooden hives for Sister Mary Deborah, whose honey harvest increased enough for her to begin trading goods with the taro and rice farmers at the foot of Kapālama Hills and the fish peddlers from Sand Island.

On Sunday afternoons, Anah began assisting Rex Soares and Ezroh in air-laying and grafting the native plants he needed for his consumption tonics. Rex Soares instructed Supang in the propagation of an extensive herb garden full of curatives for everything from asthma to toothaches to bed-wetting.

But Seth grew sadder as he stood in the current of energy between Anah and Ezroh. Anah no longer acknowledged his presence with a wink and a smile but looked over his head for Ezroh, their bodies light whenever they inhabited the same space: a dining table, a desk in the study, the stable loft, the honey house. And though their bodies never touched after the night of shared chocolate and apple slices, the space between them was tangible.

Seth felt this.

And Anah grew older, but Seth did not. Her body began maturing into the voluptuous likeness of her Portuguese aunts from São Miguel in the Azores, her forebears coastal-dwelling, sturdy, and tenacious seafaring women who had arrived with the first wave of Portuguese immigrants in 1878 aboard the ship *Priscilla*.

Anah did not look like her Japanese mother, a frail little bird, one of the very few immigrant women from Yanai City, a courtesan with a delicate face, a girl from a family of too many girls, this one a melancholy beauty with an almost translucent pallor. The family was glad to be rid of her by *tricking* the matchmaker into a marriage contract for this most somber daughter.

The holy sisters, concerned with the changing shape of Anah's body, began instructing her on the method by which she was to securely bind her breasts with a long swatch of cloth and safety pins each and every morning. She was not to remove her binding until she lay down to bed at night.

Seth remained a little boy, never aging, the little boy with wispy blond hair, blue-green eyes, a beautiful mouth; the boy with a pencil-thin neck, white shirt with black suspenders and khakis; Anah's loyal and calm friend whose silent presence comforted her through her worst nights in the infirmary.

He watched now from a distance that grew farther and wider as the days passed, watching as Anah and Ezroh assisted Supang, Ezroh laughing while sticking weeds in Anah's short hair, dirt in her pockets, bugs in her clothes; Ezroh splashing water at her in the river, whispering in her ear about Fukunaga's bushy eyebrows in Mass; Ezroh telling her silly stories about the sisters' individual odors, teasing Chong Sum's eye-blinking twitch, and imitating Supang's bowlegged walk.

They shared meals together, studied, prayed, and worked tending the grounds and the animals until the sun left the sky; they said good night to each other and then good morning, the hours of their sleep occupied with dream visits with the other.

Seth grew lonely and dark. He remained a nine-year-old boy.

THE FIRST TIME Anah left Seth on the bridge over Kalihi Stream was the day that Rex Soares and Ezroh asked the reverend mother on Anah's behalf for permission to accompany them to greet the novitiate Sister Simone at Honolulu Harbor.

Sister Simone had taken an arduous journey across two oceans from London on the SS *Majestic*. The feisty, redheaded Sister Simone called by God from the Parish of St. Joseph at Newcastle-on-Tyne to assist the weary sisters of St. Joseph in the Sandwich Islands.

Anah had never left the orphanage since the rainy day of her arrival.

The sun of that wonderful morning colored the hills of Kalihi Valley in varying shades of verdance. Anah was filled with a great excitement.

Aunty Chong Sum helped Anah make Portuguese pão doce cake with fresh butter for Rex Soares; she brewed bottles of māmaki tea for his high blood and made a batch of star fruit and coconut candy for Ezroh. Sister Mary Deborah packed bottles of honey and a basket of refreshments for Sister Simone.

"Good day, Mr. Soares," the reverend mother greeted as he pulled the buggy to a stop on the driveway in front of the lānai. "Thank you ever so kindly for your services. Our Sister Simone will be in good hands upon her arrival this beautiful morn after what I am sure was an arduous journey."

"Good morning, Reverend Mother, Sisters," he said with a tip of his hat. He nudged Ezroh, who was staring at Anah, the younger girls giggling, Glenda Nakaya pouting and whispering her jealousy to Clydina Ramsey.

Ezroh tipped his hat. "Good morning, Reverend Mother, Sister Bernadine, Sister Mary Deborah, young ladies," he said to the gaggle of tittering girls.

"Your fine son elicits much admiration and mirth from our young charges," Sister Mary Deborah said with a small smile, "for he has inherited the handsome features and cultured manner of his father."

She put her firm hands on Anah's shoulders, moving her a step forward. Anah felt awkward in her white chapel dress, knee-high white stockings, and clumsy, scuffed Mary Janes that a parishioner had donated to the church years before.

"Thank you, Sisters, for teaching my boy how to read and write. No like him grow up to be one ignorant cowboy like me," Rex Soares said, placing the reins over his lap. "I was in my fourth year when my dai put me to work on the dairy." He grimaced and shook his head. "I was milking before I was crawling and hauling pineapple bran before I was walking—" He paused, having spoken more than he had intended.

"But the Lord thy God has gifted thee with a wise and compassionate heart," Sister Mary Deborah said with another shy smile.

"Sister Bernadine informs me," the reverend mother said, breaking into the silence that followed, "that Ezroh is a wonderful and bright pupil who has had a marked influence on the girls' achievement, especially his sister in Christ, Susanah Medeiros. And he has been of great assistance to our overburdened grounds and maintenance staff."

"Good," Rex Soares said, looking with pride at Ezroh for a brief moment. "Very good."

The reverend mother pulled Anah's arm toward the buggy. "Now do not dillydally, Susanah." She pulled and tugged to straighten the creases in Anah's dress. "Mr. Soares has been kind enough to include you on today's journey. She can be petulant and quarrelsome, Mr. Soares. Please inform us of any misbehavior or discourtesy, and she will be duly disciplined upon her return. Go on, now." She pushed from behind.

Ezroh hopped off the carriage and hoisted the bounty Anah had prepared with Aunty Chong Sum and Sister Mary Deborah into the back. "What is in here?" he grunted as the girls giggled at his efforts. He was dressed like his handsome father in khaki riding pants, a starched white shirt with suspenders, and shiny black leather boots.

"A small token of our thanks for your trouble," Sister Mary Deborah said to Rex Soares.

"No trouble at all," he said as Ezroh took Anah's hand and lifted her up.

And with a snap of the reins, the buggy moved out, slow at first, then the wind in Anah's face, the dogs barking at the wheels.

Anah turned when they stopped after crossing the bridge. She watched Seth appear and disappear from the trees. He was crying as Anah, his father, and brother left for the harbor to meet the SS *Majestic*.

THE VALLEY WAS FILLED with the perfume of an early ginger season. Mango blossoms held on to thin tendrils in the brisk spring wind. The jacaranda trees hung in purple clusters overhead as Anah traveled past the fifty-sow pig farms near the first bridge, owned by the Okinawan Miyashiro and Yafuso families. A girl and her mother stood beside a lean-to, stirring slops in a barrel over an open fire. Men washed down the birthing sties. A little boy fed hens in a vast chicken yard.

Anah passed K.C. Market in lower Kalihi Valley, whose window was full of sweet anpan and manju. The Duke's American Tobacco man sat in his green delivery truck. Little Hannah Yap swept the sidewalk as manongs with shiny black hair squatted outside in a circle of dust and cigarillo smoke.

Anah passed the vast taro patches at the foot of the Kapālama Hills owned by the Chinese Do Kam Huy family. The backs of husbands, wives, sons, and daughters were stooped over the clear waters, geese and mud hens swimming in and out of leafy rows, little children catching tadpoles and crabs in jelly jars.

Anah rode down to the flower farms in Kalihi Kai near Sand Island, where Rex Soares stopped to purchase a bunch of anthurium and orchids from Mama-san Nakamura with a towel over her head under a straw hat, her infant Teruko tied to her back with obi. He put the flowers for Sister Simone on Anah's lap. Ezroh paid two pence for a single gardenia for Anah's hair.

It was all so breathtaking.

Anah had forgotten how much she had missed seeing the bustle of people, the colors of the landscapes beyond the valley, the sounds of the world outside of St. Joseph's, so many people of all ages and faces in the streets of Honolulu:

Hawaiian aunties in long, black holoku with orange ilima around black lace hats, their black-gloved hands holding beautiful parasols and straw bags;

Chinese men with gold-rimmed spectacles inside of herbalist shops filled with dried stems, leaves, flowers, fruit seeds, intestines, and various animal parts being weighed and measured from rows and rows of glass bottles;

Filipino girls in woven coconut hats and old manongs with shiny gold teeth carrying bundles of fresh marungay, wild bitter melon, swamp cabbage, and tamarind seedpods in baskets on their heads;

a haole mother and daughter still wearing fancy Edwardian couture with great bustles and high-buttoned shoes, a young coolie following them with an open umbrella;

the shirtless Chinese mea ʻono puaʻa vendor in a domed straw hat selling his pork-filled sweet buns and rice dumplings filled with sweet bean or black sugar from an aluminum cracker can and basket, the long bamboo pole over his shoulders;

saimin lady dragging her red wagon filled with two big pots of noodles and broth over charcoals and bowls of chopped-up meats, eggs, green onions, a bottle of shoyu, and barbeque sticks for a nickel;

old men chatting outside rooming houses;

haole businessmen driving Model Ts;

kow-kow man with teakettle and rice basket;

Japanese barber ladies in white;

pharmacist;

butcher man;

boys riding bicycles;

tinsmith;

shoemaker;

stray dogs;

whores;

tailor man;

sailor man;

shoeshine boys outside of the Hotel Street stables;

"Hey, you, soldier boy!"

"Ten cents shine!"

"Oxblood GI shoes, want a shine?"

"Hey, panini boy!"

"Hey, red ink boy!"

"Got change for a dime, boy?"

"Be a good tipper, sailor boy."

"Hey, you shoeshine boy."

"Hey, Charlie boy!"

Charlie boy?

"Charles! Charles!" He turns to the sound of his name but seeing no one he recognizes, he resumes shining the soldier's shoes.

They are far away now.

Anah stands up in the buggy, Ezroh pulling her to sit.

"Sit down, Anah," Rex Soares scolds. "The ship's already arrived, see?" He points to the SS *Majestic*, gangplank lowered, a steady stream of disembarking passengers, ship hands unloading cargo and supplies. "We are already very late," he says in urgent Portuguese. "We do not want Sister Simone to think she has been forgotten." He gives the reins a quick snap.

"Charles!" The buggy rolls on toward Bethel Street. "Charles, over here!" Anah waves her arms in the air. "Charles!"

He turns again, stands upright and tall, handsome Charles, handsome brother. He flips his rag over his shoulder and scratches his brow. A little girl follows him, holding on to the waistband of his trousers. They are getting smaller as he steps out onto the street, the soldier yelling at him, Charles running, running, the little girl following, running all of his might after the buggy, too late, too late, the horse's swift trot, they will be late in greeting Sister Simone, they must hurry, there will be another time.

"Anah! Anah!" he calls as his body crumples in the middle of Hotel Street.

Sister's Sweet Counsel

Why are thee so cast down, O my soul? So you are certain you have seen your brother? Can ye not be thankful unto the Lord your God for showing you that he is in good resolution and health? Yes, Anah, he is well. And you have been blessed to have seen him. Though he struggles the persecutions and tribulations of the world, he is not lost unto our Lord. No, my dear Anah. He is found.

Why do you abandon us in the streets, my sweet Anah?

How I long for thee.

So cast down. The sadness of thy countenance has made the hearts of the righteous sad. You must understand, Susanah, your brother is not your only family. For the blood of the lamb has been shed for thee too. You are of God's family. In His goodness He chose to make us His children. And the Lord our God has spoken: you are a child of God.

Forgive me, Anah, beautiful sister, forgive me.

How I yearn for thee.

Children all: be not afraid or dismayed, arise sayeth our God and be not afeared. No more sadness. No more long dark nights without the goodness of sound sleep. Wipe away your tears. For thy children's children shall know of our Lord's goodness if you, child, keep His covenants. Our Lord will deliver you from your grief.

Hear me, Anah. No Mama for us and no Thomas. But this little one, the daughter of our mother and our vovó's brother.

How I love thee and thee.

Remain no longer in the darkness of your earthly longing. For you are a child of the Highest. His suffering little children come unto him. And now abide in Him. For ye were sometimes darkness, but now are ye light in the Lord: walk as children of light.

14

1921

Anah longed for Charles, days and months after seeing him that morning on Hotel Street. She waited for his arrival at St. Joseph's, sure that the next Visitation Sunday would be the day of his return to her life. He would bring her mother, and they would sit on the lawn, reuniting in tears and laughter just like the other families.

She waited and waited, Ezroh watching her from the stables as he slowly washed and brushed their cow, Miss Donna Choo, watching her from the garden as he fertilized the cabbage patch, watching her from the lānai as he sat with Aunty Chong Sum shucking peas. Anah sat in her chapel dress, lifting her head to the sound of each approaching buggy, all for nothing.

Charles and her mother never came. It was a cruel joke. She was better off never having seen him and the girl child. Then she would not bear the want for him. Then she would not be racked with questions. *His girl child? Whose girl child?* Then she would not long for his answers as he had explained matters to her when they were children.

He was big brother, protector against Dai and Vovó, provider when they had nothing to eat, companion and confidant.

There was a reason for him not coming. Anah was certain of this. Vovó Medeiros thought this place contaminated with every incurable infirmity. Only those with leprosy were sent somewhere else. And Vovó was right. The sick got sicker here.

Even those who left for lung operations at the Japanese Charity Hospital on Kuakini Street, endowed by the divine Emperor Taisho and his empress for the many Japanese immigrants laboring on the inhumane sugar plantations in Hawai'i, never recovered or never returned.

And no one, not even God, had found a cure for poverty and abandonment. Anah was one of the fortunate. Sister Bernadine reminded her of this each day when the girls prayed fervently for the millions of Russian children dying from famine or for Catholics in all parts of the country being persecuted by the Ku Klux Klan.

Anah knew that she would not blame her brother. She had seen the urgency of his love for her that day near the Hotel Street stables in Chinatown.

She would wait for him in her best dress with her hands folded on her lap, wait for him with dignity even as the sisters whispered, curious about Anah's vain expectation, finally attributing her newfound hope to repentance and prayer.

But Anah died inside of herself each time Sister Bernadine rang the school bell that signaled the end of Visitation Sunday and the start of Mass.

And on the Sunday when Anah could no longer bear the emptiness of the immense space around her and inside of her, the sad gestures of *farewell* and *see you again soon* and *aloha nō* from the families that did come, she gathered up her gifts of flowers and honey, sweet bread and hand-crocheted lace doilies, removed the ribbons from her hair, the socks and shoes from her feet, and dropped them across the lawn as she walked toward the river.

"Susanah! Susanah!" Sister Mary Deborah called after her.

Anah would not stop. She continued her march to the river. She would submerge her body, float away downstream, be spit out into the sea, and carried away by a riptide to drown.

"Let all bitterness, and wrath, and anger, be put away from you with all malice," Sister Mary Deborah said, catching up to her but out of breath. She placed her hands on Anah's shoulders, stopping her midstride, then turned her around.

"And be ye kind to one another," Anah said, sarcastically, continuing the scripture the sister had taught her in catechism, the scripture that began to choke in Anah's throat, "tenderhearted—" She could not finish.

"Forgiving one another, even as God for Christ's sake hath forgiven thee," the sister said, putting the gifts she had picked up from the lawn in Anah's hands.

Anah threw them onto the grassy riverbank. "I forgive my brother," she said matter-of-factly. "And if he cannot come to see me, then I will—"

"No, Susanah," the sister said, directing her toward the river's edge. "You must not." She lifted her heavy habit and walked over a few rocks. The sister sat herself on a boulder near the water that gurgled clear and swift. "Please sit with me awhile so we may speak of your dilemma with reason."

"No, thank you, Sister." Anah stood away from her in anger and disobedience. "I like stand right here."

"Suit yourself, then," she said, not looking at Anah. The sister began removing her manly black lace-up boots, cracked and beaten with wear, then her black socks.

Anah's eyes widened, her mouth agape. She had never seen the flesh of any of the sisters except for the pink flesh of their faces and hands often tucked away in the folds of their woolen sleeves. The sister's skin, aglow with a translucent iridescence, seemed to sparkle in the sunlight.

"Yes, I have the feet of a mortal, Susanah," the sister said without looking at her as she lowered her albino-white toes into the clear water. "The water feels so refreshing to my tired feet. Won't you join me?"

Anah stared at her for a moment, then took a step toward her. The sister coaxed her forward with a wave of her hand. Anah steadied herself on the sister's shoulder and lifted her dress as she waded knee-deep into the river. She let her dress fall, the white cotton floating out around her, her feet sinking into the soft silt of the river's bottom.

"Do what you must," the sister said all of a sudden.

"What?"

"For if you trust in the Lord with all thine heart, He shall direct thy paths." The sister lowered her eyes, her longing, a small sadness or regret. "I am certain of this. Trust in the Lord," she repeated, suddenly picking herself up and turning to leave, "and thou shalt be like a spring of water again, sweet Susanah, a spring whose waters fail not."

SO ANAH TRUSTED the Lord God.

She woke before dawn on the following Visitation Sunday. She tiptoed out of the kitchen door and ran barefooted to Ezroh down the driveway, through the banana grove, and then crossed the bridge over Kalihi Stream. She was sure the sisters would wake to the small noises amplified by her guile. But they did not. No rooster crowed, no dog yipped or yapped, no squawking goose chased her for bread this early dawn.

For Anah trusted the Lord God.

When the sisters finally awoke, they would think them already busy raking the lawn or cleaning the coops or duck pond while they harriedly supervised the many families who arrived for the day, then prepared for Mass.

Tora-san paused at the bridge with the milk delivery buggy, the heavy dipper clanging in a half-empty can, banging and clanging into the other cans full of the morning milking. Ezroh jumped aboard and pulled Anah up as the buggy began to move.

"Me no like pilikia with the sisters and yo' papa, you boy, betta not make trouble for me," Tora-san said, his breath still reeking of sake from the night before. "Me no like them hu-hū wit' me."

"My father told them that we was—" Ezroh began to lie. "I mean, I promise, I take the blame. This we do fo' Anah, Tora-san."

"You betta not eva lie to me, you Es-rah," Tora-san said, his eyes fixed on the dark road that led out of the valley. "You make pilikia fo' me, I give you one-two pa'i pa'i, I tell you," Tora-san grumbled and mumbled as he hurried the buggy out of the valley with the quick jingle of his reins.

He brought the horses to an abrupt stop near the Do Kam Huy taro patches. "I see nothing. I know nothing," he said to Ezroh. "Now get the hell away from me."

They got off the milk wagon on King Street. Lights flickered from windows in straw huts along the taro patches as the Do family began their morning rituals of planting the cut huli or plowing to prepare the vast lo'i, the little Do children gathering the flopping o'opu, freshwater eels, and goldfish left in the wake of the plow.

"Aloha nui! Ai poi," Ezroh called to his classmate Je Do, third son of Kam Huy. "Pai-ai?" he asked, "for Kahalelehua 'ohana plenny keiki."

"I tell Wing Tek save one tin fo' you," Je Do said, promising the half-pounded poi for Ezroh to take to the paniolo's big family. They would complete the pounding by hand at home for their evening meal.

Ezroh waved to him in thanks. They continued walking toward a group of people waiting near the intersection of Houghtailing and King streets.

"The streetcar comes by here all the time," Ezroh said in Portuguese. "And it goes straight to Chinatown. There." He pointed. "Hurry, Anah."

"But we do not have money to pay for the ride," she told him.

He took Anah's hand as they ran behind the streetcar, jumping on and riding until the ticket collector made his way to the back, then jumping off to his cursing and yelling, then hopping the back of yet another streetcar.

They laughed and ran along the crowded sidewalk, hopping an eastbound streetcar that took them past the downtown Honolulu train station where Anah had arrived years before on her way to St. Joseph's with Charles. The streetcar took them over to River Street, where they hopped off and began their walk toward Hotel Street, where Anah was certain she would find her brother.

For Anah trusted the Lord God.

The whores were still out, sailors and ship hands drunkenly milling about the corner of Merchant and Bethel streets. The doors to the Mid-Pacific Café opened, the smell of coffee and cinnamon snails moving onto the sidewalk. Ezroh took two handfuls of warm, roasted chestnuts from a basket outside of Chun Hoon Market and ran into an alley, where they peeled off the rubbery outer shells and ate the steaming insides.

"I have a couple of dimes," he said, his mouth full of the crumbling chestnut meat.

"Then why did you steal these?" Anah asked, holding out her fistful of chestnuts to him.

"I want to take you to that place. It is called Sweet Shop. It is where I bought chocolate for you. And I want to buy some Canton dainties for you to try," he said with a smile. "I think the Chun Hoons will not mind if we had just a little bit for our hungry stomachs."

They finished the chestnuts, Ezroh wiping his mouth with the back of his hand. He peered both ways after emerging from the alley and gave Anah the signal to run. They moved swiftly around old ladies bustling about baskets of ginger root and araimo, cooks hanging shiny whole chickens and slabs of red pork from hooks, and maids squeezing papayas at the fruit stands for a haole luna's breakfast, as they headed up Fort Street in the direction of the Hotel Street stables.

Soldiers stumbled by as Anah and Ezroh sat on the sidewalk near the wooden stairs leading to the small chairs that the shoeshine boys used for their customers.

They waited.

The mea ʻono puaʻa man sold Ezroh three hot pepeiao and three ʻōkole for a nickel. They took turns savoring small bites of the glutinous rice and seasoned pork.

They waited.

Nearby, a Hawaiian man with a long white beard, red palaka shirt, and worn work boots spread a mat and began weaving lauhala. They watched him and waited. Two little girls in white sailor-collared dresses arrived, shiny strips of hau woven into their braided hair.

Oxcarts rolled slowly by with bags of rice bound for the harbor.

Oxcarts rolled slowly by with bags of raw sugar bound for the harbor.

The Japanese candy man in his white jacket and white hat strolled by, carrying a big tin pan full of pink, yellow, and white taffy. "Kan-di, kan-di," he called. Ezroh gave him a nickel, and the candy man broke pieces of his ware into a package. Anah put a small piece into her mouth.

The shoeshine boys began to arrive.

"Eh, you know Charles Medeiros?" Ezroh asked the first.

"No."

And then the second.

"No, beat it. You in the way."

And then the third.

"Nope."

"Hey you, bring the girl o' hea."

"The soldier boy like the girl."

"Shoeshine, sailor boy! You can sit with this girl."

"Who? Charles Medeiros?"

"He the stealer, huh?"

"Yeah, Charlie. No mo' hilahila him."

"Yeah, him sleep under the bridge."

"Pilau bugga, steal all the money and run."

"Never see the bugga again."

"I kill the hapa dog, I see him again. Damn half-breed."

"No come o' hea long time."

"No come o' hea eva again."

"Why you ask about Charlie?"

Ezroh backed away from the angry mob of shoeshine boys. He slumped down beside Anah. She rested her head on his shoulder, and he patted her gently.

The sisters would find them missing by now. It was almost noon.

"Maybe I was not trusting in the Lord," she whispered in Portuguese. "That is why my path is not direct."

"You do not know the Lord's mind, Anah," Ezroh said. "You do not even know mine. What am I thinking right at this moment?" he asked, squeezing his eyes shut, trying to make her laugh.

"That I am a foolish girl," Anah said.

"You are wrong." He laughed. "I am thirsty." He got up and offered her his hand. He hoisted Anah up. They began walking toward River Street. Ezroh stopped at Coffee Dan's, squeezing his way between the sailors and soldiers eating lunch at the counter. He emerged with a Coca-Cola. It would be Anah's first drink of soda, that sweet burn bubbling in her mouth. She spit out her first sip.

"No waste. Try again," Ezroh said, pushing the soda bottle back to Anah. "We find yo' brother," he consoled as they trudged toward the Sweet Shop. "And if the Lord does not want to direct your path—" Ezroh stopped to smile at her.

"Then what?"

"Then I will," he said, taking a long last swig, then throwing the empty bottle into the river that opened to the sea. Anah stood there for a moment on the River Street bridge, a gentle concrete arc on the edge of Chinatown. She watched the bottle bob jauntily in the tide, then sink in a sudden spiral suck of water.

WHEN THEY RETURNED to the orphanage at dusk, Sister Bernadine stood waiting on the bridge over the river. She looked like a huge white phantom in the dark shadows of the trees, the mottling of light across her red face surreal, her honeycombed headdress, wilting and sweat stained.

She said nothing to Anah but lifted a large guava stick from the folds of her habit and began savagely beating her head even after she covered her face and fell to the ground. Ezroh tried to stop her. And she did.

"You are to leave the premises immediately, Master Soares," she hissed. "Your father is to send his man for your belongings in the morning."

"But, Sister," he began. "It is not Anah's fault. I tempted her—"

"Enough of your blasphemous disobedience, erbärmlich lügner." She grasped Anah by her hair with her strong man-hands. "Yes, you are a liar, Master Soares. I advise you again to leave the premises posthaste. You are also a trespasser here. Leave us to our business. Leave us now."

"No," he said, looking at Anah as she writhed in fear and pain. "Not without—"

"Then you will be arrested and shackled," she said. "The constable is waiting for you in the rectory with Father Maurice."

"Sister Mary Deborah, she—" he began.

"No, stop, Ezroh. Say nothing about her," Anah pleaded in Portuguese. "I trusted God, not her, I promise you." Twisting and turning, she wrestled herself free from the huge nun. "Run, Ezroh!" she yelled as he reached for her.

Anah took three steps toward him, when the sister's grip on her body nearly dislocated her shoulders as she yanked Anah back. The sister locked her arm around Anah's neck as Ezroh screamed, "Let her go, you foul whore of Ephraim, let her go!"

"The devil take you now to the pit of hell," Sister Bernadine snarled in German as she began praying in a voice severe and unearthly. Ezroh was struck dumb by the saints, his feet paralyzed as the sister dragged Anah by the neck, Anah's hands digging into the sister's forearm, Anah's teeth cutting the inside of her own mouth.

Sister Bernadine pulled her through the kitchen door, Aunty Chong Sum screaming at the blood drooling out of the sides of Anah's mouth, up the first flight of stairs, her feet *thunk, thunk, thunk*ing on each step, then up another flight of stairs.

She threw Anah into the dark prayer closet on the third floor, the smell of old beeswax, rotting wood, rat and roach feces, and stale incense filling the small space. Anah heard the snap of the padlock, then the jingle of the keys hanging from a ring on a nail outside the door.

She could not breathe, her trachea collapsed, the air dusty hot in the closet on the third floor where the heat from the day rose into the rafters like a fire heating the inside of a forno.

"Are you prepared for repentance and reconciliation?"

"I trusted the Lord God." The pungent vinegary smell of Sister Bernadine was on Anah's dress and on her skin. Her eyes could not adjust to the dark. It would be a long night. Anah's throat burned and her bladder filled to bursting.

Then with the thin light of day under the door, again, her voice: "Are you prepared for repentance and reconciliation?"

"I trusted the Lord God."

Day had come and then gone. Anah had urinated all over the floor. She was dehydrated from vomiting at the smells of her own excrement.

Again: "Are you prepared for repentance and reconciliation?"

"No. Let me out. I get the beri-beri."

Night. Anah had taken off all of her clothes to try and clean the slime that pooled around her, not knowing how long she would be punished.

Day came with her voice: "Repentance? Reconciliation? Answer me or you will receive the punishment due your sins, Susanah."

A long silence followed.

"Susanah? Susanah?"

Sister Bernadine shoved the key into the padlock and pulled open the door.

Anah fell naked at her feet, the smell of the room intensified by the heat, a thick noxious cloud hurling out at her. The sister stumbled backward, dropping her rosary beads to the floor.

"Chong Sum!" she called.

The cook came stumbling up one flight of stairs and then the next. She saw Anah's stinking body a few feet away from the prayer closet. She gasped, falling to her knees to help Anah gain consciousness.

"How can you do this to our Anah, Sister?" she cried, cradling Anah's limp head in her lap.

"Not a word, Chong Sum. Do you hear me?" She struck the cook across the back of her head. "Not a word to anyone. Do you understand? Or I will have you removed from your duties for stealing the salted meat and sugar. It is true, ya, the bags of sugar missing from the pantry were your doing, Chinesin."

"I no steal," Aunty Chong Sum said, wiping Anah's face with her apron.

"It is your word against mine, Chinesin heidnisch." The sister's words were glassy and cruel. *Chinese pagan*. "Now clean her up." She held the back of her hand over her nose and mouth. "And then have Susanah thoroughly clean and disinfect this room." She bent down and whispered in Anah's ear: "Are you prepared now for repentance and reconciliation, mein kind?"

Anah looked up at her blurred form. "I trusted—" she began.

"Yourself and young Master Soares," the sister finished.

"In the Lord—"

"Turn from your wicked lies—"

"God direct me—"

"You are defiled by what you say and do, temptress, the devil take you with your paramour." She spoke in German, praying again with vicious consonance.

But unlike Ezroh, Anah was not struck dumb.

"My path—"

The light behind her intensified. And then the light opened. The sister's horrid voice buzzed on like a fat cow fly. Anah saw Aki, Leah, and Seth on the outside of that light, their shining faces in a shivering orb of light, Seth's hand pulling Anah closer and closer to them with each beckoning wave, and then, water, water on Anah's face, on the floor around her, Aunty Chong Sum on her hands and knees scrubbing away the bile and excrement in bitter silence.

Anah's Path

And Sister said, "For he that soweth to his flesh shall of the flesh reap corruption, but he that soweth to the Spirit shall of the Spirit reap life everlasting."

Dear Anna,

Do not listen to their lies. We are not corupt. We are not indesent. We have done nothing wrong. Be strong. Get well. I will wait for you.

Love,
Ezroh

And Sister said, "She that liveth in pleasure is dead while she liveth."

Dear Anna,

Aunty Chong Sum has told my father what the sister did to you. You must tell the reverend mother what she did to you. Now that my father knows the truth, he is not angry at me anymore. He is filled with regret for beating me. He said I will go to high school with my cousins and children of the ranch hands. But my heart is broken for you. No one sings to the cows and bees here. No one laughs at my silly jokes. I miss you, dear Anna.

Yours,
Ezroh

Dear Ezroh,

Listen, let us love one another: for love is of God; and everyone that loveth is born of God and knoweth God. None of them listen to their own Bible. Why should they listen to me? For every scripture that I say, they can say ten back to me. I am afraid. But I will trust in the Lord's path. Do you think I was on the Lord's path?

Love,
Susanah

Then Sister said, "For men shall be lovers of their own selves, covetous, boasters, proud, blasphemers, disobedient to parents, unthankful, unholy; without natural affection, truce breakers, false accusers, incontinent, fierce, despisers of those that are good; traitors, heady, high-minded, lovers of pleasure more than lovers of God."

Dear Ezroh,

I must repent. You must repent. Their list is getting longer.

Yours,
Susanah

So Anah asked the sister, "Do you speak of Ezroh or do you speak of me?"

And Sister said, "For of this sort are they which creep into houses, and lead captive silly women laden with sins, led away with diverse lusts, and never able to come to the knowledge of the truth."

Dear Anna,

Tell them what the Bible says. A new commandment I give unto you, that ye love one another; as I have loved you, that ye also love one another. Shall I come for you, Anna, to take you away with me?

Love,
Ezroh

And Sister said, "Flee your youthful lusts: follow righteousness, faith, charity, peace, with them that call on the Lord out of a pure heart."

Dear Ezroh,

My answer is yes. I will not die a prisoner here. I would rather risk eternal damnation than die here like Aki and Leah and your brother Seth. Even they cannot flee this place. Their spirits are bound to suffering. I beg you to take me with you. But I am a heavy burden laden with sins.

Love,
Susanah

Dearest Anna,

Do not worry, pure heart, I will come for you with my father. The day will come soon, I promise.

Love,
Ezroh

And the Lord said, "I will guide you along the best pathway for your life. I will advise you and watch over you."

And Anah said to the Lord of the Heavens and Earth, Dominions and Principalities:

"Amen."

1922

Anah knew it was the buggy coming at night, the sound of creaking wheels and horses' hooves on the wet, unpaved road. Her body stiffened as her eyes searched the darkened courtyard outside the window. Sister Mary Deborah paused, her tortoiseshell comb poised above Anah's head until she fixed her eyes again on the crucifix above the mantel. The sister resumed combing Anah's hair with sweet ambergris oil from a tiny green bottle.

Anah knew the squeak of the wagon bed as she tried in vain to concentrate on her fancy work, sweet jacaranda and maunaloa vines choking the borders of pillowcases, her embroidery stitches intricate and taut. She turned her eyes to the window, seeing nothing but the twist of moonlight on the shifting leaves. She resumed her needlework.

A harness jingled. Her eyes probed the darkness. Sister Simone paused with her crocheting to ponder Anah's concern over the nothingness outside.

A horsewhip cracked. Anah stepped to the window and pressed her hands to the glass. Sister Bernadine placed her sewing needle between her thin lips to glare at Anah, the older girls around her stopping in their mending and darning.

A horse whinnied in the cold night.

Sister Mary Deborah put her needlework on the table, her warm hand on Anah's face, a sad, knowing smile, her eyes tender. She guided Anah away from the window and walked her to the third floor. She bade Anah good night, the hour late, the moon full on this night, another night in a series of many that Anah believed her Ezroh would come.

TORA-SAN HAD CONTINUED to deliver Ezroh's letters to Anah daily, placing them under a cup and saucer, "More o-cha and senbei, onegai shimasu, Miss Anah-san."

He tucked them into Aunty Chong Sum's apron pocket, then patted her buttocks with his, "Deli-berry for our Anah-san." She hit him with her dish towel as he shuffled out of the kitchen door.

He hid them in the feed buckets, guiding Anah's hand deeper into the cool depths of corn and grain. "Gifuto for you, Anah-san, way, way in-sai, but no feed to the chicken, o-kay?"

Or he pressed them directly into her waiting hand in the early morning, passing with a greeting of "Ohayō gozaimasu, Miss Anah-san."

Tora-san, who smelled every morning like last night's empty bottle of bootleg sake, worked hard on repairing the fences, the chapel roof, the new outhouse, the honey house, the piggery, the broken stairs, the rusty attic doors.

By midday, the alcohol of his sweat made him stink of body odor mingled with the rank musk of homemade rice wine, the sisters covering their delicate faces with hankies whenever he passed by. His work continued for months after Ezroh's banishment as Rex Soares's way of holding out the proverbial olive branch to the reverend mother for his son's misconduct.

"For a drunkard becomes poor in body and spirit, and drowsiness and churlishness clothe him in rags," the reverend mother complained out loud in the kitchen one day, shaking her head at Tora-san as he lumbered by the window with a bundle of wood. Anah rushed out to help him, knocking the wood from his arms. "But God bless his kind and patient heart for tolerating our Susanah," she tsk-tsked.

Each day, Anah ran with her letter to the dark comfort of the honey house to read Ezroh's words, *I will come to get you soon,* placed each dark stroke that formed the words then sentences then paragraphs onto her body. *I will come to get you soon.* She longed to see his face again, the shape of his broad shoulders, the vulnerability of his open palms, his sweet wrists, *get you soon,* Ezroh who pressed his heart into his thoughts and then with each letter a small gift of rose petal, *get you,* a drawing of his house, his bicycle, his favorite dog, wild violet blossoms, *you,* a feather for Shizu's jar, a self-portrait, *you,* and then a beautiful sepia-toned photograph stolen from his father's desk:

Ezroh, his father Rex Soares, his mustachioed Uncle Marcus, and a Hawaiian paniolo named Kahalelehua—four handsome cowboys poised on horseback, the wind in the movement of horse tail and mane, in the eucalyptus and ironwoods on the rugged Koʻolau Mountains behind them, the ruddy-faced boy whose eyes drift away from the camera:

I am looking for you, sweet Anna, in the hills of Kalihi above St. Joseph's for I promise that I will come to get you soon.

Anah believed him, as she clutched each letter to her breast, that she would die for want, that she would die waiting for him to come, she would never get well, she would never leave this place, she would never again see the boy who fed her apples and chocolates, the boy who called her name from the bridge over the stream, the boy whose gaze held hers across rooms full of people, the boy who saved her life with his father's herbs and tonics, now the young man whose sweet breath warmed her dreams and whose words held the promise of love, forever, theirs was the stuff of poets and scribes:

I am yours, forever, I am yours.
I promise, dear Anna, I will come to get you soon.

She waited each day on the arrival and departure of his father's man, the old Okinawan mule skinner who had come to work on the 'Ewa Plantation with the first twenty-six Uchinanchu immigrants aboard the SS *City of China* in 1900. He ran away from the plantation following Ezroh's grandfather, João Soares, begging him for work at the dairy.

Tora-san never missed a day of work. He came to the orphanage early each morning, a groggy, bent figure on a tired mule named Makana. Anah knew when he had lost money gambling the night away with the hooligan cowboys in the bunkhouse.

He would complain throughout the day, "I bad luck, no can win, chimu gurusan—me good for nothing," the black cloud of his debts viscous and dark, his mood dour and his tongue sharp. "They cheat me all the time, them no good kanakas, that no good Pa-ke, goddamn haole farrier, and that one-eye borinque Camacho he the worst for cheat, cheat, cheat, think I not watching him, think I saki jōgu," he said, tippling his thumb into his mouth. "Think I no can see him steal all my jin, even my kaijin from my pocket no mo'," he said, turning it inside out.

Until the day he put two bits in Anah's hand, calling her his Lady Luck after she shoved a handkerchief embroidered with four-leaf clovers, stars, crucifixes, snakes, and horseshoes into his pocket. He never lost after that, and breaking even was winning as far as he was concerned. He wrapped all of his winnings in that handkerchief.

Anah followed him from chore to chore as his self-appointed assistant after her schoolwork and catechism with questions and thoughts of Ezroh. Tora-san was the only one with whom she could freely speak of her beloved. They spoke in hushed tones, sometimes in a code of broken Japanese and pidgin mingled with his native Okinawan. And the old man became Anah's extremely gruff but tolerant confidant who entertained most matters of the heart.

On the chapel roof: "I think Es-rah tire, so tire when all pau school and chore. No, no, no Anah-san. Now you talking pupule. No talk crazy. I no can tell him write some mo' to you pau hana time. Tired after work, you know, you bakatare, you. Watasun the tar brush—o'dere by yo' feet."

Repairing broken windows: "Hai, hai, he talk about you, hai, sometime, not all time, most time no, not like you, Anah-san, all time jaba-jaba Es-rah, Es-rah, Es-rah. He chikariton, you know. Es-rah so very tired, you know. Now go 'way before you fall off ladder. No bodda me."

Chopping pineapple bran and corn stalks for the cow and donkey: "Every day all same-same kine day for Es-rah. He do all kine chore, then benkyō so he get good grade in school, then kaukau with everybody in the cookhouse, then bocha in the bathhouse, then moe-moe his room in the main house. I no know when he kaku you—maybe when he study he write you letter. Watch out before I cut yo' finger. Move yo' hand, Anah-san."

Fixing honey frames: "Maybe he cry for Okaasan. I no know. See now, you make me get bee sting. Ai-ya itai, itai. O-kay, maybe, *maybe* he naku fo' you. Me no know. Now go 'way befo' *me* make you cry."

Watching Supang slop the pigs: "Chinu yūsandi he read yo' letter." He snapped his fingers. "Fast, sugu yonda," he said again, snapping his fingers emphatically. "I no know if he smile. I not watching. I no look long time at him. Yo' okaasan no teach you no stare? O-kay, hai, hai, maybe he smile small one. Now leave me alone. I like talk story otoko-otoko with Supang," he said, thumping his chest and then Supang's. "Man-to-man we like talk. Now go away."

Cleaning leaves from the gutters: "I busy man. He kaku yo' letter when he pau schoolwork. I see lantern late at night in Es-rah room. Now get the hell away. Who you, my shadow?"

Riding on his mule to the bridge: "No bodda me no more. I think he say *aishiteru*." He stopped, looking at Anah's sad face: "Maybe one time, I think he say *love*." The mule moved forward, slow: "You happy?"

Anah nodded.

"Then go back in-sai. You good-u girl-u, Anah-san. Go now, hekuna, getting dark. Hurry, hurry, go now before Sister scold you. I see you tomorrow."

ANAH WATERED and fed Tora-san's old mule, older and smellier than him. She unhitched him in the morning with kind words and fed him a fresh pile of chopped corn stalks and timothy grass with a cool bucket of water; she washed him with sweet coconut soap, brushed off his winter coat, combed the tangles from his mane and tail, and braided his long bangs with wild heather; she picked his hooves clean of mud and manure, fed him ti leaves and rose apples, and oiled his broken saddle with kukui nut oil; she did this every day before saddling him up in the evening. Tora-san surreptitiously watched her and shook his head, saying nothing to her but for his grumpy, guttural responses to her constant questioning.

In the morning, Anah brought the old man hot coffee and biscuits covered with butter and honey, cold water and corn bread before lunch, a big musubi filled with pickled vegetables and salted fish for lunch. She asked Aunty Chong Sum to purchase a package of genmaicha from Chinatown with the two bits he gave her for his afternoon bowl of chacha rice and tsukemono.

Anah passed Tora-san a letter for Ezroh as he patted her head each night. "Oyasuminasai, Anah-san. I no answer no mo' question. Me erai, nei. I so tired, tired work all day." He'd climb up onto his mule, "Mata ashita nei."

Anah ran after him.

"I see you tomorrow." He'd wave to her, the dogs barking alongside him.

Then she'd stop on the bridge over Kalihi Stream. Tora-san never turned to wave good-bye even as she yelled his name that echoed deep in the throat of the valley.

Anah only wanted to tell him good night, sleep tight, don't let the bedbugs bite.

AND THEN ONE DAY, he did not come.

And then for many days after.

"I NEVA HEAR NOTHING about Tora-san," Aunty Chong Sum said, busy swatting flies from her rising loaves of bread. "No worry, Anah. I sure sure he a-okay. Maybe the boss man need him at the dairy."

"They might have taken the herd into the mountains," Sister Mary Deborah said one morning during breakfast. "We've had quite a dry spell in the last month or so. And Mr. Toranosuke was probably needed to conduct affairs at the ranch. Mr. Soares has said that he's very dependable in spite of his drunkenness."

"He gamble my mo-ni away, the no good Uchinanchu, talk big he get Lady Luck on his side," Supang complained as Anah harvested bush beans. "He shame show face, no can make big buck for me."

"No, we will not send word to Mr. Soares like common beggars," Sister Bernadine scolded as the girls washed laundry at the river's edge. "He is in no way vital to our operations here at St. Joseph's. We are managing quite well without the drunken heathen's assistance."

"He sick. Too much sake." Fukunaga laughed, tippling his thumb over his mouth, then fake staggering as Anah raked the red hau tree leaves in front of the statue of the Blessed Virgin. And then he spoke to Anah in Japanese. "He is a crazy, drunken fool, that big-talking, old Okinawan dung heap."

THEN ONE NIGHT, many nights later, Anah was awakened by the sound of many hooves in full gallop up the unpaved road to the orphanage. In a drowsy half sleep, she lifted her head and peered out of the window on the third floor.

Below her, she saw Ezroh on horseback, a spirited stallion leading a mule and a small filly. He looked up and frantically searched each window for Anah's face behind the dusty glass. She thought him a dream, his form ripping a thunder of mighty white fire through her, but only a dream, until she heard him call her name.

"Anah! Anah!"

She ran down the first flight of stairs, her feet not touching the surface of the floor, then down the second flight. She saw Sister Bernadine run out of the kitchen door. She pushed past Sister Mary Deborah, who paused on the lānai, and Sister Simone, who wrapped herself in a tattered blanket.

"Please help me. You must listen. Tora-san, he is—" Ezroh said to Sister Bernadine through his tears. "My father ask that Father Maurice come to perform last rites. Please come with me." Sister Mary Deborah hurried down the stairs toward the rectory.

Anah ran to Ezroh, who searched for her in the crowd of sleepy girls, nuns, a cook, a groundskeeper, and janitor, Ezroh, who took Anah's hand to lift her up. Sister Bernadine grabbed the back of Anah's nightdress and pulled her away, ripping the thin white cloth. Anah fell to the ground, the big nun picking her up by the scruff of her neck. She clutched her nightdress to keep it from falling.

"My father ask that Anah come with Father Maurice," Ezroh stammered.

"O my soul, O my Lord, from lying lips," the sister answered. "Father Maurice will never allow it. The reverend mother will never allow it. I will never allow it."

"Tora-san asking fo' her," he said, panicked. "He keep calling her name, Anah-san, Anah-san, no can stop."

The reverend mother moved forward, pulling her old shawl tightly around her. "Take the girls back inside before they catch their death," she said to Sister Simone. "Do it now, Sister, make haste." She stared at Anah and then at Ezroh. "Leave Susanah to me."

Sister Mary Deborah hurried Father Maurice to the courtyard.

"No, Reverend Mother," Sister Bernadine began. "If you allow the girl to go, she will disobey you again. I tell you, the girl will not return. She has a foolish and hurtful lust for the young man in her Jezebel's heart and he for her. His lying lips are a foul abomination."

"Our friend is dying," Ezroh began, the tears on his wet face. "He like say good-bye to Anah. Please, Reverend Mother, he no mo' nobody. No mo' 'ohana."

Aunty Chong Sum began to cry for the old man. She draped a blanket over Anah's shoulders. "I never say nothing, dear Mother," she said, sobbing, "but this time, I ask you in sweet Jesus name, let the girl go. She the only one show the 'elemakule little bit kindness when her life mo' hard than his. Ezroh no lie. It's true. The old man no mo' family."

Father Maurice mounted his mule. "We need to leave immediately," he said, Ezroh's horse stamping the dirt in an anxious prance. "The girl must stay. She cannot go—a young, unmarried girl, unaccompanied—to the Soares ranch."

"Then I will go with her," Sister Mary Deborah said, stepping out from under the eaves of the porch. She hurried over to the small filly, Supang helping her up.

Anah broke free from Sister Bernadine and took Ezroh's outstretched hand, a soft rippling filling her, then surging as he lifted her onto the back of his horse. He released the ropes towing the mule and the filly. His horse turned, then moved briskly into the darkness. And in that dark, Anah wrapped Ezroh in her blanket, pressed her face into the hollow between his shoulder blades, breathed in the sweet smell of his body, and moved her hands under his loose nightshirt, his skin warm and alive. He placed his hand over her hand, weaving his fingers between hers.

He led them out of the grounds of St. Joseph's, stopping on the bridge to wait for Father Maurice and Sister Mary Deborah, Aki shrieking in the trees, Seth and Leah standing on the bridge holding hands, crying, Ezroh turning the horse in the direction of his father's dairy, taking them deeper still into Kalihi Valley.

Aki Speaks in Their Mother's Tongue, the Holy Sister Whispering the Rosary for Tora-San, Anah Asleep on the Floor of His Room

"In the name of the Father, and of the Son, and of the Holy Spirit. Amen. Our Father, Who art in heaven, hallowed be thy Name; thy kingdom come, thy will be done, on earth as it is in heaven."

I saw you leaving, Anah. You leave us, you die. I will kill you. I see you with the old man. He is not your father. Your father is here with us. See him in the corner of the room. See him waiting under the tree. See him scream at the children in the trees. See him touching me.

'He is touching me too, Anah.'

". . . and forgive us our trespasses as we forgive those who trespass against us; and lead us not into temptation, but deliver us from evil. Amen."

When will you take us home? You promised Leah.

'You promise, Anah.'

You promised me.

'Promise, Anah.'

When are you coming to take us with you? Hurry, take us home.

'Take us home with you, Anah.'

Anah is a liar. I told you, Leah. I whispered in your ear, remember: your sister is a liar.

Mentirosa!

"Hail Mary full of grace! the Lord is with thee; blessed art thou among women, and blessed is the fruit of thy womb, Jesus. Holy Mary, Mother of God, pray for us sinners now and at the hour of our death. Amen."

Vovó hates Charles.

'I love you, Charles.'

Charles loves Anah.

'I love you too, Anah.'

Vovó hates Charles.

"Vovó, I saw Anah riding on a buggy, I swear it was her. I saw her on Hotel Street."

Vovó hits his face for telling lies again. "Stupid boy, how many times have I told you? You have no sisters." Calls Uncle Floyd. Tie him naked to the tree. Beat him with the horsewhip.

Run away, Charles. And take the bastard child with you. Live in the streets, dirty streets, plenty Chinamen and whores. Stealer-robber, Charles. Scram, Charlie boy, panini boy, shoeshine boy.

Vovó hates Mama.

'I love you, Mama.'

Vovó hits Mama. "Why do you make more half-breeds with Floyd? Do you not realize, whore, that he is your dead husband's uncle?"

It is nighttime. Mama is leaving. She steals the money from the coffee can in Vovó's kitchen.

The money Mama made for Thomas.

"You iron clothes for the luna, Sumi. You deliver tōfu to the Japanee camp, Sumi. You make the lunch for the Filipino, Sumi. I will hold the money."

The money Charles made for Thomas.

"You pick the kiawe beans for the dairy, Charles. You shine the sailor shoes, Charles. You golf caddy for the officers, Charles. You work the cane field, Charles. I will hold the money."

The money for Thomas.

"Thomas will go university. Thomas will be a doctor. Thomas will take care of his vovó, won't you, my sweet Tomas?"

Mama takes all the money. She hides it in her yanagi-gōri tied with rope. Mama is running away from the house.

'Do not leave me, Mama! Wait for me! Take me with you!'

Mama is on a big boat.

'No!'

Good-bye, Mama.

'Mama!'

She turns around. She hears her little Leah. She is hearing things. Only her mind playing tricks again. She has no daughters.

'Mama!'

Mama is crying. Mama throws our picture in the water.

The picture:

"Sit still, sit still, Mama-san, keep the children still, don't cry, little girl, you will ruin the photograph, little boy, little boy, no, no, little boy, don't do that, everyone, please don't move. Mister, whassamatta you? Restrain them, please. Missus, keep your doggone children still."

Our picture sways on the oily waters, then sinks.

Mama is gone, gone to sea. Mama is going home.

'Home?'

Where is home, Anah, when there is no home?

'Anah knows.'

Where is home, Anah?

'Anah knows.'

Tell us, Anah. Take us there.

'Take us.'

Anah hates you.

'I love you, Anah.'

See Anah leave with Ezroh. She is leaving us here.

'Come back, come back!'

See Leah crying. See Seth crying. Stop crying, stop crying, you are hurting my ears. Crying for Anah.

"Hail, hail, hail Mary, blessed art thou among women . . ."

Seth chases you to the bridge. How Seth loves the living. He sucks your breath inside of him at night. We are here with him, but he wants his Anah. Suck her breath, suck, suck. So sorry, Seth, no more Anah for you, stupid boy. Anah loves Ezroh. Seth hates you, Ezroh. I hate you too, Ezroh. Give us back our Anah.

'Give us back our Anah.'

Behold the children in the trees, the many with no homes, we are hungry, we are scared, love me, my chest hurts, love me, I want milk, I am cold, Mama, Papa, when will you come? They are screaming all at once, the children in the trees.

'Can you not hear us, Anah?'

Why will you not listen? It is my birthday.

'Sweet cakes and gumdrops. The kittens came to Aki's party, remember, Anah? We made paper hats for everyone there.'

No one comes. My grave is a stone that looks like a toad. Where is my name?

'Beloved Aki.'

It is written on the wind. Beloved Aki. Daughter of no one.

'Wind.'

Wake up now, Anah. I said, wake up!

'Wake up, my sister, my Anah.'

"Glory be to the Father, and to the Son, and to the Holy Spirit. As it was in the beginning, is now, and ever shall be, world without end . . ."

Listen to me:

". . . world without end. Amen."

Where is home when no one is home?

16

1922

Anah woke the first morning to Ezroh crawling into Tora-san's room; he lay his head at her feet. He closed his eyes, his fingers stroking her ankles. Father Maurice snored in a chair near the window.

Sister Mary Deborah gave Ezroh a small grimace, then cleared her throat as a signal for them to cease and desist in their display of affection. Ezroh offered Anah a hand up, her nightdress slipping off her shoulders; Anah had forgotten it was torn. She covered herself with the rough horse blanket.

Tora-san stirred, his sleep distressed, his waking distressed.

Sister Mary Deborah signaled for Ezroh to find something for Anah to wear, pointing with her quick fingers and mouthing, "shirt, trousers, top and bottom, wrap her breasts, give her anything to put on, hurry."

"I will let Anah wear my clothes," he whispered to the sister, who nodded, her finger over her lips, then pointing them out the door. Ezroh quietly led Anah to his room down the hall, a spartan space, a bed, a desk with a lantern, and a chair.

Anah looked at him, the months and months she hadn't seen him or heard his voice, laughed, shared a meal, a beautiful poem, his comforting silent company, all in this moment:

No more questions, no more doubts, life is short, my beloved, too short, each second significant, eloquent.

The blanket fell to the floor. He slid his hands into her torn nightdress, his fingers over her breasts and then across her back, drawing her near: Anah moved her hands under his shirt and they held each other for what seemed an infinitesimal forever because forever would never be enough.

My Ezroh.

Warm skin, his hand on her head smoothing back her hair, petting her, she was his treasured one. They wiped the happy tears from each other's eyes.

He handed Anah a clean white shirt and a pair of khakis, watching her wrap her breasts with strips of the torn nightdress with the interest of a child and the desire of a man.

Anah put on the clothes of a man. Ezroh helped her button her shirt. He passed a belt through the loops of the trousers and cinched it around her waist. He adjusted the length by folding up small cuffs.

They sat on his bed and said nothing for a long time, each memorizing the shape and form of nose, eyes, cheek, chin, and lips, not knowing when they would see each other again. Anah had no words, her skin shivering involuntarily at his touch, his hands on her face, shaking his head in disbelief.

Is it really you, my Anah?

He pulled Anah's hands to his face, wet with tears, and sobbed into her open palms.

"Get ready for school, Ezroh, or you will be late. I will not have you disobey me," his father called in Portuguese from the cookhouse. "Ricardo is taking everybody on the wagon. It is too muddy to walk. Go now, Ezroh."

"I want to stay with you," he said to Anah, panicked. "What if they make you leave while I am at school?"

Anah sighed heavily, lowering her eyes. "No, no, I will stay."

"Have you heard me, Ezroh?" his father yelled. "You will be late to school. I will not tell you again. Do not try my temper."

Ezroh changed into a white shirt and khakis, pulling his suspenders over his broad shoulders. He stared into a cracked mirror nailed to the bare wall. Anah followed him across the room, putting her arms around him, then slipping her hands under the waistband of his trousers. Their faces reflected in the dusty mirror. He rubbed brilliantine between his palms, then slicked back his hair, doing the same for Anah. He chuckled when she took the comb from him and parted her short hair like his.

"If they make you leave before I get home from school," he said, "run away into the valley and I will come to find you when it gets dark. You promise me, Anah."

"I promise," Anah told him.

He grabbed his book strap and ran out the door.

FROM BEHIND the closed door of Tora-san's room, Anah listened to the doctor who spoke in hushed tones to Sister Mary Deborah, Father Maurice, and Rex Soares.

"The Oriental's got the dengue fever," the doctor said. "It's all the rainfall we've been having with the tropical climate. The mosquitoes love the taste of the Japanee. With his advanced age and his weakness for spirits, he most certainly will not last the week." The doctor snapped his black bag shut.

"I had serious misgivings about bringing the girl here," Father Maurice said. "But the family, well, the good Mr. Soares requested last rites and that we bring along the girl for the old man who had been asking for her—"

"He will only get worse," the doctor replied. "They're falling like flies"—he smiled wryly at his pun—"in these Pacific islands. He will go any day now. So if he wants to say good-bye to his loved ones, then by all means. But yes, the girl's consumption surely compromises the old man's condition, I'll have you know that, Rex," the doctor said.

"Then certainly in good conscience we must send the girl back to the orphanage," Father Maurice responded.

Anah's heart stopped.

No. Run into the valley. Ezroh will find you after dark.

Someone placed a hand over Anah's mouth. She turned. It was Ezroh. He had not gone to school with the others. "Run away with me," he said. "You promised."

Wait, Anah mouthed, lifting her hand. She put her finger over her lips, *listen*.

"The girl can stay as long as Father Maurice allows her to stay," Rex Soares said.

"You sure, Rex?" the doctor asked. "The consumption's very contagious for you and everyone else here as well—"

"As was the Pa-ke's leprosy, the Spanish flu, the kanaka's dropsy, the Filipino's diphtheria, the borinque's whooping cough, and now this," he said about Tora-san.

"As you wish, Mr. Soares," Father Maurice said. "But I will be returning to my duties at St. Joseph's within the hour. The sister and the girl will remain here to assist you in getting your house in order." He looked at Rex Soares. "To the righteous, good shall be repaid. The good Lord smiles upon thee, brother Soares, for your continued generosity to the orphans of St. Joseph's."

The door flung open, nearly knocking over Anah and Ezroh. Rex Soares glared at Ezroh. "Son, go saddle up Makana for Father Maurice," he said to him. "Then escort him back to the church. And hurry on back. Since there is no *school* for you, there will be much work to do with the old man down." He looked at Anah, tipping his hat. "You will both be put to work."

◈

ANAH AND SISTER MARY DEBORAH STAYED at the Soares Dairy for eleven days, cooking hearty meals and boiling load after load of laundry for the cowboys and ranch hands. The cookhouse was a filthy mess—pots, floors, dishes, windows, tables, linens, and curtains dusty with fine sod and old spiderwebs, mouse and roach feces collecting in every corner.

In the afternoons, Anah and the holy sister helped tend the enormous vegetable garden with Ezroh, his cousins Matthew and Bert, and Abigail, the eldest daughter of Kahalelehua.

They helped feed and water the chickens, geese, ducks, turkeys, peacocks, pigs, dogs, cats, goats, sheep, donkeys, mules, and horses. The ranch hands and paniolos spoke in whispers of the death of their beloved ali'i Prince Jonah Kūhiō Kalanianaole in Waikiki, his body laid to rest at the Royal Mausoleum in neighboring Nu'uanu Valley.

They woke before the sun to assist the ranch hands with the morning milking transported to the Dairymen's processing plant downtown, then packed lunches for the children and ranch hands before they left for school or the mountains.

She spoke with much excitement of the visit of Prince Edward, the Prince of Wales, to the city of Honolulu and his brief stay at the "First Lady of Waikiki," the beautiful Moana Hotel.

Tora-san remained bedridden, delirious with the dengue fever that threatened to take his life, his body covered with a horrific rash and the delirium of unrelenting fever. He begged Anah in muffled gasps to let him die, his mouth full of white boils.

Anah followed Rex Soares's instructions, sponging the old man with a solution of crushed a'ali'i shoots, 'ulu sap, and rock salt boiled into a creamy paste. She cleaned him three times a day with a cool towel bath, careful not to break the liquid pustules, making him prone to further infection.

Anah forced him to gargle with a solution of iodized salt and hydrogen peroxide that made him gag and heave bile into the washbowl on his nightstand, the boils in his mouth growing more creamy and phlegmy with each day.

When his fever would not break, Anah covered him with ti, overlapping the big green leaves from his head to his feet. When he rasped for water, she gave him small sips. She prayed and prayed for him, the holy Rosary constantly on her lips, as she covered him with heavy blankets, his fever still advancing.

At Rex Soares's behest, Anah gathered a gallon full of ko'oko'olau, the beautiful oriental lantern plant that grew in abundance in the valley, and ground it with rock salt, straining it through a cheesecloth three times, then wiping the refined liquid on Tora-san's burning head, neck, armpits, and groin.

Anah made him her vovó's sopa do espírito santo, a hearty beef stew full of fresh chunks of beef, blood, and vegetables from Tora-san's garden. She added many sprigs of mint and cloves of garlic, much more than she did for her vovó who beat her if the flavor was not to her liking. Anah fed Tora-san her soup of the holy spirit spoonful by spoonful even when he turned his face from her. She fed him, knowing that he could fight the fever with a strong body.

Anah would not let him die.

She slept in his room at the foot of his bed, woke to his every moan, turning his body to prevent bedsores, shifting his limbs that stiffened, every inch of his skin a prick of bone-deep pain; he was now thin and pale, her friend who called out in dementia one night, "Oi Pilipine, I bet two-bit on your rooster this cock fight! Oi tui! Nice niwatori! And strong, just like me. Two-bit, Pilipine! Lady Luck on my side."

Anah whispered in his ear every night, "Good night, sleep tight, don't let the bedbugs bite." He'd grimace. She knew then that he had heard her voice.

⟐

AS ANAH WORKED on the ranch in the days that followed, Ezroh made sure she was always within eyeshot. If Anah worked at the kitchen sink, he worked outside the kitchen window. If Anah tended to Tora-san, he swept the lānai outside of his room. If she gathered vegetables for meals, he dropped his feed buckets to help carry her heavy basket full of produce.

Sister Mary Deborah allowed Anah to assist Ezroh with his lessons when, on the third day, confident that her stay would be lengthy, he returned to school with his cousins and the other children who lived on the ranch.

Anah read with Ezroh after his return from school. They learned of the great leader of India, Mohandas Gandhi, who had been seized and again imprisoned by the British government and of Cardinal Achille Ratti, a studied librarian, becoming Pope Pius XI and of the purchase of an entire Hawaiian island by a missionary descendant, James D. Dole, who now owned the largest pineapple company in the world. They did their studies at the table in the kitchen, their legs touching, as Sister Mary Deborah prepared dinner, hitting their hands with a wooden spoon when skin-to-skin their arms lingered together and their gazes persisted long and doe-eyed.

"Keep thy heart with all diligence," she reminded, dusting flour from her hands, Ezroh entwining his foot with Anah's under the table.

"Yes, Sister." Ezroh smiled.

Late, late at night, when Sister Mary Deborah retired to her quarters, Ezroh crawled into Tora-san's room and moved his warm body under Anah's heavy blanket; they slept on the floor of Tora-san's room, Anah and Ezroh exchanging breath-heavy kisses, slow and hungry, eating each other's lips and tongues, their exposed, vulnerable necks. He woke before the light of dawn to return quickly to his room down the hall.

BUT THE DAY CAME SOON, much too soon, the day of Anah's departure.

◇

RYOKI SUNABE, the midwife, had come to deliver Kahalelehua's eleventh child, hurrying into the cookhouse with a kettle full of pigs' feet soup to assure the mother's speedy recovery.

"Keep jiru hot, keep hot," she blurted as she rushed out in the direction of the living quarters of the few married hands. "Very danger, no mo' keiki, no mo' baby," she repeated, lifting her kimono to run. "No listen, the hard-head kanaka-man never listen me. Keep making keiki, keiki, keiki just like the usaji. Hippity-hoppity baby all over the place."

Anah lifted the lid of the pot, the thick stock full of the smell of shiitake, ginger, and garlic. The gelatinous pig knuckles glistened. She remembered her mother drinking this same soup, the buta ashi no shiru brought by another Okinawan midwife she insisted upon calling for Leah's birth even when Vovó demanded she be attended by the Portuguese midwife who had delivered the rest of the children.

The Okinawan midwife became Okaasan's friend, Anah's Japanese mother who lived among the Portuguese, shunned by her own for marrying outside of her kind. The midwife didn't care. She too was cast aside by the Japanese who thought themselves better than the dirty Okinawans whose contact with pigs made them unclean, whose hairy bodies and round eyes made them a mongrel breed, whose unsavory women tattooed their hands. The midwife imbued Okaasan's soup with shots of home-brewed sake that made her warm from the inside out in the hours after Leah's birth, their mother's breast milk thick with nutrients.

The smell of the soup sank into Anah, bringing a wave of sadness. *Little Leah, infant girl in my arms.* She sat down at the table. Sister Mary Deborah lifted a kettle of ham hock stew from the stove and carried it to the long table in the cookhouse. She paused to look at Anah.

Nutrients.

"This soup," Anah told her, "is very good soup. I can make one bowl fo' Tora-san lunch?"

At first the sister hesitated. "Just a bit," she said, taking two baskets of bread to the table. "The midwife brought it for Nohea. She is having a very difficult delivery. I will be assisting Miss Ryoki as soon as lunch is served." She hurried out with two plates of butter. "Will you assist me, Susanah?"

Anah did not respond. She moved the ladle through the pig feet soup. She picked out a piece of daikon and konbu, one shiitake, a clove of garlic, and a piece of meat dangling from a big knuckle with a serving of the thick broth. She grated a small piece of fresh ginger root into the bowl. She took a small sip, the ginger sharp. The soup needed sake. She searched the cabinets in the kitchen and found nothing. She stared out the window for a moment and saw Ricardo scrubbing his hands in a metal bowl by the washhouse.

"Ricardo!" Anah called to him. He turned to the sound of his name but, seeing no one, resumed cleaning the dirt from under his fingernails. She ran out to the washhouse. "Ricardo, I need some sake," she told him as he walked away from her.

"Who don't." He laughed, heading toward the cookhouse. "We no break the law o' here. No mo' booze," he lied. "No kickapoo, no 'ōkolehao, no sake, no arak, no nothin'."

"For Tora-san," Anah blurted.

"He no need sake. Might make the makule bas-ted keel over," he said, full stride as Anah hurried alongside him. "The sake is all fo' me." He winked.

"Ezroh said you betta show me where Tora-san hide his sake," Anah lied.

He stopped. "Ezroh said? You sure?" he asked.

Anah nodded.

"Betta not be bullshit, damn lying wahine," he said, turning toward the butter house.

Anah paused. "I not," she said, tripping over an 'ōhi'a post, "a liar."

He did not stop to help her up. Anah dusted herself off and ran behind him. He opened the door and lifted the lid of an old churn, the room cool with the smell of old milk. He handed her a white bottle, uncorking the top and taking a whiff that made him wince. "No wonder he ready fo' ma-ke," he said, "drinking this kickapoo shit." He corked the bottle and tossed it to her.

"Thank you, thank you," Anah told him. He burped, spit, farted, and walked off.

Anah put a jigger of sake into Tora-san's soup and a jigger into the kettle for Nohea. She heated his portion to a boil, then hurried to his room. The smell of the soup entered before her. His eyes opened slightly.

"Buta ashi no shiru," Anah whispered, placing the bowl on the nightstand and taking a spoonful to his lips. She blew on the hot pigs' feet soup that eddied near the rim of the spoon. She lifted his head and tipped the broth into his mouth. His lips moved, his tongue taking in the flavor. Anah fed him another spoonful and another.

"Oi, atsui," he complained. "Hot, hot, hot, you bakatare Anah-san, you burn my mouth." Anah put the spoon down and smiled even if he had berated her. It was the first time he had spoken to her in days. "Gimme some mo' yo' sake soup."

Anah fed him bits of mushroom, vegetable, and pork, then tipped cold water into his mouth. She lifted the bowl to return to the kitchen, but he held her hand in his and would not let go.

Anah sat down again beside him in the sister's chair, humming a Japanese lullaby unknown by name to her, the same lullaby her okaasan hummed to her, holding the old man's hand until he fell asleep.

"WE WILL LEAVE in the morning," Sister Mary Deborah said to Anah late the following night. "Mr. Toranosuke will find ample assistance in the wives of the kanaka and the borinque."

"But he still very sick and—" Anah started. Ezroh poked at the small fire in the hearth.

"The children at St. Joseph's are my first priority. They need me to return immediately," she said matter-of-factly. "The reverend mother, Sister Simone, and Sister Bernadine have labored long and hard in my absence and it is time for us to go home."

"I want to—" Anah began.

"I want you to be prepared for our departure in the morning with your belongings packed," she said, not looking at Anah.

"But I want to—"

"I know what you want to do. The sisters and holy mother all know what your flesh wants, Susanah. But I made a solemn vow to them that you would return with me."

"No, Sister, Anah like stay," Ezroh said. "If you take her, then we going run away, right, Anah?"

Anah looked at him, unresponsive.

"You promised me, Anah," he whispered in Portuguese.

Anah turned her eyes away from his urgent gaze.

"You want to stay here with me, do you not?" His voice cracked with uncertainty.

Anah nodded, her face in her hands.

"Then we will run away tonight," Ezroh said, taking her hand in his.

"It is rude for you to speak a foreign tongue in my presence," the sister scolded. And then she looked sadly at Anah. "Do not make a liar out of me, Susanah," she said, standing up now. "And do not make a liar of yourself."

Anah looked at Ezroh, her eyes full of sadness.

"Anah is not a liar," Ezroh said with great conviction.

Sister Mary Deborah put her folded hands under her chin and looked down at Anah. "A liar giveth ear to a malicious tongue. God help you, Susanah. I will pray for you tonight."

"O Lord," Anah whispered, her body breaking from the weight of her decision, "keep falsehoods and lies far from me."

Ezroh stood and walked out of the room.

"Ezroh!" she called to him. But he would not return. Anah watched his shape move out of the lantern light, absorbed slowly by the darkness.

He would not come to lie with her that night at the foot of Tora-san's bed. She waited awake all night for his quiet footstep, his sweet breath saying her name, his hungry mouth eating hers, their lips devouring the words whispered between them even as they were spoken. But when the morning came, Anah was alone.

"I SEE YOU sugu when I get mo' betta, Anah-san," Tora-san rasped as he tried to snap his fingers together. He hacked and coughed. "Oi-ya, shi shi come out, gunfunnit," he said, holding his groin. "I see you soon, sugu, very, very soon," he said, then waved her off.

Ricardo lifted their bags onto the buggy, then helped Sister Mary Deborah up. Anah stood in the dusty wind, wearing the white shirt and khakis Ezroh had dressed her in the morning she first arrived at the dairy. The ranch hands, cowboys, their wives and children bade them a fond farewell. Rex Soares stood on the lānai of the cookhouse, his arms folded across his broad chest. Anah climbed up next to Sister Mary Deborah and turned as the buggy pulled away.

Ezroh had not come to say good-bye.

Anah's Letter

Dearest Ezroh,

It is raining in the valley. I like the rain. Do you remember the times we sat on the lanai listening to the rain on the roof and on the leaves? Do you remember when we said we both loved the taste of the rain?

I have hidden your shirt and trousers under my pillow. That way, you will always be near me. It smells like you and me together late at night.

I am so sorry, my Ezroh. I did not mean to hurt you. But I could not bear the word, liar. My sister Aki often called me a mentirosa. I did not want to hurt Aki and Leah so I told them many things that were not true. In a way, Aki was right. I was a liar. But I no longer wish to be one.

I could not lie to Sister Mary Deborah. I could not lie to our heavenly Father. I could not stay or run away with you like a thief in the night, hiding like a criminal. I feared that they would send the constable to hunt me down with the dogs as they did when Aki ran away into the valley.

You see, we are inmates here at St. Joseph's. If we are ever released, we are parolees like Shizu. Do you remember Shizu? When she was cured of the consumption, her family came to get her. But you see, my dear Ezroh, I have no family to get me even if I did get well. I must remain an orphan here at St. Joseph's until my eighteenth birthday.

Do you think for a moment that all of this did not run through my mind when Sister Mary Deborah told me we would be leaving in the morning? I did not want to bring shame to you or to your father or to Tora-san. I would have been arrested and shackled. I did not want to bring shame to myself.

But I love you so, my Ezroh, of that I am certain. I have never spoken these words to you. Everyone I ever loved has left me behind. I did not believe in such a thing as love. I did not think myself worthy of love until I loved you and you loved me. Do you love me, Ezroh, the way that I love you?

If your answer is yes, I will ask you now to please make me a promise. Promise me you will come to get me on the day of my eighteenth birthday, April the 17th of the year 1923. I promise you that I will go with you in love.

Let it be morning when I walk out of this horrid place.

Let me lift my head high.

Let me not leave like a thief in the night.

Let me stand in truth.

Let me leave this place like Shizu into the waiting arms of family.

Be my family, Ezroh.

We did not say good-bye to each other when I left. That is a good thing, for good-bye is so very final.

I will see you soon, Ezroh.

Until that day, my beloved, I remain yours always.

Susanah Medeiros

APRIL 17, 1923

Early in the morning, Anah gathered her few belongings into a rice bag duffel that Aunty Chong Sum had sewn for her birthday. She placed in it:

a honey jar filled with baby teeth, hair, and fingernails, little Leah's.

Anah listened to her sad little voice, a child's singsong whirling above over and over in a monotonous wail, 'A-nah Ma-ma, A-nah Ma-ma, A-nah Ma-ma.'

Anah sat on the edge of her bed on the third floor, Fukunaga's mop bucket wheeling across the wet surface. She covered her ears with her hands. He stopped to look at her. Puzzled at first, he leaned on his mop, then gave a small wave hello, or was it good-bye, as Anah placed in her duffel:

a bottle cap, her first Coca-Cola shared with Ezroh in Chinatown.

Seth appeared in the far corner of the third floor, his eyes glazed over and sad, gesturing to her over and over again.

Hands over heart, hands breaking stick.

Heart broken.

Hands over heart, hands breaking stick.

Heart broken.

Anah closed her eyes. She heard the Reverend Mother Magdalena from the courtyard below as she welcomed the families to a special Visitation Sunday. It was Easter morning. Girls gathered around her in joyful reunion, girls in their white Sunday dresses, ginger blossoms in their hair. Mothers held daughters. Fathers cried for their sick children. Brothers and sisters spilled across the lawn, hunting for colored eggs. Supang showed the little ones his fluffy yellow chicks, ducklings, and baby bunnies. Anah continued packing:

a honey jar filled with baby teeth, hair, and fingernails, Aki's.

Her voice sounded jagged and shrill, a macabre union of Japanese and Portuguese, frantic with threats, her earthy breath circling around, slashing Anah's arms with what felt like thin sewing needles.

'Where are you going, Anah? Take us with you. Take us home. So many dead ones, Anah. All around you, dead ones. Can you see us, Anah? We are many.'

The window rattled in a brisk northerly wind, the dramatic exhale and suck of the curtains against the glass. The bed stand shook, the empty washbasin falling to the floor, bedsprings creaking, bedspread pulling.

Anah closed her eyes and listened to the coming of a light rain. How she loved the rain. Anah placed in her duffel:

a bottle of lemons soaked in honey, crisp waxed paper under the cover.

"No like you eva get sick again. All pau sick," Aunty Chong Sum told Anah as she placed it in her hands the night before as they cleaned the kitchen. "I make plenty, just like you show me when—" She stopped, unable to complete her thought, pressing her hands to her face, her eyes welling with tears. "Fo' yo' happy birthday," she managed to say.

Anah packed:

packets of bitter melon seeds, kabocha and mitsuba seeds, cuttings of basil, rosemary, dill, thyme, and gobo, the bulbous roots of chive, daikon, and carrot tops.

Supang patted his dusty hand on Anah's cheek as she milked their cow the afternoon before. He said nothing, letting his hand linger on her face, before turning to give the cow another armful of chopped corn stalks and sweet alfalfa. He sighed deeply, pressing the packets of seeds into her hands, then shuffling out of the stable.

This morning Anah packed her few belongings: gold paper stained with melted chocolate, a red ribbon, Christmas gifts from Ezroh.

Anah took off her Sunday dress mended in so many places, folded it neatly, then placed it on the pillow at the head of the bed.

Seth cried, his body melting to the floor, squatting, fetal.

Anah placed in her duffel:

violets pressed between waxed paper, drawings of a favorite dog, a ranch house, a red bicycle, a photograph inscribed, *I am looking for you, sweet Anna, in the hills of Kalihi above St. Joseph's for I will come to get you soon.*

Anah took off the binding from her breasts and then her underwear, laying them on the pillow. She sat naked on the bed, the sunlight warm on her skin, as a draft of cold shivered over her. Aki scratched at her breasts, tiny drops of blood appearing from white flesh, but Anah was not afraid. Anah knew that Aki could not kill her.

She held in her hands for a moment, letters hidden under her mattress, so many letters:

I am yours, forever, I am yours. I will come to get you soon.

Anah dressed herself in Ezroh's white shirt, a small circle of blood spreading over her heart, his khaki trousers hemmed above second-hand Mary Janes. She combed her hair with ambergris oil.

Little Leah screamed.

Anah lifted her duffel onto her shoulder and walked out of the ward on the third floor. She stopped in front of the prayer closet, the door ajar to darkness, the smell of incense and beeswax pungent still.

Little Leah screamed.

Anah shut each of the attic doors, the smell of urine and vomit embedded in the wooden floor, fingernail scratches on the walls, some little girl whimpering behind the closed door on the makai side facing the ocean.

Little Leah screamed.

Anah walked down the first flight of the steep staircase, pausing at the closed doors of the second-floor infirmary. She peeked through the hole she had etched in the paint when Aki lay dying in the same bed where a tiny Korean girl lay under the isinglass, the rasp of the camphorous humidifier repetitive and hopeless.

'The Yobo's dead; she is dead in a day; climb the tree, stay with me; nobody is coming to get you anyway to take you home, to take you home.'

Anah walked down the second flight of the steep staircase, pausing at the door to the kitchen, Aunty Chong Sum laying clean dishcloths over the Easter bread she helped her to bake before sunrise.

"Nice and yellow, and very shiny," she said to Anah, patting the bread. She took a second look at Anah's duffel. "You o-kay, Anah? You be happy. Today yo' birthday and the day our sweet Jesus Lord rise up be in heaven with his God the Father of all. How you like that? You and Him get same-same birthday. You count yo' many blessing," she chided Anah. "You stay here help me," she said, almost pleading.

Anah shook her head *no* and walked slowly out the door.

"Anah!" she called. "Anah, please, you listen me!"

Anah walked across the lānai, the chatter of grateful mothers sipping sweet tea with the nuns, walked under the staccato shadows of the fragrant banyan tree and sat in the gazebo alone, waiting on yet another Visitation Sunday, this time waiting for Ezroh. Anah sat there:

the sound of children's laughter, agonizing,
the gathering of mothers and fathers, wounding,
grandmothers and grandfathers, excruciating,
sisters and brothers, their joys Anah's death again and again.

Anah had convinced herself that today would be different, but it wasn't. The pain of waiting and the crush of blighted hope had not diminished over the years.

Sister Bernadine crossed her arms as she stood on the lānai across the lawn, observing Anah's every move, her every attention to arrivals at the orphanage. She whispered to Sister Simone whenever another girl's family arrived, then sniggered behind a closed fist at Anah's disappointment.

Anah would not let the sister see her hoping and wanting. She would not let the sister see her break. How could *this* hurt her? She'd been through too many Visitation Sundays to care anymore. Anah stared back at her, devoid of expression.

The sun rose overhead, the sisters hurriedly excusing themselves from the families to prepare communion for Easter Mass, Sister Bernadine finally leaving her observation post on the lānai. Anah breathed deeply, anxiously resuming her vigilant watch of the road.

Someone laughed at her from the branches of the tree.

'Monkey, Monkey, look at Anah! Nobody coming to take her home. Look, look at her. But do not fall off the tree, Monkey, Monkey.'

Then more laughter, a chorus of vicious mockery.

'Sad, so very sad. No Mama, no Papa, all alone, pity, pity, pitiful you.'

Sister Simone rang the church bells as families headed for the chapel, the scurry of nuns in heavy woolen habits welcoming all of them to Mass.

'Do not fall, Monkey.'

Sister Mary Deborah stood at the open doors of the chapel, calling Anah with her eyes to come, her lips saying, "For yet a little while, and he that shall come will come, and will not tarry."

And when Anah did not stand, she made the sign of the cross, nodded sadly, then closed the heavy chapel doors.

'Happy birthday to you. Happy birthday to you. Happy birthday, sweet Anah. No one's coming for you.'

No one's coming. Anah almost laughed out loud. What did she expect? No one was coming. No one had ever come. No one would ever come.

Anah heard little Leah praying, 'Never let my heart look for the joys of this world, but for the true joys of heaven.' Or was it some other little girl reciting the Second Glorious Mystery in the chapel?

Anah would leave this day if she had to leave alone. She would find Charles and make a family and a home with her brother. She said her own prayers:

"Let it be the light of day when I walk out of this horrid place."

The sun faded on the Koʻolau Mountains, a stripe of white light caught in its high peaks, spidery ironwoods, grassland rising. A cold northerly pulled down the valley.

"Let me lift my head high."

The seconds Anah waited on that day deepened into minutes into hours, the diminishment of her hope, love disappearing. She lowered her eyes, the litter of newborn kittens at her feet, the mama cat's gift to her.

And Aki whispered, 'Take them when you leave for nowhere, then drown them one by one in the river.'

"Let me stand in truth."

'Mentirosa,' she snarled.

"I love you, Aki, no matter what you do or say to me. I have always loved you, little sister, even if we never returned home. I told you lies to give you hope," Anah said aloud in Japanese. Her eyes began to bleed again. "I love you, little Leah, my baby girl. I am so sorry I let you die here. And I am so sorry our mother and brother never came to take you home." Anah wiped her eyes. "I love you, Seth. Thank you for saving my life. Thank you for being my loyal friend."

'Liar. Anah is a Liar.'

"Mass is ended!" The chapel doors opened wide, the sun moving behind the upper reaches of the Koʻolau Mountains, always an early sunset in a valley, the cool of spring, a blue sky.

Anah prayed, "Let me not leave like a thief in the night."

The cold of day's end ushered in. She placed the kittens in the bread basket woven from lauhala fronds by Pa-ke Doh Nee. Mama cat slinked down the stairs of the gazebo, disappearing under the orphanage building.

'Mama does not love them. Mama does not love me.'

Anah lifted her duffel bag and her basket of kittens. She walked across the lawn. She would leave alone before the fading of this day.

"Susanah Medeiros!"

Anah stopped to the sound of her name.

"Susanah Medeiros!"

She looked around but saw no one, then heard the mighty rumble of phantom hooves thunder on the road until she was surrounded by a swirl of dust and the overwhelming sounds of horses and riders.

Cowboys wearing fragrant maile, ʻōhiʻa lehua, aʻaliʻi, and palapalai lei around their lauhala hats galloped on horses wearing matching lei. They rode over the bridge and into the courtyard, around and around her.

Anah put her belongings down and ran to each rider, searching each face through the whirlwind of dust and leaves to find Ezroh. The cowboys tipped their hats to her as she frantically spun herself around in the din.

"Susanah Medeiros!"

Tora-san rode in on Makana, the two of them adorned with gardenias and pua kenikeni blossoms. "Haisai, Anah-san!" he called to her, waving his straw hat in circles from atop his slow mule.

"Haisai, Tora-san!" she called back to him. "Where is Ezroh?"

"Susanah Medeiros!"

Anah ran across the courtyard toward the bridge over Kalihi Stream, the road lined with cowboys and ranch hands, wives wearing paʻu velvets and satins, sons and daughters singing Christian hīmene in beautiful Hawaiian, cattle dogs yipping, a favorite dog depicted in a boy's drawing wearing a lei of wild violets and fern.

"Anah!"

The bridge strewn with white ginger blossoms, Ezroh stood in the light rain of early evening, holding a bag of apples and a bag of chocolates.

He ran across the bridge, their bodies meeting in the sweet rise of ginger around them. He took one apple and one chocolate out of the bags and put them in Anah's pockets.

"Fo' Sister Mary Deborah," he said, putting the bags down. "From my father." He held out his hand, taking hers, kissing her fingers.

The cowboys whooped, "Whoo-ta! Yi-haa!"

And then they walked hand in hand toward the orphanage. "Let it be the light of day when we walk out of this place," he said.

"It is almost night," Anah told him.

"We had to work," he said, his father riding alongside, pulling Ezroh's horse.

"Lots of work to do, Anah. Every day we work, even on Easter Sunday," Rex Soares said in Portuguese. "But especially today. We worked first, then prepared for your arrival home."

Home.

Anah would leave this place on her birthday and never return. She climbed onto the back of Ezroh's horse, Tora-san packing her duffel and stuffing her kittens in each of his pockets.

No one came out to wish Anah farewell. The cowboys began leaving one by one. They waited for a moment longer.

"Let us leave with our heads held high," Ezroh said to her.

The kitchen door creaked open. Aunty Chong Sum looked both ways, then waved, *Hurry, hurry, come outside now.* Supang helped Sister Mary Deborah carry her heavy Victrola out to the lānai. Fukunaga rushed over from behind the building. Anah watched as the sister carefully cranked the gramophone and placed the needle gently onto her record. The slow trill, then rise of strings.

Bach's "Air from Suite no. 3 in D."

Anah remembered the sister's words to her while she did her fancy work. "Susanah, I want you to meet Mr. Johann Sebastian Bach. He will help our mending and sewing each night to be a pleasant time."

She walked over to them with a package wrapped with twine. "For you, Susanah," she said.

Anah looked at the beautiful sister, no words to say good-bye.

"Please, open it," she said, lifting her gift up to Anah.

Anah pulled the twine and removed the paper. Her bee hat and gloves.

"Remember always, dear Susanah, love is sweet," she said, a crack in her soft voice. "God be with you always." She tucked both hands inside her habit, turned slowly, then disappeared inside, the music continuing, cellos, violas, and violins.

Anah collapsed onto Ezroh's back. Aunty Chong Sum, Supang, and Fukunaga remained on the lānai, their good-byes sad and brief.

"We need to go now," Ezroh said, giving his horse a kick.

"Wait," Anah called to Ezroh. She got off the horse, stumbling onto the ground. She got up then ran toward the apiary on the south side of the lawn. She scrambled into the nativity shack and dug furiously in one of its corners for her gift from Shizu.

Anah remembered the words of Shizu's letter: *my special bottle of red feathers . . . You can make wings and fly away from St. Joseph's in case your mommy and daddy don't come back at least you can fly over the valley and go home.*

Anah opened the bottle of feathers to the north wind, the stirring bluster of delicate nestling lace around her, whirling and lifting into the trees.

"Make wings, all of you, fly away from here," she called to the trees in Japanese. "Your mama and papa not coming to get you," she called out in Portuguese. "Fly outta this valley, Aki! Fly all-a way home, Leah," she said in pidgin.

Anah left St. Joseph's Orphanage on April 17, 1923.

SHE NEVER SPOKE of Leah, Aki, and Seth again. She never wanted to hear their voices or feel their urgent and constant presence.

She left over the same bridge that she had arrived that rainy winter of the year 1915, the little girl in the yellow dress, the naked girl dressed in the valley's foliage, and the little boy who never aged, holding hands, weeping.

The tiny girl figures disappeared into the trees as they had done so many times before. Then he of the sad, longing eyes opened his mouth, widening into a spiraling black hole, a screaming maw, the rest of his body dissipating into the wind.

Farewell, Sweet Susanah

Curse your life for leaving me. Your home is here, turn around, come back.

Curse my love for you. How I loved you those many years, passing myself from sister to dying sister.

Hate you. *Heart.*

Hate you. *Broken.*

Curse the ground you walk on. Burn your feet on earth's hell.

Curse the food you cook. Poison to the tongue.

Curse your body with affliction. Rot of flesh, broken bones, galloping cough.

Die. Die soon.

Curse your womb. Dirty waters break between your legs.

Curse what issues forth. Sickly, crying beasties.

Curse you with girl babies. No namesake, no heirs. Dead babies, deformed, crippled.

Curse your days with sweat. Labor in the sun, the days never end.

Curse the ones you love. Husband, father, brother, child.

Curse you, Anah, brief our love and gone.

Curse your God. He will forsake you as you have forsaken me.

Curse your love.

Curse my brother. Bastard son of a bitch, why have you stolen my Anah?

Curse my father. Paipa, why were you not watching me when I fell from the tree?

"Too high, son, too high. Paipa loves you. Come down, Seth. It is time to go home now."

Blood, so much blood, the Monkey has fallen. Round and round beneath the tree, dead children, rosies ring just like me. Come, dead little Yobo, hurry through the dark, come out, come out wherever you are.

There is no light here, dark the tunnel through which we come. Curse the light, too bright. I came to you whenever you called, through the dark tunnel, so cold, so scared, I came.

I called to you from across the bridge. Did you not hear me? I called your name today. I called you, Susanah Medeiros! You heard me. You turned.

Why have you left me here? It is me. Seth. It is cold here, Anah. I want to go home too.

18

1924

How Anah wished her mother could see her wedding day.

How Anah wished for her mother to place upon her the beautiful silk kimono with ornately embroidered obi lifted out of a chest that smelled of sandalwood and senkō.

How Anah wished for her mother's soft touch, her quiet presence, her many blessings whispered mother to daughter.

Ezroh's Aunty Tova lifted a heavy wedding gown onto the long dining table in the cookhouse, Tora-san sidestepping her huge girth with a kettle full of hot oxtail stew. He grunted an obscenity at her in Okinawan, then ladled a serving of stew for Rex Soares.

"You wear this, Anah," she commanded. "I am certain it is not bad luck to wear someone else's dress, especially if it is family," she said in Portuguese. "And especially since you have no dowry. You make do with what you are graciously given." The yellowed lace was frayed over the bodice, the skirt spotted, the hemline torn.

"No, Aunty Tova," Ezroh began. "Not for Anah. I want to buy her a—"

"And that is the trouble with you, nephew," she said, flicking Ezroh's forehead with the first syllable. "In matters of the heart, so very pitiful and sad. You are without wisdom, just like your father—"

"Tova—" Rex Soares interrupted. Then he turned his irritation at his older sister to his son. "You mind your aunt, Ezroh. I will not tolerate your disrespectful tone of voice."

"Do you think your father is made of money?" she spat at Ezroh with the backing of her brother's authority. "What, is your girl too good for this dress that your own mother wore on her wedding day? God rest her soul such a disgraceful son."

"Tova, that is enough," Rex Soares said, not even looking up as he dunked a piece of hard bread into his hearty stew.

"Tova nothing," she began with a huff. "I told you, Rex, if this dress was good enough for Mary Anna, it is good enough for *her*." She looked at Anah, shaking her head. "Half-breed orphan," she whispered. "Our mother warned us against intermarrying, especially with the Orientals. You did not heed her admonition. Now look at what your son has chosen for a bride. Even worse than a negra portuguesa."

"Hush now, Tova," Rex Soares scolded. "You made Carlotta wear it too, you know," he continued, his eyes lingering above his plate. "It is a wonder she did not take it with her to the Azores. She took everything else. Maybe Ezroh is right. It is time for—"

"You listen, Rex, and you heed my good word. Let me remind you that it was yours truly who told you over and over even with the first one, do not marry that illiterate Maldonado girl. They have bad blood and bad teeth, those Cape Verde Island Maldonado women. Sure enough, she dies in childbed, the keiki perishing too, God rest their eternal souls. And then that Barboza harlot from who knows what kind of Madeira gypsy lineage, I told you, Rex, I said, 'Rex, do not marry that whore.' Sure enough, she runs after that Graciosa sailor with all your keiki. You are so sad. Your life is so very sad," she said, wiping the sweat from her flushed brow with a lacy handkerchief clutched in her tubby fist. "But as our beloved mãe said time and time again, the blessed saints attend her soul, 'Whose fault is it when you do not listen to your big sister?' "

Anah stepped to the kitchen window. Nohea's daughters followed her as she gathered ferns and blossoms that she would weave into beautiful haku lei. Ricardo sharpened his knife, then picked his teeth with its tip as he stood by the pigsty. The noisy hens gathered around Kenji and Ai-chan as they walked around the chicken yard.

In just one week, Anah would no longer live in the small, dusty room in Aunty Tova and Uncle Marcus's home way beyond the feeding sheds near the vast north pasture. In just one week, she would no longer cook three meals a day, sweep and mop the rooms, wash and iron the laundry for Aunty Tova. She had forbidden Anah to stay in the main house upon her arrival at the ranch.

"Over my dead body," she'd said, pounding the table with her thick fist. "Tell your brother, Lydia. Our mother would turn in her grave, God bless her eternally resting soul, to have this Jezebel lay in sin with her grandson before marriage. And what, with Rex in the doggone main house, he is a bachelor man, and Ezroh, the Jezebel shalt not tempt my nephew, and that drunken old Okinawan, who knows what he will do in his soused state. Heaven forbid, lest they all commit adultery and walk in lies. Never."

Anah stared out the kitchen window. Nohea secured infant Brittania in her sling as she headed to clean the bunkhouse for the bachelor men. Ricardo spat at the slow, coconut-fattened boar in the slaughtering pen. Kenji gathered eggs in the chicken yard and Ai-chan carried them in the scoop of her apron. Anah listened to Aunty Tova's excuses in Portuguese as she justified her own laziness from the next room.

"Because if Lydia was not lugging around that ten-ton load of pregnancy, Rex, you know I would be of more help to you down here. I do not know why she and Nohea both hāpai at the same time. Does it not seem that they conspire against me with their pregnancies? It does not make sense with the two of them unable to perform their duties and chores. I cannot do all of the work for three women, you know. How many times did I tell you that? And now you want to have this big wedding? Right after seven weeks of the Festa de Espírito Santo. We are all so very worn and tired. I will do what I can as is humanly possible," she said, "but Lydia is of my utmost concern and I hope and pray—"

Anah let her voice trail off.

Outside, Kahalelehua and Ricardo soaked old bread with kava to feed to the fat European boar they planned to slaughter for the wedding. The boar ate heartily, his sad eyes rolling before he stumbled headfirst into the concrete trough and passed out. Ricardo quickly slit his silent throat, the thick blood gurgling and spurting into a bucket for the morcelas. They hoisted the pig by the hind legs from a tree with rope and pulley, then scalded the coarse, mottled hair from its body. Ricardo sliced its gullet open, the swift flicking of his knife removing quivering heart, liver, kidneys, lungs, stomach, and fat, as he and Kahalelehua cleaned it for the viewing celebration. Tora-san turned the intestines inside out to scrape them clean on a metal tube contraption he rigged up for making sausage casings.

At pau hana time, the cowboys and ranch hands gathered around the huge pig, Uncle Marcus strumming his ukulele with Uncle Stanley on his old rajczo. Ezroh sang a sweet falsetto, looking for Anah's face in the window as Aunty Tova supervised her preparation of the pig head soup and the delicacy of lung and heart stew.

Tora-san sliced the raw pig ear and cheek meat into a mimiga nu sashimi, showing Anah how to make his secret peanut and vinegar dipping sauce, so secret that, "I no tell nobody, even though everybody like know my secret. And you no tell Ai-chan, o-kay? She ask me all the time, ask, ask, bodda, bodda. No tell now, or else, sugurarindo," he said, playfully threatening Anah with a closed fist in her face.

"You better hurry and get the brine and salt crocks ready for the pig, Anah," Aunty Tova called from the table. "And stop wearing Ezroh's clothes. Do you not have anything of your own to wear?

Mince the garlic, hurry, and the onions. Did you pick the hot peppers like I told you? Didn't I say we were making the sausages today? She is so slow minded," she whispered to Aunty Lydia. "And such a slow-moving snail. I pity you, Anah, when they slaughter the steer. No time for your dillydallying."

"I would help you, Anah," Aunty Lydia said, her hand on her enormous belly. She looked so tired and swollen. "But I cannot take three steps without hurting myself. Oh, I need to hānau this child soon. I am way past my due."

"Oh, stop it, Lydia." Aunty Tova grunted. "Why should we feel guilty about letting her do all the work? After all, it is *her* wedding. They did not make this much of a fuss for *you* or *me*. Why must I always question Rex's decisions? Our father should have never made him the head of this ranch because it implies that he is the head of this family when we all know that I am the matriarch as our mother was and her mother before—" Her voice droned on.

It was all so overwhelming and difficult. Anah didn't know where to begin, how to plan, what to do next and next and next, how to prepare all of the foods that would bring good fortune and happiness.

How Anah longed for her mother who knew the meaning of each dish she prepared every New Year's day at their home in Portuguese Camp Four at the O'ahu Sugar Plantation. Soba the buckwheat noodles for longevity, kuromame the black beans for good health, konbu maki the seaweed for happiness, sekihan the red rice for good luck, mochi the glutinous rice for prosperity, kazunoko the herring roe for fertility.

How Anah longed for her brother Charles who assisted her with her many chores and comforted her. Her brother who would give her hand in marriage to her betrothed.

Anah hadn't even begun to fix the dress Aunty Tova had brought out of her rotting beech wood chest full of mothballs. The dress looked like the clothing of a lost wraith, crumbling at Anah's touch.

"Oh, Tova, let bygones be bygones. Do not hold on to what is already long past. Our mãe and paipa smile upon all of us. This is a time for celebration." Aunty Lydia sighed, fanning herself with a strip of woven lauhala. Her two-year-old David tried to climb onto her lap. "Do not be so overbearing, sister. Mind your tongue. It is the girl's wedding, she knows that. That is why she is working so hard."

"My point exactly, dear one. It is *her* wedding. Not even a mama-san to help, imagine that! Do not even *think* we will be doing any of the labor. I am not her mother. You are not her mother. And I am not overbearing," she said. "Make some coffee with that fresh cream for Lydia and me, Anah," she demanded. "And stop listening to our conversation. We know very well that you understand Portuguese."

Anah kept her silence. Her place in the household of her husband-to-be according to its matriarch was beneath that of the animals. She made that clear to Anah as they sat to dinner every night in their home in the north pasture.

Anah lifted David into her arms, his brother Michael running about her knees with a fistful of wilting dandelions. "Leave them, Anah," Aunty Lydia said. "You have so much to do." Anah placed her swollen red feet on a small stool. Aunty Lydia managed to smile at her.

"Look at her tending to you, Lydia, like a kowtowing coolie. Please, Anah," Aunty Tova said with a laugh, "your Oriental blood is becoming all too prominent." She looked out the window. "They should have slaughtered the pig long ago. Marcus told him to slaughter the steer too, long ago. But does he listen? I do not know what in heaven's name is wrong with Rex," Aunty Tova complained, shoving a biscuit slathered in butter and honey into her mouth. "He never listens to me. And you think he listens to Marcus? No wonder Carlotta ran away. You would have run away too. Our mother was right, Lydia, when on her deathbed she told me to watch with vigilance over the affairs of our brother, especially the affairs of his heart—"

"Monkutare," Tora-san whispered, placing two cups of coffee on the table. "Gachimayā buta-chan, no do nothing but monku."

Anah did not even look up when she responded to him in Japanese, "Calling her a big fat pig and a complainer will do nothing to change her."

"Eat, shit, and complain," he said to Anah.

"Watch your tongue, motherless orphan. And you keep muttering under your drunken breath, you decrepit old man, and I will have Rex send you packing. Heathen Okinawan thinks he runs the whole dairy. Did I not tell you, Lydia? Even this idol-worshipping pagan thinks he can speak to me in this way. That is what happens when our brother gives him the woman's run of his house. We should have stayed up in the north pasture and left them to their own wedding preparations."

Nohea sat on the porch with her newborn, her daughters Mariah and Joyce at her feet, sorting the washtubs full of liko lehua, a'ali'i, bougainvillea, Spanish moss, gardenia, and kukui blossoms they would weave into haku lei for the wedding. She was humming a lullaby Anah once knew.

How Anah longed for her mother who would brush her hair with sweet oil, place flowers in a crown of blossoms, hum a lullaby Anah still knew by heart.

How Anah longed for her brother who would defend her against the constant brutal attacks of Ezroh's Aunty Tova.

Ezroh sidled up behind her as she stood at the kitchen sink, pressing himself against her back. "When this is all over," he whispered into Anah's ear, his breath on her neck, "my terrible aunt will go home to the north pasture for good and you will come home as my wife to the main house forever."

Anah turned her body to face his, his lips on hers.

"Ezroh, get out of the kitchen!" Aunty Tova yelled, waving her lace handkerchief in the air. "Rex, Ezroh is in the kitchen! With her! Bad luck, such bad luck. What is wrong with you, Rex! Our beloved mother is turning in her grave—"

"Ezroh, get me two bottles of Comet Whiskey from the liquor cabinet," his father yelled from the fire outside, all of the men gathered near the pig hanging from the tree. "And join the menfolk for a wedding toast."

The cowboys yipped and hollered. Kahalelehua got up to dance a jig with Kenji. Ricardo fell backward off a log in laughter. Uncle Stanley swigged his homemade kickapoo from a jelly jar. Uncle Marcus sang sweet and high.

Tora-san cussed over his kitchen duty. "Make me slave. I not wahine. How come I do all woman work? Me, ikiga!" he said, hitting his chest. "Me, man!" He coughed. He swiped the metal plates from the sink.

Anah began to pick them up. "Go," she told him. "Go. I clean 'til all pau. You are," she told him in his native Uchinanchu, his eyes meeting hers, "a very good man."

"What in hell's name is going on in there, Anah?" Aunty Tova yelled over the rising festivities outside. "You make that old man clean up that doggone mess you both made."

"You no mo' mama," Tora-san said sadly, "and no mo' papa." He placed Anah's face in his rough hands. "I tell myself when I sick, 'Toranosuke Goya, if you live, you do everything to repay Anah-san and Sister Mary Deborah take care you and make sure you no ma-ke'—"

"Never mind, you go numun with Ezroh," Anah said, giving him a gentle push on his shoulders. "And have a drink for me too. That make me happy."

"Arigatō," Tora-san said, wiping his hands on his apron, "sank you, Anah-san, sank you." Bowing, bowing, his hands pressed together. "Anah-san, I not saki jōgu, you know," he said, tipping his thumb toward his mouth, then staggering like a drunkard.

"I know," she told him, "you not saki jōgu." Yet later that night, she would cover his drunken body, passed out on the roadside, with a warm horse blanket.

He looked at Anah from the doorway for a long time, then left the kitchen. Was it a look of compassion? Pity? Shame? Anah told him again, "Go, go. No worry." He disappeared into the darkness. She stared at the mess. She did not know where to start.

ANAH AWOKE the next morning at the kitchen table to the sound of eggs being beaten in a bowl, the smell of fresh bread coming from the forno outside, fofas and cavacas rising under damp kitchen towels. She squinted at the face looking down at her, the face framed by the sunlight that hurt her tired eyes.

"Aunty Chong Sum?" Anah was barely able to utter the words.

She smiled. "No, not Aunty. Good morning, sleepyhead," Pa-ke Doh Nee said. "I making Chong Sum 'Hoping for Good Husband' cake," she said. "Very sweet, this wedding cake." She held Anah and patted her head. "Yo' pig head soup very ono, Anah. Bumbye me and you wash-wash the pig guts, we make the fresh blood morcelas. You marry the Pukikī, you better cook the Pukikī food. Thass what Chong Sum say."

"They like me make coelho guisado, but they neva skin the rabbits yet. And the cream laranja, that Mr. Soares's favorite, and the arroz doce, and the taro fritters."

She put her hands on Anah's shoulders. "Thass why Chong Sum tell me go, go, hurry, hurry. I hup, hup help Anah-san."

"And me kokua the Pa-ke girl," Aunty Lydia said from the doorway. She sat at the small table in the kitchen. "I no can hali nothing too heavy, but I get mouth like luna tell the Pa-ke what fo' do and how fo' do the Portuguese way."

"Me know how to cook the Pukikī food," Doh Nee said to her with mild arrogance. "Me work the cookhouse Samoa. Many Pukikī sailor man. No humbug," she reassured Anah. "Look," she whispered, pointing out the window.

"What?" Anah's eyes searched the yard. "Pa-ke Melvin!" Anah yelled. He stopped arranging huge bouquets of red torch and shell ginger, giant heliconia, wild vanda, and stalks of green and red ti to wave his whole body at her. He pointed toward the main house, mouthing something over and over.

"Look-see, look-see. All nice-nice."

They had already wound strands of fragrant maile, pakalana, and stephanotis vines around the banisters and poles. The mule cart by the lānai was still full of huge floral bouquets and tall banana and palm fronds to decorate each window, post, and step with the bounty they all had harvested from the valley.

Pa-ke Doh Nee placed her hands on Anah's shoulders. She led her to the dining table.

"Sister Mary Deborah?"

In the morning sunlight, her face was so beautiful. How many days Anah had spent memorizing each line that smiled, the curve of jaw, weathered skin, her lips saying a silent Rosary, murmuring a passage of Scripture.

Anah placed her face inside her hands.

She sat there at the dining table with a threaded sewing needle held between her teeth, her hands intent on darning the frayed edges of Anah's borrowed wedding dress. She stopped to look up at Anah, weaving the needle into the garment before speaking. "I have treated the fabric with some lemon juice and Clorox liquid bleach. It will take the yellow discoloration and these stains right out."

Anah fell to her knees before the holy sister. "Thank you, Sister Mary Deborah."

"Get up now, Susanah," she said. "Chong Sum has been gracious enough to send her family to assist you in your preparations; however, I regret that the reverend mother has forbidden her to leave St. Joseph's. But there is plenty of work to do and much assistance, for our labor is not in vain to the Lord our God."

"How you knew I was—" Anah stammered. "I neva think I would eva be ready befo' they drove the herd up mauka. Then I would have to live with *her* way up there in the north pasture for another year because I wasn't married. How you knew?" Anah slumped down beside her. "Get so much work fo' do. I dunno where fo' start. Who told you?"

Tora-san tripped, hitting his hip on the edge of the table. "Owee, itai, itai, move outta my way, Anah-san, ai-ya, shi-shi come out now, see? Itai, itai," he complained, rubbing the sore spot. He poured a cup of tea for Sister Mary Deborah, placing a plate of soft honey and coconut cookies on the table. He burped the stale smell of last night's whiskey and Bull Durham. "Gomenasai, nei."

"You are excused." Sister Mary Deborah smiled. "I knew because our good Lord, sweet Susanah, sometimes works in very mysterious ways," she said, looking with fondness at Tora-san.

Near noontime, the cookhouse brimming with the activity of Pa-ke Doh Nee, Tora-san, Ai-chan, and Anah's labor with Aunty Lydia's supervision, everyone stopped at the sudden thunder of horses' hooves. Clouds of fine dust moved into the cookhouse.

"Stampede!" Tora-san yelled, pulling off his apron and running to the door. "Get the keiki inside the cookhouse bumbye they get trample!"

"Anah! Anah!" Ezroh called from the makeshift festa grounds near the butter house. "Come, quick, come!"

Anah rushed outside.

There was no stampede.

Tora-san smiled meekly. "Gomenasai. Mistake, mistake. So sorry. No mo', no mo' stampede," he said, waving his apron in the air as if to erase his error.

Matthew and Bert rode alongside Ezroh, their hats and horses adorned with fresh plumeria lei. Uncle Stanley and Uncle Marcus followed with Rex Soares and Ricardo, cowboys and horses wearing Nohea, Mariah, and Joyce's beautiful strands and strands of plumeria lei.

Anah ran toward Ezroh, who released the towrope pulling Miss Barbara Mullen, a gentle quarterhorse mare he had given to her. He had named her for his favorite teacher. Anah got up on Miss Barbara, her mane and tail braided with delicate lavender heather, and lifted David and Michael on the saddle with her. They followed the cowboys, the little boys squealing with excitement.

Ai-chan, Nohea and her eleven children, Sister Mary Deborah, Pa-ke Doh Nee, Pa-ke Melvin, and Tora-san threw flowers as they gathered along the roadside when, from the north pastures, Kahalelehua and Kenji drove a mighty steer adorned with plumeria lei and ti leaf streamers through and around the ranch in his final parade before slaughter, everyone clapping and cheering, dancing and laughing, the bright of this day filled with clouds of flowers and dust.

ANAH WOULD MARRY Ezroh on the morning of May 25, 1924.

THE MIST LINGERED along the cliffs of the Koʻolau Mountains, veils of white, the fairy terns gliding in and out of the high ridges, blue sky lifting into the cool of spring's breath, the valley walls wet with morning.

Nohea placed a haku lei of orange kaunaʻoa on Anah's head, then a lei of kaunaʻoa wrapped with thick maile around her neck.

"The motherless plant," she whispered. "Fo' you who no mo' mamasan, yet you get plenny mamas o' here."

Pa-ke Melvin placed coins wrapped in red paper in one hand and a huge bright navel orange in the other.

"Orange mean good luck and leesee for you—take-take. Chong Sum save leesee fo' you, please accept from Chong Sum. She like give to you, *her* Anah."

Tora-san peered at the women from the door to the kitchen. He whispered something to Ai-chan, then hurried away.

"Tora-san say give this to you, Anah." She placed in Anah's hand a clean handkerchief embroidered by a girl's clumsy fingers with four-leaf clovers, stars, crucifixes, snakes, and horseshoes folded around a wad of money. In his crude scribble, Anah read his note, Good luck me. Now good luck you. T. Goya.

Anah lowered her eyes, unable to take in their kindness.

"I want to be set free," Sister Mary Deborah whispered into the still of that moment.

No one spoke for what seemed forever.

"I want to free," Anah responded at last.

"I want to hear," she said, her voice sure, strong.

"I want to be heard," Anah answered, the memory of these words choking in her throat.

"Sweetness dances," she said, taking Anah's hand in hers.

"I want to pipe; all of you dance." Anah held her warm fingers, the soft of her palms.

"I want to make you beautiful," she said, standing Anah up and straightening her white wedding dress.

"I want to be beautiful," Anah said, meeting her eyes at last.

"I have no house," she said.

"And I have houses."

"I have no ground," she said.

"And I have ground."

"I want to join with you." Everyone turned toward the voice from the kitchen door. Ezroh stood across that threshold, his shirt starched white, a handsome black tie, black trousers, new suspenders, fancy leather boots.

Nohea placed a lei of kauna'oa and maile on his neck. She wove another lei around his black cowboy hat. Ezroh placed his hat on the table as he stepped into the room.

"And I want to be joined," Anah answered him.

Sister Mary Deborah placed Anah's hands in Ezroh's.

"If you look at me, I will be a lamp," Anah said to him.

"If you see me, I will be a mirror." He smiled, remembering their many days of catechism, Sister Bernadine's strict memorization drills.

"If you knock on me, I will be a door," Anah told him, as he put his arms around her waist, drawing her to him, encircling her in his protection.

"If you are a traveler," he whispered to only her, petting her with his gentle hand, "I will be a road."

They wept together, Anah and Ezroh, the room still but for the hushed breath of mothers and daughters, someone humming a lullaby Anah once knew.

"This is my dance," Anah told Ezroh, his eyes in hers.

"Then answer me with dancing," he said, spinning her around once for him alone to see.

Sister Mary Deborah put her arms around both of them, Father Maurice calling them outside to "Hurry, children let us begin the wedding ceremony," the invited nuns and neighbors restless and hungry.

Aunty Tova yelling, "Bad luck, I tell you, bad luck, the groom seeing the bride like that. Cursed, I tell you cursed, you mark my words."

Aunty Lydia fanning herself. "It is so doggone hot out here. Where are they? Why has the father not started the ceremony? The children are hungry."

The musicians playing traditional favorites from the Azores on their ukulele, taro patch fiddle, rajczo, and braguinha, dogs barking, chickens squawking, the children running about up and down the stairs of the cookhouse.

"Remember always, my children," the sister whispered to Anah and Ezroh, "the kingdom of God is within you."

Three Days, Three Nights

His room is filled with flowers, on the floor, on the bed, blossoms in bowls of clear water. He lights beeswax candles, the slow igniting of wicks, the delicate drip of wax away from trade wind.

The man and woman sit on the floor. He begins to unhook the clasps of her bodice.

She places her fingers under his suspenders and drops them from his shoulders.

The lantern breathes, the candles glint.

The cowboys are serenading the night outside, singing and dancing under the paper lanterns, round and round under the canopy of night, this night of white stars over valley ridges etched against the black canvas of sky.

The wedding dress falls around her waist.

He removes the pins from the binding cloth around her breasts, lifting her arms as he slowly unwinds the length of fabric. She closes her eyes to the slow circular motion, feels his warm hands, his warm lips on her naked breasts, kissing the halo of aureole, the gentle motion of his tongue.

His shirt open, she moves her hands over his skin, the width of his shoulders, removes his sleeves one by one, shirt falling behind him, his chest bare and shiny.

Hours they sit on the floor of his room, mouths moving over skin, touching each other, smelling each other, tasting each other, the brine of his throat, the spice of her spine, the varying ecstacies in crevices.

There is no hurry.

Has he known this love before her?

He leads her hands. She touches him there, the length of him there, smells the palms of her hands, her fingers. He leads her there. She eats him, his back arching as she takes him into her mouth, his soft moaning, a child's soft whimper. She kisses him there, the sweet heady musk of horses, dust, and flowers.

Has she known this love before him?

The moonlight enters the room from the window facing the sea. She stands naked in that light, pours cool water into the washbasin and puts it on the floor between them.

She dips a sponge in the water and bathes him, the water falling between the floorboards, washes his eyelids, his cheeks, his chin, runs her fingers through his hair, wets her fingertips and he drinks from them, his body wet, flesh shivering with her light touch, she washes his feet.

He bathes her with the cool water, tracing the outline of face, hollow of throat, breasts, circling and circling, circle belly, circle back, circle buttocks, the V of pubis, he spreads her legs.

They look at each other with tenderness, the tenderness of history and childhood, knowing always, longing a tangible entity, as he enters, slowly, she does not cry out, her vaginal mouth opening to him wet and warm.

They are the moment of one body, his heart melting into the empty spaces of her heart.

The hours pass in a numb euphoria.

A soft knock at the door. It is already early morning. The smell of blood sausages and biscuits, hot coffee, a fresh pitcher of water, cold milk, two shots of sake, and a plate of honeycomb left for them on a tray.

Outside, the muffled lowing of cows come to morning milking in the barn.

They feel the cool trades carrying the scent of night-blooming jasmine over naked skin, see the veils of white over the Koʻolau Mountains, white stars on a lavender canvas, listen to a quiet braguinha strumming to a fading fire, taste the inside of wrists with a hungry tongue, as you enfold me, my only love, in your favorite yellow blanket.

19

FEBRUARY 28, 1925

The moon was full. Its light slipped into the room a lunar yellow. Anah listened to the slap of reins, the jingling of bell spurs, the muffled clop of horses' hooves, dawn's departure of the cowboy gang to repair fences, build the new pipelines, plant the pines along the north side of the property as windbreaks.

She sat in a rocking chair by the window. She had not found sleep for two weeks, the discomfort of skin pulling taut with the extra weight of child when she lay on her side, the breathless crush of internal organs when she lay on her back, the ache of neck, shoulders, and breasts, her hands and feet swollen to a translucent pink shine, her thoughts vague and clouded.

She closed her eyes and remembered her okaasan heavy with another girl child. She was crying in a rocking chair by the window of their house in Portuguese Camp Four. It was 1908, the year a new group of sea-weary immigrants arrived from the sugar district about Málaga, Spain, some dark skinned, some light skinned.

Anah remembered her okaasan's rejection of the child, the Okinawan midwife chiding her to breast-feed, *quickly Sumi-chan,* the child hungering for her mother's milk. *Too soon, too many keiki, these Portuguese. Much too soon*. Anah remembered the look of absence on her okaasan's face, her spirit hollow, her soul bare.

Anah stared at the shape of the child inside her, two weeks late now, conceived on her wedding night, the slow movement of a protruding arm or leg in the perfect orb of her moon belly, the child inside restless, as she rocked slowly in the chair, the snuffling of the milkers known to Anah by name moving to the barn, to warm and clean stalls, Kenji pitching timothy grass, corn stalks, and pineapple bran in heaping portions for each of the udder-heavy cows.

Tora-san knocked at her door. "Anah-san, you awake? I see light under the door. You hungry?" He paused for her answer.

Anah sighed.

"Keiki no come yet, Anah-san?"

"Not yet," she answered. "Come in."

"Maybe I call midwife just in case you hānau today," he said, coming into the room with a glass of cool milk, fragrant tea, and a slice of his banana bread. "Maybe you give birth today."

"No. No call her," she told him. "Bumbye she hu-hū come all the way up here fo' nothing."

"You not nothing," he said, rubbing Anah's back. "She get smart with me, that doggone Ryoki-san, I tell her, 'Go hell and no come back. This Anah-san numba-one baby.' I tell her, 'She have no mama to help her. You be little mo' nice, you flat-nose jefe-san.' "

"I know what you mean. She talks and talks and talks," Anah muttered. "She get answers fo' everything." She tried to get up, gripping the armrest of the rocking chair. She groaned, sitting back down. Anah closed her eyes.

"Yukuimi sōre," Tora-san encouraged her.

"I no can rest," Anah said. "This baby no like me sleep."

"Maybe you drink this lemon balm tea, make you go moe-moe little while."

"No can sleep," Anah told him again.

"Try, you try, yukuyan." He put a light blanket over her shoulders. "Rest, rest," he said, patting her head. "I bring you papaya later on so you make big kūkae, clean you out then you feel better," he said, closing the door behind him.

The morning appeared through the dark.

'Anah,' a voice rasped behind her. 'Anah.' She turned her head slowly to the corner of the room, a small figure standing there, weeping.

Seth?

He stared straight at her:

'Curse you, whore.'

Anah screamed. And then her water broke.

THROUGHOUT ANAH'S ENSUING LABOR, Tora-san refused to leave the room. Even when Ryoki Sunabe, the chatterbox midwife, berated him for getting in the way, for intruding on women's business, for bringing his stinking yang into the room, he remained beside Anah, holding her hand when the worse waves of contractions clutched at her body, soothing her with his gentle words, a cool towel refreshing her brow.

As far as he was concerned, he was second in command, ordering Nohea to bring the bottle of pain tonic he had made by mixing the juices of moa, the primitive chicken feet plant, and pua kala, the prickly poppy, with Hawaiian salt, shaking the dregs from the bottom of the bottle, then feeding Anah a tablespoonful every half hour.

Ryoki Sunabe winced, calling him a meddling woman, a māhū mu'umu'u-wearing busybody, a no-good maiden sister, and even an irritating white-haired, old hāmē with no teeth. Still, he stayed, orchestrating the vigorous boiling then thick simmering of the pigs' feet soup by ordering Ai-chan around. He told her to imbue the broth with a whole bottle of his homemade sake. And he made sure the gelatinous pig knuckles were precisely soft enough for the moment the baby arrived to ensure the free flow of Anah's breast milk.

He updated Ezroh himself with a quick whisper at the door. No one dared to sit in the chair he left empty beside Anah's bed. "No, you no worry, Ezroh. Anah-san screaming anykine crazy things when water broke."

"What she was telling me Seth, Seth?"

"No, no mo' Seth. Anah-san little bit lōlō. Talk any kine crazy. Keiki coming thass why—"

He'd quickly return to her bedside. He even ordered Ezroh to boil kettle after kettle of water and to go wait outside. *He* was in the way. He comforted Ezroh that Anah's awful words about him were the result of a momentary insanity.

Anah had never known this kind of pain, the maddening rush of violence seizing the muscles and nerves of her body. She would never enjoy relations with Ezroh again, she vowed to herself. She would tell him all about his brother Seth. Tell him from beginning to end. Call Seth to comfort her. Seth who would never do this to her. Never let Ezroh touch her, do this to her ever again.

Anah gritted her teeth and bore down in her delirium whenever the midwife yelled for her to do so, Tora-san supporting her aching back as she pressed and pressed, her child's head crowning at last but unable to come out into the world for what seemed forever.

Anah lost consciousness for a moment when, all of a sudden, she was awakened by a burning fissure between her legs as Ryoki Sunabe sliced her from vagina to anus with a razor blade, screaming, "Usun! Usun!" as she clutched the baby's head in her slippery forceps, pulling fiercely on an eye that would be lost. "Push! Push!"

"A girl," she said at last, the lanugo covering the newborn's bluish body in a fuzzy, white-gray membrane.

"Look, look what you have done to Anah's baby, you horrible mule," Tora-san said to the midwife in their native Okinawan.

She continued cleaning the infant.

"Oh, my goodness, what do I say to Ezroh?" he cried, hitting her with a damp towel. "You useless old woman."

Ryoki Sunabe turned to face him. "The girl did not push. The girl did not listen. You saw her fall asleep. If I hadn't pulled the baby out, it would have died inside her. You should be grateful to me. I saved the lives of both mother and child. It is the girl's fault, not mine." She bandaged the bloody eye with strips of rag. "Next time, you call the Pilipine. See if she will come all the way up here into this valley with no road. No, you call the Portagee. I hear she lost three keiki and a young mother last week. No blame me."

The midwife swaddled the infant and placed her in Anah's arms. Anah did not scream at her bloodied, bandaged little eye, Ezroh's quiet tears of pity as he sat beside her. It would make her daughter strong.

Anah thanked God with endless hosannas as she held her first beautiful child in her arms, her *only* blood relation, her breast milk coming in abundance thanks to Tora-san's soup, better than the soup the midwife brought on the day of Nohea's birthing.

"Sing hosanna to the King of kings," Anah said to her soft tufts of brown Portuguese hair, her tiny Japanese nose on her round face, her strong pink hands:

Hosana Soares, the one-eyed girl who would one day break her cousin David's finger for trying on her eye patch for fun;

the one-eyed girl who beat up Kahalelehua's eighth son Kawelo for hitting her blind side in a muddy game of pasture football;

the one-eyed girl who *accidentally* dropped a hammer on her cousin Michael's head from the mango tree for teasing her sister, the prongs embedding in his skull;

the one-eyed girl who spit in Ricardo's food and drink for months for nicknaming her Makapa'a;

the one-eyed girl who raised an injured pueo she found after her grandfather amputated its gangrenous wing;

Anah bore the secret and pain of her child's curse, never telling Ezroh of Seth's appearance in her room that day. He was only a figment of her vague delusions.

Still, she faced the pillow of her infant southward like her mother had instructed to ward off the dead; she placed azuki beans in the four corners of her room to keep spirits at bay; she spit on her comb before grooming her baby as was the good luck superstition of her Portuguese grandmother and aunts; she placed a crucifix above the doorway to their room, a crucifix above each window.

Over many years, she nurtured her one-eyed Hosana Soares who sat shotgun to her father on business and supply trips downtown, driving the new delivery truck for him or loading bags of rice and grain onto the bed;

the young woman who roped and mugged calves for branding and castration with the cowboys, inoculating the calves for pinkeye and dehorning with her own pair of large, sharp cutters;

the young woman who rolled a sturdy Bull Durham with home-grown, charcoal-roasted tobacco for her grandfather Rex from his hand-carved pahu puhi paka tobacco box every evening, keeping him company on the lānai as he told her the stories of his mother from the Azores, a founding member of the Portuguese Ladies Society of Honolulu and his father, a burly Cape Verdean whaler out of New England;

the young woman who stood by her mother in defiance of the horrible jibes and innuendo of her Portuguese aunts, her mother's true blood relation;

the young woman who fiercely defended her sister Elizabeth, the lohi'au who seldom spoke throughout her childhood, carrying a hunting knife to school to defend her sister from those who unmercifully teased and taunted, the retard, the idiot lohi'au, the cuckoo bird Elizabeth Soares.

SHE WAS CURSED from her conception in Anah's womb just weeks after Hosana's birth. Of that Anah was certain. *Too soon, too many keiki, these Portuguese. Much too soon.* The festering little worm inside of Anah that failed to make her belly grow large and robust. So when the girl child came much before her time, the earliness of her birth was confirmation of that bad omen.

But it was the time of Epiphany, the cowboys and ranch hands singing and folk dancing in a circle of lanterns outside of the cookhouse, the women and children in colorful clothing and feathered masks, Aunty Lydia baking her famous Bolo de Reis full of raisins, nuts, and candied fruit, a true crown of the magi full of sweet jeweled morsels.

Anah put all thoughts of misfortune and doom out of her mind, indulging Ezroh's daily partaking of her voluptuous body. He had never questioned her after the birth of his first child: *Why did you call out my dead brother's name?* And she, grateful for his silence and disregard, grateful for never questioning her superstitious practices to ward off the dead, gave even more freely and willingly of herself to him.

They would all take a moonlight ride in the wagon to attend a late Mass at St. Joseph's, then return to the ranch for more celebration. Anah, still small in her seventh month, had decided to go to Mass on the new Raleigh bicycle Ezroh had given to her as a birthday present months before.

Ezroh had taught her to ride that bicycle before he knew she was with child again, promising to take her with him through the streets of Chinatown to find a Chinese herbalist. She wanted a vial of powdered deerhorn to hang around the neck of her newborn infant until her christening to ward off evil spirits.

Ezroh began by balancing Anah from three feet away from the steps to the main house, moving to four feet, then pushing her off at five. He ran alongside as she took to the open road with a kind of giddy freedom.

Ezroh was always surprised at Anah's agility and perseverance, dodging stones and climbing small pu'u in the pastureland, riding her bicycle along the road taking baby Hosana tucked snugly inside the wire basket for a short ride. Anah's strong baby squealed with glee.

"Get that crazy fool of a wife in here, Ezroh," Aunty Tova scolded in Portuguese. "Does she not realize that she is seven months pregnant? And very small for seven months, if you ask me. Is that fool wife of yours nourishing herself, Ezroh? My vovó always said, 'A goose, a woman, and a goat are bad things lean.' Look at how thin she is. Are you sure she has counted right? Maybe she is only four or five months along."

Ezroh did not answer. He watched his Anah with great joy for her unbridled happiness, for her childlike gaiety, for that moment as he stood on the porch watching his wife and child ride a red bicycle in the sunlight of the valley.

"You want her to lose your child and take the first one with her while she is at it? Is that what you want, nephew? Your carelessness is appalling. You are worse than your father, who was utterly careless with his wives and children," Aunty Tova yelled at him. "And look what that has gotten your father. No wife and no children. Tell Anah to get over here and help us load the wagon with the food for Mass."

"You are right as usual, Aunty Tova. You, of all people, have never been wrong. No, not you. Anah!" he called to her, laughing from the lānai of the cookhouse. "We need to take the malassadas and the farturas to the church." The smell of the fresh pastries rose around him as he waved his arms for her to come over. "Hurry, you need to dress the children in their costumes."

In the wonderful Christmas pageant at St. Joseph's, Mariah would be the Virgin Mary in a dress of blue and a veil of white; David was a handsome Joseph with a beard made of rabbit pelt; Aunty Lydia's twins Sammie and JohnJohn were the front and back of the donkey that carried the Virgin Mary to Bethlehem; and tonight, her beautiful Hosana would star as the baby Jesus cooing in the manger.

Anah turned the bicycle around, the cool of the winter evening in her face, her eyes lingering shut for a peaceful, happy moment when there by the mango tree a small figure stood, just over there, weeping, rasping her name, 'Anah.'

Seth.

He stared straight at her:

'Curse you, whore.'

Anah screamed, the bicycle crumbling like crushed tinfoil into the tree outside the main house, Hosana crawling out of the basket, Anah's body splayed on the dusty roadside.

Her water broke.

ELIZABETH WEIGHED just two pounds, fit in the palms of Anah's hands, her head deformed and wrinkled, eyes bulbous and insectlike, a bald-headed, varicose-veined, pink creature with labored breathing and soundless cry.

Ezroh, lost in his own grief and blame, remained in a drunken stupor for weeks, taking bed in the bunkhouse and comfort in the bottle. No one dared speak to him as they washed the separator or console him as they took the cream cans to the roadside shack, his temper quick and mean.

"We must baptize her now," Father Maurice said to Anah and Rex Soares. "If we do not, this child will not be an heir of heaven but be eternally in the place of limbo.

Do not let Susanah become attached to this child," Father Maurice whispered to Rex Soares. "I am certain that our merciful Lord will take the child into his loving fold soon."

"Get Ezroh from the mauka paddock and bring him o' here," Mr. Soares said to Tora-san, who lingered by the door.

"Me no know where he stay," the old man said. "I wen' go look-look up in the mountains for him already. No mo' Ezroh."

Anah held her fragile child. Ezroh's weakness only made her stronger. Her child would not die. Anah would not let her die. Anah would not allow Father Maurice to baptize her just hours after her birth in anticipation of her death.

Her Elizabeth would live.

Tora-san boiled honey jars for Anah, sterilizing them for the breast milk she poured into baby bottles. Anah rolled balls of condensed milk and placed them in her tiny baby's mouth to soothe her just as Aunty Chong Sum had done for the orphaned babies. Anah fed her constantly, as much as she could drink, hour upon hour, alternating and sometimes overlapping feeding times with Hosana, who was still on the breast as well.

When Ezroh finally returned to the main house after severe chastising from Tora-san, he slept at the foot of the bed, waking with Anah through the night, feeding her foods rich in nutrients, Rex Soares forgoing his Portuguese meals for Tora-san's Okinawan fare.

Aunty Tova complained nightly about the horrible Oriental meals being served in the cookhouse. "They eat the flesh of swine every day, even on the Sabbath with those horrible root vegetables that taste of dirt. Everything he cooks tastes so primitive and ghastly," she grumbled, "like he does not take the care to wash off the chicken manure he uses as fertilizer in his dreadful garden." She stayed in the north pasture and forced Aunty Lydia to cook separate meals for their families.

The ranch hands and cowboys who ate to their absolute fill at the cookhouse were healthy and strong that winter season. They ate rich ōpū soup filled with pork stomach sliced thin; chi irichi, the sauteed pig's blood and fungus in a thick miso broth; sweet potato rice with the finest Japanese herbs Tora-san grew in their garden; the rich mountain oysters and beef tongue soaked in ginger, chives, garlic, and goma oil.

Anah remained sequestered in her room, her days and nights a determined blur of incredible food and water, prayers to the Holy Virgin, food and tea, incense and offerings of rice to appease the dead, food and milk, chanting her mother's nembutsu *Namu Amida Buddha* again *Namu Amida Buddha* and again, her body getting leaner and leaner with each passing week no matter how much she ate, her body depleted by an abundant production of thick milk.

Anah had no mother to help her, no sisters, no aunts, no grandmothers. Nohea, busy with her own eleven children, did what she could, sending her eldest Abigail along with Mariah and Joyce to assist Tora-san after school in the kitchen. Her sons Kaleiali'i, Kanae'aupuni, and Ethan helped Ai-chan, who performed Anah's chores along with her own chores.

Ezroh left with the cowboy gang before dawn but remained with Anah through each long night. He checked on Elizabeth's breathing, his sighing helpless and afraid. Anah knew that he and everyone else at the ranch blamed him for the child's early birth, so she vowed never to burden him with her acquaintance with Seth. She would keep Seth away with prayers, offerings, and incense. She comforted Ezroh with relations even as she slept, praying all the while that the next child and the next would not bring more catastrophe and sorrow.

ELIZABETH WOULD SURVIVE, a lean, shadowy child holding on to the hem of Hosana's shirt, thumb in mouth, blanket slung over her shoulder. She said not a word again until the day of her sixth birthday, when she looked at Hosana with her bird's talons locked onto the cloth wrapped around her arm and said, "Sista. Owl." She watched the world, her eyes bright, hair dark, handsome features of her father, but said nothing of its meaning to her.

Anah loved the purity of her simple heart. Her daughter cried over drowned field mice. She loved picking the wild violets by the bunkhouse. She gave rose apples to the tired cow ponies tethered in the shade of the shower tree. She fed motherless ducklings at the river's edge, then lured them to the goose pond crumb by crumb. She drew circles in the dirt as she waited for her father's return from the hills in the evening. She sobbed for the calves separated from the milking yearlings. Then one night, screamed insanely in the next room, for when she was just over a year old, Anah birthed the next, stillborn.

◇

IT WAS THE YEAR of Charles A. Lindbergh's solo transatlantic flight in the *Spirit of St. Louis*, electric plugs, flapper dresses, and international airmail. And it was a very prosperous year at the Soares Dairy.

Aunty Lydia was certain Anah would bear twins, recalling her own girth at the time of Anah's wedding. "You are as big as me, maybe even bigger," she said in Portuguese, running her warm hand over Anah's belly.

Anah groaned as she shifted her weight.

"Do you recall our vovó's Portuguese saying, 'What was hard to bear is sweet to remember'? Do you remember, Tova? Maybe Ezroh has two fine sons in here. That is why Anah is bearing the terrible discomfort of this pregnancy."

Aunty Tova looked at Anah and shook her head in disgust. "Two sons? Think again, sister. Then she would have birthed *four* babies in just under three years. We should all be praying she does not have twins. The girl can barely manage the two she already has. My goodness, she is better breeding stock than the Guernseys Rex purchased from the haole dairyman from Montana."

"Tova!" Aunty Lydia scolded. "You must watch the wickedness of your words. Do not judge Anah so harshly." She shooed several loudly crowing roosters from the lānai, then put a wedge of tangerine in Hosana's open mouth.

"Marcus told me the cowboys were laughing at you, Anah. They are calling you and Ezroh rabbits," Aunty Tova went on. "Just count back the months, sister," she whispered to Aunty Lydia. "Just like the coehlo in the hutches by the barn. No, I tell you what. Our nephew has little to do with her predicament. These are typical Oriental heathen behaviors. She has no regard for propriety. They do not even wait until her afterbirth bleeding finishes. How filthy is that? Even the breeding animals wait another season."

They both winced at the thought.

Anah was ashamed but would not let Ezroh's aunts have the benefit of her reaction to their remarks. She had already heard from Torasan how Ezroh's virility had been the subject of many a night's tales out in the fields. And if he was proud of his ardor, then so was she. They continued to have relations deep into each of Anah's pregnancies and just days after the birth of each child.

Anah had told herself, no matter the pain, no matter the outcome, she would never refuse Ezroh her body. *Never*. His children were a blessing unto her. They were her only *true* blood relations. All else was a figment of her imagination. She had left all of that behind on the bridge to St. Joseph's. She would give freely of herself to him. For he hungered for the taste and comfort of her flesh many times a day. And he desired many children, he had told her, many more sons than Kahalelehua.

"Enough already," Aunty Tova scolded Anah. "No more keiki. After this, you keep your legs closed. You do know that it is your frequent relations with my nephew that bring the children into the world, don't you, my dear?"

"Tova!" Aunty Lydia scolded. "Of course she knows. You do know, don't you, child?" she asked Anah in a whisper.

Anah nodded.

"Sleep in separate rooms," Aunty Tova commanded. "That is what you must do to tame the ardor of the menfolk. Marcus and I have not shared a bed for years now. I simply refused him the pleasures of the flesh. You must refuse my nephew the marital bed or you will be like the kanaka Kahalelehua who breeds like the field mouse in the summer. How shameful."

Anah said nothing, the heat of this August muggy and oppressive. The summer days were long ones. The women spent their afternoons in the cool of the expansive tree-shaded mauka lānai of the main house. David and Michael played in the dirt as twins Sammie and JohnJohn napped in the adjoining front room. Hosana stood on the corral where Ezroh spent his pau hana hours with Matthew and Bert, breaking a beautiful Hawaiian horse mix that would become Hosana's beloved companion.

Elizabeth lay asleep in the bassinet after a long afternoon of colicky crying, her body arched and tensed for hours, then finally withdrawn and twitching convulsively in a restless sleep. She fussed as she nursed, screamed and screamed inconsolably, then cat-napped day and night.

The weight of Anah's pregnancy, the heat of the summer's days, the need of her tiny infant daughter, the exuberance of her toddler daughter, the constant droning and nagging and heckling of Aunty Tova, chore upon chore, do this upon do that, Anah had succumbed to a kind of silent insanity that helped to let needs and wants, thoughts and words flow easily in and away from her, the moment of an eye's blink, a long, drawn-out slowing of her body's movement.

She had not prayed for weeks. She had not lit a stick of incense for a month. Nor had she offered rice, azuki beans, or rock salt. The ceremonial green ti leaves withered. Her mother's nembutsu was gone from her memory.

She was benumbed, even with Ezroh inside her body, believing and hoping that he would perceive her growing melancholia.

He did not.

Days into weeks into months. She believed she would tell him everything. Her fears of Seth's curse. Her silent dementia.

She did not.

Why would she not share with her beloved her fears for herself, for him, for their children? She could not. He would know, then they would all know:

It was *she* who was cursed. It was *she* who had brought the evil to their family. The misfortune. The calamity.

She was absent from her own body. She knew this when one afternoon, even shame and decency left her. She stood washing dishes at the kitchen sink. Ezroh returned from the branding, the air thick with the smell of burning hair, fat, and hide. She turned her face to him in greeting. He did not smile but came toward her, lifted her day dress, lowered his trousers, and took her at the kitchen sink. It lasted only a minute, she reasoned. No one saw what he had done. And he was able to continue his work in the corral for the remainder of the day, she reasoned.

Anah closed her eyes on the lānai to the constant need and want, the infant Elizabeth stirring awake in the bassinet.

Earlier in the day after the first milking, Anah watched Ai-chan help Tora-san clean up the breakfast dishes. She put a hearty serving of ukara irichī over a hot scoop of rice for Anah.

"You so skinny, Anah-san. Eat, eat plenty. C'mon, open yo' mouth," she coaxed, "bumbye you no can push this baby out."

"Nō, nihe dēbiru," Anah said, clamping her mouth shut to Ai-chan's spoon. "No, no thank you, no."

"You too good talk-talk the Uchinanchu," Tora-san said with pride. He ate a spoonful of his specialty, sweet ukara with honey, finely chopped green beans, carrots, spinach, shiso, and chives. "I dunno why they call this ukara buta kaukau. This too ono feed to the pig. My old hāmē, ninety-five year old, and my own anma, who still live in same shack where she had all us thirteen keiki, all time make this kaukau fo' us."

Ai-chan giggled. "They think we buta-chan eat the piggy food, no? They dunno"—she laughed—"that this not pig food." She cleaned the spoon in her mouth, smacking her lips and rubbing her belly. "C'mon, you try," she said to Anah.

Anah pushed the bowl away. She could not eat, her chest burning with each mouthful of food that lingered and fermented in the hollow space beneath her throat. She felt certain that if Ezroh understood her constant discomfort in pregnancy after pregnancy, he would be moderate in his relations with her. But he was not.

Anah was past her birthing date, again, the movement inside her diminishing from lack of space. There was no more room, not even for a spoonful of ukara and hot rice.

She sat at the table in the cookhouse, Tora-san trying to soothe Elizabeth as he mopped the floor, Hosana fighting off both David and Michael's advances on her kukui nut tops on the lānai. The juices inside Anah gurgled. Then all movement stopped.

"Tora-san!" she called, panicked. He put his mop down and shuffled over.

"No worry, keiki o-kay," he said to her even before she said a word. "Ai-chan, come, come. You all time tell me you yuta."

"Yes, me good fortune-teller just like my old hāmē and all before her."

"Then you tell the future to Anah-san what kine keiki, boy or girl, she get," he said, laughing.

Ai-chan lifted Anah's day dress and pulled her undergarment just below her huge swollen navel to examine its shape. "So, so," she said, probing with her finger. She put her ear to Anah's belly. "Nei, nei," she said with much seriousness. She closed her eyes and rubbed her hand briskly over the mound of skin. "Hai, hai," she said at last, patting Anah like a proud mother. "Two inside here. Two inagun gwa."

"Two girls?" Tora-san nodded. "Ai-ya, *two* mo' girls? You sure? How come only girl keiki, you, Anah-san?"

But Anah did not care. She would be blessed with two more healthy daughters.

Ai-chan held out her hand to Tora-san. "You, old hāmē-chan," she teased him, "pay up yo' two-bit, you old hag, to the fortune-teller."

"Akisamiyō!" he said, slapping her hand away.

AUNTY LYDIA PEELED another tangerine. It was an off-season fruiting of all of the citrus trees in the orchard. A strange abundance in a year of great profit.

Anah watched the cows running toward Kenji's voice for the afternoon milking, two brown pueo circling slowly overhead.

"And Marcus told Stanley and Rex, 'Looks like Ezroh's shooting only wahines. He must be a single-barrel, one-shot.'" Aunty Tova laughed. "They are all hoping you have a boy in there, Anah. But I do not think so," she said to Aunty Lydia in Portuguese. "Look at how she is carrying so low. She has another girl in there. Somebody sure has bad luck around here. At the rate they are going, we will have twenty Soares girls at the dairy in as many or less years. That's some dowry. Enough to keep Rex and Ezroh working the rest of their days. Such a pity to not have a male child."

Bad luck. Such a pity. Did they already know?

Anah watched the horse go round and round the training pole, her spirit unbroken even after hour upon hour of running, the swirl of dust, the swirl of heat waves, a brisk wind southerly, a brisk wind northerly, kona winds in the trees, the movement of low clouds in the evening sky, cattle dogs running and howling, mud hens appearing with loud croaks and cries, Ezroh running, Matthew running, Bert running, Aunty Tova talking, babies waking, whining, and demanding, Elizabeth screaming:

Hosana falls backward into the mad swirl of the corral, pushed by small invisible hands. No one sees her fall but Anah. All motion stops.

Anah heaves her body up from the chair, moves down the stairs and over to the corral, the moment of an eye's blink, long and drawn out. Anah will not get to her daughter before her face is trampled.

Hosana is lifted off her feet and up onto the unbroken filly.

In the swirl of dust and hooves, wind and leaves, heat and sod, a child squeals, high and giddy. Anah's daughter Hosana holds on, two white shapes riding with her on the back of that beautiful horse that comes to a slow trot. Ezroh then takes hold of the bridle.

Anah's water breaks.

Fortune-Teller

How come, Ai-chan? They big, healthy keiki, the first one Beatrix, the second one Bertha, but stay dead even when inside. You say you yuta. Then tell me how come. Tell Anah-san how come."

"I TELL YOU, Lydia, somebody sure has a curse on her."

"Do not talk like that, sister. We are not in the old country anymore."

"And she has brought the bad luck here, I just know it. It is so clear that the girl is cursed. Do you think our nephew knows? How can he not know?"

"Maybe it is our nephew who is cursed."

"Maybe it is our brother, and he has passed the curse from father to son."

'IN THE NAME of the Father and of the Son and of the Holy Spirit,' Ai-chan dreams, wandering free from her body.

Mud hens cry from the heart of themselves, sad and long. She listens to the story they tell her of a girl now woman at the river's edge alone, all night, alone. A small towheaded boy watches the woman from behind the trees.

Go away, Seth. Leave me alone, Seth.

Dogs howl into the hollow, dark spaces of forest, round vowels full of foreboding, the dark clouds filling the trees with more of the many, so many. But the woman sits at the river's edge alone.

Take your curse from me, Seth.

Horse eyes, red and yellow glow, ears pricked up, nostrils aflare. 'What do you smell, brave Nma, what do you hear, tell the woman, what do you see?'

See the brown owls circling overhead in an ominous prelude when Ai-chan dreams, wandering free from her body, a night of no moon, low clouds in a cloudless sky, citrus blossoms caught in the swirling winds.

'Anah-san, Anah-san, wake up,' she says to the woman. 'Let us meet beyond the light of the seven sisters.'

But the woman is tired, her vitreous heart shattering in the magnificence of this loss, dead babies wrapped in swaddling, she shrouds them with feathers her first child keeps in jars.

'Anah-san, wake up and see your two baby girls. See them with a girl in a yellow dress and a girl clothed in the valley's foliage, all holding hands, there standing under the pine trees.'

The woman will not see. She will not hear the festeras howling like hungry spirits on the day she falls onto the soft mulch that dirties the buried faces of her infant daughters, digging madly until she unearths their bodies, wiping away the dirt and leaves from their frozen eyelids with the hem of her dress, breathless nostrils, blue lips filled with dirt.

'Open your mouth, Anah-san, and call them to you, for they run, run from the small boy who throws glass at them. He catches them when they stumble, burns feathers in the palms of their tiny hands.

Oh, Anah-san, he is hurting your babies. Quick, call them to the light, the light beyond the light of the seven sisters.'

The woman opens her mouth in a grief so profound, her entire body moans from deep inside her; she calls out to her babies, calls her babies back to her.

Brown owls fall from the sky.

'No, Anah-san. Call them to the light beyond the light of the seven sisters.

'Oh, Anah-san, do not call them home. Only *you* must return home. Hosana is wandering, you must find her. Elizabeth is hungry, you must feed her. Your husband is crying, you must comfort him. Their avô is calling, you must answer him.

'Your God is waiting in light beyond light. Lift your dead ones to him.'

Ai-chan dreams, wandering free from her body, 'Listen,' she pleads:

'Give them up to God, Anah-san. For God is the author of life, life is sacred, sacred as the Sabbath, sacred as this valley.'

Listen:

'Please, Anah-san, quickly, you must pray the small boy away.'

Pray:

'Eternal rest grant Seth Soares, O Lord. And let perpetual light shine on him. May he forever rest in peace. Say it, Anah-san. Say it. Hurry. He calls the akua lele over the hills, more and more, many more spirits are coming for he is calling them. Say it':

"O God, be not far from me when I say, 'Get thee behind me, Seth!' My God, make haste to help me!"

20

1928

Ezroh rode home from the fields each day, the flowers of the forests and pastures he rode through woven into haku lei around his hat, flowers woven into his kanaka mustang's mane, flowers filling his work bag. This was the custom of the paniolos, burly and brusque cowboys, who in their long days in the fields filled their hours with picking and weaving blossoms into lei for holding down their hats in strong winds. And for their sweethearts at home.

Anah's heart quickened each day when she heard the jingle of his kepa pele as he ran to find her. The bell spurs sounded like wind chimes. She was always with their daughters in the garden, harvesting vegetables. He lifted their little one high in the air as they gathered eggs in the chicken yard. He put their eldest on his shoulders in the kitchen helping with dinner. He put his mouth on Anah's neck, his hands over the length of her arms as she rocked in the chair by the window, Hosana nursing still, Elizabeth asleep on the bed.

She had a family now. A good husband and sweet daughters. A

gruff but kind father-in-law. A doting Okinawan grandfather. She thought of her okaasan with a fond bitterness that faded with each passing day. She still longed for her brother Charles who had disappeared from the streets of Chinatown far away from their childhood home on the O'ahu Sugar Plantation. She prayed for his health and well-being every day.

Ezroh always removed his hat upon entering their room, slowly putting flowers in Anah's hair, on her pillow, on the small table, on the bed next to the sleeping baby. He placed his valued kaula'ili already oiled with tallow on the dresser. This rawhide lariat, his prized possession woven for him by his grandfather João Soares, came with him into the house every night. He smelled of the deepest forest, a man's hard labor, sweet flowers, as he kneeled at Anah's feet, his head on her lap, fingers lifting the hem of her dress, his thick hands on her skin, Hosana's toes playing in his hair.

He planted an expansive garden for Anah outside of that window, a garden full of flowers and herbs he cultivated with a delicate hand, pruning and shaping each bed, each plant to perfection. There, Anah watched the English daisies bow to the morning wind. There, Anah observed the slow bloom of the Chinese forget-me-nots, chamomile and rosemary near sweet alyssum nodding, mei sui lan and lemon balm fragrant, statice in multifold colors, the delicate thyme and the sturdy kwai fa. There, Anah saw the fragile crawl of the lei loke lani, each pink rosebud reaching upward on the white latticed archway.

When they walked in the garden over stepping-stones drawn from the river that ran through Kalihi Valley, Hosana picked the wild violets and pansies, dahlias and geraniums, held the balls of pink, lavender, and blue hydrangea in her hands, filling their room each day with bowls full of flowers, placing a bowl of flowers in Tora-san's room and in her avô's room as well.

She picked flowers and fruits for their visits with Beatrix and Bertha, whom her avô buried at the foot of the Ko'olau Mountains with his ancestors.

There at the grave of her sisters, Hosana placed flowers from her garden for the dead, for Seth, her father's brother.

Anah offered rice balls and tangerines, holy water and purification salt, incense and coins for Seth's fare, for her daughters' fares and their safe passage across the River of Three Hells to the heaven of her mother's ancestors.

She spoke Japanese folk stories told to her by her okaasan that ended the same each time: "We will be apart for now. Until we meet again. Even if I travel ten thousand miles, my love for you will remain the same."

She sang songs to all of them upon leaving, songs of the Land of Nod, the land they visited every night in tales and rhymes.

Anah's strong one-eyed girl who shared her sweet cakes and sugary filhos cookies with the dead as Elizabeth lingered over the graves.

Anah's dead babies fully formed inside her, dead in the world, never left her thoughts.

She rode out one night to their graves in a grief she could not let go of, through screaming wind, ferocious winter rain. She saw a small campfire under a large banyan. Ezroh and his father, Rex, sat near a mound of dirt, small rivulets veining down its sides. Shadow and flame mottled their faces. They were drunk, shouting to the lonely night, "Droga morte! Bebida, bebida!"

Then Ezroh spoke softly to his "Mama, sweet Mama."

Rex Soares toasted the dead. "To Mary Anna, my beautiful wife, the saints abide your eternal soul."

Rex Soares toasted the lost. "To my beautiful children, gone, all gone back to the land of their father's fathers." He held himself in the brisk cold. "Seth!" he cried. "My fault, all my fault. O my son, how I miss you so."

The wind screamed.

"My daughters, my daughters," Ezroh sobbed, the slender reedy trill of kōlea this cold, rainy night. "I should have never given her that bicycle." He drank long from the amber-colored bottle.

Rex Soares openly wept over the spitting fire, his swarthy big hands covering his face. Ezroh leaned into him, his father taking him into his arms.

"Are we cursed, Father, as Aunty Tova says?" Ezroh asked.

"Curse of the father," Rex Soares cried. "Curse of the son."

Anah watched them from behind the trees, their horses spooking at the sound of her mare, but before she turned to leave, she willed the ghosts away to the country of the dead, there beyond the flames of the banishing fire.

She did not want to feel this pain, the pain that found her again and again: the pain of losing her beloved ones, *Okaasan and Charles*, her sisters, *Aki and Leah*, many children, *behold, behold*, her daughters, *Beatrix and Bertha*. And *Seth*, her once cherished friend.

What heartache her mother must have felt. Her daughters were as good as dead to her. Anah had to believe she fell into a silent hysteria to cope with the pain of loss in her heart. Anah lived that hysteria.

Anah had to believe her mother wiped her daughters from her thoughts, to leave them, to return to a land far away from this place of such great sorrow.

Anah did not want that pain anymore.

"No mo'," she begged Tora-san that night, her clothes dripping, her body shivering as she stood at the doorway to his room. "Help me. I no like no mo' babies."

He looked at her, his face full of sadness, her sadness. "No," he said at last, removing his glasses and placing them on his nightstand. "Bumbye Ezroh mad with me. I no play God."

"Ask Ryoki," Anah pleaded. "Ask Ai-chan. I cannot . . . this just like when my father sent us away to . . . and my okaasan, she stood there . . . and then my sisters . . . but this time, the babies was *mine* . . . please, no mo' keiki."

"No, I no can," he said, pushing past her. "I dunno how. Not my business."

"Please. I begging you," Anah pleaded. "Why you no like help me?" she screamed at him.

"Leave me alone, Anah-san," he said, running from the main house, tripping over stones, falling on the muddy road.

Anah did not see him for all of the next day.

But he returned to her in quiet acquiescence later that evening, his arms full of an assortment of plants and flowers. Anah watched as he snipped and crushed, grated and strained, the smells sweet and bitter. "O-kay, Anah-san." He sighed. "We do just like Ryoki say the ancient Okinawan way," he said, taking a sip from a hot spoon. "But you never tell Ezroh that me was the one—"

He served Anah the tea of geranium and mountain apple blossom three times a day. He massaged her wrists and feet with rosemary, pine, and basil ground into an oily paste. He strained the juices of the ʻōhelo and ʻākala berries with cheesecloth, picking out the seeds and the skins, then grinding them with his pestle and mortar. Anah drank a tablespoon of this tonic four times a day.

Ai-chan placed three large stones in the center of Anah's garden, calling them the kami of the hearth. She offered daily prayers in her lilting Uchinanchu with salt, water, and incense, asking the kami of the hearth to lift her requests for Anah to the higher kami.

She told Tora-san to plant wild raspberry outside her room and passion fruit vines over the windows. The ample prickles and thorns on the thick branches of the ʻākala and the chaotic, ligneous vine arms of the lilikoʻi would keep the kami of fertility away from Anah's bed.

And all that they did, Ezroh did not know.

ANAH WAS WITHOUT child for two years.

"SHE IS CURSED, I tell you, cursed. First the fruit of her womb, then the crops of our land, the calves of our herds, and the lambs of our flocks will all follow. It is written in God's word," Aunty Tova whispered in Portuguese.

Anah threw the first bucket of water over the dusty floor of the cookhouse. Hosana laughed, the cool rush of water over her legs.

"Or else my nephew is not having relations with her," she surmised. "Maybe he has finally realized that he should have married Abigail. Marrying a kanaka would have been a little better than marrying an Oriental. He must be sleeping outside the marital bed. How else can you explain no more keiki after four in a row like that?"

Aunty Lydia said nothing, wiping the dusty windowsills as Anah pushed the mop over the floor. "At least she keeps this place spic and span for Ezroh and Rex," she said. "And she is a hard worker with the old Okinawan gone with the cowboy gang in his cook wagon for such a long time. Kenji even has her doing the morning milking with him. Why don't you get up and help us dust, sister?"

"Hmph." Aunty Tova scoffed. "I clean and tend to the affairs of my own house, thank you very much, Lydia. She must be barren, I tell you. I knew it. I always knew it. The Lord our God's curse is upon her."

"Stop that kind of talk, sister."

"She is cursed, I tell you," Aunty Tova whispered, leaning closer to Aunty Lydia. "Good. Better for Matthew and Bert. And David and Michael and Sammie and JohnJohn. They will inherit all of this," she said, sweeping her arms wide. "It is as much their endowment from our father as it is Ezroh's from our brother. We must stand up for what rightfully belongs to *our* children, sister."

Aunty Lydia changed the subject. "When have you ever seen the vegetable garden so healthy? And the flower gardens she tends are beautiful." Aunty Lydia smiled, rinsing her rag in a bucket. "Who has the time or vigor for the luxury of flowers? Not you or I, sister."

"Something is not right," Aunty Tova remarked, squinting her eyes, glaring at Anah. "And the vegetable garden is full of produce fit only for pigs and Orientals."

Elizabeth wandered out onto the lānai. She dragged her tattered security blanket and a rag doll Anah had made for her with dark yarn hair and a simple yellow dress.

"Good fruit never comes from a bad tree," Aunty Tova scoffed at the child. "When are you going to talk?" she barked. "Cursed tongue, just like your mother. How will you ever attend an English Standard School if you never speak? Lydia, did you hear they are allowing Orientals to attend the English Standard Schools? I cannot imagine not a one of them proficient in written and oral English. Appalling, I tell you, absolutely appalling."

Aunty Lydia did not respond. Elizabeth stared up at Aunty Tova, tilting her head like a curious dog, her eyebrows furrowed.

"It is not like the government hasn't been trying to Americanize you Orientals," she ranted at the child. "What with half of the children in our schools being Japanese." She made the sign of the cross and shook her head. "These Orientals act as though it is owed to them. That they have *rights* to an American schooling, if you will. When will Governor Farrington realize that educating them will not make a lick of a difference. Look at them—their traditions, their appearance, their innate tendencies, their very blood is still so Oriental."

Hosana stepped up to her huge Aunty Tova, knocking a glass onto the lānai, shards sparkling in the spill of sweet tea.

"How dare you, you wicked little one-eyed makapaʻa—" She hit her across the face. "That is for being such a clumsy little fool. You are worse than your mother with her minimal housekeeping abilities learned at that dreadful orphanage. She is no better than the foundlings taken from the brothels in Iwilei. Now clean up this mess."

Hosana picked up a big piece of glass. Anah scooped up both little ones in one arm, the dusty rugs in the other. She ran with them toward the corral, draping the rugs over the ʻōhiʻa posts. Hosana beat them with her tiny, angry hands, the dirt sticking to the rivers of sweet tea on her arms and legs, the rivers of tears on her face. Elizabeth sat down in a tuft of grass, thumb in mouth.

"Do not listen to her," Anah whispered to her daughter in Japanese, watching the mountains for Tora-san's return. "She is a foolish old Portuguese woman who speaks before she thinks. Much chatter, little wit. You must not grow up in her likeness or with her vicious words in your thoughts."

Hosana looked up with her one good eye fierce. Anah saw Aki's fire in her, the fire of sweet revenge. She pulled the piece of glass from her pocket and hurled it into the pasture.

Anah was afraid for her. Anah was afraid for silent Elizabeth. Anah was afraid for herself. Aunty Tova was right. And she was running out of Tora-san's infertility tonics.

EZROH RETURNED the next night alone. The babies asleep, he put his hand over Anah's mouth and lifted her quietly from the bed. His body hungry for her and her for his after days apart from each other, he carried Anah to his mother's empty room at the end of the hall, where they made love that night again and again and again.

The cowboy gang would return in two days with the herd. Ezroh was to oversee operations at the ranch for his father, prepare for the tagging, branding, castration, and inoculation of the late-born calves, deal with the infectious pinkeye, supervise the maintenance and shoeing of all the horses by the Spanish farrier, consult with the Dairymen's Association about the new motor-driven bottle-washing machine, discuss business with the newly hired ice cream manager at the Purity Inn.

But he spent night and day overseeing Anah's body. Between each of her chores and Hosana and Elizabeth's sleep, they met in his mother's darkened room, its windows painted black, making desperate and insatiable love in his mother's bed. It felt wrong, but every time he called Anah's name, she went to him quickly, her garments falling to the floor before she pushed the door shut.

Anah was without her tonics. He begged her to let him enter her, promising to remove himself before the moment of his final moaning, but caught in that moment, their bodies joined, breathing together, moving together, arms and legs entwined, he could not remove himself from her.

By the time of Tora-san's return in his sturdy cook wagon, Anah was with child.

Again.

ANAH'S FIFTH CHILD was born on the night of July 13, 1929, the first night of Obon, the night the Okinawans and the Japanese welcomed back their dead with lights in the doorways guiding them home.

Ryoki Sunabe refused to come until after Obon, too busy making jushi with grated ginger, hiya sōmen, mochi, konbu maki, and the many other Obon ryōri food offerings, cleaning and purifying her family shrine, offering incense, bowing at the door with her husband and children, aunts and uncles, first cousins and second cousins, nieces and nephews, saying, "Uchin kai imisōre," welcoming home their many unseen dead.

Anah's baby would not wait for the midwife, Tora-san quickly taking her place, Nohea at her bedside, Ezroh assisting her. Rex Soares had allowed Kenji and Ai-chan to pay homage to their dead at their ancestral shrine on the other side of the island, the childless couple leaving the ranch the morning before.

"You sure she be o-kay?" Ai-chan had asked Tora-san as he lifted a basketful of purple sweet potatoes into the buggy.

"Hai, hai, no worry, no pilikia," he said. "I go call Ryoki Sunabe pretty soon." He did not know she would refuse them her services during the Obon.

This birth would be a difficult one, labor going on into the night, yet Anah's cervix not opening. Near dawn, Anah felt her baby dead in her as she had felt Beatrix and Bertha dead in her, the hysterical shock of each wave of contractions, the pillows, the bed, wet with her sweat and the sour odor of her brine. Anah's cervix would not open. The baby would not come. Anah knew Tora-san feared the worst.

"Maybe you hurry up, Ezroh, go call Ryoki. Tell her come ʻāwīwī right now bumbye keiki die," he stammered. "Bumbye Anah—"

"No," Ezroh said, "I staying here."

"Go!" he commanded, shoving Ezroh, the room silent but for Anah's delirious groaning.

"No!" Ezroh insisted, pushing back at the old man.

"Ai-chan!" Tora-san yelled suddenly.

"I come back help Anah," she said, hiking up her sleeves at the doorway. "I tell Kenji, you say to my hwā fuji for me, 'Welcome home, honored grandparents, from Ai-chan. I see you soon, but now I have work to do.' "

"The razor," he said, "go hurry, get the razor. Usun, Anah-san, get ready to usun!"

He pulled Anah's cervix open with the might of the angels, the bones separating inside her. "Usun!" he yelled through the grit of his teeth. "Push!"

Anah lifted herself again, Ezroh supporting her back, the baby's head finally crowning. Anah pushed and pushed in a kind of stunning delirium she had known only in childbirth, screaming at the faces of unseen wraiths and demons.

Seth.

He stood there between her legs, pressing the baby's head inward.

"No! Your brother, get him away!"

"What? Who?" Ezroh asked.

"No talk crazy, Anah-san!" Tora-san scolded.

"C'mon, Anah, you can do it," Ezroh said, Seth smiling right at her.

Ai-chan hurried back from the kitchen with a kettle of hot water and fresh towels. "Chiyun," she yelled at Tora-san, pouring the hot water over the razor's blade.

"I cutting now, Anah," he warned her.

"Go away. Go away. Get away from me," Anah pleaded.

Nohea steadied her legs. "Watch the keiki head," she warned him. "No cut the keiki head. Akahele, old man." And then he sliced her open to beyond her anus. In one final push, Ai-chan took hold of Anah's baby, slipping out from between her legs.

Anah heard nothing, no cry, Tora-san siphoning out blood and vernix from its nose and mouth with the tip of his agile tongue.

"Girl!" he said to Anah. "C'mon, you cry," he said, scolding the infant. "Cry, cry," he begged, the baby's small mewl a breathy staccato above Anah at last.

Ezroh collapsed himself on Anah's belly, stroking her face and her wet hair, as Nohea wiped down the infant, then lay her on Anah's body. Ezroh counted ten fingers and ten toes, surveying the baby girl from head to toe and then back again.

Someone laughed at Anah from the corner of the room.

Ai-chan opened her legs and began stitching her, the smell of buta ashi no shiru entering the room. "Hey, you, old man," she said to Tora-san, needle poking and pulling through flesh, "go check on the jiru. Make sure soup hot, hot, hot. Now, go hurry, 'āwīwī," she mock-commanded him.

Little girl with the dark hair of Anah's mother, her name Claire for the saints, the daylight coming in through the window. Her name Tori for the old man who brought her into the world. Anah's Claire Tori Soares, little To-chan, little bird who came, though Anah did not call her name.

THEIR DAYS-OLD INFANT WAS colicky and jaundiced. Hosana stayed with Aunty Lydia and her cousins up in the north pasture. Elizabeth stayed with Ai-chan, who doted over her. Anah spread a small blanket before the kami of the hearth in the center of her flower garden.

She fervently offered incense, threw handfuls of purification salt, poured cups of fresh river water over each stone, imitating Ai-chan's gestures the best she could, whispering her prayers to the tombstone-cold kami of the hearth to lift to the higher kami.

"Infertility. Empty womb. Stop. No more."

Anah knew that these prayers if offered to the Blessed Virgin or St. Joseph or the Sacred Heart of Jesus would be futile.

She asked nothing of them.

Mist hung in the Ko'olaus like shaggy apparitions, as she watched a rider on a kanaka mustang move down the rocky, steeped pali through mountain paths full of the smell of ironwoods and camphor, brown owls rousing from late afternoon roosts.

He would find her sitting in the garden, weeping amid the flowers, white and yellow ginger in tall bloom, night-blooming jasmine coaxed into a sweet arch over a bed of heather and violets, 'awapuhi brilliant red torches sweet with sticky water.

He cut one at its base, tipped her head back, and squeezed the perfumed waters of 'awapuhi into her hair, massaging her forehead and temples with strong hands, the sweet water slipping down her face, her neck, between her breasts.

The night dark, a lantern lit in the window of their room above them, he pulled the bloody rag of afterbirth from between her legs and moved atop her slowly over a bed of wild violets, the stitches straining with the slow, slow pleasure of him entering so soon, so unexpectedly, the moment full of joy, grief, longing, fear, commingling in a night full of flowers.

Anah never refused him her body, never, though tired or aching, always wanting him more than the time before. Ezroh moaned and the infant inside the window stirred awake. Anah rose, gathering her clothes, wrapping the blanket around herself, and hurried inside.

◇

NINE MONTHS LATER, on April 17, 1930, the anniversary of her departure from St. Joseph's, the day of her own birth, Anah birthed another child.

Another girl child.

Miriam.

She would be Anah's last, her insides irreparably scarred from the damage she had done to herself in secret to end the life of her unborn child.

Anah was never alone in her darkness. Seth came to watch her revulsion at her attempts to end her own pregnancy. They wept together every day, her hands holding the poison of tonics and herbs.

Miriam's birth was a miracle.

Anah was certain:

Her Miriam was her miracle.

She was breech, her way of surviving the beating, the horrible tonics; she turned herself around, kicking away the poison of Anah's harm.

Ryoki turned her with the might of an angry kami, *my eyes see a green-dotted, fading consciousness*, shoved her forearm inside Anah with the strength of the furious saints, *my eyes see an explosion of white light*, twisted the innards with the gnarly hands of a pantheon of ancient gods, *say good-bye, Ezroh, my love*.

Anah left her body there on the bed, unable to manage the pain of one hand inside her, more hands pressing outside her, contractions, nausea, delirious fever, her cervix finally cracking. Seth reached out his hand to her. He was cold when he grasped hold of her. He was happy at last, smiling, pulling her into the tunnel that led away from this world. And then she heard Ezroh's voice calling her name.

"Anah! Anah!"

Anah let go of Seth's hand, and he spun away into the dark tunnel wall.

"Anah!"

She returned to fight one last time, following the voice of her beloved with a rabid, bestial resistance.

They tied Anah's arms to the bedposts, her legs strapped open.

Ryoki and Tora-san kneaded the baby toward the birth canal; Anah screamed at them horrid obscenities in their Uchinanchu until blood spat from her mouth.

So they gagged her.

"I know it is a boy, Anah," Ezroh encouraged with a hysterical calm. "Our boy is coming. We will name him Charles for your brother. C'mon, Anah, you can do it."

She nodded, biting into the rag between her teeth.

The baby came, one arm reaching for Tora-san before the emergence of a face, a broken collarbone, a body frightfully bruised.

"One mo' girl," Ryoki sputtered, flinging rags onto the floor, then rinsing her hands in a basin of cloudy water.

Anah saw her little one breathing heavily as Ryoki laid her bloody sprawl on Anah's breast. Her breathing soon mirrored Anah's. How determined she was to be with Anah in this world. No prayer or offering, no beating or poison would stop her.

Anah admired her tenacity and will from the moment she saw her.

She did not care when, from beyond the flower garden, she heard the cowboys' drunken laughter at Ezroh and her.

"Six keiki all girls, two dead."

"What he going do with four wāhine keiki?"

"Mo' better he stop fucking her."

"Mo' better he fuck the cows in the pasture like this lōlō borinque's cousin."

"Then no mo' girls."

"One mo' humbug. One mo' girl. One mo' mouth fo' feed."

Anah did not care even when she heard Aunty Tova going on and on. "She cursed, did I not tell you, Lydia? One more deformed girl. Her bad luck followed her from that godforsaken orphanage. And it is bound to infect the rest of us soon. I tell you Lydia, you mark my words for these are the words of the Lord our God—first the fruit of her womb, then the crops, the calves, the lambs will follow. You know, Ezroh should run off with Abigail. He is still young. He can start another family. He would be the better for it. You know it is because she is a half-breed making more half-breeds that they are all tainted and diseased. Rex is so ashamed he cannot even come down from the mountains to greet another girl grandchild."

Anah did not care even when she heard Seth's childlike giggling outside of her room. She did not know how to appease him anymore. She did not have the energy or will.

No one celebrated.

But a goodness was written on the child's face.

Tora-san served Anah her first bowl of pigs' feet soup soon after Miriam's birth with a cup of geranium and mountain apple tea and a bottle of ʻōhelo and ʻākala berry tonic. He massaged Anah's wrists and feet with rosemary, pine, and basil oil as he whispered the holy Rosary, prayers to the Blessed Virgin for intercession on Anah's behalf.

"No mo' keiki. All pau," he said, patting Anah's head. "This is the last one. I make promise to you."

Ai-chan hurried outside to offer prayers to the kami of the hearth to lift to the higher kami. Then she too held her rosary in prayer. "No mo' keiki. All pau."

Miriam cried.

Claire Tori cried.

Elizabeth cried.

Hosana cried, holding Anah's hand in hers.

Anah cried, all of them around her, because she remembered Seth on the bridge:

Memory of the Little Boy on the Bridge over the Stream Unable to Go Home to God

It had rained for days and nights. You were wet and cold.

'Curse your womb, waters that break from between your legs.'

The stream raged, a thick torrent, the whip and thrash of low-hanging wiliwili branches. You stood there holding hands with a naked girl and a girl in a yellow dress.

'Curse what issues forth. Sickly, crying beasties.'

The waters churned beneath us.

'Curse you with girl babies. No namesake, no heirs.'

When my sisters disappeared into the trees, I begged you to come with me, you who never aged. But in your anger, you would not hear the voice of my heart.

'Dead babies, deformed, crippled.'

You looked at me, sad eyes, mad eyes.

'Curse your God. He will forsake you as you have forsaken me.'

Your mouth opened, a spiraling black maw.

'Curse the ones you love. Husband, father, brother, child.'

You dissipated into the wind. I remember now. This is when I heard your voice for the very first time, the only time:

"Curse you, Anah."

The emptiness of a life without you.

My living damnation.

But your curse is my blessing, don't you see?

Turn the page.

Their lives have been written in destiny.

Hosana of the one-eyed ferocity, Elizabeth of the seeing plane, To-chan the face and heart of my okaasan, and Miriam, beautiful Miriam, the light of my own brother that shines from deep inside her.

Don't you see?

You have given their light to me, that day on the bridge, the waters of the river churning beneath us.

See us all:

The morning is cold. We sleep on the bed near the window over the flowers. Sweet breath of the babes, their father's arms encircle us all, as one by one they suckle and doze under warm familiar blankets, the promise of another day rising in the hills of Kalihi Valley.

21

1931

"Build many hives," Rex Soares had encouraged Anah at the feast day of the Epiphany. The music of the cowboys came into the cookhouse from the porch as the family sat at the long dining table. "I remember when the holy sisters traded their honey with the ranchers and farmers and fishermen of Kalihi," he said in Portuguese. "They rivaled the production of the Sandwich Island Honey Company. Everyone said the sisters bottled the sweetest, darkest honey they had ever tasted. Even better than the Vitalic and Crystal brands. Do you remember, Marcus?"

His brother-in-law nodded over a huge bite of boiled potatoes with codfish. "There was so much honey, and a high-grade honey, I might add," he said at last, pointing his fork at Tora-san, "that this penny-pinching old Okinawan did not need to buy sugar."

"Hmph, stop stretching the truth," Aunty Tova scoffed. "And who, pray tell, will manage these ridiculous hives?"

"Anah will," Ezroh said.

"Anah?" Aunty Tova laughed, poking her elbow into Aunty Lydia's side. "She cannot even boil water or embroider a handkerchief, let alone wipe the mucus from her baby's nose. Look at the child," she said, lowering her eyes at Miriam as she crawled across the dining room floor with a wet cookie in her fist. "And she is of an uneducated Oriental stock, clearly incapable of—"

Anah stopped cold in the doorway to the kitchen, the kettle full of hot canja in her hands. They all turned to look at her.

"Anah, show my sister your drawings," Rex Soares said in Portuguese. "The drawings you showed me when the old man and I were fixing the ʻōpae baskets on the lānai. And tell her your thoughts on acquiring those good-quality imported queens from the Territorial government office." He picked Miriam up from the floor and wiped her face with his handkerchief.

"This I have to hear," Aunty Tova said. "Well, c'mon, speak up. And serve the soup while you're at it. It's getting cold."

Anah shook her head.

"Show us your drawings, Anah, and tell us," Aunty Lydia encouraged. "Stanley has been telling Rex for years to produce honey, but nobody had even a rudimentary knowledge of beekeeping."

"Anah," Ezroh said, taking the kettle of soup from her hands and placing it on the table. "The sweet, dark honey my father spoke of from St. Joseph's was *your* honey. Show them your drawings."

Anah slowly reached into the pockets of her trousers and opened the papers full of numbers and lines, the three-dimensional sketches she had made while sitting in the gazebo Ezroh had built in her garden. As her babies napped, Anah spent hours watching the wag-tail and the circle dances of the bees over the flowers, watching and sketching.

Uncle Marcus and Uncle Stanley leaned in to see the dimensions for the wooden boxes and frames. "The frames have grips," Anah said, pointing to her drawing. "It is easier to take them out of the hive. This is the food chamber," she muttered, Aunty Tova's eyes boring into her, "and this is the brood chamber." She pointed.

Uncle Marcus nodded at Rex Soares. Uncle Stanley smiled at Anah with a shaka and a wink.

"Tell them what you plan to do with the hives," Ezroh told Anah, as he lifted To-chan onto his lap.

"We can consider purchasing some of the queens the government has imported to the Territory. Queen bees of any nature are well received by worker bees in overcrowded hives," Anah said, her voice barely a whisper. "They brought in the queens from abroad, extracted them from their existing hives, then destroyed their colonies to prevent bringing in foreign diseases. I wish to put the newly established queens and their hives in many different places here in the valley according to season and bloom."

"Not near the north pasture you will not. I will not tolerate the placement of one of her ridiculous hives near my home in any season or bloom," Aunty Tova scolded. "Over my dead body."

"Because—" Ezroh prompted her, sighing deeply at his aunt's rude interruption.

"Because rather than having a central apiary that would produce the same kind of honey, I want the bees to make certain kinds of honey. The quality of the honey would vary from season to season as the taste depends upon—"

"O ye who speaks from limited knowledge," Aunty Tova said. "You frighten me, Anah, with your brazen need for attention. You did not even finish school. You can barely read. You do not know mathematics. And you know nothing about beekeeping."

Tora-san stared at Aunty Tova, then put Elizabeth down. "Honey good," he said, "save money, maybe even make little bit mo' money. Now hard, no kabi jin in this Depression times, very hard time fo' Mr. Rex. Stock market crash and all pohō, even Mr. Rex. Every year mo' harder, mo' harder."

Hosana pressed herself into Anah. She put her arm around her daughter. "And honey is better for us for its many curative properties. And we will produce it here at the ranch. I am positive that we would not be yielding cooking honey as did the Sandwich Islands Honey Company when they sold the honeydew honey from the sugarcane leafhopper but a higher-grade honey. Ours will be thick enough to be spread like a fine jelly—"

Rex Soares nodded, deep in thought. "We all need to tighten our belts," he said at last. "So very hard on all of us, this Great Depression. There does not seem to be an end in sight. We all need to chip in however we can. There is talk of exporting honey and beeswax to the Orient. All of us," he said, looking hard at Aunty Tova, who snubbed him, "must be more prudent in our expenditures."

"She will need expensive equipment," Aunty Tova complained. "How will you afford that, brother, with your talk of hard times and prudence?"

"I will barter with the holy sisters," Anah told her. "They have not produced honey for a couple of years now. I am sure Sister Mary Deborah would not mind letting me use her extractor. And we will build our hives with material we already have here at the ranch."

"Then it is done," Rex Soares said with final authority. "Matthew and Bert," he said to his nephews, "you help Ezroh build the hives, then place them according to Anah's plans. Anah, you secure the purchase of our queen bees."

"The Lord our God help you if I am stung but one time," Aunty Tova said, wanting to get in the last, bitter word.

"Hush, Tova," Uncle Marcus told her. "The bees are swarming everywhere in the valley. You would have been stung long ago."

They laughed as Tora-san served the dessert of rice pudding and Bolo de Natal, laughed at Aunty Tova who whispered something sibilant to Aunty Lydia, Ezroh taking Anah and his cousins out onto the lānai.

"To Anah," he said, holding up a glass of whiskey.

"To Anah," Matthew toasted.

"Anah." Bert smiled, lifting his glass.

"Me," Anah whispered, Ezroh's eyes in hers.

◈

IN EARLY SUMMER, the ʻākala and thimbleberry blossoms produced a tangy, amber honey from the cool patches beyond the north pasture. The avocado blossoms from the shady grove near the main road yielded a thick honey rich in vitamins.

In the fall, the chamomile and sage Anah had planted in abundance around the wild kiawe trees to the south produced a spicy clear honey, the hives placed amid the end season of yellow and white ginger.

In the winter, the mango and mountain apple blossoms produced a sweet, light honey full of the flavors of fruit. The hives in the still, wind-breaking line of eucalyptus trees produced a minty-sweet menthol harvest.

In the spring of heather and violet, pansy and geranium, kukui and strawberry guava, lavender and phlox, the hives produced a robust honey from the center of Anah's garden.

It would be a honey of renown, her bottles of Hosana Honey, served at the tables of foreign dignitaries, commissioners, and government officials, sugar and pineapple barons, businessmen in drawing rooms, ladies of polite society, and afternoons of high tea in the island's finest hotels.

TORA-SAN AND ANAH PACKED UP her daughters and her frames full of the glistening honey of her first harvest onto his sturdy mule wagon. He was not allowed to drive the new Divco milk truck or the Ford Model A pickup. They would ask Sister Mary Deborah's permission to use her extractor at St. Joseph's.

The sister stepped out into the courtyard of St. Joseph's Orphanage at the sound of the wagon. She did not recognize Anah in the distance. As the mules pulled to a slow halt, she waved happily at last in recognition, "Susanah! Susanah!"

She took each of Anah's daughters' faces in her hands, followed by the sign of the cross, and placed a sweet kiss on each forehead. And then she held Anah by her shoulders, pulling her in and then away from her to study Anah's face and then into her warm habit again.

Aunty Chong Sum ran toward them from the back door, sweeping Anah's children into her arms. "Ai-ya, many keiki, so big now. My, my, look just like the mama. Too bad no mo' boy yet. Maybe later. Plenny time for more suk-suk, make plenny mo' boy keiki." She laughed, nudging Anah hard.

Supang put down his rake and Fukunaga paused in his mopping of the lānai to wave at them.

The children of St. Joseph's surrounded them.

So many, many more.

An eight-year-old girl took Hosana by the hand when, in the flurry of greetings, the other children began pointing and teasing Hosana about her eye patch.

"What so funny?" the little girl said to the other children, putting her arm around Hosana and leading her away, Elizabeth and Tori following behind them. "No laughing. No be mean."

"Little Anne's a feisty one," Sister Mary Deborah said to Anah, putting her arm around Anah's shoulder. "I may have found a fine apicurist apprentice again. It's been a few years," she said, smiling.

"Her name Anne Yap," Aunty Chong Sum said, nodding in agreement. "Her daddy owner the Chinee market down the road, K.C. Market."

"No call her Annie," Supang added, "and no call her Pa-ke bumbye she yell you, 'My name is *Anne* not *Annie*, and I Chinese not Pa-ke, you lōlō or what, idioto-to.' "

Fukunaga laughed, mumbling, "idioto-to."

"She stay here all by herself?" Anah almost hesitated to ask. "Like me?"

"Not all are orphans or the infirm," Sister Mary Deborah said. "Some are students here like Ezroh was. Anne is our student. You must send Hosana for schooling," she said, taking Miriam from Anah's arms. "She's already made a fierce ally," she said, lifting her chin toward Anah's daughters playing with Anne Yap under the huge banyan tree. "Send them all to school and catechism. We will make them into fine, upstanding Catholic women."

The sister peered at the honey frames in the back of the wagon. She ran her her finger over the honeycomb, then tasted Anah's harvest. "The nectar of berries," she said, "simply divine." She ran her finger over the yellow glaze again, placing it in Miriam's mouth. Anah's daughter clapped and laughed. "As I told your mother many times, Miriam, remember always, love is sweet," she said, taking the mules by the reins and leading them toward the honey house.

"Love is sweet," Anah repeated.

"I've been incredibly occupied with the children," Sister Mary Deborah said. "Especially after Sister Bernadine was called to São Paulo, Brazil." She shook her head and made the sign of the cross.

"She not here?" Anah asked. "Brazil?"

Tora-san pushed Anah's shoulder from behind. They exchanged genial looks.

"Brazil so far away," Anah said as sincerely as she could.

"The smiles on both your faces is not becoming. Our Sister Bernadine was called to serve many children in great need in the terribly dilapidated orphanage of the Catholic Church of Echapora by the Lord our God," she said to them, though she could not see them. "The sister has been sorely missed in the schoolroom and the infirmary. But as I was saying, I have not been able to keep up the hives. The extractor is not in very good condition and Mr. Toranosuke may have to adjust the spigot, oil the rusted gears, and replace some of the broken filters."

She opened the door to the honey house. The smells of the room infused with nectar and honey, the heady smell of the beeswax, and the decay of the wooden frames and boxes made Anah step back from the doorway.

Beeswax is the brightest of all candle flames.

How many days she had spent in this room.

How many times she had stolen from this room.

I place a cube of honeycomb in your dying mouth.

Sister Mary Deborah always found her here, always ready with a scripture for her like this day, the sister's hand on Anah's shoulder to steady her. "Fear not, for the Lord's commands are more precious than gold, they are sweeter than honey, than honey from the comb. Bring your children to the Lord our God."

Anah brought them all into the honey house, glazed their hair and lips with the honey of her first harvest, then placed a cube of honeycomb in each of their little mouths.

"In remembrance, little ones, remember always, love is sweet."

ANAH KNEW that Hosana possessed the rebellious streak of her sister Aki and the love-filled filial piety of her brother Charles. Or was it all an overcompensation for her damaged esteem, her blind eye? Hosana would run faster than her cousins, beat them into a bitch's submission, always be first in line, stand up to the cowboys' taunts, ride standing on her father's kanaka mustang, and she would defend her sisters to the bloody end.

From the time she could speak, she declared her love for Kahalelehua's son Ethan, one day expressing her whole heart's desire to the children as they played on the lānai. "When you and me marry-marry, Ethan," she said, "you going come live in this house with me." She gestured. "I be the mommy, and you be the daddy, and we have plenny keiki." Surely he would not say no.

Everyone stopped in their activity. No one spoke, stunned by her honest forthrightness.

"Marry?" Kanaeʻaupuni, his brother a year older, laughed. "You and my bradda? I no think so." He paused. "Look at you. You one makapaʻa. Bumbye you and Ethan get all one-eye baby look like their ugly mama."

The children began chanting, "Maka-paʻa, maka-paʻa." It was a cruel, conscienceless child's taunt, some of them covering one eye as they teased.

Elizabeth pressed her ears shut. Tori slid behind Hosana. Anah held Miriam in her arms as she watched from the window, her eldest daughter looking face to face for someone to stand up for her. And when no one would look, she knew to stand up for herself.

She said nothing, the dust from their chanting and dancing rising around her, steeling herself from tears, little as she was. Anah watched as the resolve of her sister Aki seeped into her daughter's heart.

Not one tear fell.

But when the teasing turned to Elizabeth, squatting with her back to the mob, making odd sounds with her fingers in her ears, "Lōlō Lizabeth. Crazy girl, crazy girl. Lōlō lohi'au," their own cousins joining in as children do, Hosana with the fury of Aki and the love of Charles would not stop until blood was drawn.

It was the rage of a cornered animal, the bloodied noses and mouths, blackened eyes left in the wake of her anger, as Aunty Lydia and Nohea pulled Hosana off their children, screaming and crying.

Anah did not intervene. She stood at the window, seeing the face of her sister, the heart of her brother again in Hosana. Her daughter would have the might of Aki. The compassion of Charles. Her daughter would survive this world.

THEY TRADED their farm and dairy goods for schooling. It was all she could give the sisters of St. Joseph's in this time of the Great Depression. Anah put Hosana and Elizabeth in the back of the Ford Model A pickup truck every morning with the rest of the schoolchildren. She stood with Tori and Miriam on the lānai as they waved goodbye.

Anah sent cut flowers for the chapel, herbs for Father Maurice's roasts, fresh vegetables and fruits for Chong Sum, pumpkin, banana, and taro bread for the children, and bottles of honey and sweet cream for the holy sisters and Anne Yap, the little girl who befriended both the one-eyed Hosana and the silent Elizabeth.

"She can talk now, Mama," Hosana said to Anah on a Saturday morning trip to K.C. Market to pick up the mason jars Mr. Fatt Yap had ordered from the Ball Company in Muncie, Indiana. Anah would pay with a small sum of money given to her by Ezroh. She vowed never to buy anything on credit, remembering her father's enormous debt to the O'ahu Sugar Plantation's general store that was passed on to his children after his death like many of the other low-paid contract workers.

"What she say?" Anah asked her daughter, humoring her. Elizabeth sat absentmindedly with her thumb wedged in her mouth in the back of the mule wagon with Ai-chan, who held Tori and Miriam.

"Anne Yap taught her in hello-cue-shuns."

"Elocution." Anah smiled at her, dismissing her remarks as she pulled the wagon to the dusty curb outside of K.C. Market.

"She say 'frien', frien' and 'Mama, Mama,'" Hosana said proudly of her sister.

"Oh, is that so?" Anah smiled.

Hosana jumped off the wagon before Anah brought it to a complete stop, Ai-chan yelling at her, "Yonna, yonna! You be careful, you hear? You wanna broke your leg, roughneck? Hosana, sugurarindo! I give you licken, you no listen me!"

Anne Yap peered out from behind the big glass window from between rows of doughy anpan, chewy jin dui, delicate custards, glutinous gau, and jelly rolls. She ran to the doorway, wiped her hands on her soiled white apron, and took Hosana by the hand.

"Ba, this my friend from school, Hosana Soares," she said to her father, who stacked a heavy bag of chicken feed next to the Coca-Cola cooler. He bowed to her as the two of them ran off. "C'mon, Elizabeth," Anne called to the slow-moving one with her thumb still in her mouth, stopping before turning the corner to the back of the store. "Ba!" she yelled. "This the lady that I told you about. The one that make the honey."

"Do jei, sank you, sank you, very good honey, very like the jelly, and very 'ono, do jei," he said. "Missus, you have plenny bee?" he asked, lifting the boxes of mason jars into the back of the wagon.

"Many," Anah said, gesturing wide arcs with her arms.

"Many?" He laughed. "Then you sell here?" he said, winking. "I pay you. And make small profit for me too."

"Yes, yes," Anah stammered at his unexpected offer. "I have many." It would be the beginning of the Hosana Honey Company.

"Good," he said. "You bring. I pay." He finished his loading and put several diamond-shaped pieces of spongy rice cake and jin dui filled with black sugar into a paper bag. "For keiki," he said, pointing at Miriam and Tori.

"Ippe nihe dēbiru," Ai-chan said, bowing and bowing. "Say sank-you, sank-you to Mr. Yap," she said to Miriam and Tori, pressing their heads to bow too.

"I go home and bring back fo' you," Anah said, breathless with excitement. "Hosana! Elizabeth!" she called.

"Go behind," Fatt Yap said. "They play o' there." He pointed.

Anah ran to the back of the store. The three of them hid in a large cardboard box turned over on its side, a dirty, torn blanket covering the opening. Anah pulled the makeshift curtain open to the stench of urine, unwashed sheets and a brown-stained pillow, dirty tin dishes, a jelly jar, crumpled newspapers.

"We going right now," she told them. "Say thank you to Anne. We come back again. Play later on." Anah reached in for Hosana, who reluctantly stood up, Anne behind her. Elizabeth pulled herself deeper into the corner. "Elizabeth!" Anah scolded, "you come with me right now." She did not want to leave, clutching the filthy pillow to her.

Anne stopped. "Sweet dreams for thee," she sang.

"Sweet dreams for thee," Hosana sang with her.

"There's not a comb of honeybee so full of sweets as babe to me," Anne finished, holding out her hand to Elizabeth.

Anah's silent one took that hand in hers, pushing the blanket aside. "And it's o! sweet, sweet!" she whispered with much pride.

"See, Mama?" Hosana said. Anah watched her walk away with Anne Yap and Elizabeth.

See.

"What you got in yo' hand, Elizabeth?" Anah asked as she shoved something into her pocket.

Hosana turned. "Leave it there, I told you, Elizabeth," she scolded. "Thass not yours. Sister Mary Deborah said 'Thou shall not steal.' "

"Leave it there, Elizabeth," Anne Yap said. "That one not yours. That one belong to the skinny man."

Hosana reached into her sister's pocket and pulled out an old tortoise comb. "Give it to me," she said, holding out her hand.

Elizabeth clutched at her pocket. Again, Hosana reached in and this time pulled out an old photograph. "I dunno why you like this. So old and dirty," she said, holding on to the edge of the photo and the tip of the comb.

Anah took them from her to return them to the box.

But when she looked at the photo, she saw:

Dai, the stiff discomfort of a Western collar.

Okaasan, the severity of her dark, formal kimono.

Leah, frilly white dress sitting on Okaasan's lap.

Aki, long hair in ribbons beside her.

Thomas, standing between mother and father in a schoolboy's white-starched shirt and suspenders.

Anah stands alone beside her father.

And Charles, one hand on Okaasan's shoulder the other hand on Aki's.

None of them smile for the long moments after the burst of light and smoke.

"Sit still, sit still, Mama-san, keep the children still, don't cry, little girl, you will ruin the photograph, little boy, little boy, no, no, little boy, don't do that, everyone, please don't move. Mister, whassamatta you? Missus, keep your doggone children still."

ANAH LIFTED the photo and the comb to her face, the smell of her okaasan's scented oils still there, the smell of diesel fuel and ocean on glossy sepia.

Anah's body collapsed in the alley behind the market.

Fatt Yap and the Tale of Hop Charlie

Me find Hop Charlie outside my store. He just sitting on ground in hot sun. All day like that. Face all pāpaʻa just like beef jerky. Look like old man but I know not old man. I tell him come inside bumbye he drop dead so hot. I help him walk inside, right o' hea, he sit down on crate. I give him soda water and anpan.

Then little mo' I help other customer, I turn around, and he sweeping floor, he fixing shelf, he clean window. Say sank-you, sank-you, no can stop say sank-you to me. I give him job. Him very good worker.

But Hop Charlie, he come, he go. Every time I pay little bit, first he give little bit back to me, then he buy candy for Anne, then he go, no come back four day, five day. Then one day, I look, and he sleeping in box. Thass his box, Hop Charlie's house. He no bother nobody. And he kind man, very kind to my Anne, very kind to customer.

I help him because he just like my uncle. He my favorite small uncle. Good small uncle, all time play with me, take me ride on his horse, give me plenty rock candy, take me Ringling circus see lady with beard and man on flying trapeze. He say I the best one of all Yap brothers. He say he can tell I good on inside, mo' better than all ten older brothers. One time, he take me on boat ride in harbor, me and small uncle. One time, he take me downtown Washington Place see the queen, our very sad queen.

But him too, he smoke the hop, go down Chinatown spend all the money on the opium, skinny, skinny, just like Hop Charlie and all sweats. My father love small uncle. I love small uncle. We go get him down there where all the Pa-ke man smoke the hop. We bring him home, but little while mo' he go back. Oh, how he need the hop.

"No can, no can, so-wa, so-wa," he yell at my father. "I need the hop bumbye I die."

I feel sorry fo' small uncle when my father tie him to the bed.

"You listen me," my father tell small uncle, "you no smoke the hop. All pau opium. Bumbye you lawbreaker. America president say no mo' opium in territory of Hawai'i. You like go jailhouse with all the kolohe sailor man, no good Pa-ke, all no good Chinee who smoke the hop?"

Small uncle talk all kine, cry, cry, he like die.

"Let me go, youngest nephew, you love me, you hemo rope. Take off rope, hemo, hemo."

And mo' he cry, mo' him all blue his skin. He no like eat, no like drink water. Pretty soon he no breathe. Him, my small uncle, he dead. But I never forget him. Show me how bow to the queen. She put her hand on my head, you know. Small uncle tell the queen in kanaka words I am the best Yap brother in the Kingdom of Hawai'i.

But Hop Charlie, I no see him long time. This time, long time he no come back. Sometime I so very worry him. I go Chinatown take Anne help me run inside the alley look fo' Hop Charlie just like when I small boy I go look for small uncle.

My Anne, she find Hop Charlie, and we drag him out bring him home to sleep in his box and kau-kau, drink water, so skinny. How many time we bring him home. He okay one, two, three day, try hard no go back there, but little mo' I pay, and he go again.

I no like pay. I know where he go. But I think of small uncle drop dead when he no mo' hop. How he cry like me the one wen' make him sick and mo' sick, when I the one wipe his vomit and turn him side so he no choke. Small uncle tell me I no love him. If I love him, I hemo the rope. Take off rope, hemo, hemo. I no listen. I too much love him. Then he dead. I no like Hop Charlie dead. So I give.

You go take Anne go find brother. She know where. And here, you take money buy hop from fat Pa-ke man sit by door. I show you how give little bit hop, then mo' little bit, so he no so-wa, cry, cry for the hop. Go, go get brother, take the money, go now, hurry, hurry. Bumbye Hop Charlie never come home again.

22

1933

Fatt Yap and his daughter Anne drove Anah and Hosana to Chinatown early the next morning in his five-passenger Phaeton. It was a rainy morning in the valley, fog on the windshield, the jerky flap-flap of the wipers on their cold ride down to the Kapālama Hills into lower Kalihi.

He drove along King Street through a predawn Chinatown, stopping on the corner of Merchant and Bethel, whores and drunks still lingering at the corner, a shirtless hobo curled asleep on the sidewalk, a stocky mama-san setting up a makeshift noodle shop in a small wagon.

He pointed down a narrow, unlit alley. Anne took Hosana by the hand, Anah behind them. They ran along the mossy wet cobblestones on the dark, rank path, the buildings on either side of the alley etched with thick lines of dripping black fungus.

Anne pushed a heavy metal door that opened to another long, dark hallway. The smell of sweet almonds burning, kerosene fumes, wet animal hair, and the musty odor of men full of sweat and alcohol hung in the windowless corridor. A fat, perspiring Chinaman sat behind a counter to the right of the open door in a small, cluttered room lit by a single lantern that gave off a disturbing sallow glow. A mangy calico nursing six newborns slept on a pile of old newspapers.

He barely moved when Anne said, "I come get my uncle." He opened one eye, looked her up and down, then jerked his head toward the darkness ahead of them. The heavy door clanged shut. Anah reached for Hosana in what became an almost total darkness.

The hallway was a maze of doorways that opened to small, barely lit rooms, the opium addicts deep in early morning stupors, men of all ages spread out like stone statues on double-tiered shelves lined with torn bamboo mats. Nearly all the bunks in each room were occupied by two men, a small tray lined with a horn box filled with thick black opium and a bamboo pipe between them.

Anah searched each face, placing the back of her hand over her nose when out of the corner of one room, a haole woman sat up, passing her pipe to the Chinaman beside her. She looked like the granddaughter of the rich missionary family that owned the O'ahu Sugar Planatation, her eyes glazed and vacant, dry lips stuck to white teeth.

"Smoke?" she rasped at Anah.

Anah shook her head.

"Do not stare at me so," she said. "It is terribly impolite of you." She reclined, her body slumping against the wall.

Anne Yap took Anah by the hand and led her to the next room, the occasional sound of groaning, the slow shuffle of bodies, the gurgle of a shared water pipe, but otherwise silence and stench, everything around them, tables, bunks, walls, even the faces, a brownish-gray pallor.

Anah looked at Hosana. She was not afraid.

Then, in a small room near the end of the hallway, Hosana pointed. "Look."

"Charles."

He did not recognize her at first, the languid bodies of the men reclining on wooden crates, some asleep under dirty burlap blankets in this yellow-lit room filled with the sweet, rancid smoke of opium.

He sat on the floor, a fat gray tomcat curled beside him, next to a Chinese man with a graying goatee long and tangled. Their legs entwined, the older man pulled Charles closer as Anah crouched next to him in the dark.

"Charles, wake up. Open your eyes. It's me, Anah," she said to her brother in Japanese, shaking him awake.

The old man with wire-rimmed glasses and a rich Western suit pushed Anah away.

"Charles—"

Her brother's eyes barely open, he reached out a limp hand to her, the doped smile of his contentment as his arm dropped to the floor. A long bamboo pipe rolled between her legs.

"Aki," he whispered, his mouth dry. "I told you to wait for me outside," he said in Japanese. "Go now, Aki. Be a good girl and listen to what I ask of you. Wait for me. I will only be a little while. I promise I will buy you some candy on our way home, Aki."

"It's me, Anah," she said, taking his face firmly in her hands. "Look at me, Charles."

"You dead too, Anah?" he asked, his eyes squinting to see. "Leah said you went away, went way, never came back. Anah ran away from us. Good Anah, when did you die? Leah is cold. Are you cold too? Even the small man is cold. He is so sad, so sad. And hungry. He wants bread and milk. Can someone take the small man to the hospital? Do you know his name?"

The old man laughed. "Small man." He moved his hand between her brother's legs.

"I broken o' dere," Charles said to the old man.

"Yo' small man broke? I fix. Make big man," the old one said, his hand on her brother's groin.

"No work no mo'," Charles said, angry. "I said broken. How many time I tell you, old man, no touchee."

"I have come to take you home," Anah told him. "Get up now. You must leave with me."

He could not even lift his head, but he nodded slowly as if remembering a long ago dream. "Home. Home."

"He stay with me," the old man said. Then turning to Charles, "You promise you stay with Goong-goong if Goong-goong make you happy. I buy plenny hop fo' you and me share-share. We so happy today and you like go?" he whined.

"Go, we go then," Charles managed to say, flicking his hand toward the door. "Aki tired of waiting."

The old man leaned over and kissed her brother's slack mouth. "O-kay, we go. Goong-goong take care you. Then you take care Grandpapa like you promise." The old man looked at Anah, his gray-blue lips pursed.

"Not you, no," Charles said. "Aki stay waiting fo' me outside. We going home." He tried to lift himself, collapsing back onto the floor.

The old man giggled a high, sucking sound. "No, you stay with Goong-goong." He pushed at Charles's shoulder. "Stay, stay, we smoke some mo' hop, o-kay?"

"I going with my sister," Charles said to the old man, staggering at first, then hitting him across the face. "She dead, you know. You better listen to the dead or they will haunt you day and night, you hear me, old man?" he said in Japanese, striking the Chinese face again and again until the old man fell over.

"Oh, take him," the old man said to Anah, rubbing his cheek, then slumping back down to the floor. He fumbled in the dark for his pipe, then lit it. He sucked deeply. "He broken down there anyway. He no good fo' me." Her brother's fingers reached for the pipe. "No, you cannot have," he said, pulling himself away, then relaxing into the haze of smoke. "You bad boy. Go home with yo' *missus*," he teased. "I neva know you like the wahine too, Cha-rwee." Anah pulled Charles away. The old man grabbed her hand hard. "He owe me money, lady," he said.

Anah looked at Charles stumbling toward the open door. She took the coins from her pocket and threw them at the old man's face. He laughed, the money falling to the floor around him. Anah lifted her brother, Anne and Hosana on the other side, and dragged him down the dark alley and into the street.

EZROH CARRIED Charles into the main house, then lay his bird-like body on his mother's bed, pulling the heavy quilt over him, his body cold and twitching in a restless stupor.

Tora-san took the glass vials of opium from Anah's hands, Ai-chan taking her little ones away from the dark room. Anah pulled open the curtains. Charles tightened his closed eyes, turning his face away from the sunlight, as she settled into the rocking chair beside the bed.

"How will I do this?" Anah asked Ezroh, who looked at the shell of her brother and shook his head in dismay.

"My father said to give you this." Ezroh put his old treasured kaula ʻili on Anah's lap. "Matthew is almost finished with my new rope. He is oiling it tonight." He put his hands on Anah's shoulders. "Use this rope."

Anah let it fall to the floor. "No, I cannot," Anah said to him. "Maybe when he wakes up and sees that it is me, he will not—"

"My father said we are going to have to tie him up or he will run right back. Or he will stay and steal money or things he can sell and lie to you. Anah, listen—he will not be Charles again until the opium is out of his body."

"But he will die just like small uncle."

"Who?" Ezroh asked.

"We give him little bit in tea Mr. Rex make from his plant medicine," Tora-san said from the doorway to the room. "When he crying, he all so-wa, like die, we give him little bit in the water, in the soup. Make mo' little bit, mo' little bit every day. Still yet, he going biri-biri in his own pants, all shake-shake, pilau sweat, stink like the pig, but we no can let go the rope, bumbye he go back. And then we start all over again. Maybe next time, he hide from you. No can find. Next thing you know, he dead. You listen Mr. Rex, Anah. He know what he talk this kine."

"Oh, Charles," Anah cried, her body sobbing over his, the sweet mossy smell of opium glazing his skin.

Her brother groaned, a strange pleasure on his face, a bemused chuckle, his eyes moving back and forth under his closed lids.

Tora-san lifted Anah off her brother. "You be strong, Anah-san," he warned. "All pau cry, no mo', wipe your eye. Your brother walking between the alive and the dead. You be strong, you call him back. You cry, cry, cry, then you good fo' nothing—he good as dead."

Hosana came up from behind Tora-san. She placed her small hand on Anah's shoulder, squeezing with a child warrior's reassurance. She took the rope off the floor and handed it to her mother.

Anah wiped her eyes and stood up from that chair. She removed her brother's filthy clothes, handing them to Hosana. Then she pulled the mattress out from under him. She bathed him thoroughly with hot water, then tied his naked body covered with ti leaves and old blankets to the wooden bed frame.

As the hours passed, Anah wiped up his cloudy piss and foamy diarrhea even as he slurred angry words at her, "Go away from me, ghost daughter," vile words about their mother, "Jezebel Japonêsa," their father, "stupid Portuguese donkey," and Anah again and again, "dead sister, you are dead to me."

Vomit and frothy yellow bile gurgled out of his mouth in the days that followed, Charles moving in and out of a volatile consciousness of horrid daydreams. "Duk Ho, no, Aki watching. I bleeding. Stop it, old man. Get it out of me. I no love you. Yes, I love you. No, this not love. Yes, I said I love you."

His body full of sores, Anah rubbed honey and noni juice into the open wounds on his arms, feet, and back, on his anus, ripped and infected.

Rex Soares grated arrowroot tubers into a fine starch that he mixed with poi to stop the diarrhea, the gray gruel melting out of the sides of her brother's mouth. Anah put drops of opium into everything he ate and drank, as he gagged and heaved in the nausea of his withdrawal.

Anah woke in a half sleep on the chair beside his bed one night to the sound of wind chimes, the trill of a shakuhachi, *a flute's high notes*, and the sadness of a distant koto, *a zither's resonance*.

"Do not play with Okaasan's koto, Aki," Charles whispered in Japanese as the zither's music grew closer and louder. Anah turned to him, his eyes closed, his lips mumbling. "Sad, so sad, playing your koto like that. Put it away, Okaasan, hide it quick before he takes it from you."

A marble rolled across the bedroom floor.

"Draw a circle in the dirt outside by Vovó's swing," he said with great longing. "My marble bag, over there by Thomas's books. I am coming," his voice trailed off. "Play marbles with me, hurry, before he comes home."

Anah listened to heavy footsteps coming toward the room from down the long hallway.

"Ezroh?"

The footsteps stopped outside the door. The door creaked open to a bitter wind.

"Abba, no!" Charles writhed in his bed, his body shivering, his teeth chattering. "No, Dai, no! Stop!" The ropes cut into his wrists and ankles. "Go away, Father. It hurts."

Anah lay herself over him, brushing hair away from his brow, calming him, his eyes wide and afraid looking up at the ceiling and into the corners of the room.

"I must be home," he whispered to her.

Home.

Anah turned toward the empty doorway.

"Get away from him and go back to the hell from where you came," she snarled in an earthy Portuguese.

The door closed, the heavy footsteps moving down the hallway, the patter of children's feet following behind, all of them disappearing into the nothingness of the night's silence.

Anah picked up the marble from the floor and held it in her hand.

A child giggled in the corner of the room.

HOSANA SAT with her uncle when Anah tended to her sisters or to her chores, running to get her mother at the first sign of trouble.

"He choking."

"He crying again."

"His so-wa bleeding."

"He no can stop shake-shake."

She cleaned her uncle's body, trimmed his fingernails and toenails, wiped his hands and his feet with a cool washcloth, and combed his hair.

She fed her uncle the familiar dishes Anah cooked for him: cabbage with tōfu and dried shrimp; tender pumpkin with belly pork; tsukemono, his favorite pickled vegetables on hot rice.

Hosana prayed: "Bless us, O Lord, and these gifts which we are about to receive from your bounty, through Christ our Lord. Amen. Uncle? Uncle, you in there?"

These dishes Anah prepared to lure him back to her, Hosana blowing on the hot spoonfuls until they cooled, then feeding him with a maternal patience. She wiped his face and slowly poured water into his dry mouth.

Her daughter prayed: "We give you thanks for all your benefits, O almighty God, who lives and reigns forever. Amen. Uncle? You can hear me, Uncle?"

She recited the holy Rosary at his bedside with the vigilance of the saints as Anah listened at the doorway. She sang to him, "Sweet dreams for thee," songs she learned from Sister Mary Deborah, "Angel of God, my guardian dear," songs Anah sang to her own sisters, "Nen ne yo, Aki, nen ne yo, Leah, nen ne yo, imōto," Anah's sisters who died in her arms.

Then one day, Charles awoke.

"What happened to your eye, Anah?" he asked her that day.

"The owl came and took it away," Hosana answered. She was calm and unafraid.

"What owl, Anah?" he asked.

"See the owl in the tree?" She pointed to the aviary as though she had been waiting all of her life to tell him.

Charles turned his head toward the sun on the Koʻolau Mountains. He squinted his eyes, then nodded.

"He lost his wing so he cannot hunt anymore," she answered in Portuguese. "I gave him my eye so he could see better."

"Tell me a story," he asked her.

"Once upon a time, there was a kind prince—" she began.

"Does your story have a happy ending?" he asked.

"Yes," she promised.

"Then take the ropes off me, Anah," he begged. "Let the prince go. My body ache fo' the pipe. I going come back, I promise."

"No, Uncle."

"Uncle?"

Anah stepped into the room.

"Anah!" he said, looking at her and then back at Hosana, back and forth at their alikeness. "Oh, my Anah!"

Anah put the tray of food and tea on the small table.

"Charles!"

Elizabeth and Tori wandered into the room.

He looked at Anah's three daughters and began to weep.

"No cry, Uncle," Hosana consoled, smoothing his hair away from his eyes, wiping the tears from his cheeks.

Anah loosened the rope that bound his hands as Hosana helped him to sit up. He took her in his arms, sobbing, reaching for his sister. Anah loosened the ropes that bound his feet. Elizabeth and Tori, serene in his presence, sat on the bed frame.

Ai-chan came in with Miriam in her arms to gather up the children. "So sorry, so sorry, Anah-san. I turn around and the keiki all gone," she said. "Come, come away from Uncle."

"Please get my brother's clothes," Anah told her. "Their uncle has come home."

IT WAS the worst year of the Great Depression. Still, Rex Soares promised not to let go of any of his workers at the dairy. He had been forced to turn his prized Model A into a tractor when the old one broke down in the summer. But his workers would remain. He did not welcome another mouth to feed, one who was too sick and weak to earn his keep. Yet he was Anah's beloved brother.

Anah watched Charles improve day by day, week by week, playing with her children as she fed and milked the cows. How he ran with the clumsy Elizabeth in the pasture, how he fed the baby calves with Tori, how he carried Miriam on his shoulders, how he loved Hosana as he had loved Anah.

Anah listened to his voice as he spoke of their mother and their sisters as he bathed the children, his stories of their okaasan's long black hair, her beautiful face and tiny hands that played the koto, Aki's trickery with the mead-drunken Floyd at the old stable, Leah's precious collection of olivines in a tin can under their small house in Portuguese Camp Four. He told the children stories of their mother, Anah, whom he loved most of all.

Anah watched him as he wandered about the aviary feeding mice and chicks to Hosana's owl, her daughter running to get him when he lingered too long, taming the rabbits and hens, feeding the stray dogs and feral cats, taming the owl who soon lighted on his arm wrapped with old rags.

Anah wiped his tears as she tied him to his bed at night.

Anah kissed his brow as she untied him in the morning.

This Anah did for one year. Not once did he complain.

The cowboys laughed at him as they drank freely of celebration crates of Old Tub and Seagram's, Prohibition repealed this year, laughed in drunkenness at Charles's feminine ways as he walked with a feline's gait, his lack of skills as he tried to pitch alfalfa to the cows or mulch and seed the vegetable garden. He was better at women's chores, and they laughed at him, but he did not care.

When he looked at Anah from across the table as they shared their meals or from the shade of the gazebo as the children gathered olivines or from his bed as she sat with him until he fell asleep, he looked at her with a knowing:

He was home.

And she had found him.

They would never lose each other again.

Charles Tells the Children Fairy Tales

Sunday night:

Once upon a time, there was a prince. He once had a beautiful mother. But she left him alone on the docks for a faraway land called Nippon. He once had a cruel father. But somebody poisoned him. He once had an older brother and a little half sister. But they became slaves to his evil vovó who lived next door. He once had three sisters. He loved them more than he loved himself. But one by one, they were taken away from him. He cried for them every day, years and years of crying. For you see, he never saw them again.

Monday night:

Once upon a time, there was a prince. But nobody knew he was a prince. He lived in the most dirty part of town after his vovó threw him out of the house. He did not have a family. He had no one. He shined the sailors' shoes. He picked the beans for the cows. He carried golf bags for the rich haoles. He slept curled up on the streets, and he was always hungry and afraid. One day as he was shining shoes, he heard someone calling his name. When he looked up, it was the sister he loved most, but she was riding away in a buggy. He cried and cried, "Come back, come back!" But the buggy did not stop. And you see, he never saw her again.

Tuesday night:

Once upon a time, there was a prince. He was a very lonely prince. One day he was walking the dark streets of his kingdom. He came upon an old man. The old man had a magic pipe. This magic pipe could cure the prince's loneliness. He took the prince to a dark room filled with other lonely men. And then he lit the magic pipe. Soon, the prince was happy. He fell asleep for long hours and dreamed of his mother, the queen with long black hair. He dreamed of his three sisters and his little half sister wearing pretty dresses. He was no longer sad. For you see, with the help of the magic pipe, he saw his loved ones again.

Wednesday night:

Once upon a time, there was a prince. One morning when he woke up, he had no clothes on. Someone had taken his fine robes and shoes. There was blood on the bed. But he did not know where he was. He wrapped himself in the sheets and ran out to the streets. The old man with the magic pipe called to him, "Come back, come back, you bad boy!" He ran all the way to his kingdom. The queen was packing her willow reed suitcase. He followed her to the docks, where she boarded a big steamship. She did not say good-bye to the prince. "Take me with you, I beg you, take me with you," he called to her. Instead, she threw a package into the waters below. The prince dove in after it. Inside, he found a tortoise comb and a picture of his family. He never saw his mother again.

Thursday night:

Once upon a time there was a prince. He lived in a little box. In the little box, he kept a tortoise comb and a picture. They were his only possessions. He kissed his mother and his sisters good night before he went to sleep. He became sick with sadness and longing. He wanted to see his loved ones again. He went to look for the old man with the magic pipe.

Friday night:

Once upon a time. The old man wanted money. I had no money. I gave him my love. It was all I had left. If I loved him, he let me smoke the magic pipe. Aki came to visit me all the time. She did bad things to the old man. Leah came with her. She sat in the dark with us, crying all the time. I wondered why I never saw the sister I loved the most. She never came to visit me. So I smoked more from the magic pipe. My father came, laughing at me all the while. I smoked the magic pipe. I dreamed of my mother in a faraway land with a new husband and new children. I smoked the magic pipe. I was not sad. At least I saw my family.

Saturday night:

Once upon a time, I knew love. Love went far away. I searched for love. There was no love.

Then love found me. Love brought me home. Love made me well. Hello, my love. Good night, my love:

Nen ne yo, Hosana,

Nen ne yo, Lizzie-beth,

Nen ne yo, To-chan,

Nen ne yo, Miriam,

Nen ne yo, Anah,

Nen ne yo, Aki,

Nen ne yo, Leah.

Go to sleep, my love. I will see you when you wake up in the morning.

And they all lived as happily as they could forever after.

23

1939

Hosana grew strong through the years tending to injured animals and birds brought to the ranch by the neighbors of the valley. Ezroh built her another aviary for the brown owls too small to survive or abandoned by their parents. She hand-fed her nestlings strips of raw chicken meat. They roosted in the aviary during the day and took flight in the row of pine trees to hunt at dusk, always returning home by morning.

Anah walked with Hosana through the grove of pines, watched the yellow-feathered faces of her owls and the stretch of their wings. The brown silence of their flight through the boughs stilled her. They walked along a path of pine needles, her daughter selecting stones to bring home for Elizabeth's vast collection.

She studied the scat, black orbs filled with delicate mouse bones and undigested hair, the tip of her walking stick dismantling the tangle of skeleton and skull. Her owls kept her in sight, their faces turning to find her as she hid behind trees covered with the fine chartreuse lace of lichen.

By late afternoon, clouds drifting along the upper reaches of the pines, the heavy buzz of bees diminishing, the fog like Baba Yaga's fingers reaching toward them, Anah and Hosana would start home.

She called to them with a high *kuri-kuri-kuri-ko*, her owls low-gliding along the path ahead of them then rising into a high circle over the treetops, the detail of branches and leaves blurred by a darkening sky and the intensity of what appeared before Anah:

One day, she saw a girl walking along a path.

Then one day, she saw a young woman walking along a path.

The owls in the trees watched her too, their soundless brown bodies soon venturing beyond the confine of the pines.

ANAH COULD NOT say she loved her most, her big-boned, one-eyed daughter who began riding out with the cowboy gang at twelve to repair fences or maintain pipelines on the range paddocks or rescue injured calves. By thirteen, she wielded the inoculation needle with a surgeon's precision as the muggers branded and castrated the yearlings.

Anah loved her for riding with her as they searched the valley for the retarded Elizabeth who was saddened by the departure of her sisters for school every day, bored with Anah's constant tending to the many hives and Ai-chan's preoccupation with milking and meals. Elizabeth wandered away, following her invisible friends, the cold and hungry ones with names she kept forgetting, choosing instead to call them by nicknames.

Anah knew of whom she spoke. With the strength of her mind, she willed away the presence of the invisible ones. But Elizabeth kept calling them:

Goldie. Monkey. Smiley. Twiddle-dee and Twiddle-dum. Sausage, Sausage, catch me if you can, you can't catch me, I'm the Sausage Man.

ANAH LOVED the way Hosana tended to Elizabeth, always frightened by her ordeals. She loved how she told her stories or repeated prayers or sang children's songs. She loved how she calmed her sister by sitting with her to collect olivines near the gazebo, filling a soda bottle with the tiny volcanic stones that glistened as Elizabeth held it up to the sunlight, admiring it from all angles with one eye shut tight.

When Ezroh converted the old butter house to a honey house for Anah, Hosana built sturdy shelves along the walls for Elizabeth's collection of stones and soda bottles filled with clay and Bennington marbles, Job's tears, olivines, or koa seeds. She collected odd knickknacks—a tarnished bronze Mr. Tod, a metal pram, its paint chipped, and a musical tin egg. She kept broken trinkets—half a Mickey Serviette ring, the head of a Jaymar Red Riding Hood, and pewter horses and dogs without a leg or tail. She loved collecting corroded horseshoes. And she filled bottles with feathers. Hosana humored her sister by marveling at the bizarre treasures.

Anah loved Hosana's bravado, her apiculturist's apprentice, learning from her mother the skill of beekeeping as she had from Sister Mary Deborah. She took the inevitable daily bee stings with gritty resolution, biting out the wriggling green stingers from her skin, then continuing on with her work. She wore her bee hat and gloves with great pride, later fitting Elizabeth and Tori with bee hats that she had Ai-chan sew for them.

Anah loved her. Her imperfection. Her warrior's spirit. Her swaggering optimism. Her sharp wit. Her wry certainty. Her kind heart.

She was not the beauty of Tori, a delicate Japanese bird with porcelain features, gentility, a whisper of voice and presence. The vanity of an elegant courtesan's face reflected in a window, water, or mirror. The precision of voice and manner.

She was not the sickly frailty of Miriam, light haired and fair skinned, favored by her aunts for her completely Portuguese appearance, instructed early to never reveal her Japanese heritage, to lie if she must. A shadow girl who followed her To-chan.

Hosana was a hearty and bawdy one-eyed cowboy, spitting Skoal dip farther than her cousins David and Michael, riding faster as they raced on horseback through the forest, skinning hides with the buck knife given to her by her Avô Rex with greater precision than most of the cowboys, learning more quickly, she outwitted them all easily, Anah's firstborn, her first blood relative when she had no one but herself.

She never called herself ugly, as had the other children and the cowboys, standing firm in some center place of herself inhabited by the holy sisters of St. Joseph's, the beautiful Virgin, the blessed Christ, God himself. There was no ugliness therein.

But there was ugliness without.

Anah could not stop the taunting that took place in the fields when, with the vulgar cowboys, Hosana traded jibes and obscenities, narrowing in on their weaknesses and hurling at them the most brutal insults. And they at her.

She could not stop her Aunty Tova from making remarks about her. "Such an ugly duckling." Remarks made at dinner. "A homely, half-breed girl." Remarks made at celebrations. "Hosana is the family eyesore. She will never be married off. But never mind, it is one less dowry for Ezroh. And someone to tend to him when Anah dies."

Clever remarks in Portuguese that made Rex Soares and Aunty Lydia chuckle. "The girl has an eye. But so does a potato. And the girl has a head. But so does a pin."

"Tova is just ribbing the girl," Rex Soares would say with a chuckle. "Where is your sense of humor?"

Anah could not stop the incessant teasing from Hosana's schoolmates or cousins who blindsided her with their ridicule *a hand over an eye* and mockery *a blind man's bump into a tree, a trip, a spin, then a fall.*

Hosana pummeled them all into deferential submission.

And Anah could only love her more.

But it was not enough.

Anah found her in Charles's room one night before she strapped him into his bed. She stared into the small mirror above his bureau, her eye patch strewn on the floor.

"Uncle, why do tears come out from here?" she asked him. "There is nothing there." She moved her finger into the empty socket. "Do you know why I cry from both eyes even if this one is no better than dead?"

"I know," he said.

"Why, Uncle?" she asked.

He paused for what Anah thought cruel moments filled with his unintended answer:

Because you are ugly, a hideous, unlovable creature with one eye. You will never find true love. You will know only the love of a mother and father, sisters and uncle.

"One day," he began, "true love will find you. This I promise you, my sweet Hosana. This man will see your heart's beauty. The beauty that I see." He did not look at her but turned to see Anah standing at the door.

Hosana wiped the tears from her face, picked up the eye patch from the floor, and tied it over her blind eye.

"Mentiroso," she whispered.

Liar.

IT WAS the summer that Kenji's youngest brother arrived at the ranch. He had first run away from a young common-law wife and three little children in the impovershed district of Naha, Okinawa, then run away after seducing his thirteen-year-old paramour in Honokaʻa, the plantation store owner's youngest daughter, pregnant with his bastard child. And in running, he had broken his contract with the Hāmākua Sugar Plantation on the Big Island by stowing away on the SS *Malolo*, a steamship headed for Oʻahu. Kenji hid him from the plantation's bounty hunters in the shed behind his small house for months.

Shifuku, handsome and cocksure. Shifuku, unmarried and brash. Shifuku, deep voiced and magisterial with black-slit eyes, began venturing out of the confines of that enclosure.

When he could no longer remain a secret, Ai-chan pleaded with Rex Soares. "He our family. Kenji promise Mama he take care of Shifuku. No like lose face with Papa and Mama and ancestors in Okinawa. Please, Mr. Rex, he hard worker. Now Kenji back so-wa, he not so good worker as befo'. Now Kenji makule old man. Shifuku work for Kenji. No need pay. Times is hard. No kabi jin. No money."

Rex Soares sighed, shaking his head in deep thought.

"I told you no make humbug fo' Mr. Rex, you Ai-chan," Tora-san scolded. "Go, go inside kitchen." He pushed her toward the door. "So sorry, Mr. Rex. I tell Ai-chan no humbug you. She no listen—"

"Where is Kenji?" Rex Soares asked.

Ai-chan began crying. "Kenji no like ask you," she said. "He shame. You very good man to us. We have good life. We no need work hō hana like dog in cane field. Like Shifuku and Kenji papa and mama. So sorry, so sorry," she said, bowing as she spoke.

"I no can pay him good wage," Rex Soares said.

"No need. No need pay." She bustled, waving her hands. "Bumbye he go. Only stay chotto," she said, her thumb and pointer indicating the brevity of his stay.

"Tell Kenji his brother work with him. And he help Anah with the bees. We make mo' money. Go get Kenji and his brother. And go get Anah."

Ai-chan was out of breath when she found Anah in the honey house. "Anah-san, hāyē, hāyē, Mr. Rex like talk to you. Run, run, Anah-san. Go to the cookhouse!" She pulled at her arm. Hosana closed the spigot and passed the bottle of the avocado grove harvest to Tori, who labeled it and placed it in a box for delivery.

"Right now?" Anah asked, wiping sticky honey from Elizabeth's face with the bottom of her shirt. "We busy. We delivery today pau hana time."

"Hekuna, hekuna," Ai-chan said, pressing her hands against Anah's behind to scoot her out the door. "Hurry, he like talk to you good news."

"But I have to finish, then clean up—"

"Good news?" Hosana asked, removing the empty frames from the extractor. "Hurry, Mama," she said, taking Elizabeth's hand. "Avô get good news." Miriam ran after them, and Anah followed out the door.

Shifuku stood on the lānai of the cookhouse. He was not wearing a shirt. He stared at them as they approached the steps, looking them over, all of them, one by one with his black-slit eyes.

"Shifuku, this Anah," Ai-chan said. "She your boss lady."

He crossed his arms over his chest and stared down at them with a smirk and a sarcastic nod. He looked long at Tori. She demured in an embarrassed flirtation, gazing up at him again and again. He looked at Elizabeth. She slumped down and sat on the dirt road, her legs splayed. He looked at Miriam, who ran inside the cookhouse. And then he looked at Hosana. She looked right back at him. He raised one eyebrow at her haughtiness and intensified his gaze.

"I no need help," Anah said. "I get plenty hands," she said, putting her arms around her daughters. She tried to move them all toward the main house. Elizabeth refused to stand. She wrapped her arms around her knees and began rocking slowly.

Rex Soares stepped out onto the lānai, holding Miriam's hand. "Anah, Kenji's brother only here for short while. Why you no come inside. We talk story little bit."

"But I no like—"

"Come inside, Anah," he said with authority.

Shifuku watched Anah like an angry snake poised to strike, lifting his eyebrows in approval at a giggling Tori, sucking his teeth as Hosana passed by him, Elizabeth comforting herself by looking for olivines on the road.

"Eh, hāberu," he called to Elizabeth, laughing, mocking. He batted his slit-eyes at her.

She was not a butterfly, dirt smudged onto the sticky honey around her mouth. She was not a butterfly, hair tangled and wild. She was not a butterfly, her dirty hands poking the dusty road.

It was the first time Ai-chan did not defend Elizabeth.

Hosana turned in a quick fury. "Nun naran," she hissed in his Uchinanchu.

"What you said? I good for lots of things," he shot back, staring her down. "You watch," he challenged.

SHE DID WATCH him. Every day, watching and waiting for a morsel of his seductive attention like a needy, neglected dog. He stole secret glances at her and whispered beguiling words in passing for only her to hear, "Churasan, churasan, call the owls to me."

He brushed against her as they worked in the heat of the honey house, the man who called her beautiful, meeting her in the darkness of the pine trees, waiting for her near the musky feed bins in the barn or in the shed behind Kenji's small house. Always locked in his prolonged gaze. Always an excuse to be off alone and near to him.

But Anah watched him too. How he leered at her daughters, lingering around the bathhouse or the apiary. Throwing little stones at their private parts to tease and titillate them. Touching them, all the time touching them. Taking their schoolbooks or tablets, Anah's daughters chasing him, laughing and screaming in the pasture. Sitting on the fence post with a stalk of grass in his mouth, watching Hosana in the breaking pen as she trained Ezroh's spare horse. Anah watched him throw the cat like a rag doll off a lānai chair, put his feet up, then lean back into the nothingness of his days.

Anah watched a man play sister against sister. "Who like me ride with them? You, Hosana? Or you, To-chan? Who like come with me to the north pasture? Who should I choose?"

He played daughter against mother. "Hosana, why your mama no like you go with me? She no trust you? You not doing nothing bad. Maybe *she* like come with me. Tell her mind her own business."

Then Anah watched as he turned Ai-chan and Kenji against her. "Anah, why you talk like that to Shifuku? He no do nothing to you.

You the one all time make humbug to Shifuku. Shifuku our family, you know."

Even Ezroh began questioning Anah's disdain for Shifuku. "Tell me, Anah. Just tell me plainly. What has he done to offend you?" he asked her in Portuguese one night. "He has been polite and hardworking in my presence. You are making him out to be a villain, but I am afraid you are only making yourself look bad."

She was to blame for the growing distrust among all of them. Her words planted seeds of hatred in everyone. She needed to accept him as *family*, as Ai-chan and Kenji had accepted her when she arrived at the ranch, and as Ai-chan and Kenji had loved each of their daughters.

To all of them, he was happy-go-lucky Shifuku.

"Hoi, Shifuku, you nice voice, you sing with me the old time Uchinanchu song pau hana time. We drink the sake and ʻōkolehao with the cowboy at the bunkhouse." He became Tora-san's late-night, sake-drinking buddy.

To all of them, he was charming Shifuku.

"Nohea say Shifuku just right for her Abigail. And he treat her so kind. Maybe they marry," Ai-chan whispered to Charles over breakfast. "Maybe we family with Kahalelehua. Maybe they let us be grandma and grandpa to their keiki!" she beamed at the prospect of her and Kenji being hānai grandparents.

He was kowtowing, humble Shifuku.

"He will not accept a penny for all of his back-breaking labor," Rex Soares said to Uncle Marcus on payday. "He will not be compensated according to his wishes."

He was hardworking Shifuku.

"The coops, the pigpens, the stable, the barn, all clean. And the gardens all fertilized," Matthew marveled one pau hana on the lānai.

He was smart Shifuku who outwitted the plantation luna.

"And all the way from Hāmākua Sugar, he been follow that rugged coastline down Laupāhoehoe, hide down the point, then go way up mauka in the forest hide under the waterfall so the dog no can smell, all the way back roads he go Nīnole stay in the gulch eat guava 'til the bounty hunter go 'way, then go Honomū stay little while like one monk with the old bonsan who the priest at the church, then when the coast clear, the bugga run all the way down Onomea, Pāpa'ikou, then go Hilo, hurry up hop on the steamship. Even their best dogs no could track him—he hide under the flume, inside the cliff cave, by the drainage ditch, way up mauka in the forest," Uncle Stanley told Ricardo by the corral. "He leave one cold trail, that Shifuku."

For heaven's sake, he was a Catholic, Shifuku.

"Mama," Hosana called to her mother from the back of the delivery truck each Sunday. "Hurry, Shifuku taking all us to Mass. Please come with us. Sister Mary Deborah asking fo' you."

How could they all not see?

The snake slide into the garden, the snake coiling itself in some musky darkness, winding his oily body around the leg of one daughter and then the next, then squeezing tight, the snake with a lying tongue and black-slit eyes.

Anah watched him. It was all she could do. And she waited for him to steal her Hosana's heart.

SHE WAS ONLY FOURTEEN when she ran with him. He had broken his contract with the sugar plantation. And they were looking for him. He could have run by himself. Hopped a steamship to another island, leeched off another brother, hid away in another shed in back of a small house. But he took her with him.

She was ugly; she was certain.

"You one-eye blind. You deformed. Who going love you when you look like that? The world see you, they think you strange monster. Only me no think you ugly. Nobody going ever love you. Only me."

And as her Uncle Charles had prophesied, love had found Anah's daughter.

"I the only one you going ever catch. You lucky I like you. You lucky I look at you. You lucky I no say you ugly to nobody. I no laugh when they all laugh at you. You yanakāgi, nobody but me, you hear me? You not ugly only to me."

That one day had come.

"You leave with me now. And if you no go right now, I never come back to get you. No mo' second chance. This is it. You listen to me. You no go now, you never see me again. Never."

But he did not see the beauty her uncle spoke of.

Shifuku saw a hideous, vulnerable girl desperately wanting, dying inside, then wrapped his snake-self around the center of her, the center place of her self inhabited by the holy sisters of St. Joseph's, the beautiful Virgin, the blessed Christ, God himself, the center place inhabited by the mother who loved her most. He put himself inside her and bound her to him in a lover's need and want forever.

And then he stole her from her mother.

Anah did not eat. Anah did not sleep.

Ezroh forbade her from speaking to the bounty hunters who arrived at the dairy. And then Anah did not speak at all.

"Shifuku will return with her after they all leave," he promised her. "We cannot implicate ourselves for harboring him. We must all keep our silence."

Days turned into a week.

"Kenji has sent word to his brother with an Okinawan brakeman on the train who will hand-carry his letter to the other side of the island. He has written Shifuku that he can return safely now with Hosana."

A week turned into many weeks. More letters were sent with no response.

Charles urged Anah to tend to the hives overflowing with honey. "They are all swarming, Anah. There are new hives in fallen trees. You have to do something. The horses and cows are spooking."

But Anah would not leave her room.

Elizabeth's hair was unkempt, her face filthy. She did not bathe for days on end. "Sing hosanna, sing hosanna, sing hosanna to the King of kings," she muttered as she wandered the main house looking room to room for her sister. "Hosana school? Hosana school?" she asked mindlessly. Then finally she wandered away, searching for her sister.

Late that night, Ezroh and Charles found her sitting outside the Puerto Rican dance hall with a kachi-kachi band and canteen dancers on the other side of Kalihi Valley, sitting on the ground looking for olivines surrounded by drunken sailors on shore leave, sailors hungry for homemade pastilles, empanadillas, and bacalao, hungry for girls, any girl. Her white dress was ripped and soiled. She was without her underwear.

They tied her to a bed next to Anah's at night. She listened to her daughter's nonsensical babbling but could not respond. "Uncle Monkey and me. Goldie in the yellow dress." Anah listened to her crying but could not comfort her.

Anah would not speak to Ai-chan or Kenji.

She did not eat.

She did not sleep.

And in the ensuing delirium, she let the invisible ones return to her. And what she saw, Elizabeth, tied next to her, saw.

Aki was furious with the stench of the muddy river. Wiliwili thrashed the thick brown torrent of her anger.

"Smiley? Smiley mad at you, Mama, mad, mad."

Leah cried, pacing back and forth, back and forth. She did not know where she was.

"Goldie in the yellow dress want to go home, home, home. But where is home?"

Anah's father laughed at her, laughed at Charles, danced on the floor of his new house.

"Sausage man, catch me if you can."

Beatrix and Bertha, babies covered with mud, their mouths wailed, full of vomit, milk, leaves, and sod.

"Twiddle-dee, cold like me. Twiddle-dum, you can't come."

And Seth, still hurt by Anah's abandonment of him, reached out his arms to her, then pulled away, again and again.

"Monkey no love Mama. Uncle Monkey love me?"

Anah welcomed them to the madness of her sorrow, welcomed them to their new home, the invisible ones who followed her to the huge aviary one moonless night. She unlatched the doors. The hungry, dying owls cried inside. The flurry of brown wings and feathers. Their desperate talons scratched at Anah's arms and face. She released them all to the laughter and delight of the children in the trees.

"ANAH! ANAH!" Ezroh came into the room, lifting her frail body from the bed. "Listen," he said, his hands trembling as he unfolded a letter.

> *Dear Mother and Father,*
>
> *I will be home soon. Shifuku lied to me. He is drunk all the time. He is gambling all the time. He beats me. I am with child. Do not try to find me. He says he will harm you. I will come home very soon.*
>
> *I love you,*
> *Hosana*

"Get Kenji," Anah said to Ezroh. She untied Elizabeth from her bed. "Get washed up, right now," she instructed her. "To-chan, help your sister."

Anah dressed herself in Ezroh's trousers and white shirt. "Let me take care of this," Ezroh whispered to Anah as he braided her long hair. Anah said nothing.

Tora-san served her pork broth with mustard cabbage and a strong black tea. "I told Ai-chan no good that man, no good brother of Kenji. He make fool of me. He make fool of Anah-san. But Ai-chan no listen," he said, as he served Anah her first bowl of rice at the dining table in weeks.

Anah slowly finished her meal.

"Anah-san?" Kenji whispered from the door.

"Where is your brother?" Anah asked him, her voice a scratchy monotone.

"They say Waipahu," he said. "They say 'Ewa. Somebody seen him Honouliuli. Me dunno. Same what I tell Mr. Rex and Ezroh. Me dunno."

"Why you lying to me?" Anah screamed, hurling her bowl of hot soup at him. Charles scrambled around the table to stop her.

"Same what I tell plantation man," he said, stoic. "Me dunno."

"Liar," Anah snarled. "When did you become a fucking liar, old man? Your brother has my daughter. He hurting our Hosana. Where he stay?"

Kenji said nothing, then lowered his eyes. Elizabeth screamed, covering her ears and closing her eyes. He could no longer look at her, not then, not ever again.

Tori ran inside. "Hosana's owls," she cried. "They all in the sky."

Miriam ran for the house, wrapped in a moving shadow of bees, the owls circling low.

Ezroh grabbed Kenji by his shoulders. "Where is he?" he said, shaking him, then throwing him against the wall.

"Kahuku," came the answer, but it was soft. "Kahuku plantation with Kenji cousin Buntaro," Ai-chan said, holding Miriam in her arms, brushing away stray bees from her hair and pulling the stingers from her face. "Shifuku promise he come back with Hosana," she continued. "I send him letter. 'The coast clear. Come back.' But one week, two week, he no come. I send one mo' letter then one mo'. Then Buntaro write back. He tell that Shifuku stay with him little while mo'. I tell Kenji mo' betta we go get—"

"Shut up your mouth, Ai-chan," Kenji warned, raising his hand at her.

"Kenji, you the one," she sobbed, "tell me mind my own business. I say, 'Look Anah-san, no eat, bumbye she die.' He tell, 'She no die. Who your kuleana? *Her* or *me*? Me your husband. Me your business.' " She held Miriam close, sobbing.

"Go get Matthew and Bert," Ezroh said to Charles. "They must be near Kamanaiki by now."

Charles hurried out to saddle his horse.

"We will take the delivery truck at dawn," Ezroh said to Anah. "She will be home by nightfall."

"I am coming with you," Anah demanded. "Watch my daughters," she said to Tora-san, who held them close to him. "I am bringing Hosana home."

Anah stepped outside. A cold northerly storm rumbled in the evening. The owls cried, circling slowly overhead. She sat in the honey house and waited for morning.

What Elizabeth Saw, What Elizabeth Heard Tied to Her Bed at Night

'Little girl, it is cold out here. Let us in, please let us in. See us outside your window?'

'Little girl, we are hungry. You have bread? You have milk?'

'I need a doctor. His head is broken. Her arm is broken. My heart is broken. Hurry, we need a doctor.'

'Monkey is cold. See him shivering? He fell from a tree. His head cracked open. Your Uncle Small Man. Your Uncle Monkey.'

'Come play with us. Run down the hall with us. Hear us running?'

'Slide down the banister. Go now, your turn. Want me to pinch you, little girl? Want me to slap you, little girl? Then slide.'

'Jump from the roof. Watch me. Go now, your turn. Want me to pull your hair, little girl? Then jump.'

'Kick her bed, kick her. She left us all alone. Never came back. Never took us home. She is a liar.'

'Mentirosa.'

'Once upon a time, we played in the trees. Played in the wind. You hear us laughing all the time, don't you, little girl?'

'Leah is scared. Walks back and forth, back and forth.'

'Abba is blocking the light. Our dai says, Let's stay here. This is home.'

'I throw stones at your window. Let me in. It is cold.'

'Come play with me. Hold my hand. I will be your friend. Who needs school?'

'Monkey loves you. Your uncle loves you.'

'Don't mind her. Goldie in the yellow dress cries all the time with the two dirty babies.'

'Put some mead in a bottle. Leave it open on the porch. The Sausage Man will leave you alone.'

'And them in the trees? They are all friends, best friends forever.'

'Your mama is a dog. Kick her.'

'I love you, I promise.'

'We all promise.'

'Happily ever after.'

'Hold my hand and jump. It won't hurt once you fall. The doctor will come. The sister will come. The priest will come. Everybody will pray. Everybody will cry. And then they won't tie you up anymore.'

'And we can play in the trees.'

'Forever.'

24

1939

Light enters the room. She stops where the sunlight stills.

'Remember always, Mother,' she says without moving her lips. 'Love is sweet.'

And then the rain.

Anah knows Hosana is dead.

THE GRAY DAWN CAME. Ezroh passed the Winchester M70 and a 20-gauge double shotgun to Matthew, who loaded them on the gun rack. Bert climbed into the back of the delivery truck.

"Where is Anah?" Matthew asked Ezroh, the rain sliding off his black Stetson. "We need to leave before the road floods."

Elizabeth ran off the porch and grabbed her father's hand, pulling him without words.

"Not now, not now," he said, frantically looking past her for Anah. "Get out of the rain, Elizabeth." And then he asked her, "Where is your mama?"

She took him by the hand. She did not cry out as she ran through the wild swarm that hovered in front of the door to the honey house.

The heavy rain, the frenzied pitch of the bees, Ezroh yelling, Elizabeth humming to calm herself in the doorway, Anah sat in the whirling blur of the old hive. She stared at the green stinger barbs writhing in her naked skin. He tried to pull her shirt over her head.

"Anah, why are you naked? Anah, put on your clothes," he yelled. "We have to go. The road will flood soon. Hurry!"

Anah did not move, the bees stinging her face, her back, her breasts.

"Go get Uncle Charles," he told Elizabeth. "Get your uncle and Tora-san. Run," he said, pushing her out the door and into the rain.

Anah listened to their buzzing concern outside.

Moments later, Anah heard the delivery truck start up then leave down the muddy road without her. She stood, surveying the landscape of her body. The bees burrowed inside her navel. Anah walked out of the honey house fully pierced, Charles covering her with a horse blanket, Tora-san running ahead of them in the pouring rain.

"Saddle my horse," Anah yelled at the old man. "And get me some dry clothes."

"Come inside, Anah-san," he yelled at her, "bumbye you catch cold and die dead, hekuna! Come inside, hurry. I clean you up, put medicine on the bee sting."

"Saddle my horse," Anah said to Charles. He looked at her with sad, knowing eyes.

The owls swooped down, roosting under the eaves of the cookhouse.

"Are we riding out to the North Shore?" Charles asked.

"We?"

"Me and you," he said, running toward the stable. "I want to go with you."

"No, Anah-san, you cannot go North Shore in this kine rain. You crazy or what? Take you all day on horse. By the time you get there,

Hosana come home all safe and soundly with her papa in the truck. How come you no go on truck? No be furimun, Anah-san, no be stupid. No worry, by nighttime, they bring her back," Tora-san scolded as he dressed her in Ezroh's shirt and trousers.

"She is not there," Anah said. She pulled herself from him and ran toward her brother.

"Hah?"

Charles buttoned her shirt.

"She is not in Kahuku," Anah said at last. She looked at both of them, the nausea of her knowing rising inside of her.

"Then where she stay?" Charles asked.

"She is here."

O BODY.

O child.

THE VALLEY IS a woman with woodland arms outstretched and vulnerable, a woman with breasts of aʻaliʻi and hāpuʻu, lauaʻe between her thighs, the palapalai touching her there where it is wet and torn.

She is here.

CHARLES AND ANAH RODE DOWN the valley in a heavy deluge, the horses kicking up thick clumps of mud, the owls above them in the wakening day sky leading her along the flooded road.

They followed the river whose waters thrashed, a thunderstorm bellowing down the forest hollows like ghostly hooves. Mongrel dogs barked from narrow lanes leading to the piggeries of Kalihi Uka. The ironwoods and bamboo groves on the ridges bent in the whipping winds, fairy terns wavering along the cliffside in the gusts. Anah pushed on.

The constant rains had flooded the rice and taro patches of Kapālama, the sound of rain on the broad cupular taro leaves and the clanging of pots hanging from the outside kitchen of the Do family compound drummed in Anah's head. Muddy water from the lo'i washed up against the banks of the taro fields where the ducks and geese crouched under the banana trees. A large flock of rice sparrows circled the paddies in a frenetic chatter. Anah paused for a moment in the shadow of the passing darkness of the rice thieves. She continued on.

The rain bit into her face as they rode past the sugarcane fields of Kalihi-waena, where in the cold wet of the morning storm, Japanese weed women huddled under makeshift lean-tos made of cane stalks to shelter their crying infants as a Portuguese luna atop a horse ordered them back to work. The woman leading the line began singing a holehole bushi, a field song about the cruelty of the overseer on this stormy day. The other women in the work gang joined in. He did not know the meaning of the words of their song of mockery.

Anah followed the river that led to the flower farms of Kalihi Kai. The delicate petals of the vanda orchids and plumeria bruised to transparency on their branches. Even the hearty red anthurium plants under the large tangerine trees and hāpu'u ferns languished in the downpour. The farmers, their wives, and children squatted inside weathered garden shacks or under huge mango trees, waiting for a break in the rains.

And then Anah came to the mouth of the river in the shallows of Ke'ehi Lagoon. The smell of brackish brine, mulch, manure, and a dead sea overwhelmed her. She stopped, her horse turning away from the ocean.

'LOVE, MOTHER, IS sweet.'

◇

ANAH LOOKED at Charles. The owls circled low overhead.

She is here.

They began searching the basin. A goat, chest deep in water and feces, bleated gray tongued and shivering, sank in the silt of the river's mouth.

Where?

A bloated calf drifted by. A mother cat cried atop a broken stone wall, her newborn kittens, mouths snarled open, fur wet-matte, eyes white, their bodies wedged between the stones.

"Anah," Charles called, surveying the banks. "She is not here." The horses reared in the whipping water and wind. "We should look elsewhere."

Hosana is here.

Anah searched for her amid the twisted chicken wire caught in the debris of fallen kiawe trees, fragments of bridge, broken concrete, a bent bicycle tire tangled in fishnet, misshapen iron rebar tumbling downstream and into the low tide.

There.

A torn car fender, rusty iron roofing, a ripped birdcage, a cracked toilet seat, and a wicker suitcase—feathers in long black hair.

O BODY.

SHE IS limb torn. Naked, her skin floats on fragments of bones like pearly fish fins fluttering in tide. She is shiny. She is bound, but for her legs spread open and wet. Her throat is sliced from ear to ear, her head held to her body by a sinewy ligament. She is pale green. Her eyelids and lips are gray. Her fingers and feet are white.

◇

O BELOVED HOSANA.

'WATCH, O LORD. Those who weep tonight. Bless your dead ones.'

Anah dismounts, falls into the low tide, stumbles over to her daughter. She lifts her limp, heavy body out of the water, silt, leaves, and water spilling from her mouth. She wraps her daughter's body in a blanket. She closes her eyes. She holds her daughter close to her.

'O MY GOD, into your hands, I commend my spirit.'

ANAH DOES NOT KNOW who speaks these words.

A DAY PASSED.

They laid her body in the front room of the main house. The dogs howled on and on from light into dark. Anah anointed her daughter with royal jelly. Elizabeth whimpered. She placed a cube of honeycomb in her mouth. She sat beside her daughter day and night, the vigil light moving with her breath, constant prayers to assist her daughter on her journey to heaven. Open scissors for protection on the table. Upside-down brooms behind the door kept the festeras away. Inside the casket, trinkets and broken toys, stones and bottles, and feathers that lifted in the passing trade winds. The dogs howled on.

Another day passed.

Father Maurice sprinkled the casket with holy water, then led the altar boys, the pallbearers, the family, and then Anah and Ezroh into the church. Psalms, she listened to the psalms. And scriptures. All sung. Anah saw no one, heard nothing during the funeral Mass, sending her own fervent prayers on the smoke of the incense to God Himself. There would be no intercession for her daughter. No Requiem Divine Liturgy. Anah made her own appeal over and over to the Almighty God.

Another day.

They buried Anah's most beloved daughter beside her twin sisters at the foot of the Koʻolau Mountains. Father Maurice threw a fistful of dirt onto the casket.

He looked at Anah. "We are all dust and ashes. We are all earth, and according to the will of God, we all return to the earth again." He intensified his gaze at her.

He made the sign of the cross on the head of the casket, the foot, and then its sides to seal in the dead until the second coming of Christ. Someone shrieked high-pitched and long from the towering treetops along the banks of the river. Everyone turned but Anah. She fell into the grave, her fists full of broken earth.

And then a day passed. Maybe a week. It was months.

The dead surrounded her.

There was nowhere for Anah to run from them. There was nowhere for her to hide. They stayed with her day and night in her room full of spirits both known and unknown. Anah knew what her mother felt as she rocked in her chair by the window for weeks:

The presence
in the absence of presence
in the numbing passivity
of back and forth.

Anah knew it would be soon. The day she joined the many in the room, the many in the trees.

Behold.

One night she was awakened to scratching on the palm of her

hand. She thought it was Elizabeth, afraid again. She had promised to take her daughter with her on the day of her flight to the trees.

"Today, Mama? Now?" she asked several times a day.

"Soon, soon," Anah whispered.

"Me too." She pointed to herself. "Me go too."

"I promise, Elizabeth," Anah rasped. "Soon."

"Soon what?" Ezroh asked. "Please no talk like that, Anah."

This night Anah awakened to scratching on her palm. Blood dripped down her arm. A whirlpool of smoke burrowed into her navel. Anah gasped in fear, unable to scream or call out. The smoke sucked itself into the corner of the room, a shivering cloud of white.

It was her.

It was Hosana, pearly skin like fish fins fluttering, severed head, bloody pubis. She was afraid. Anah would help her. Anah would show her the way. Anah would go with her daughter to her beloved Christ.

A naked man crouched in the corner beside her. And soon through the smoke, a naked girl. Hosana looked at them, then placed her broken hands on their heads.

'Remember always, Mother. Love is sweet.'

"Tell me who did this to you, Hosana? Tell me."

'And that which he hath done shall be forgiven him.'

Night after night, Anah begged her to tell as she listened to the old funeral buggy on the road, the wailing of the ghostly mourners, the slow creak of wheels, the clop of horse hooves, the jingle of the riders' kepa pele bell spurs, the slap of reins as the procession moved farther and farther into the valley. The final shut of the casket lid. A handful of dirt falling, falling on top of it. The bells clanged.

Night after night, Anah pleaded with her as wild phantom horses galloped around and around the house. The vigil candle would not stay lit. The winds shredded the leaves of the banana, ti, and ginger plants. Mad shapes, mad shadows cast grotesque forms against the moonlit walls of her room.

By day, Anah listened to children crying. She remembered the crying of the little ones being torn from their mothers, the guttural howling of that primal separation.

It was a sound coming from her body.

"Tell me, Hosana."

In daylight, the children threw showers of stones on her window. They shrieked as they ran around the flower garden in their manic play.

"Who did this to my Hosana?" she asked them. They laughed, mischievous orphan wraiths running about the trodden beds of violets and heather.

At midnight, the Victrola played Bach's "Air," loud then low, loud then low.

"Please, Hosana, tell me."

At the hour of the dead, the radio dial whistled and strained static against a background of Glenn Miller's "Stairway to the Stars." *There's a silver trail of moonlight leading upward to the sky.* Snow-static, on and off. *And the night is like a velvet lullaby.* Screeching on and off. *There's a heaven of blue.* Off again. On again. *And we'll go there, just you and I.*

"Tell me so I can kill him."

Elizabeth put her hands over her ears. She would not leave her mother's bedside.

"Listen—"

Anah heard the labored breathing of a chest filled with green phlegm. She heard the crackle of the isinglass tent lifting. A child sat on her pillow, the room infused with the fragrance of white ginger and camphor. She heard the quiet steps of a nun's weathered black boots in the hall outside the room.

Ezroh called Father Maurice.

"Blessed are the sorrowing," he said. "I will come to assist the ailing in receiving any health God may wish to restore to the body, mind, and heart."

"What good is prayer?"

"For they will be consoled."

"Did you feed the cats, Ezroh?"

"Preserve them from despondency and despair, O Lord."

"Is your shotgun loaded, my love?"

"Receive this holy communion, this viaticum, food for the journey into the everlasting."

"Did the owls come home?"

"Conduct her soul to the vision of Jesus, there to obtain mercy for her."

"Is there a God?"

"There is one God who is Father of all, over all, through all, and within all. We will continue our prayers for you and your family," the holy father said, leaving Anah alone at last.

"Where is Charles? Where is Tora-san? Where is Tori? Where is Miriam? Where is Ezroh?"

Anah wanted them all there around her, but if they spoke to her, she felt burdened by the tedious nature of their minutiae.

"Do you want tea, Anah? Bath, Anah? Prayer, Anah? Window open? Window closed, Anah? Bread with butter? Bread without butter, Anah? You cold, Anah? Hot, Anah?"

"I fed your cat. I made ham hock soup. The owls came home. I picked the Chinese beans. I swept the kitchen. The laundry is done. The cows are milked. The hives are full."

Anah did not care that they witnessed her spiral downward into the fragility of herself.

The house was full of the many. Yet the house felt empty.

"Look who's home from school, Anah-san."

Anah saw Tori and Miriam's faces above hers, their features two-dimensional, listened to their two-dimensional faces chatting; she loved their faces; she loathed their faces.

"Mama, do this. Mama, do that. Mama, I need. Mama, help me. Mama, I want. Mama, you have to. Mama, wake up."

"Anah, I need you, get up," Ezroh begged.

"Get over it already. Do not be such a weak woman. What is done is done. Live to live and you will learn to live again," Aunty Tova scolded. "A vida, a vida."

"Tova is right. That is life, Anah. There is nothing any of us can do to change what happens," Aunty Lydia said. "You must simply get up and move on."

"Se Deus quizer," Uncle Marcus sighed.

"It is a police matter now, Anah," Rex Soares consoled.

"Let the dead rest in peace," Uncle Stanley whispered.

"I anoint the sick to receive any health God may wish to restore to your body, mind, and heart," Father Maurice prayed over her body, withering away with each passing day.

HOW ANAH LOATHED their faces. She took no food or drink, her lips dry and cracked, her pallor gray.

Father Maurice returned again and again. "Repeat after me, Susanah," he commanded. "O God the Father, do not reject me; O Jesus, do not abandon me; O God the Holy Spirit, do not forsake me," he pressed her to speak.

"And what of the woman who chooses to reject God?"

"Foolish woman, only the fool says in his heart, 'There is no God.' "

They all directed their useless thoughts, their useless prayers at her. They who looked so blasé with their concerned faces.

All she wanted was sleep.

Anah emptied herself of all thought and emotion, her mind a thin-penciled line going across pages and pages of meaningless scripture. The deeper she went into herself, the less she found.

Sister Mary Deborah entered her room. Anah felt her sitting beside her for days, silent. And then on the day Anah was certain she would die for she had not taken food or water for weeks now, she heard the sister's voice. Had she been speaking to her or praying for her the whole time?

Anah heard her:

"I want to be saved and I want to save." She paused, waiting for Anah's response.

Anah said nothing. But inside, her infected heart fluttered. She had not heard or spoken these words for years.

"I want to be set free and I want to free," the sister said softly.

'Hosanna, sing hosanna to the King of kings.'

"I want to be born and I want to give birth," she said, placing her daughters' warm hands in hers. First, a tentative Miriam, gentle child. Second, a trembling Tori, little bird. And last, a sobbing Elizabeth, so lost without her protector, her Hosana. They held on to Anah's dying hand as her sisters had held on as they lay at the moment of their death.

"I want to run away and I want to stay."

'Amen.' It was Aki's voice.

"I want to make you beautiful and I want to be beautiful."

'Amen.' Little Leah breathed in her ear.

"I want to hear and I want to be heard."

'Love—is—sweet.' It was the voice of he who never spoke, Seth whispering Hosana's words.

Anah did not open her eyes. A single tear slipped down her face. She felt her breath leaving her body.

"I want to join with you, I want to be joined."

Ezroh put his lips on hers. And she breathed in deeply of him. Anah remembered the boy who waited for her on the bridge over the stream with chocolate in gold paper, the boy who placed a fan of apple wedges in her hand, the boy who wrote her letters, who ran with her through the streets of Chinatown, who came to bring her home on her eighteenth birthday, who loved her and gifted her with children, who taught her to ride a bicycle, who planted a garden of flowers outside the window of her home with him.

"I have no houses and I have houses. I have no ground and I have ground."

Charles knelt beside Anah, weeping, he who never found her. He who was found by her. "I am so sorry, Anah, so sorry. I thought of you and Aki and Leah every day of my life, I promise you. But I was weak. Our father was right. I was useless even to you. But now that you have found me, I will never lose you again."

"If you knock on me, I will be a door."

"Amen," Aunty Chong Sum whispered, her rough, kitchen hand petting Anah's head.

"If you look at me, I will be a lamp," Sister Mary Deborah whispered.

Anah's eyes opened slowly.

"If you see me, I will be a mirror."

'Remember always, Mother. Love is sweet.'

The room was still.

"If you are a traveler," Anah's voice whispered at last to the living and the dead, "I will be a road."

"Amen," Sister Mary Deborah responded.

There was not an empty space in the room filled with sisters, brothers, mothers, fathers, aunts, uncles, cousins, husbands, wives, childhood friends, teachers, and children, so many children.

"Finish the Acts of John, Susanah, please," Sister Mary Deborah said.

"This is my dance—" Anah began, unable to go on.

"Sweet Susanah, please finish the scripture," she urged her.

But Anah could not.

Elizabeth took her mother's face in her hands. "Mama," she said, smiling, wiping the tears from their eyes, "answer me with dancing."

Anah kissed her palms, her fingers. She looked at all of them, all who had gathered in that room. Her heart knew the rest of the words. Her heart had known all along:

"The kingdom of God is within you."

This Is Who Killed Her

She tells him she is leaving him. He will not have it. She belongs to him.

She tells him she is leaving him. If he cannot have her, then no one else will.

He takes her to a bar in town. There, he introduces her to a pale man with sandy hair, light eyes. A friend, our friend, he tells her, this disheveled, young haole vagrant.

She thinks nothing of it. Her step is light. She has made up her mind. She is leaving him.

But he will not have it. Nobody will have her. Nobody but him.

She comes home from work. She is a creature of habit. She is bathing downstairs. It is early evening.

He is upstairs listening to music. He looks at his watch. He turns up the volume.

The pale man with the sandy hair bursts in on her. He hits her over the head with a heavy piece of wood. She is unconscious. He binds her hands with rope as planned. It is raining. He drags her by the hair to the open field nearby as planned. He slices her throat from ear to ear.

The pale man with the sandy hair goes back to the house. He is paid for his work.

"Why did you have to make it so fucking bloody?"

The pale man shrugs his shoulders. He leaves the house. He leaves the island. He is a vagrant. He lives in Tallahassee, Florida.

Tell no one, she begs me. I love him. I have forgiven him. Yes, that was me you saw in the sunlight. I came to see you when I died. To say good-bye. Tell no one. Do not tell the police. Do not tell my mother. I do not want her to feel the hurt of the truth. Promise me.

I promise, I tell her.

And then she is no longer naked, her body ravaged by a pale man with sandy hair then paid by the man who would not be left behind.

She is beautiful again, the motion of her hair, the motion of her dress a coral-orange gossamer, the sunlight behind her xanthous, she is dancing on a balcony of a mansion in her Father's kingdom.

Promise me:

"Dearly beloved, avenge not yourselves, but rather give place unto wrath: for it is written, Vengeance is mine; I will repay," saith the Lord.

25

1939

I want to be set free and I want to free.

'Come,' Hosana says to the many. 'I know the way.' She stands at the center of the garden, forget-me-nots and kwai fa sweet in the wind. 'The way to our Father's kingdom. The way home.'

She is wearing a beautiful orange dress.

Anah's brave warrior daughter calls them all to her. She calls the lonely and the lost, the frightened and aggrieved, the rueful and pitiful, the orphaned and abandoned. All who will listen.

She calls Aki and Leah. She calls Beatrix and Bertha. Seth is not far behind. The wind swoops through the eucalyptus and ironwoods as the children come down from the treetops, the chatter of their voices caught in that wind.

'Where is my mother?'

'Why has she left me here?'

'I am hungry.'

'Where is my father?'

'Is he coming to take me home?'

'I am cold.'

'Brother, where are you?'

'Sister, why have you forsaken me?'

'I am afraid.'

'Mama, I want to go home.'

'Papa, I do not know the way.'

'Look, Aki! It is Anah and Charles coming to take us home,' little Leah cries.

'Anah! Charles, you came!' Aki calls. 'Are you going to take me home now?' she asks.

"Yes, you are going home now," Anah tells them from the center of her garden. "And we will have a great celebration in your honor."

Charles cannot stop his crying. Aki holds his hand. Her touch is cold. Leah climbs onto his back, wraps her icy arms around his neck, and does not let go.

'Anah was not lying. I told you, Aki,' Leah whispers into his ear. 'Charles came. He came just like Anah promised.'

ANAH BEGAN PREPARING a Feast for the Dead in the time of the Feast of the Holy Ghost between Easter and Pentecost.

Ai-chan, Nohea, Aunty Lydia, and Anah cooked, as Abigail, Joyce, and Mariah cleaned, all of them working for seven days and seven nights. Uncle Marcus, Uncle Stanley, Rex Soares, and Ezroh slaughtered a huge pig, a rabbit, a chicken, and a sheep, while Matthew, Bert, Kahalelehua, and Ricardo prepared the festa grounds.

The many remained, playing in the house, climbing the fruit trees, chasing the animals, running through the flowerbeds and fields, in and about the stables, the paddocks, the honey house, the washhouse, padding their little feet along the lānai, jumping in and out of open windows.

Anah covered a long table in the garden with lace cloth. She laid out a traditional Portuguese Easter feast of lombo de carneiro, carne de bife assada, sweetmeats, egg custards, and a rich rice pudding. She offered a plate of amêndoas for the children who gathered around the table stealing handfuls of the sugar-coated almonds. They baked loaves of shiny Easter sweet bread with whole eggs on the top. She made a special plate with a symbolic serving of each dish as an offering to the dead. Anah lit many Easter candles. But it was not Easter.

Tora-san and Ai-chan lit paper Obon lanterns for the kami of the hearth at the center of the garden. They burned rice paper money in front of the shrine for their fares to cross the River of Three Hells. They adorned the shrine with bowls of fruit and sugarcane stalks, offerings for the dead to take with them into the afterlife. They made jushi, rice seasoned with vinegar, sugar, and ginger, to ward off the evil ones who had no one to feed them. They made a ceremonial plate of daikon, tōfu, burdock root, konnyaku, pork liver, kamaboko, and rafute. They offered special prayers to the kami of forgiveness for Kenji's transgressions. They lit Obon incense and prayed. But it was not Obon.

Anah prepared Aki and Leah's favorite New Year's foods just like their okaasan did. Soba the buckwheat noodles for long life, kuromame the black beans for good health, konbu maki the seaweed for happiness, sekiham the red rice for good luck, mochi the glutinous rice for prosperity, and kazunoko the herring roe for fertility. Anah prepared their favorite New Year's ozoni soup. She served a symbolic bowl of the ozoni full of soft, hot mochi as an offering to the dead. She placed the kadomatsu, an arrangement of pine for strength and bamboo for resilience, on either side of the front entrance to the main house as her okaasan had done each January first for their home in Portuguese Camp Four. But it was not New Year's.

Anah baked a chocolate birthday cake in honor of little Leah and Aki. She prepared fofas filled with sweet cream, cavacas frosted with sugar, and a Bolo de Reis full of raisins, walnuts, and candied fruits. She sewed a new yellow party dress for Leah, wrapping it in bright paper and twine. She filled a vase with blossoms of the abundant valley—ginger, heather, kwai fa, wild violets, pansies, and geraniums for Aki. They would light the candles on the cake and sing them a happy birthday. They would serve the cake with ice cream to the living and the dead. But it was not Leah or Aki's birthday.

Elizabeth brought her trinkets and knickknacks to the table in the garden, her jars and bottles of olivines, marbles, and feathers, horseshoes, and stones, emptying her shelves of found treasures. Tori decorated the table with her beanbags and jacks. Miriam placed her kukui nut tops and agates there too. Anah fashioned a small altar from their toys, knowing that the dead children could not resist a table of wonderful playthings set forth for them. She spilled a portion of sweet cocoa on the altar as an offering. "This is for you, dear souls, dear little sisters," she whispered, as Elizabeth chanted, "Come, criança, Dia de Finados! Dia de Finados!" But it was not All Souls' Day.

And when the Feast for the Dead began, the children, family, and friends gathered round to eat and celebrate. Father Maurice and the holy sisters prayed, consecrating the meat and bread as sustenance for all the families at the ranch.

The cowboys sang all night with guitars, the five-stringed rajczo, braguinha, and ukuleles, the castanets and tambourines rhythmic and strong. The women and children danced under the colorful paper lanterns. The men drank and toasted, "Seja por as almas!" raising their glasses again and again to the departed souls.

Ezroh and Anah danced in the garden of flowers and herbs that he planted for her.

AND THEN IT WAS time for all to go home.

IT IS EARLY MORNING, still dark. Rex Soares retires to the main house. Kahalelehua takes everyone back up to the north pasture in the horse-drawn cart. Tora-san falls asleep inside the patch of rosemary and lemon balm. The ranch hands stumble back to the bunkhouse, Ricardo passed out on the roadside. Miriam, Tori, and Elizabeth sleep in the gazebo. Ezroh drives Father Maurice and the holy sisters back to St. Joseph's in the delivery truck.

The Easter candles burn on.

Anah sits on the steps of the gazebo with her brother in a solemn silence.

"If you look at me—" Charles whispers.

"I will be a lamp," Anah tells him, taking all of him in her arms.

The dark sky opens up with the first rays of this dawn. Anah sees Hosana in the threshold of that light, standing before her in a kind of indomitable radiance.

'Come,' she says to the many around them, 'I know the way home.' There is a rustling in the flower and herb beds, a trembling in the trees, the sound of little feet, many feet running on the gravel road. She turns away from Anah and heads into the light, the children in the wind following her.

'I know the way home,' she calls to the stragglers, the lonely and the lost, the frightened and aggrieved, the rueful and pitiful, the orphaned and abandoned. She looks at each face behind her.

Anah knows she is looking for Aki and Leah.

Anah knows she is looking for her sisters Beatrix and Bertha.

'Aki!' she calls. 'Leah! It is time to go home. Beatrix and Bertha! Our heavenly Father is calling us.'

'Anah? Are you taking us home?' little Leah asks.

'Charles, are you coming too?' Aki asks.

Charles does not answer. He cannot answer.

"If you see me—" Anah tells Aki and Leah, Beatrix and Bertha, Seth.

'I will be a mirror,' Hosana answers. They turn toward her image.

The sunlight is warm. It begins to fill the valley. Anah looks into her daughter's beautiful eyes, her perfect symmetry.

"I want to be set free," Anah tells her beloved daughter, her first blood relative when she had no one, the one whom she loved the most.

'I want to free,' she answers, her voice full and resounding.

The sunlight is warm.

Beatrix and Bertha's spirit bodies take flight, becoming part of the sunlight. Little Leah in her pretty yellow dress follows, waving her hand at Charles and Anah as she goes. Aki hesitates at first as Charles slowly releases her hand. She takes a small step away from him. She is dressed in the flowers of Anah's garden. She looks at Charles and smiles. And then she looks at Anah. She turns to Hosana, who is softly saying her name, Hosana, her mother's mirror, her mother's child, keeps saying her name, beckoning to her *come, come home*. Aki follows her voice, dissolving into the light.

Charles buries his face on Anah's shoulder. He cannot take any more, sobbing now, wailing as he did the day he left them at the orphanage all those many years ago.

Anah lifts his face to the light. "Remember the way home," she tells him.

Seth lingers in the shadows of a mountain apple tree.

Anah stands up and walks toward him, he who never aged, little towheaded boy, the quiet one who followed Leah, then Aki, then her, a loyal friend who never complained, his calm but sad presence in her most agonizing and unbearable moments. An angry wraith who believed she had betrayed him.

"Seth, my friend and brother by marriage." Anah holds out her hands to him. "I want to hear, and I want to be heard."

'Love—is—sweet,' he says, not moving.

"Remember always, brother," says a voice behind her. Anah turns. It is Ezroh, who falls to his knees before the little boy who fell from the big tree all those years ago. Seth walks toward him and places both hands on his brother's head.

His eyes survey the panorama of the valley as if placing the horses in the pastures, the green hills, his childhood home, a father, a brother, and a once beloved friend in the sweep of his memory. When fades the light behind an errant cloud, so fades he.

Anah helps Ezroh to stand.

"Sweetness dances," she shouts into the valley. "I want to pipe; all of you dance!" The trees, the bushes, the flowers, the grasses, the lichens, and the mosses, a coterie of verdant arms and fingers, move in delicate response, the morning illuminating the deepest reaches of the valley, the valley that is a woman:

An ill-fated daughter, her sisters' mother, a nun's apprentice, a young woman, a blessed wife, a sublime lover, a grieving mother, a joyous mother, a reflection in a mirror, a prophet's whisper:

"My spirit will not leave them, and neither will these words I have given you. They will be on your lips and on the lips of your children and your children's children forever."

Grateful Acknowledgments

To my family and friends:

I would never write books without you. I want to thank you for letting me be a part of your lives. I want to thank you for loyalty and sustenance that bear more greatly than you know upon the way I live each day of my life. Even when life takes me down the rabbit hole or into my shell or inside the dark, dark abyss, whatever metaphor we use, I know you will encourage and wait for my return. Your gestures of goodness, assurance, and vivid understanding are written in my every word.

Jean and Harry Yamanaka, Grandma Narikiyo, Mona, Shane, and wonderful Samantha Rei Saiki, Kathy, Jeffrey and best nephew Charles Heima Tatsuhara, Carla Beth Yamanaka, Ellie and Zeke, Aunty Gladys and Uncle Daniel Yoon, Uncle Paul Yamanaka and family, Aunty Jan Linardos, Uncle Steven, Ross and Dustin Narikiyo;

Sista Charlene Nobriga, Ian and Ira, Charles Inferrera, Joanne and Jessica;

Claire E. Shimizu, Web master and ghost buster extraordinaire, Shari Nakamura I feel way better after a shower, Malie Chong and the whole Nakamura family, Nancy Hoshida and cats, cats, cats especially our Boop,

Melvin E. Spencer III laughter daily and joy ingrown, Mimi, Dede, Michael, Debbie, Everett Kanaeaupuni, Hannah and Ethan Spencer, Keoki Mercado pueo man, Kenn Sakamoto, Linda Conroy, Don Sumada;

Susan Bergholz and Bert Snyder;

John Glusman, Aodaoin O'Floinn, Sarah Russo, and Corinna Barsan;

Morgan Blair, light;

Cora Yee;

Tae, Sunhi, Jim, and Nora Okja Keller, Wing Tek Lum, Darrell Lum, Eric Chock, Marie Hara, Fuku Tsukiyama, Joy and Xander Cintron, Laura and Albert Saijo, and my friends at Bamboo Ridge Press;

Josie Woll, eternal gratitude;

Patricia Yu, Miss Betty, Miss Suzy, Keoni Yago, Karen Sakurai, Mrs. Abby Lyau, Diane Suzuki, Carole Matsukawa, Brandi Nishimoto, John and June from Robert's Hawaii, Shane, Ben, and Reed Pamantigan, Russell Nishimura, Uncle George, Beverly Barnard, Gerald Teramae, and the staff and students of Jarrett Middle School;

JohnJohn's beloved and trusted friend Nohea Kanaka'ole, Aunty Penny, Marlene, Kaleo and Lohi, Aunty Bridget Kanaka'ole, Skye, Adam, and the extended Kanaka'ole family;

Kathy Maemori, Michiko Sato-Escobido, Toni Miyamoto, Nadine Okazawa, Joyce, Mariah, Britney;

Lisa Lawson, Dr. Errol Hamarat, Llewelleyn Smalley, Leo Richardson, Mr. Blaine;

Joyce Allen and Vici, Cheyenne Akana and Beau, Sheila Kaimuloa and Matthew, Naomi Grossman and Vance, Leolinda Osorio, Mrs. Osorio, and Sonny;

Crisana Cook, Dr. Kimo Chan, Dr. Sada Okumura, and wonderful Boyd Slomoff;

Aunty Kui of Kualoa Ranch;

Verbano Friends Club: Clyde "Mr. Verbano" Ramsey, Jeffrey "50%" Do, Eric "Feliz Navidad" Kahalelehua, Ken "Velcro-in-Peace" Fukunaga, Glenn "Stars in My Eyes" H., Jim "Just Another Duck," Kang and sister Omi;

Treasured students and families at Na'au: A Place of Learning and Healing, teachers Kim Roman, David Ishii, Katie Uechi, Lindsay Furuya, Matt Mitsuyuki;

Friday Night Writing Club past and present: Traci Shizu Kutaka, Casey Kiyoshi Matsuo, Marisa Sue Pang, Jordan Marcus Chong Sum Harrison, David/Michael Imanaka, Mie/Emi Omori, Erin Yamada, Stephanie Miki Torige, Carrie Tribble, Sarah/Keith Elias, Reyn Yonashiro, Kevin Okawa;

Catherine Toth, Jeremy's beloved friend;

Marci Ikuta, research librarian extraordinaire;

Donna Choo and Simone Ling (see, I know);

Ai-chan and Mie, So'o, Jazmine, Miss Ula, Leilani, JazRae, Danielle, and Michelle Kang;

Eternal rest Lynn Ebisuzaki and dearest Joan Inamine of Sunday school, choir practice, and childhood camps;

Sweet friend with the yellow blanket, broken crayons, model cars, tree house, soothing orange, green tea/ginger, and go-cart;

Na'i, Chiba, Toby, Caterine, Olivia, Betty, Boop, Birdies, John Infererra, incredible Daddy and caregiving friend, and JohnJohn, blessed teacher and beloved son, I love all of you so much forever.

A NOTE ABOUT THE AUTHOR

LOIS-ANN YAMANAKA is the author of *Saturday Night at the Pahala Theatre*; the trilogy *Wild Meat and the Bully Burgers* (FSG, 1996), *Blu's Hanging* (FSG, 1997), and *Heads by Harry* (FSG, 1999); *Father of the Four Passages* (FSG, 2001); and two books for children, *Name Me Nobody* and *The Heart's Language*. She is the winner of a Lannan Literary Award, an Asian American Literary Award, and an American Book Award. She is codirector of Na'au: A Place for Learning and Healing in Honolulu, where she lives with her husband, son, four cats, three dogs, and eleven birds. She is working on a new novel written entirely in pidgin.